SO MANY PEOPLE, MARIANA

SO MANY PEOPLE, MARIANA

COLLECTED STORIES
1959-1967

TRANSLATED FROM PORTUGUESE BY MARGARET JULL COSTA

TWO LINES
PRESS

MARIA JUDITE
DE CARVALHO

© 2013 by Maria Isabel de Carvalho Tavares Rodrigues Alves Fraga
Published with special arrangement with the Ella Sher Literary Agency
Translation © 2021 by Margaret Jull Costa

Cover photo: George Marks/Retrofile RF via Getty Images
Interior Design by Sloane | Samuel

Two Lines Press
582 Market Street, Suite 700, San Francisco, CA 94104
www.twolinespress.com

ISBN: 978-1-949641-51-6
Ebook ISBN: 978-1-949641-52-3

Library of Congress Cataloging-in-Publication Data

Names: Carvalho, Maria Judite de, author. | Costa, Margaret Jull, translator.
Title: So Many People, Mariana: Collected Stories, 1959-1967 / Maria Judite de Carvalho ; translated from Portuguese by Margaret Jull Costa.
Other titles: Tanta gente, Mariana. English.
Description: San Francisco, CA : Two Lines Press, [2021] | In English, translated from the Portuguese.
Identifiers: LCCN 2023021560 (print) | LCCN 2023021561 (ebook) ISBN 9781949641516 (paperback) | ISBN 9781949641523 (ebook)
Subjects: LCSH: Short stories, Portuguese.
Classification: LCC PQ9265.A77 T3613 2023 (print) | LCC PQ9265. A77 (ebook) | DDC 869.3/42--dc23/eng/20230601
LC record available at https://lccn.loc.gov/2023021560
LC ebook record available at https://lccn.loc.gov/2023021561

1 3 5 7 9 10 8 6 4 2

This book is supported within the scope of the Open Call for Translation of Literary Works by the Luso-American Development Foundation. The translation of this work was also supported in part by an award from the National Endowment for the Arts.

FLAD

ALSO BY MARIA JUDITE
DE CARVALHO:

EMPTY WARDROBES

CONTENTS

SO MANY PEOPLE, MARIANA

I arrived just a short time ago and yet I've only the vaguest memory of having come here. My one clear recollection is of the man about to be run over, and of the hands of the driver who brought me, big and white and with short, almost nailless fingers, limp on the steering wheel, like starfish washed up on the sand. Two bloodless hands. And yet the owner of those hands was very much alive. He even insulted the old man when he suddenly appeared there, in front of his car. Just as happened to me all that time ago. "Get some specs, you old fool!" The man looked lost, his eyes blank and faded. It was as if he were somewhere very far from the street his body was walking along and where he was now standing and receiving, without hearing, the insults of the driver and the laughter of the people who had stopped simply in order to laugh. "Cat got your tongue, old fellow, or did you just have one too many?" He was so alone, the poor man, so alone!

Did I really go to the doctor? Did I really leave the house? I must have. I still have beside me my suitcase and, on my lap, the hat I bought six years ago and that, as I've only just noticed, has a couple of moth holes in it and a ridiculous feather on the righthand side. It doesn't suit me, and I don't suit it. How could it be otherwise?

The world is suddenly a pile of strange things that I'm seeing for the first time and whose existence has an unexpected potency. The peach tree in the garden about to burst into flower, the battered old armchair where I usually sit, the bed with the carved headboard that once belonged to Dona Glória's mother. Tremulous images that finally plunge into the sea of my tears.

There are so many things that we never think about for lack of time! About hope, for example. Who is going to waste five or ten minutes thinking about hope, when they could make better use of that time reading a novel or talking on the phone to a friend, or going to the movies or firing off memos at the office? Thinking about hope, really, how absurd! It's enough to make you laugh. Thinking about hope, honestly, some people… And yet hope is always there like sand in the folds and hems of the soul. Years pass, lives pass, then along comes the last day and the last hour and the last minute and hope turns up to make what we were hoping for hopeless, to make what was already bitter still more bitter. To make things more difficult.

The consultant asked if I had any family. I told him No. He seemed slightly put out, as if my being single were the most serious factor in what was about to happen and about to be said, the first pebble on the otherwise smooth path of my illness. He was looking at me, the results clutched in his hand. No one at all? he asked, as if appealing to my better nature. I shook my head, and, in the beige-framed mirror behind his reddish neck, I saw myself smile gravely. The feather on my hat moved from side to side. And for some reason, I suddenly felt very ashamed of that feather. He said: Right... He had just re-read the results. So why this whole performance? Perhaps he didn't know how to begin... But how could he not know? He must have had plenty of practice. Why all the delays? Perhaps he just wanted to spend a few more minutes with me. That was possible. After all, I'd handed over 500 escudos when I arrived—and it had been no easy matter scraping together those 500 escudos!—to the pretty receptionist with the technicolor face, immaculate gown, and conventional smile that she could turn off like a flame being extinguished when it was no longer needed. "The doctor hasn't arrived yet; please take a seat..." Perhaps it wasn't as serious as suggested by the other doctor's silence, by what he left so encouragingly unspoken, by his broad, smug smile, as false as Judas. Who knows. Perhaps...

One could always hope.

Again the receptionist's red-and-white smile, her large eyes rimmed with mascara.

"Senhora Dona Mariana Toledo."

There he was before me, the great Cardénio Santos, once again studying those complicated hieroglyphs, those mysterious numbers, which are only for the initiated and are like a code for death. I found myself studying his face intently, as if that were the most important thing in the world, more so than the words he was preparing to throw over the truth like a veil. A pink, moon-like face, two small piercing eyes embedded in soft flesh. Nothing more, apart from being the face of a good doctor, one of those rare geniuses who has never made a wrong diagnosis. Never.

As far as one knows, of course.

He said:

"Well, your situation certainly isn't desperate, far from it. What we need…"

But all I needed was the truth. I managed to dredge up another smile and showed him my sandalled foot.

"That's good, because I'm all set to go on a trip. I just need to buy my ticket, but I didn't want to do that without coming here first."

I could see he was surprised. I knew that, even without actually looking, he had noticed my faded jacket, the feather on my hat, the darned underwear, the general air of neglect.

"I don't think that would be a good idea," he said at last.

"I'm a brave woman, doctor. How long do you give me? Without being hospitalized, of course. If I'm not contagious, then I want to die in my own house, or, rather, in the house where I'm living now."

The tip of my blade had hit home, because he wasn't expecting it. Naturally, he fought back. He laughed, and I was filled with admiration, because his laugh seemed genuine.

"You're not one for half-measures, are you? You immediately assume you're going to die…"

"Please, doctor. It's very, very important. You can't imagine just how important. I'm not going anywhere. You just have to look at me. Do I look like a traveler? It's just that…when you're alone as I am, with no one, you can't allow yourself the luxury of being deceived. You need to be prepared."

He mumbled a "Yes, well…"

Then he presented me with a very grand truth, laden with difficult, highly technical words. When I unwrapped it, I found myself face to face with death, and face to face with the hope that I would survive despite all, screaming to myself that it simply wasn't possible. Perhaps he was wrong; you never know. Everyone makes mistakes, even professors at the School of Medicine. The very idea! How could he be wrong when the numbers were all clearly there in the results? And what about the laboratory? It wouldn't be the first time they'd made a mistake. I remember reading about just such a case in the papers… Oh, who am I fooling! It's all true, both what the doctor said and what's written in those reports. It's hope…not wanting to lose hope, clinging to the slenderest reed, however frail, however insubstantial.

Today is the 20th of January, and in three or four months' time, I will begin to wait for death.

I feel very alone, more than ever, even though I always have been.

Always.

One night when I was fifteen, I woke up crying. I don't know now what path led me to those tears; it's all so long ago now, lost somewhere along the white ribbon of the past. I remember only that my father heard me and came into my room. He sat down gently on the edge of my bed and began stroking my hair, wanting to know what was wrong.

"I'm all alone, Pa; that's what's wrong. I was crying because I was so alone and it seemed to me… How silly, eh? I mean I'm not alone now, am I? You're here."

I tried to cover my embarrassment with laughter, regretting having been so frank, but he refused to collaborate, and that refusal saved him from the anger I might have felt for him the following morning. He didn't laugh, and when he spoke, his voice was very gentle, almost sad.

"So you've felt that too," he said softly. "Yes, you've felt that too. Some people live for seventy or eighty years, sometimes more, and never notice. And yet you, at fifteen... We're all of us alone, Mariana. Alone, but with lots of people around us. So many people, Mariana! And not one of them can help us. They can't, and wouldn't want to if they could. Not a hope."

"But what about you, Pa?"

"Me? The people who fill your world are different from those who fill mine. Well, some of them will be the same, and yet if they ever met, they wouldn't even recognize one another. How can we help each other? No one can, sweetheart, no one can."

No one can.

Not even my father, who, poor thing, died just a few months later; not even António, or after him, Luís Gonzaga. My life is like a tree on which all the leaves have gradually withered and died, followed, one after the other, by all the branches. Not a single one is left. And now it's about to topple over for lack of sap.

The maid, Augusta, spends her days uttering huge, heartfelt sighs. Then she says, Sometimes, I think I'd be better off dead! And yet she's a plump, healthy woman, always cheerful and smiling, with a real penchant for policemen, which she does nothing to hide. The words that accompany those sighs are completely meaningless.

Unlike me, she doesn't have nightmares about lying in the dark under the heavy earth. She couldn't, and even if she could, she'd find it childish to think about such things, to imagine the worms devouring her body. She didn't see, as I did, the mound of earth on my father's grave. The earth from the graves being dug on either side. My father who, only months before, was stroking my hair with his warm hand. No one can, sweetheart, no one can.

I didn't believe him because I was just a little girl, still hoping for great things from life. So many that I can no longer remember what they were. I felt alone, but I knew that I wouldn't always be. I was sure of that. When, a few years later, I left school and met António, I thought my father had been quite wrong. Well, I don't know that I even thought about my father. I had time only to think about António and about me. Time was slipping through my fingers, and I wanted to grab hold of it.

We had a few difficult years. My in-laws didn't approve of our marriage and did their best to ignore us, which was easy enough because they lived in the provinces.

Now that any egotistical thoughts I might have had, any resentments and enmities large and small, are about to die with me, I'd like to think they were right, or at least feel able to understand their attitude. Who knows: Perhaps I wouldn't have been pleased if Fernandinho had married a mere typist with no money and no family, who wasn't even pretty or attractive or brilliant. Who knows what we would be capable of doing or thinking if this or that had happened in this or that way? If my son had grown to be a man, for example. If I had been rich like

António's parents. Money changes people in the most extraordinary way. Those who were secretly, modestly evil become ostentatiously so when they grow rich. They can be as aggressive or indifferent as they like, and all will be forgiven.

For six years, we lived in an attic apartment on Rua das Pretas. António was teaching math in a girls' school in Largo do Andaluz and giving private lessons in the evening. I worked as a typist and did the occasional translation job. Our joint income, plus the few investments left me by my prudent father, was just enough for us to pay the rent and keep from starving.

Sometimes, in the evening, we would walk down the Avenue to the Baixa, as far as the river. On sunny days, there were always children standing by the harbor wall staring in astonishment at the ships, or happily chasing the pigeons. Filled with sudden sadness, I would say to António:

"Perhaps things will be better next year; then we could have a baby, don't you think? I would love that."

He would say, yes, perhaps things would get better; then he would clasp me to him. We'd have a baby, then we'd go to Paris. Agreed? Sometimes he would get angry at the thought of all the land his family owned around Gouveia, the properties in Viséu, the gold bars that his parents kept under lock and key in some bank vault.

"If it's a boy, we'll name him Fernando, after my father," I said to him once.

He laughed purely for the sake of laughing.

"All right, my love, if that's what you want."

His eyes were bright with tears.

Life is a strange thing. When António's mother died suddenly, we both went up to Gouveia for the funeral. His father was utterly distraught, terrified by a death he had never thought possible. He embraced his son, weeping, and asked our forgiveness. He, too, felt suddenly alone, and this seemed to him so dreadful that he immediately began to ingratiate himself with those he had previously despised (he was a simple soul really and was merely in need of human company). He would begin by ingratiating himself, and then, of course, would ask for something in return—just to be sure he wasn't being duped, the wily old peasant! A little money for us to spend in Paris, which was António's dream. Then a nicely furnished house, where he would expect to have his own room. When he said this, he would turn to me with a triumphant look in his eye, because he assumed this must be my dream come true. I would smile and say nothing. I would smile and think of little Fernando.

I feel so sluggish, and somehow sick of myself too, as if I am a much-chewed piece of bread that ends up tasting sour, tasting of me, of my own juices. In sheer disgust, I spat myself out onto the bed, and here I have stayed, limp and insipid. It's a state of mind somewhere between calm and despair, with a slight admixture of anxiety. Sometimes I feel afraid of this solitude, which is far greater, far vaster than any I've known before. Whichever way I turn, I bump into myself, but I've seen quite enough of me and realize that I have nothing more to say to myself. Nothing.

From time to time, I feel afraid, but the room protects me. When I closed the door just now, I thought it made a different noise, one that didn't just hang in the air as it usually did, but stood there in the silence like a full stop. Time stopped too. The hands on the clock continue to move, but the hours are all the same. The hours set aside for eating and sleeping, for talking to other people, for working—but that's all in the distant past—and those hours that were mine alone have ceased to exist. Now that they are all mine, I don't even notice them. There is only day and night, but morning is no longer the beginning that smoothes the rough edges off things. Everything has stopped. Even the cars that pass in the street and the voices from outside, because they no longer touch me. Even the rain beating on the window, because that noise has become silence.

I'm in my room. It's no longer dark in here and no longer smells like an unwashed body that can't even sweat now because it's run out of juice, or like decaying paper and ants, which is how many old women smell and how this house smelled when I first moved in. It was a smell that kept me company, that wrapped about me even in the street, that entered my nostrils and my mouth, and that probably hasn't left me for the last few years, although I no longer notice it. The room has gradually stopped being horrible. I had to look around me very carefully just now in order, once again, to notice the low ceiling with its large areas of flaking plaster, like constantly watching eyes weighing on my shoulders, the ugly old furniture, the florid wallpaper, of which Dona Glória is perhaps overly proud.

She pops in sometimes wielding all the diminutives she has on hand. Why don't I go for a little walk? Would I like her to bring me a little something from the shops? No? It's such a lovely day, a little bit of sun would do me good…

Go out? And what if I met someone I knew? I can hear them now, as if they are here in front of me. "Oh, my dear, you're so thin and pale. You should see a doctor. Why don't you go to Dr. So-and-so? He's wonderful, you know." Followed by a litany of all the people saved by Dr. So-and-so. Or else, "I hardly recognized you, you know. Look, seek help while there's still time. Remember What's-her-name? Well, she started to look unwell too, lost all her energy, and when she did go to a doctor, it was too late. Nothing to be done. Poor thing, she's in the cemetery now." In the Lumiar cemetery, or Alto de São João, or Prazeres.

Even if they didn't know, even if I didn't tell them I was going to die, they would still feel sorry for me. People love to feel sorry for themselves and even more so for others. "You're ill, my dear: I can see it in your face. How much weight have you lost? Oh, that's terrible." And they would be sure to wear that look, at once resentful and indifferent, that the truly unhappy or anxious (which is to say, nearly all human beings), even the best, even so-called good people, are incapable of concealing. "These things happen, you just have to be patient. Take me, for example..."

I've had it up to here with examples, I've had it up to here with other people.

The worst things are the nights. Long. Endless. Full of ghosts. Some old albeit recent, almost without faces or voices, others young and yet ancient, airy bodies that had not yet begun to decompose, a process that chose not to start just yet even though time is flying. António, Luís Gonzaga, and Estrela of course. She more than any of them. Thoughts of them come into my head unbidden, even when I try really hard not to let them in. They come, despite everything, and stay there. I see them as they were before and also as I imagine them now. They're all so immensely happy since they batted me out of their lives like some annoying insect. Did they? No, they didn't. It's not their fault my life has ended up like this. It just hurts me that they have managed to be happy at my expense. It was me and my silence that gave them their good fortune. One word would have been enough, a scream or a tear, but I couldn't squeeze out either. Now it's too late, because I'm going to die. It would be too late even if death wasn't already on its way.

Fortunately, in Portugal you can purchase sleep without a prescription. One, two, or three tubes of sleep. If I were in Paris... *L'ordonnance s'il vous plaît... Interdit, Madame...à cause des suicides, Madame...à cause des suicides, Madame...* *À CAUSE DES SUICIDES, MADAME...*

That voice comes from so far away! It's so clear. And real. Six or was it eight years ago? I think the pharmacy was called Heudebert. Or was it Saint-Michel? It was on the left side of the boulevard on the way down to the Seine. *Je vous l'ai déjà dit, Madame. C'est impossible. Je regrette.*

I wandered the streets. An icy cold drizzle began to fall, and I went into Café Biard because it occurred to me that I hadn't eaten since the previous evening, and this fact seemed suddenly very important. Afterward, I went down into the metro, but I can't remember which station it was. I don't know where I resurfaced either, but I spent a long time down below, one hour or two. It was late evening, and there were loads of people. They carried me along: it was comfortable like that; they chose where I should go. It smelled good, that bustling night spent going nowhere in particular. Dubo... Dubon... Dubonnet... The night was coming to an end. Barbès or Place Clichy? *Mangez les pâtes Lustrucu... Les enfants aiment Banania... Marignan... Les Amants de Venise...* Being propelled down two corridors then out again into the night. *Vous ne sortez pas? Alors permettez...permettez...permettez...* A girl next to me was reading *Confidences*. It's odd how clearly I remember her face. As if she were a close friend. *Omo lave plus blanc...* Jean Marais about to kiss a motionless profile with long blonde hair. *Messieurs, rasez-vous avec la lame...*

A few days later, I went to sort out our passports for our return to Lisbon. António insisted on coming with me.

Just hours before, it had been night: a cold February night with lights spilling on to the greasy asphalt of the boulevard and neon signs forming luminous puddles outside the cinema and the cafés. In the air, a light mist like the city's breath. We went into the Royal. Costa, a friend of ours from Lisbon, was already there; he had a scholarship at the Centre des Recherches Scientifiques. With him were a group of Brazilian friends and a Portuguese woman I didn't know. Her name was Estrela Vale, and she was a sculptor. I barely noticed her at first. Then, when I saw the unusually insistent way António was looking at her, I began to observe her more closely. She was short and skinny and wore her dark hair combed very sleekly over her small, round head and a dash of cyclamen-pink lipstick on her thin, tight lips. She was wearing a very low-cut top and had a mole at the base of her overly long, white neck. She talked a lot, but very slowly, as if she had to sculpt each word, meticulously, carefully.

It all began not with a presence or a look or even

a conversation, but with a few words that came out of nowhere and that were, perhaps for that very reason, inevitable, yes; it's odd how I instantly felt so sure about that. Ordinary words, as innocent as so many others that are spoken only to dissolve in time and be forgotten. Those words, though, remained engraved on my memory. Everyone was talking. What a great poet Apollinaire is. Have you read *Alcools*? You know Julinha Reis, don't you? Well, Julinha Reis... They suddenly plunged into a conversation "for Brazilians only," in which they were trying to ascertain whether a particular person was actually married. Estrela raised her glass of white port to her lips, and António gazed at her, forgetting his own glass of beer. At one point, he said in a voice I didn't recognize:

"That mole is really pretty. It looks like a flower being blown by the wind."

I was so shocked. It was so unlike him to say such a thing. He always called a spade a spade. Had it really been António who had spoken, who had said those words?

She placed her hand on her neck to hold on to the flower those words had created and began to laugh, for no reason, as if filled by one of those all-consuming joys that sometimes rise up in people and that, when they go—as unexpectedly as they came—leave behind them a memory of a whole week spent with a mouth like sawdust and dark circles under eyes closed to any light. But I have no idea what Estrela thought or felt... António continued to look at her as if oblivious to everything and everyone. She laughed; she laughed a lot. I can still hear that laugh, secret, subterranean, coming lightly to the boil, but without ever spilling over.

Why do I remember that night so clearly? The voices of the others kept elbowing each other aside, scrambling and trampling over each other in their desire to reach a vantage point, where they could claim that they were right. All I could hear was Estrela's muted laughter.

At around one o'clock, the fat Brazilian with the flat face—what was his name now?—already maudlin with whiskey and full of an irrepressible, nauseating nostalgia for the family he had left behind in Curitiba, started talking about his wife (or as he called her "his other half") and their two "precious" children, all the while staring doggedly—as if the two subjects were related—at Simone's vast decolletage, which barely covered her nipples. António was talking to Estrela, but so softly that I couldn't hear what he was saying. The others, distracted and utterly indifferent to anyone other than themselves, continued the topic of the moment, laboriously washing down with alcohol the few, tired words they could still muster at that late hour.

We returned home crammed into either the swarthy Brazilian's Renault or Simone's Vedette, with Simone, as usual, advancing and retreating and turning back on herself in the old, deserted city, sometimes getting lost in the narrow backstreets or in the broad boulevards, which she couldn't tell apart even in broad daylight, because, in her view, they were all equally gloomy and ugly. Simone didn't like Paris. She agreed when people talked about its many good qualities. Far be it from her to say otherwise. The night life was amazing, yes, but don't talk to her about how elegant the Parisians were (the women in Rio were far better dressed) or about French cuisine and about how beautiful Paris was. Beautiful! She was fed up to the back teeth with *bifteck* and *frites* and the all-pervading filth. Her dark eyes danced in the small, rectangular rearview mirror, eyes so dark they seemed to have no iris. Her slender hands with their scarlet nails tapped impatiently on the steering wheel, because she had once again gone the wrong way.

"Rio is something else entirely," she said suddenly in a dreamy voice. "That huge sea, eh, Etelvino? Do you remember? That vast, never-ending ocean."

In the back seat, to my left, Etelvino Cruz's teeth were a white gash in the darkness.

"Why did you come here, then?" he asked in a slurred voice. "Why don't you catch the first plane back? Or did you come here just to criticize everything? That's sick."

They were talking, and, suddenly, I was alone, so alone that, just as I had years before, I felt like crying. Except now I had no one to stroke my hair. António was beside me, yes, but I knew he was really with Estrela in the car belonging to the fat Brazilian, whom I now remember was named Garibaldi.

Simone started singing. She had a low, husky voice, and the songs she sang were almost always sad. They spoke of godless, hungover eyes, eyes that are like nocturnal harbors where ships run aground, like deep lakes where men disappear forever. Her voice droned never-endingly on.

Costa, who was sitting next to her, asked her to sing something cheerier. It was too depressing, he thought. Simone shook her dark, glossy Indian hair. Impossible, she said. Drink made her sad, and there was nothing to be done about it. She felt really low. So much so that, one night, she'd even considered suicide and had taken six Gardenal tablets. She didn't know anyone else who felt like that. Jandira, the fair-haired girl, who was sitting near the door, her arms around Costa, confessed that it was only after the fourth whiskey that she began to enjoy life, and she suggested that we finish the night in a bar in Montparnasse that was *ouvert la nuit*. Simone stopped the car to tell the others about this new plan, and, a few moments later, we were all sitting around another table. António sat down next to Estrela and resumed their whispered conversation. Simone, eyelids drooping, seemed to believe that the only solution to life was death.

It's odd how I remember every detail of that night. At one point, Jandira started singing a samba, and António got up to dance with Estrela. Their faces were very close, and their two bodies seemed to form one body. They weren't talking. Simone suddenly cried out as if inspired:

"I'd give anything for some *feijoada*."

Etelvino said:

"Well, there's a restaurant somewhere that serves *feijoada*."

"Really?"

"Yes. Salustiano told me where it was, but I wasn't paying attention. It would be hard to find now, because he's gone off traveling."

António and Estrela returned to the table. Etelvino was rhythmically shaking a box of matches.

"*Garçon, une demie*."

That was me. António said:

"You've drunk too much already. You know you can't hold your liquor."

I drank the beer down, then another and another. Everything became quite different then. The other people were suddenly much nicer, and I even felt an impulse to embrace them all. I began to feel so fond of Estrela that I almost wanted to cry. It was more or less then that I spotted the white hair, so coarse that I couldn't keep my eyes off it. Estrela started looking at me equally hard, doubtless because my drunken state put her at her ease. Then she transferred her gaze to António. How could that man have married this woman? It was easy to guess her thoughts in that piercing look and the puzzled crease that appeared between her plucked eyebrows. I then leaned over the table and pointed at her head:

"Let me pull that hair out for you; you might make a mistake and pull out the wrong one, one you might need later on. After all, you don't have much hair as it is."

My words emerged with difficulty, slightly garbled. But they emerged all the same. There was a tense silence, interrupted by Jandira's nervous giggle. Then António helped me to my feet, helped me on with my jacket, wrapped my scarf around my neck, and told the others not to worry about us. There were taxis nearby, the waiter said.

At the door, we passed the Bible man who had just come in. *Rappellez-vous de la vie éternelle*… I laughed at him as if he were some very witty comedian and even turned to wave goodbye to Estrela, for whom I clearly remember feeling genuine friendship.

I think that as soon as my head cleared of alcohol—that is, the next morning—I considered killing myself, which is not the same as saying that I really intended to. Far from it. There are very few suicides, and it's the ones who never talk about it who, sooner or later, actually do kill themselves. The others, those who spend their lives talking about it, are just using death as a form of blackmail. I'm going to kill myself because I've just found out that you're the lover of this man or this woman. If you leave me, I'll kill myself. Usually, this works because human credulity (especially male credulity when personal vanity is involved) knows no limits.

I only considered suicide as a way of increasing my suffering. A kind of chess game I was playing with an absent partner—António: a game he knew nothing about. And even when I went into that pharmacy on the Boulevard Saint-Michel, it wasn't because I wanted to kill myself, but because I wanted to sleep and thought this would be impossible without a sedative.

Much later, I did mean it. There was a day when I did want to die. The day when Estrela came back to Portugal, just to take away from me all that was left—the memory of the child I never had.

Even today, I'm amazed that I was so sure about what was going to happen between António and Estrela. Something—I knew it, knew it at once—was going to be spoiled, and no one would lift a finger to stop it happening. Not Estrela and not him or me. I was certain, but that certainty was still full of doubts. I told myself, more emphatically with each passing day, that perhaps I was wrong and it had been nothing but a mild flirtation, already relegated to the past. Inside, though, that certainty had already put down roots I couldn't see. My doubts were hard workers, but even when I put them into words, I still didn't really believe in them. That's why the surprise I felt was only relative—mixed with a kind of bitter satisfaction that made me say to that other part of me, You see, didn't I tell you? I was right, wasn't I?—when, one afternoon,

António told me, without looking at me and while he was rummaging around in a desk drawer for something he never found:

"Guess who arrived yesterday: Estrela Vale. I just met her downtown. She's come back for good."

"I just don't understand why he told you that," my oldest friend, Lúcia, said to me much later on (she had always been my friend and always would be, or so I thought). Lúcia knew António only superficially. For her, he was just a man; for me, he was António. That was the difference. He was in love with Estrela, as I had seen at once that night in Paris. He wanted her entirely to himself and, as I realized later, wanted to be entirely hers. António was like that. Never, even when he was single, had he gone with a woman he didn't like or stayed with one he no longer liked. He just couldn't do it.

At the time, we were living in the first-floor apartment in Avenida de Berna, which, during our absence, António's father had had furnished in exquisitely bad taste, all very ornate. He had not yet visited, and his room at the far end of a vast corridor was still empty, but on the wall there was already a big, blown-up, full-length picture of his late wife.

I invited Estrela to supper, and that very night all my carefully constructed doubts dissolved before the evidence. António was incapable of hiding his feelings, and maybe he didn't want to. She settled her narrow, invertebrate body into an armchair, her head always very erect, her lips half-open even when she was listening. She brought with her all kinds of stories, the sort of gossip that usually irritated António, yet that now, on the contrary, he appeared to find positively delicious. Did we know that Costa was now engaged to Jandira? He was going back to Brazil, of course. Her father was very rich, some sort of factory owner. She had never thought Costa would allow himself to be seduced by money…

"But Jandira…"

"Oh, Jandira! A complete ninny, *une tête de linotte*. But then, between you and me, Costa isn't exactly a genius either…"

António laughed. He was a friend of Costa's, yet he laughed at Estrela's words. So that was Costa out of the way; what else did she have to tell us? What about Simone? What had happened to Simone?

She had taken Gardenal again one night when she got drunk and was now spending a lot of time with the doctor who had treated her, Jean-Claude. As for Garibaldi…

António drank in her every word.

Estrela visited us on other nights too. I needed to see them together. I needed their presence. I would watch them, and, oddly enough, I felt very calm.

Lúcia, who visited me almost every day, said straight out:

"Mariana, your husband is deceiving you."

"Deceiving me. What a horrible expression. António never intended to deceive me. The only reason he hasn't told me everything is because I've been avoiding having that unpleasant conversation."

"And are you determined to continue avoiding it?"

"I suppose I am. I'm waiting for António to say something."

"You're in for a long wait."

"I certainly hope so, but I'm almost sure he'll say something soon."

Lúcia gave a puzzled frown.

"And you still keep inviting that great…" (She stopped on the edge of the next ugly word, just as in life she had always stopped on the edge of anything she found embarrassing.) "You still keep inviting her so that she can throw herself at YOUR HUSBAND, IN YOUR HOUSE?"

Lúcia always spoke in capitals when she was angry. She had an over-developed, almost medieval sense of ownership. Perhaps because she had a ruined great-uncle, who was a count. I tried several times to show how exaggerated her views were, but Lúcia either couldn't or didn't want to understand. I think she probably couldn't. When she was still a child, she had been given a set of infallible opinions by her mother, which she will doubtless pass on to her own children in their entirety, enriched still further by her husband's views.

I wonder what Lúcia is like now. Even then, it was clear she'd do well for herself. As far as she was concerned, *my* husband was a man who belonged to me, body and soul, and *my* house was a kind of impregnable fortress from which I could hurl down rocks or boiling oil on any attackers. Poor Lúcia didn't realize that the possessive is, in most cases, purely ornamental.

We went to spend a weekend in Gouveia because António's father was feeling unwell. In the end, it was nothing serious, and he was already up and about when we got there, working away as always, and worried because there were so few flowers on the olive trees. It was a lovely day, so we went for a walk. For some reason, perhaps to avoid having to talk, or to fill the hours in some way or another, António decided to take some photographs. I remember I was leaning against a tree with my arms by my side. There was a click, and I shuddered.

"That's it. It's all over," I said, letting my arms hang loose by my side.

"What's over?" he asked in a faint, hesitant voice.

"I don't know, but something is. I was looking at you just now and feeling very good about things. Despite everything. Then you took that photo, and somehow you and I changed position. And there's no real need for us to change…"

"What do you mean? Of course there is. We can't possibly stay like this for the rest of our lives."

I said:

"No, we can't."

António came over to me.

"Listen, Mariana. I've wanted to tell you for a long time…to explain. But it's so difficult, Mariana. I would never have believed it could be so difficult. I look at you and I can't… Perhaps it's better like this; yes, it definitely is."

"I know what you're about to tell me."

I said this without so much as a tremor in my voice. I spoke a little abruptly perhaps or a little too loudly, but I couldn't have said it any differently. António was silent for a moment, then he said:

"I thought you probably knew, that it was almost impossible for you not to know."

"It was only natural, wasn't it?"

"Yes."

It was so difficult; he would never have believed how difficult. And I had to help him; otherwise, in my own relationship with myself, already so tense at times, there would be a kind of schism.

"Look, António, I'll go along with whatever you want to do."

I feel quite calm today, which is why I am once again writing to myself. Who else would waste their time listening to me, given that my life is now empty of everyone? Of António, Luís, Lúcia—who had always been my friend... Always... How deluded I was! The stage is bare even of those pals who enter and then leave having spoken their few lines but who are, after all, so necessary.

Around me there is only the death that gets closer by the day, that and the silence of the house, the silence of the noises in the house, the cracked monotone voice of the landlady chatting to the neighbors who come each evening to talk about other neighbors and about embroidery and about the maids (they're the enemy within, Dona Glória!), the cars passing in the street, the women crying their wares—vegetables or fish. Sometimes there's only silence, and sometimes there are noises I don't want to hear, because they are no longer my noises and long ago ceased to belong to me. They belong to others, to those who are alive. I close the window, put a pillow over my head so as not to hear them, so as to be alone. And also so that I can feel the tears welling up and feel sorry for myself. Then it's as if I have finally reached the top of the mountain and am feeling perfectly calm, ready for the descent. There are other days, though, when I go out onto the balcony to watch the passers-by. I already know the barber who spends his days standing outside his shop, the Barbearia Chique, enjoying the cool or the sun, depending on whether it's hot or cold; the old lady with the cat who always smiles when she sees me; the pretty girl who lives in the next building and who sometimes leaves in a car driven by a bald gentleman, an older man, apparently very respectable; the children who play on the sidewalk when they come back from school. It's when I see them and hear their fresh, green voices that I close the window and step back into my life, which is mine alone and is spent in my room.

For years—how many exactly?—I tried to flee from solitude, the mere thought of which terrified me. I would believe in people, then just let them slip from my open hands. Luís Gonzaga said I expected too much from God's creatures, forgetting that they were just that, God's creatures. Perhaps he was right. Then there were days, months even, black and empty, with no beginning and no end, days I had to get through somehow, leafing through other people's lives in detective novels with happy endings, in which the villain was always punished and virtue richly rewarded, watching stupid films, smoking one pleasureless cigarette after another, or wandering the streets. Alone. But that's all in the past...

Now I'm here and can't even bear to read a book. I know I'm going to die, and that certainty is enough; it's rather soothing actually. In the face of death, everything disappears. But sometimes everything comes back too, depending on what color the day is. The gray days pass, flaccid and glum and tear-stained. I spend the black days trying to unpick for myself the whole of my failed existence. I sometimes wonder if that existence would have been different, better, and if not longer at least more profitable, if I had behaved differently, taken different paths.

But no. I wasn't the one who made the decisions. I wasn't the one who let it all slip away, but I see now that I did exactly that. I was forced to act and, at the same time, to do nothing. I would sometimes be walking down a wide street, the sidewalk ahead of me clear, and suddenly, unexpectedly, I would find a wall blocking my path. It would be too late to retreat, and then I had to find a way of getting out of there or else give in and stay where I was. I wasn't the one who built that wall, nor was I the one who was causing time to speed up. It was all there, ready for my arrival, waiting for me.

My life in this room has lasted for five years, and now it's the only possible life for me. Now that I know what awaits me, there's something deathly about it, or at least something provisional, nebulous. It isn't yet death, but it's not entirely life either. I suppose it never was. I wouldn't be capable of living a real life, because I've lost the habit. Besides, life always was far too difficult for me. I never got used to it, which is strange, because other people find it simple and natural, the simplest, most natural thing there is. I always made such a fuss about it and didn't behave as I should, as other people did so easily, even the coarsest, most vulgar people. I spoke loudly when the most elementary rules told me to speak softly; I said nothing when I really should have said something; I didn't know how to *be*. Yes, that's it. I didn't know how to *be*. I always chose the wrong moments to speak and not to speak. I got everything the wrong way around; I got so muddled that, in the end, I didn't even know where I was. People like Estrela, or even Lúcia, know how to choose their moment, know the value of what is appropriate—that is, they know how to live. I always chose badly. Even the moment for Fernandinho to arrive, had he been born, was wrong. Estrela herself said to someone that, in her view, it could not have happened at a worse moment. Even Estrela.

My son died inside me. One afternoon, I was crossing Restauradores when I spotted Estrela. She was wearing a close-fitting, tailored yellow suit, and, from a distance, her head seemed to me even smaller and blacker. Without thinking, I stopped to look at her. That was when the car drove past and struck my legs. I fell to the ground unconscious. I think I cried out first.

That's how it came about that my son wasn't born and why I could never have any more children. Looking at Estrela. She probably didn't even see me. She didn't stop, because she never was the sort to stop in the street just because someone cried out; she may not even have heard. Her crime was to have passed close by me, for the second time in our two lives. Sometimes, though, all it takes for another person to die is a look, a word, for someone to laugh or walk on by.

Later, many months later, I found out that, at the time of the accident, Estrela was abroad with António. For me, though, that is purely secondary. I could never free myself from the idea that Estrela was that woman. Her or her deceitful shadow, what difference does it make? She was the person I saw even if her actual body was, at that moment, in Paris or in London. It was because of her that Fernandinho never arrived.

I don't want to leave anything behind me. I spent this afternoon tearing up papers. Among them, I found that photo of me, arms by my side, leaning against a tree. Why had I kept it? I don't know; I can't remember. I put it on top of the chest of drawers. I enjoy looking at it.

So many papers, so many pieces of paper filled with my scribblings! Diaries, letters that never reached their addressee because, when I thought about it, it didn't seem worth sending them… Papers written in a tiny hand that I no longer recognize. Firmer, neater, rounder. My writing now is as shriveled and flaccid as my face and my hands, as my slack-breasted body, my lonely faded flesh.

The wastepaper basket is full of my life. Torn bits of paper, fragments, phrases that someone once said to me and that I can't even recall having heard, words I once said to someone and have forgotten. It's all jumbled up in my memory. Postcards from Luís Gonzaga bearing Italian stamps and views of cathedrals. Words from a stranger addressed to someone I no longer am. The weather's been lovely… Rome is just amazing…sending you my very best wishes. I can't even laugh about it.

It's perhaps because of those postcards that I dreamed about Luís last night. His real or imagined presence was—and still is—very pleasant company. For a long time, I would often find myself thinking of him when I woke up. He would appear to me as he was when I first met him or when we said goodbye to each other forever. Forever, despite the postcards that he continues to send me every few months. It was a time when I would wake in the night and gradually become aware of the dim, still strange and vaguely aromatic light of my bedroom, my mouth still tasting of sleep. I didn't want to wake up, because then I would begin to become conscious of myself again. I would close my eyes, wanting to return to the nothingness I had just left behind. In the back of my mind were images I could not see. I wanted to know who I had dreamed of, but couldn't make them out. Sometimes, though, from the deepest depths of my night I would manage to haul to the surface the occasional, almost drowned figure, vague and dull. Were other people's dreams so colorless? I once asked Luís this question, and he said his dreams were like that too. But then Luís accepted everything, never made fun of anything or found anything strange or ridiculous. He always thought deeply about any idea and tried to understand everything, even things too trivial to merit his attention. And in that respect and others too—his voice, his way of smiling—he reminded me intensely of my father.

He and Lúcia were distantly related, and I first met him at her house. He belonged to a wealthy, very devout family from Minho. He was the youngest and most fragile of their sons and had been destined for the priesthood when he was still only a child. He had dutifully gone to the seminary, but, when he had finished his studies there and before taking orders, he was gripped by doubts. Did he really have a religious vocation? That was when he came to Lisbon to study classical philosophy. And yet the first time I met him at Lúcia's house, he said quite spontaneously that it was very likely that he would still become a priest.

Now, writing his name and recalling his face, I feel less alone. As I do when one of his postcards arrives. They don't really say much, but the handwriting is his, and it's so lovely to know that someone actually thought about me, however briefly.

I wonder for how much longer Luís Gonzaga will

continue to send those postcards. In the last one, sent six months ago, he told me that after five years spent in universities and on retreats, he was coming back to Portugal, where he was looking forward to being given a small parish in his own province. This was followed by a banal sentence, in which he hoped that I, too, had found my direction.

My direction… Perhaps I have found it. Could there be a better one for me, however hard I looked for it?

Perhaps he will continue to write to me even when I'm dead, who knows? But no, there will be so many things to prevent him from doing that. His reputation, for example. What would people say and think if they found out—as they surely would—that he was writing to a woman? And you have to protect your reputation, as Lúcia knew. Who cares about friendship when your reputation is at stake? Friendship… As far as Luís is concerned, it may simply be a matter of rooting out a memory that is now nothing more than pity. Yes, perhaps he will continue to send me those postcards out of pity. No, what an idea! What about his reputation? And don't forget egotism. We only give others the gift of remembering them if they thank us for it. And I think I've only written to him a couple of times. We are, after all, only God's creatures. Once, twice, ten or perhaps twelve times in exceptional cases… But then boredom sets in and forgetting, along with those words we cling to so as to feel we're in the right. She doesn't answer because she's not interested in my news. Perhaps my letters bore her. Or: She may have moved again. Or even: Perhaps she's remarried. That is the absolution we give ourselves.

How will I remember Luís Gonzaga? We're incapable

of remembering a person or a landscape, except perhaps on the very first day we saw him or her or it. How can I possibly summon him up as he was then, when I'm now thirty-six, an old woman of thirty-six? An old woman with a lined face and white hair who ceased—how long ago now?—to be a woman? I'm sure that Lúcia's mother still goes to the hairdresser's every two weeks, has her nails manicured, and even plucks her eyebrows and still applies her anti-wrinkle cream each night. What a joke! Lúcia's mother doing all that and me...

How shall I remember Luís Gonzaga? I was twenty-eight at the time. I was going through a divorce; I was unhappy, but I was still only twenty-eight. And I still loved António; there's no doubt about that! Oh, I suffered, yes, but I can't remember how much. It's odd: The years pass, and we remember ancient details with almost photographic clarity, we hear a few words along with the voice that said them, but what we actually felt at a specific moment gets left behind in the past, dies with the moment itself. It's because I was in pain and unhappy that I clung to Luís Gonzaga with something verging on despair. His eyes had the kind of serenity I needed. His calm voice and the way he had of looking at me calmly, almost absentmindedly, brought a feeling of well-being I had never known before and never again found in anyone else. That serenity was perfectly in keeping with the slight flicker of anxiety that sometimes appeared in his eyes and that he did little to suppress. He never again spoke to me, or to anyone else, about the possibility of becoming a priest, but the idea never left him; I knew this from his silences, the sentences begun and never finished, whenever the conversation, however remotely, touched on the church or the seminary, or even the Catholic religion itself. I also knew this from the fact, which will be incomprehensible to some, that he never tried to convert me.

We often went out together. I had an almost physical need to walk, to see people, to go places, to keep my eyes fixed on things outside myself, far from myself. I had finally found a job as a typist in a shipping company, but after work, and whenever he was free, I would meet up with Luís Gonzaga and we would visit exhibitions, go to cinema matinees, and, on Sundays, for lack of anything better, we would even go to the zoo to look at the animals. On bad days, I would talk to him about António, about Estrela, and about myself. He would laugh and remind me that I was still only twenty-eight and had many more years ahead of me.

"Just you wait, I'll officiate at your wedding one of these days," he said once.

He had his bad times too. He would seem preoccupied and silent. Once, he told me that the seminary had damaged him. Other people had made his decisions for him, and now he didn't know how to set himself free.

"I can see the marks," I said. "Anyone could. Just think, out of five siblings you were the one chosen by the family to be a priest. Don't you think it would be a tremendous coincidence if you also happened to have a religious vocation? Unless you think you're in a state of grace and are thus committing the sin of pride."

He smiled:

"We all commit the sin of pride sixty times an hour, sometimes more. You saw my marks and know you're right. And I know I'm right in knowing that I don't yet know. Ah, yes, pride…"

Estrela and António were married one June morning. A church wedding, of course. As Luís Gonzaga always mentioned, mine had merely been a registry office affair. Alice Mendes, an old colleague of Maria Amália's with whom I'd always stayed in touch, phoned me to give me the news. Purely by chance, of course. The matter came up in conversation by a simple association of ideas. Or so she said. "And speaking of fools…" Perhaps it was true. Among other snippets of news—Alice always had plenty of news and couldn't distinguish good from bad—she mentioned a former rather unpleasant classmate of ours, whom she had bumped into a few days before in Versailles. "And speaking of fools, do you know who got married today? Your husband, António."

I would have preferred to find this out the next day or a week or month later. Alice could not resist though. Poor thing, you couldn't really blame her; she'd been the same at school. She wasn't a bad person, merely a victim—as we all are—of the quality of our chromosomes. It's a real curse being such a blabbermouth. You're not in control of yourself; you never know what you should or shouldn't say. And you can cause other people real pain.

That afternoon, I went in search of Luís. I couldn't be alone with Estrela and António, and they wouldn't go away. I even phoned Lúcia, but she had gone to the cinema with her mother. I had visited Luís Gonzaga's room on other occasions to borrow a book or to take him one I'd promised to lend him. It was a small, modest, self-contained room in Rua do Conde do Redondo. A bachelor room, tidy and anonymous, and that gave the impression of being uninhabited. There was a cross above the head of the narrow wrought-iron bed. By the time I left, it was dark. He had told me earlier, looking me in the eye, that he couldn't marry me.

"I know."

"Because it's almost certain, almost inevitable that I'll go on to become a priest."

"That's OK."

Before I left, just as I was about to open the door, I asked, and I still don't know why:

"Will you go to confession first thing tomorrow, Luís?"

"Why do you ask?"

"Good question."

We met frequently after that, then, one night, he phoned me. He needed to speak to me urgently. The following morning, I found him looking tired and sunken-eyed, like someone who has spent a sleepless night. He had finally come to a decision. It was all arranged. He would be leaving in a couple of days.

I put my hand on my belly, where my son was not yet stirring, then held the same hand out to him. I spoke (I don't know now what I said), but I remember that my face and my words were those of a very bad ham actress.

"So, this is goodbye, then," I said at last. "We won't see each other again."

"We can always see each other again, Mariana. After all, we were friends before, weren't we?"

"Aren't we friends anymore?"

"That isn't what I meant, but, yes, we can be friends as we used to be. If you ever need anything..."

"I'll ask. But why these empty words, Luís? Goodbye means goodbye, nothing more."

The world had not fallen in on me as it had that other time, when António gazed into Estrela's eyes. Now it was more as if a screw had come loose or a small beam had broken, but both things could be mended. And I didn't feel alone either, because I had my son with me, a son all to myself.

I went over to Luís and thought very coolly that, under the circumstances, a tear or two would make him happy, but I had none to give him. At first, I had felt sad, despondent, but now I was beginning to feel strangely liberated, which was rather troubling at the time. Luís seemed to be waiting for some response from me. I found myself silently thinking things like "abandoned and with a child on the way" and "what a terrible situation to be left in" and even "how am I going to pay for the birth?" And these words suddenly made me feel like laughing.

"You're hurt, Mariana," said Luís. "Go on, cry if you want to."

The vanity of men! Why would I cry when I had my son with me? Just because he was leaving. Ah, the vanity of men, the incredible, ridiculous vanity of men…

I was at Lúcia's house. She hadn't yet come home, and her mother was telling me about her daughter's new boyfriend, whom she liked enormously. Her eyes were shining, and, in her enthusiasm, she had put her knitting down on her plump knees. She was a woman of a certain age (Lúcia had been a late child), but she took great care of herself. Her now somewhat ill-defined mouth resembled a withered flower, her lipstick leaching into the concentric lines surrounding it.

"He's an excellent young man," she said firmly. "Excellent."

For Dona Corina, a nice young man had no age or physical or intellectual qualities, let alone moral ones. He had, and this was very important, a salary worth more than three *contos*. The description I had just heard told me all I needed to know about Lúcia's new boyfriend, whom I had not even met: namely, that he must be earning well over five contos.

"How old is he?" I asked merely to ask something. "The same age as Lúcia?"

Dona Corina took off her glasses.

"No, he's forty-five, but you'd never think it. You must meet him. You'd think he was thirty at the most. And he's just mad about Lúcia, you've no idea. He wants to rent an apartment and get married this year..."

"What does he do?"

"Oh, I thought you knew. He's an engineer, and highly respected. He works for Tabor. He has a good salary too, very good."

I managed to suppress the "How much?" that was on the tip of my tongue. Not out of curiosity, no one could accuse me of that, but simply to discover what qualities were necessary to merit the description of "excellent." But what was the point? Dona Corina resumed her knitting, and I turned on the radio. I felt at home in Lúcia's house, my "always friend," as much as I did in my own house, which I no longer had. And infinitely more than in the boarding house I was living in at the time. I didn't like the music they were playing, and so I twizzled the knob. Lúcia was late. I began to think it odd that she hadn't yet introduced me to that boyfriend to whom she was soon to be married. It probably just hadn't happened. What other reason could there be?

Without even stopping her knitting, Dona Corina returned to the subject preoccupying her.

"He's from very good stock, you know. I'm sure you've heard of the Vale de Pomar family. You haven't?"

She frowned in disbelief, as if I had just confessed to not knowing that the British royal family existed. Then she abandoned her knitting to go into the kitchen to see what the maid was up to.

"Oh, it's nothing, just the usual. You'll excuse me, won't you, Mariana, but if you don't keep an eye on these maids..."

I was left alone to wait for Lúcia. I thought to myself, "What am I doing here when I have nothing to say to her?" I stayed out of sheer inertia. The armchair was very comfortable and the flower painting opposite so pleasant to look at. My already heavy body was filled with a great languor.

Lúcia arrived at around seven o'clock. She was in high spirits and looked prettier than usual; she asked rather indifferently if I would be staying for supper, then, without waiting for a reply, asked what I'd been up to recently. For nearly half an hour, we spoke of matters of no interest to either of us. In the end, I laughed. She always did keep her cards close to her chest, I said. I hoped she'd at least invite me to the wedding.

She gave a rather embarrassed laugh. Oh, so her mother had told me, had she? The blabbermouth! Not that she had been keeping it a secret, what an idea, but nothing had yet been decided. Her mother always oversimplified things. After all, a person can't get married just like that...

"But you've never even mentioned him to me!"

Really? No, she must have.

I got up. I had to go, I said. No, I wouldn't stay for supper. They were expecting me back at the boarding house. I went over to the window to see if it was raining. When I turned round, I saw Lúcia's eyes fixed on me, on one particular part of my body. The keen, interrogative eye of someone who wanted to be absolutely sure about something.

I hoped with all my heart that I was wrong, and, while I waited and hoped, I didn't return to Lúcia's house. She knew where I lived, didn't she?

I heard nothing from her for months.

One day, my boss called me in. He was usually a very autocratic type and rather unpleasant, but this time, I felt sorry for him. He looked at me, not knowing how to begin. He cleared his throat. He riffled through some papers. He was very pale.

"Someone told Senhor Bruno (the owner of the company) that you've, well, that you're…"

"Going to have a baby. As you can see, that's perfectly true. It's so obvious that the 'someone' who told Senhor Bruno could have saved him or herself the bother. Senhor Bruno just had to look at me."

"Senhor Bruno has charged me with asking you to leave the company quietly, and nothing more will be said." Those were his words, which he repeated twice: "nothing more will be said." "And that's all, Dona Mariana. I'm really sorry. You can collect your wages at the cashier's office. Believe me, I really am very sorry."

His hands were trembling. Not that he was a nice man. On the contrary, he was coarse, unfair, and bossy.

He was simply experiencing his one moment of kindness. I didn't say this to him, because I knew he wouldn't understand.

I had to survive on the meager interest from my father's investments until Fernandinho was born and then try and find another job. I started saving up so that I could pay for my stay in the maternity ward.

One morning, I read about her wedding in the society column. Her uncle, the bankrupt count, had given her away, and her bridesmaid had been a friend of the family, whose forebears had been in trade, but who had inherited substantial wealth. The bridegroom's best men had been João Frederico de Castro and Nunes Vale de Pomar, long names that meant nothing to me. I couldn't be angry with Lúcia, poor thing. How could she possibly present me to her new family?

"This is my friend, Mariana, who, as you see, is about to have a child."

"And your husband?" someone would ask.

"I don't have a husband, Senhora."

"So who is the child's father?"

And Lúcia, in very worldly fashion, would say:

"No one knows. Do you, Mariana? I mean, you might know, mightn't you? It does happen..."

I had exactly these conversations several times a day, but I couldn't be angry with Lúcia. The time it must have taken her, her fiancé, and her mother to arrive at a solution! The hypotheses set aside and the shortlist of possible strategies drawn up before making a final decision. Should they put the situation to me frankly? They wouldn't have the courage. Introduce me anyway? "Are you mad, Lúcia?

And what about my family and the Vale de Pomar family?" Silence was the best option. They forced me to understand that I was simply not a friend they could introduce to anyone. "What do you think, Mama?" And Dona Corina would state very firmly, "I think a lady should know how to preserve her reputation." I can hear her now. She would have taken off her glasses and put her eternal knitting down on her lap. The hours they must have wasted on my account. Poor, poor Lúcia!

That was yesterday. Today, it's poor me. I'm going to take some sleeping pills.

The landlady woke in a bad mood. She's spent all morning scolding the maid, who responds with the silence of her great sighs. Today's topic is that the girl got up late. Despite the general disorder and lack of cleanliness, which surprised me at first, Dona Glória considers herself to be a good housewife. Lúcia's mother also used to say sometimes, "I'm a very good housewife myself, and the man who marries my daughter can think himself lucky. She can do everything. That's very important in a woman. Men like to have a tidy house: the clothes put away and meals on the table at the proper time. I've always been a real slave to housework."

What would my mother have been like? She died when I was only three, and my father would always cry when he talked about her. I longed to know what the mother I'd never really known was like, but I couldn't bring myself to ask him. Sometimes, I would spend hours looking at the photo on my father's bedside table. I would gaze at it so hard that it seemed to me that her eyelids moved and her mouth opened in a smile.

No, she hadn't been like these other women; she couldn't have been. She cooked the meals, did the washing (they didn't have a maid), but I'm sure she wasn't a "good housewife."

I loathe good housewives. If they're poor, they wear themselves out working; if they're well-off or rich, they employ one or more other women to wear themselves out working instead. Either way, they are the slaves of that work or of keeping an eye on the other slaves at their beck and call. Life goes on outside—husbands and children can get on with their lives, can plunge into it—and the housewives have to stay home scrubbing and cleaning and polishing the brass. Or watch others: Look, you've missed a bit of dust there. That tap isn't shiny enough. Things can't go on this way. Life, meanwhile, has passed them by and they haven't noticed, haven't noticed a thing. They've been left alone, and they haven't even noticed. The husband has died without ever being there; the sons have fled in order to marry the housewives hidden inside other pretty, jolly, passionate girls. And life goes on. Look, things can't go on like this. And the sons of those sons dream of running away and meeting other passionate girls…

Then I saw Estrela on Restauradores. Well, Estrela or someone who looked like her; it doesn't matter. And Fernandinho died forever and ever. He and all the brothers and sisters he might have had. The nurse told me he was a boy. As if I didn't know! The nurse had seen him, but I knew far more about him than she did. I was sure he would have fair hair, large, slightly almond-shaped eyes, António's pale hands… António's?

"It's such a shame. He was a lovely baby."

The nurse was sharing professionally in my grief. I said only:

"Yes, he was."

And I closed my eyes tight to keep the tears in.

The nurse came over to me and stroked my hair. I screamed at her to leave. I screamed so loudly that the women in the other beds fell silent, and, for a long time, all you could hear in the ward were my sobs and the frightened cries of newborn babies.

I moved from the boarding house where I was living to a private house that suited me better, Dona Glória's house. She knows nothing, either about my life or my death. Nothing, except that I'm divorced. On several occasions, at mealtimes, she's tried to draw me out by talking about herself. She tells me about her husband who died of septicemia (that was in the days before penicillin, Dona Mariana); about the younger sister who, at seventeen, ran away with an ensign and was, alas, very unhappy. I've even seen the photograph of her sister, Ermelinda, a plump girl with vacant eyes. Ermelinda is dead now, God rest her, Dona Glória always says very reverently, and you can tell that she's dead from the faded photo where there is neither gaze nor smile.

"What the poor creature went through, Dona Mariana! The heartbreak, the money problems, that man's disgraceful behavior…everything. And she was so pretty, too, as you can see from the photo."

"Yes, she had lovely eyes," I say, just to please her.

"Lovely."

You can never go wrong with eyes. Everyone is convinced that they, and all their family, have lovely eyes. They run in the family! Even I had—yes, "had" is the word—lovely eyes. Like your mother, my father would say dreamily. Just like your mother's eyes.

Dona Glória sometimes sighs gently.

"But that's life, and we all have our cross to bear. As you yourself know all too well."

There's the hook. I smile and nod. Don't I know it, say that smile and nod. But I offer her only an empty phrase:

"Who doesn't, Dona Glória?"

"Oh, not everyone does, Dona Mariana, not everyone. You know, sometimes I think..."

But I never find out what Dona Glória thinks. She sits there, gazing off into the distance. When she speaks again, she's already onto another subject.

"Now, tell me what you'd like for supper. You're so thin and have no appetite at all. Isn't there anything you really fancy? Really? I was thinking of making some fish pasties with tomato risotto..."

That woman, Dona Glória, has photos of her husband and her sister. I don't have any of my father or of António. I was in such a hurry to leave the house in Avenida de Berna that I left all my things there. I know now why I've always kept the photo António took in Gouveia, the one of me leaning against the tree. Because it's the only one I have of him. He's there in my wide eyes.

I went back to work, this time as secretary to a semi-famous writer, who, every day, produced several pages (he, poor man, thought he was giving them to posterity) that were then typed up by me in single spacing. That job lasted as long as it took me to transfer onto new paper all the vicissitudes of a very wealthy family living on an estate close to

Viseu. And then I again found myself unemployed, with very little money and with nothing close by to which I could cling. But I felt almost contented.

Sometimes I go to bed and spend hours staring up at the ceiling or at the wall on the lefthand side of the bed. The floral wallpaper has a background that must once have been white, but is now yellow with age, and it's full of spots of mold where I can make out smiling or sometimes very troubling faces. Strange, almost diabolical, silently snickering profiles, which grow more perfect the longer I spend looking at them, unblinking, as if my gaze were unwittingly completing the design, bringing life and relief to the outline. At other times, the faces are horrible, looming out of the peeling ceiling plaster or formed by the shadows cast by the furniture when I turn on the light. Sometimes, one of those profiles gradually mutates into Estrela laughing her quiet laugh. I close my eyes, but she's still there inside me. I take a couple of pills, but sometimes it's only with the fourth pill that her face and her laugh dissolve into a deep, heavy sleep.

One day, I was reading the classifieds in the paper, and I found one that interested me. An English couple with two children needed a Portuguese companion to go abroad with them. I thought my English would be good enough, and so I replied. They arranged to meet me in a hotel in the Baixa. The wife was a tall, thin woman, not in the first flush of youth, with very pink, freckled skin. Her husband was a fat, imposing man, with a short brush of almost white hair. The boys gravely shook my hand. They were both fair-haired and rather lackluster, with a deep, precocious gaze that was older than their years.

The proposed conditions suited me perfectly. The

Harpers wanted their children to learn Portuguese. They were going to spend a few months in London, possibly a year, and only then settle in Oporto, where Mr. Harper had business interests. On the way back, they intended to spend a few days in Paris. Oh, I knew Paris, did I? Then I would doubtless be pleased to make a return visit. After all, anyone who has ever been there always dreams of going back, wasn't that so? Mrs. Harper smiled. Should I tell her that it was in Paris that...? No, why tell anything to a woman who was a matter of complete indifference to me? She continued to talk. If, at any point or for any reason, I should feel ill or even bored or simply miss my family (as was only natural!), they would consider themselves free of any further obligation toward me—which did not mean, she added, that they would be shocked by any decision of that kind. It was also agreed that I would enjoy relative freedom. The husband said almost nothing, merely underlining with smiles and nods what his wife was saying. The house and the children were clearly her domain, while he dealt with the business side of things. When I got up to leave, having first given my prolix author and two or three other people as possible references, the two boys accompanied me to the door of the hotel.

At last, a job I would really enjoy and one that I had never even considered. I had often thought I would like to be a nurse or a primary school teacher, but I didn't have the necessary qualifications for either profession. My experiences working for the shipping company and for the novelist had been real nightmares. I really couldn't face the idea of spending weeks, months, years, the rest of my life, sitting at a desk in front of a typewriter, writing boring letters or typing up horribly tedious, vapid novels. Getting older and fatter (because I think boredom does make you fat), always mired in the same problems, other people's problems. When the writer had finished his "novel of manners," he offered to recommend me to some under-secretary or other who often featured in the newspapers at the time.

"I'm sure he'll find something for you. He's a great friend of mine and will be glad to do me a favor. He's an excellent fellow, as admirable in public life as he is in private. Why do you laugh?"

My old habit of laughing at things that others didn't find funny. Men could have a public life, but women? Or only women of the street. Perhaps there was a connection. I stopped laughing, and he continued to praise his friend and admirer.

"I'll give you a letter of recommendation."

I turned down his offer, even though all I had in my purse was a twenty escudo note. I had asked to be paid the rest as an advance during the month I had worked for him.

Now I would have a job that interested me. I once again placed my hope in life. Not too much, just a little. Consciously, I mean. Perhaps a change of air, a job I enjoyed, and spending time with children would bring more cheerful thoughts, would sweep away those obsessive ideas that kept me from sleeping. It was with something verging on enthusiasm that I sorted out my passport and the necessary visas. So great was my desire to return to a normal life that I even phoned a few vague acquaintances, including Alice Mendes, to say goodbye. I think I needed to convince myself that things would get better and that the best way to be sure of that was to hear it in my own voice.

Then, just two days before we were due to leave, Mr. Harper called me in a terrible state, stumbling over his words. His wife had just been taken into the hospital for an urgent operation. The doctors had clearly thought it was a serious matter, and he feared the worst. And of course, for the moment, he had dismissed all thoughts of traveling. Even if everything went well, Mrs. Harper would be left very weak, and he had just phoned one of her sisters, who lived in London, to come and take care of the children. He was expecting her on the first plane the following day. Naturally, he insisted I tell him of any expenses incurred.

Mrs. Harper recovered, I found out later. In fact, I telephoned the hotel one day to ask. Mrs. Harper was convalescing, I was told. She hadn't left Lisbon, and I was still chained to my old room, an eternal prisoner of its walls.

"It's just as well, Dona Mariana," said the landlady. "I was dreading having to get used to a new face... That would have been very hard. I even prayed to St. Teresa for you not to leave."

The Englishwoman survived, and Dona Glória was content. It was all for the best, thanks to St. Teresa.

I began to feel more and more tired. Tired of living and incapable of seeking out my own death. Tired of existing and tired of the ghosts that continued to come at all hours of the day or night to saunter past me. Tired of everything, both near and far. I became so thin and looked so ill that the landlady insisted I go to the doctor.

"Has it never occurred to you that it might be

tuberculosis, Dona Mariana? And that's very serious, a contagious disease. I'm not saying that because I'm afraid I might catch it, I've never been afraid of illnesses, but Augusta's still a young girl..."

I went to the doctor. He examined me carefully, then sent me off to have various blood tests. It was probably nothing, but just in case... I asked him if what he suspected I had was contagious.

"No, what an idea!"

And he laughed. I couldn't see what was so funny. Neither could he.

One evening, I went to the cinema. I've no idea why. How long had it been since I last went to see a movie? I walked past the Tivoli. There weren't many people going in, and I felt something calling to me. Why not? That was life after all. I used to love going to the cinema, and later on, I just enjoyed being there when the lights went down and having a dream appear right before my eyes. I used to enjoy it; perhaps I still would. Yes, now I remember: that's why I went in, just to find out if I was still capable of enjoying something.

It was early, and the place was almost empty. Behind me, two women, sorry, two ladies, were talking. They both had the kind of voice you'd expect to hear coming from a buxom contralto bursting out of her dress, the kind of voice that, for some reason, certain well-heeled ladies always have.

"You were quite right; she's really nice. And so unaffected!"

"Yes, she is, isn't she?"

"Absolutely. I was just utterly *charmed*. As a couple, they seem very close too, which is quite a rarity these days. But not embarrassingly so. And they're quite well-off too. With a big house and all. How long have they been married?"

"Four years, I think. They met in Paris, he got divorced, because, fortunately, his first marriage was just a registry office affair. It was a real *coup de foudre*..."

"Hm, unusual, but then Estrela always struck me as remarkable, not as a sculptor, let it be said. I mean that 'Seated Bather' she has in the living room, really...but as a person. Attractive, pretty, a complete woman."

"And she's nice too, really decent. She won't have a word said against António's first wife, because there was a lot of talk about how the silly woman, just a few months after her divorce, could be seen swanning around town with a belly on her...well, you can imagine what people were saying..."

"I didn't know that. I assume she must have had a lover while she was married. Who was she?"

"No one you'd know. There was a lot of gossip because she was the ex-wife of Estrela's husband, but Estrela has always defended her. She agreed, of course, that the woman couldn't have chosen a worse moment to make a mistake like that, but that, in view of the circumstances... Anyway, she's a lovely person. A good wife, a good mother... When her two-year-old had tonsillitis, she couldn't have been more..."

"Oh, I didn't know they had children..."

"Yes, two, and the oldest one, Fernando..."

The lights had dimmed. I got up and struggled to the end of the row, stepping on the toes of various loudly complaining people. The usher said something I didn't understand; what it was I don't know, but I remember hearing his voice. I only breathed freely again once I was out in the street and had started walking down the avenue with no idea where I was going. At one point, I realized I was standing by the river. At the same time, I noticed people looking at me, and some were laughing. Two boys stopped right in front of me, then ran away. I raised my hands to my face, and when I removed them, they were wet with tears.

That day, I really did consider killing myself. I was still considering it the following morning when Dona Glória and the maid went out to do the shopping. I was alone in the house; I couldn't let the chance slip by. I closed the window and the kitchen door. Then I turned on the gas and waited. And I did all this without thinking, without wanting to think. Just as the air began to grow thick, someone rang the doorbell. I turned off the gas, slowly opened the kitchen door, then went to the front door. It was the mailman with a postcard from Luís Gonzaga.

Then life went on, if you can call it life.

"Why don't you go out for a while? Go to another doctor, Dona Mariana. Everyone says Cardênio Santos is wonderful. My sister, God rest her... We all have our cross to bear... But there are people... How about some rabbit stew, Dona Mariana? How about a little rabbit stew?"

"I love rabbit stew, Dona Glória. I adore it."

In the end, I did go to Dr. Cardénio, one of those people who never ever makes a misdiagnosis. I only went because I wanted to know for sure. Now I do know, and I'm waiting. I'm not having any more tests, nor do I intend to see the doctor again. Why bother if, in a month or two months, I'm going to die? I know I can't expect any more from life, and that's why I just want to feel calm. I want... Yes, that is my goal, my only goal. I can't choose another one; there aren't any. For the first time, someone is coming to find me, seeking me out. Why, then, shouldn't I be happy, me, the chosen one?

But I can't. I feel at once violated and a virgin. There are so many things in me, and yet I'm completely empty. Empty because all hope is gone. Hope, but not the desire to live. Even though I'm stuck in this room with its sour smell that I can't smell anymore, even though António is far from me and Fernandinho is kissing a mother who is not me, even so, I still want to live. As best I can. And life is ticking away with each day that passes, without me having lived it.

I can't get out of bed now; I don't have the strength. Dona Glória came today and sat across from me in the old armchair and talked for half an hour. I don't know what she said because her words somehow didn't enter my brain.

"Don't you agree, Dona Mariana? Don't you think that would be better?"

I didn't know what she was talking about, but I nodded. She looked very pleased.

"It's the best solution, Dona Mariana, believe me. You'll lack for nothing there. And don't worry, I've already spoken to Dona Manuela, who's a nurse at the Hospital de Santa Marta. She's a kind woman, a real gem, no disrespect to yourself, of course. She immediately agreed to ask them to help."

Why say No? She was, after all, in her own house, in

her castle. Lúcia had been right about that. How could I say No? Without opening my eyes, I simply said:

"Won't St. Teresa be upset with you, Dona Glória? You asked her to make me stay, remember."

"But it's for your own good, Dona Mariana, for your own good."

"Oh, well, in that case…"

I go to the hospital today. I thought I would be able to die here in this room, but it seems not. I put my photo in my bag; perhaps they'll let me look at it, I don't know. Dona Glória dressed me as if I were already dead. She put my hat on my head, the hat with the feather, put my jacket over my shoulders, gave me a pair of her stockings because I didn't have any that didn't have holes in them. Now we're both waiting for the taxi that Augusta has gone downstairs to call. Dona Glória is coming with me. It's as if we were both going to my funeral.

voluptuous pleasure, he would say out loud (mangling them horribly) just to hear those names spoken.

Then the years had passed almost without him realizing, years full of long, tedious, identical days. He began working at the counter; he was given his own desk complete with briefcase and finger sponge (this was, after all, a job with a future); he met women—a few—and he married. And now he was the one to shout "Boy! Boy!" Whenever he did, though, he felt a tightening of the throat, a feeling of embarrassment that even he could not explain, a pang of guilt too—yes, mainly guilt toward those serious, energetic, eager young lads.

He didn't often think about things (why go delving into them?), but he did sometimes catch himself thinking that perhaps this wasn't what he had been born to do and that there might still be time to escape. But escape from what? And where to? He liked his work. Did he? The truth is, he didn't know anything else. Numbers, numbers, days, months, years of numbers, years that to him were abstract but that for many other people were clearly very real. It was quite possible that he hadn't been born to do this job, but then who is born to do anything? he thought by way of consolation. He was a placid fellow, accustomed to putting up with life's vexations. A man who knew no strong pleasures and found no sorrows too unbearable. A methodical man with impossible dreams and no ambitions.

On Sundays, he would don his best suit—the blue one—and his birthday tie and set off to watch football. His wife would also get dressed up and go and visit her mother. Sometimes, they would leave at the same time and only say goodbye at the end of the street, exchanging kisses without even realizing they were. Spending Sunday afternoons apart was an old habit that both had always found perfectly natural. As natural and immutable as going to the local cinema on a Saturday night to watch some film or other, whatever happened to be on, and attending eleven o'clock mass on Sunday at São Domingos.

Sometimes, over supper, his wife would ask:

"Bad game?"

Adérito would reply with a "so-so" or a "pretty average." And he would also blush slightly because he was a man who disliked all lies. The reason he lied was simply because he felt that his wife would find it easier to understand the lies he told than the truths he could have told her. He couldn't imagine—and he had often thought about it—what her reaction would be if he told her where, for years and years, he had been spending his Sunday afternoons. Every single one. Come rain or shine. She might not believe him; women always find it hard to believe simple, transparent things. No, she would never believe that he went down to the harbor to watch the boats leaving or to the airport to see the planes taking off. One day, he had mentioned this hobby of his to Costa, his colleague at the bank, and Costa had smiled a slightly superior smile. If Costa couldn't understand it, how could a poor, insignificant creature like his wife... Costa had even asked:

"But what possible interest can you have in watching those people heading off on a plane or a ship?"

And that was the strange thing. Adérito didn't go to the airport or to the harbor to watch the people who were leaving. Nor did he go there to see the boats or the planes. It was more complex than that. Even he didn't know—for he was a simple man—what he was hoping to get out of those moments, which were the happiest, richest, most complete of his lifeless existence. It was everything and nothing at the same time. The strong, slightly putrid smell of the dark, mysterious water so close by; the salt air on his skin; the excited voices; the hustle and bustle; the shouts; the occasional tears; those calm, collected, adventurous words filling the air: Destination Karachi…or Destination Brazil…or New York… Then, and this was the best bit: the great bird roaring down the runway before slicing through empty space or the enormous ship moving as quietly as time itself over the light waves of that river-cum-ocean.

Sometimes, he would stay watching until the ship had vanished from sight. He experienced a kind of anguish, as if some much-loved person had left forever. Except that isn't quite what it was. What he felt was a terrible grief for the person—namely, himself—who had to stay behind.

He would then walk along the quayside, and there were always men—whether very dirty or just burned by the sun; he couldn't tell—unloading or loading bundles onto the cargo ships that had arrived or were about to leave. Men with the faces of adventurers. Men. Sometimes, he would stop to look at other boats: small, ancient-looking boats, slowly rotting away in the water, always in motion and always still, tethered to iron posts by thick ropes. Tethered there to prevent them going to sea. Tethered like him.

He would always return home in a melancholy mood. He would see the table laid for supper, the scarlet lampshade, the statuette of the boy eating cherries (the cherries would sway when he came in); he would see his own wife—who had already grown plump and soft with age—and he would see all this with different eyes, with the new eyes of someone come from far away and who suddenly, unexpectedly, falls back into ordinary everyday life, into his old life, into the life that was there waiting for him: his life.

As she was serving the soup, his wife would ask:

"Bad game?"

And he would blush and say:

"So-so. How's your mother?"

Sometimes, at night, it would rain. The drops would beat hard against the window panes; the wind would sweep over the entire street. She would put down her knitting and wrap her shawl more tightly around her because she always felt the cold.

"It's good to be at home," she would say. "But do you know where I'd be happiest? In Africa..."

He would smile faintly, go over to the bookshelf, open *Robinson Crusoe* or something by Jules Verne, books he had read so often that he knew certain passages by heart.

The following morning, he would return to the bank to do more addition, subtraction, multiplication, and division. "Boy!" "Come here, Boy!" But the guilty expression on his face meant that the boys didn't respect him. He was always the last person they would rush to help.

One day, one of the directors called him in and had him sit down on one of those green leather armchairs that, up until then, he had seen but never sat in. The director was a fat man, very perfumed and smiling, with diamond rings on his fingers. He looked intently at Adérito as if trying to read his thoughts.

"Do you know why I asked you to see me?"

Adérito did not. Nor did he have any thoughts worth reading. He was perched on the edge of the chair, his hands on his knees, which he kept respectfully pressed together.

The director started talking. The board recognized how valuable he was to them, his dedication to the firm, his love of his work. As he must have heard, the bank was going to open a branch in Lourenço Marques in Mozambique. And the board had immediately thought of him, Adérito, as the right person to manage and run the branch. This would, of course, mean an increase in salary. He would go so far as to say that it would be a considerable increase… Considerable… In short, it was a highly advantageous, not to say, prestigious post. But he should go away and think about it, then tell him Yes or No.

Adérito did not think, or rather, he thought about it very little. Nor did he mention it to his wife, because she would be incapable of understanding the decision he had made even as the director was setting out his proposal. She, poor thing, had always dreamed of being a lady. And a lady like her might have ambitions. With lots of hats and lots of dresses and lots of cakes to offer visitors. The wife of a bank manager in a colonial city… She would, of course, never forgive him for turning down the offer. He spoke to the director about his wife's health, about his own very delicate liver. All lies, needless to say. Why, though, why? He himself didn't know. Then again, perhaps he did. Perhaps it was because there were people who could dream and live at the same time, the swarthy men on the quayside, the actors and actresses he saw on Saturday nights at the local cinema, and he had grown accustomed to dreaming and living. Perhaps that's why. Now it was late, too late. He would no longer know how to actually *live* a dream. He felt old, horribly old, and tired, yes, terribly tired. Terribly sad too.

It was his colleague Costa who later set off on a lovely steamship. Adérito stood watching on the quayside, his eyes wide open, and he felt a dreadful, overwhelming sense of anguish. He stood there until the ship had disappeared completely into the thick mist covering the Tejo that morning. Then he went to the airport to watch the planes leave.

pretending to like someone or not to like them anymore. Perhaps old people and children were more authentic because they were closer to the void... Those about to depart and the new arrivals... New arrivals... Oh, bother! She had just typed those two words on the ad for Victoria milk: the very finest powdered milk. Another torn-up piece of paper because the boss didn't like crossings-out. It had been like this all day. Even the very first thing she had done that morning had gone horribly wrong (she had torn her new blouse as she was putting it on), and she had then headed off into fresh disasters, and, still worse, knowing full well where she was heading. She had bent her knee more energetically than usual and caused a run in her stocking, and she didn't have money to buy any more. Not until the end of the month! Then there was the heel on her shoe: the Sunday-best pair that she usually only wore when she went out at night or to visit her family—because she wanted them to think she was doing relatively well—and that, when she was hurrying, afraid she was going to be late for work, had become stuck in between one of those gaps in the floor of the tram, one of those horrid little gaps purpose-made for heels to get stuck in them, and that had almost torn the heel off and left it very wobbly. So there was that, and then, behind it all, lay the man she loved and who was about to get married. But she didn't want to think about that. What was the point? The wastepaper basket was full of crumpled bits of paper because all morning and all afternoon she had been accumulating errors and more errors. She felt like smashing her typewriter; smashing her desk; smashing Alda's dark, bold, soppy eyes, which she occasionally trained on her, eyes overflowing with unrequited sometimes asked herself if she would know how to live with another person now; she was so used to not having to explain what she did and always, always doing what she wanted. Always? What about the man who was going to be married in three days? She could still hear him saying, "Clara, I have to tell you something, and I don't know how to begin..." She had said, "You're going to get married, aren't you?" And she had said this out of pure intuition, not really believing her own words, but when he didn't laugh, she had suddenly felt afraid of what she was about to hear. He had talked and talked, but Clara hadn't heard a word he said. The room had suddenly ceased to exist, as had the man who was speaking, and only she remained. She felt empty and incapable of making a sound. With other men, it had been different. With them, she had been the one to write the words "The End" on the final page—not that she had been in love with any of them; she had only been with them out of loneliness and a need for warmth. And for that reason, it hadn't been difficult or painful or unexpected to find she was staring at the bottom of the glass. Sometimes, this even brought her a certain feeling of calm. All right, the glass was empty, but life went on. As it would now, of course, but it would be a different life. An empty existence, from which he would be absent, but where he, as she well knew, would always be present. But she didn't want to think about him. Why was he clinging to her thoughts? Why did he appear in all of them?

She took the bus to Restauradores and had to go upstairs because there were so many people. She hated doing this because she was afraid of having to come down the stairs while the bus was moving, which made her nervous, and she almost always stumbled, and almost always there was some kind gentleman getting on in years who would catch her, and she never knew whether to thank the person or get angry or even slap his face, because she really didn't feel it was necessary for him to touch her breasts or tug at her skirt. That afternoon, though, she was sorry to see that there was no elderly gentleman at the bottom of the stairs, because in his place was the very first man she had been with: the one who had led her to flee her parents' house, the one she had believed in enough to think they would marry. She had believed in him and in herself, but it was all his fault, because he had said so many things that had made her think she really did love him and could set aside all her fears and uncertainties and, with him for company, never again feel alone. That had been years ago, and yet there he was, but he didn't even see her because he jumped off the bus while it was still moving, as he always used to do. Clara even opened her mouth to call out to him, but he was already far away and wouldn't have heard her. And why call out to him anyway? It was always so sad going back in time, so disheartening…

She needed some new stockings. She was going to visit Grandma Cândida to ask her to lend her some money. Before handing over any money, her grandmother would inevitably take the opportunity to give her a brief sermon on morality. "I hear that you're living a life contrary to God's law!"—"What is a life contrary to God's law, Grandma?"—"You were seen in Bénard's café, smoking. And you were with a man. Shortly thereafter you were seen in the street with another man. What do you have to say to that?" Her grandmother would skewer her with her very steady gaze, still crystal clear despite her eighty years. "What do you say to that, Clara?" What could she say?

That one disappointment had been followed by another? No, not even a little romanticism and a few pretty words could persuade Grandma Cândida, so old-fashioned and so puritanical. She would lie to her; it was the only option. "Really, Grandma, the very idea! And all because I made one little mistake! I was very young then, you know. I'm most offended, Grandma. They were probably colleagues from the office. I can't honestly remember who they were now, but I think in Bénard's… Ah, now I know: I was with Chico, yes, it was Chico, who wouldn't hurt a fly, poor thing. People even say he's homosexual." Her grandmother would almost leap from her chair, and her voice would echo round the room: "Really, child!"—"Sorry, Grandma."

When she rang the bell, she immediately heard Gertrude's footsteps coming down the corridor. "How is she?" she asked. The maid said very softly, "Not too bad, but not great either. The doctor came yesterday. The usual problem, he said: her heart. He gave her some medicine, and she had a good night. But she woke up saying she was dying and immediately went into her study and started tearing up papers. She's been in there for ages now."

Clara half-opened the study door and said, "Can I come in?" But she saw at once that Grandma Cândida had fallen asleep. She was bent over the desk, her large head with its soft, fluffy white hair resting on her left arm, which was so plump she could barely bend it. A drawer had been left open, and beside it stood a wastepaper basket full of crumpled and torn-up bits of paper. Clara tiptoed in and sat down in the old fringed armchair. She remembered that when she used to spend the afternoon there as a child, her grandmother would tether her to the foot of that same armchair with a piece of string so that she wouldn't get up to mischief. And she would sit there very quietly. She suddenly wished she knew why she had kept so still. Was it because she was an obedient child or because she was afraid of her grandmother or because she thought she wouldn't be able to break the string? She would have to ask her grandmother when she woke up. She glanced at the clock. It was almost half past five; Grandma Cândida was still fast asleep, but Clara couldn't leave because she needed money for stockings and to have her shoe mended. She would have to wait. There was no way she was going to wake her grandmother up, because she was always very grumpy when woken. She was perfectly capable of saying No, just like that, without even waiting to hear her reasons for asking. "Don't even think about it. I've had a lot of expenses lately—income tax, repairs around the house, you name it! So don't count on me." It wouldn't be the first time this had happened.

Clara stood up and went over to the little watercolor she had bought for her grandmother as a souvenir of Paris and that her grandmother had hung on the wall because she thought it pretty. "But where the devil did you find the money to go to Paris?" she had asked on the day she came to say goodbye. "You've never had a penny to your name, and now you're off to Paris... Did you win the jackpot, Clara?" She had come up with some story about it being a very cheap trip—"incredibly cheap, Grandma"—and how a friend of hers who lived there was letting her stay in her apartment. "That's your business...but don't count on me for any money, all right? It's one thing helping you out of a little difficulty, but as for you going off to Paris, to that den of iniquity..." It was a banal little watercolor, nothing special, but full of memories. Now that it was all over, she would like to have it with her and hang it in her bedroom so that she could look at it every day. She would have to ask her grandmother to give it to her. There was the little café in Place de la Contrescarpe, where she had sat with him drinking a glass of rather gray, insipid *mistela*. He had said, "If you only knew how happy I am. I don't think I've ever been this happy." And she had sensed that memories of his time there as a student had a great deal to do with the happiness he was feeling. However, without a trace of resentment, she had placed her hand on his and she, too, had felt happy. "Who were you with when you were here? Go on, tell me." He had shrugged and smiled a long, contented, fatuous smile. "A very poetic, dark-haired English girl who was studying something or other at the Sorbonne. She wouldn't leave the hotel, or to be precise, she wouldn't leave the room, which was somewhat compromising. Her name was Daisy. She's sent me a few postcards from Birmingham harking back to those days and suggesting we revisit Paris, but I never replied." She had smiled; yes, she remembered clearly that she had smiled. She also remembered the table where they had sat, next to the entrance, on the righthand side. When her grandmother woke up, she would ask her for the painting. She wouldn't mention money for the moment. She would get by somehow or other. And at this, her eyes filled with tears, tears streamed down her cheeks, and her jacket was spotted with the large, dark drops.

At this point, Boga the cat appeared from behind a chair. She was a shaggy, very stately tabby. An appropriate cat for Grandma Cândida. She sat down and regarded Clara with serene, yellow eyes. Then she lost interest and tapped the wastepaper basket with one paw. A few balls of paper scattered across the floor. Boga again nonchalantly tapped one of these, and it rolled over to Clara's foot. She instinctively bent down, placed the paper on her knee, and smoothed it out: "My beloved Cândida..." It was a love letter full of the overinflated language of the age. I adore you, worship you, my heart burns for you, my soulmate, and so on. It must have been from Grandpa Albino. What would he have been like? She had never known him—how could she, given that her father was still only a boy when Grandpa died—but she could piece together a kind of picture from what her grandmother had told her. "Your grandfather was an excellent man, none better. But the poor thing could only see what was there before his eyes, nothing else." That was what her grandmother said about Grandpa Albino, who, poor man, had committed suicide over money worries; Grandpa Albino, the writer of that passionate letter full of details that...details that... But why on earth would Grandpa Albino write such a letter to his wife? Unless... She turned over the piece of paper. Of course. The letter wasn't from Grandpa Albino, but from someone named Augusto. "Much love from your Augusto, who adores you."

Clara was now very excited. She picked up all the balls of paper, pieced together the torn sheets, and began hurriedly reading them, keeping a close eye on Grandma Cândida, who might wake up at any moment. And as well as "your Augusto who adores you" there was "your Mário who thinks of you often" and "your Jorge who never for one instant forgets you" and another man who, very prudently, signed his letter with only a beautifully formed F. In the midst of all this muddle there was one

THE MOTHER

She was a tall woman with very white skin and thick, pale hair; of late, she had grown a little flabby and faded, almost colorless, like a reclusive nun. She was starting to put on weight, not out of inertia, but possibly out of apathy, because taking pills or following a diet was not strictly necessary and this way was easier, less bother; mainly, though, it was because she felt it was no longer worth worrying about such things, now that she was past her prime as a woman and would soon become a sexless human creature with no desires, en route to death or waiting for death to arrive. She had married very young, but never had children. Not that this was a source of regret, not consciously at least, perhaps, she thought, because her maternal instincts had withered away or were nonexistent, perhaps because in her immediate family there were no children whose presence might make her miss the children she'd never had. As everyone said, she lacked for nothing. And she did have a very comfortable house and could buy whatever clothes she wanted and had no need to worry about material things; her husband was what is usually known as a good husband; she was in reasonable physical health; and her life had been so easy that, before she knew it, she was forty years old. Forty years that had raced by, slipped past like a gentle river with no dips or boulders to block its flow or hurry it along, a river that would soon reach its end. For the first time, she thought about the years she had lived and about the years that remained to her. Not that she was afraid of death. With the passing days, she had gradually lost, without even noticing she was losing them, the innocent, mechanical prayers that, as a child, her mother had passed on to her from her mother and that, even when she was married, she had always said before going to bed. No, the end of life seemed to her, quite simply, like the end of everything: a mixture of permanent night and calm sea and nothing at all. What she did think about were the gray hairs that had already appeared and the lines around her eyes and her large empty hands, with no past and no future.

It was then, for the first time in her life, that she fell gravely ill. Death almost touched her with its stone-cold fingers, but she somehow found the necessary strength to draw back in time. Inevitably, she felt utterly exhausted. During the worst moments of the most difficult days, she would find herself pleading with someone or other—perhaps herself or her own ailing body burning up with fever: "Not yet, not yet. I mustn't die yet. I must live for another year, just one more year..." As if that year were the time required for her to experience something of great importance.

Her husband couldn't waste much time keeping her company because, although he had never really loved another woman, he had to earn money, always more money. What for? Who for, if he had no children? Lately, she had begun to ask herself many things that had never occurred to her during all those years. She looked for satisfactory answers in the smooth, white ceiling of their bedroom, but the ceiling either said nothing or told her things she had known for ages, even if she couldn't remember having thought them: for example, he would never ever be capable of doing anything else, he would never be able to sit beside her chatting or simply reading a book. No, he would never be able to do that. All he could do was earn money for no reason at all, to store up human sweat, his own and that of the people who worked for him, sweat that was then transformed into money to be put in the bank. It wasn't his fault; that's what he had been born to do. He was a man, a simple man, a poor rich man who lived his life swept along by the circumstances he had created, glued to his wealth, obliged to keep it, to increase it, without knowing why or for what.

She knew all this and would like to feel a little pity for him when he returned home in the evening with the lines on his face made still deeper by weariness. However, all her pity died the moment after she saw him. He wasn't a man to inspire sorrow or pity or even tenderness. It would have been good to do something for him, even if only by saying a single word, a simple word that he needed to hear. But what word would that be?

Her husband was short and skinny and full of vitality. He had been born poor and had worked his way to the top. He would sometimes recall A, B, or C, his friends in high school, the one school he had attended before joining the factory. A, B, or C, who were now fathers, some of them already grandfathers (poor people marry young), still mere workers or clerks. The only friend who had made more of an effort to become "someone" was the boss of a small office. Whereas *he* owned three factories. He used to say, "I'm a winner." And a winner doesn't want pity or tenderness or sorrow. Only admiration. She, alas, had no more admiration to give him. Lately, while convalescing, she had even grown accustomed to viewing him with new eyes, eyes heavy with a critical spirit she herself didn't know she had and that quite alarmed her.

One day, when visiting a female friend, she met a tall, rather charming man, mild-mannered and soft-spoken. This was what first impressed her. Otherwise, he seemed rather ordinary. When he left, having first come out with a series of rather trite remarks about America, a country he claimed to know well, her friend looked at her and laughed. Then she said:

"Mateus was very keen to meet you."

"Why?" she had asked without a hint of false modesty.

It seemed to her strange, even impossible, that a man, him or any man, should still be interested in meeting her in her own right.

Her friend shrugged.

"I've no idea."

Then the woman had said very firmly:

"He probably wants a job in one of my husband's factories."

"You're joking! He's rich; he doesn't need a job. Work? He wouldn't know how. He's a landowner, and you know what they're like. They think making other people work is quite exhausting enough. Maybe they're right, after all, lots of people think the same."

That evening at home, without knowing why, she said to her husband:

"I met a man named Mateus Porto today. Pleasant enough, but pretty insignificant. Do you know him?"

Her husband looked at her with abnormal curiosity, but said only:

"Yes, the name rings a bell, but then I know so many people."

He stood up and gave her a kiss. He had a business meeting to go to.

The two happened to meet downtown a few days later, and only then did she notice that he had a limp. Mateus gave her a long, warm handshake, and she saw in his face an almost forgotten light that made her blush.

"Are you going to your friend's house on Thursday?" he asked.

Probably not, she said, but immediately regretted not having said Yes. She would have liked to see him again and talk to him. Why? That afternoon, when she got home, she looked at herself in the mirror with the old attentiveness of youth, and her scrutiny did away with any illusions she might have. A few wrinkles, some gray hairs, a dull, almost lifeless complexion. No, she wouldn't go. And she didn't, although she spent all of Thursday feeling on edge and unable to concentrate on the embroidery she was intending to do.

Then he began phoning her. The first few times, she told the maid to say she wasn't in. There followed a long week with no calls, a week that seemed to her endless and empty. Then she decided she would answer the phone, telling herself she was doing this so that the maid wouldn't have to waste her time, and every time the phone rang, she felt her heart beat faster. But it was never him.

One afternoon, though, she heard his slow, calm voice. She said "Hello." What else did she say? She would never be able to remember clearly what he had said or what she had said in response, or even what they had said in the following days, or how and why she had finally agreed to meet him. A kind of mist covered everything. It was a voyage on the North Sea, just them and the surrounding mist. However, the voyage was brief, and the mist suddenly lifted and the sun laid bare everything, and all the veiled words and images and gestures went back to being what they really were: words and images and gestures. Nothing more. Now everything was hard, brutal, and all too real. The dream had gone, and before her stood a man, a stranger, who shared with the other man only the soft, familiar voice. Now, though, he was no longer speaking to her of his love or asking her to run away with him.

He was sitting opposite her, and she was standing looking at him as if hypnotized. He had a faint smile on his lips, but this, she realized, was his usual expression, even when he was saying those words to her that she had thought genuine. Except that now she was standing stark naked in a public square, exposed to all eyes.

"There was probably no need for me to tell you this, but I decided I would, just to show you at least a minimum of loyalty," he was saying casually. "I wouldn't want you to be too surprised by what you'll hear when your husband comes home. As I said, a long time ago now, he and I knew the same woman. He treated her like the utter bastard he is, and I swore I would have my revenge. Now we're even or, rather, we will be in a few minutes."

As if all this were some peculiarly complicated story

that had occurred on another continent and that she had not yet fully understood, she asked very calmly:

"Why did you wait so long?"

"As I said, I lived for some years in America. Then I had my estate here to deal with, and I only rarely come to Lisbon. Besides, it wasn't easy getting to meet you. It took time. You live a very solitary life."

"Yes, very solitary."

It didn't even occur to her to beg for pity. She would be incapable of doing that, and he would be incapable of hearing her. It was enough to see that half-smile, which only now did she fully understand, that hard gaze, those hands with their stubby fingers. Nor did she even consider denying the evidence. She didn't know how to lie and never had. She simply asked him:

"Do you have to tell him absolutely everything?"

"Of course. If I didn't, it would all have been a waste of time…"

She interrupted him, saying:

"Yes, you're right, what was I thinking? And are you counting on me to tell him?"

"No, not at all. I'll do that. In fact, right about now," he said, looking at his watch, "he'll be getting a phone call. A mysterious phone call of course. Just to arouse his curiosity. I'll do the rest. Your husband isn't a man to wait around; he'll be on his way right now. His office is really close, and he always drives very fast."

"Has it occurred to you that he might kill you?"

"Who? Him? You don't really believe that, do you? I know him well. Like I said, at one time, we were almost friends. He's incapable of killing anyone. He's the kind who keeps any kind of canker locked away inside and slowly rots away with it, not telling anyone… He can't bear to look foolish."

She nodded. It was strange. She didn't hate this man at all, nor was she surprised at this denouement. It was as if she were on his side, happy to collaborate. As if she had always expected this.

She got up and opened the drawer in her writing desk. The man went on talking—he knew there were no weapons in the house. She, however, wasn't listening. She was thinking about her husband. She could see him getting up from his chair after putting the phone down. There was a look of perplexity on his face. He didn't quite understand what he had just heard. Why were they telling him to go home? He would go home, though; of that she was sure. He was a man who liked to clear up any problems quickly so as not to waste time worrying about them. He was a businessman. He might already be on his way. He might even be coming up in the elevator now. As never before, she desperately wanted to clasp him to her, to stroke his hair. But it was late, too late.

When the blood began to gush from her wrists, the man screamed. She said in a tremulous voice:

"Leave now, quickly. Take all your things with you. Your gloves are over there on that chair… There's no one here; I gave the maids the afternoon off so that we could meet in private."

She fell onto the sofa, and the red flowers of her blood began to bloom among the white flowers of the blue upholstery.

She tried to say something that would wound him, that would make him suffer a little, even if only his vanity, but she could find nothing worth saying. Personal pride, remorse, her shame, all of that was beginning to be left behind, lost, of no importance. Of not the slightest importance.

In a soft voice she said again:

"Leave now."

The man left without a word, and she heard the muffled sound, the oddly muffled sound of the door slamming. Far away, in another world.

Then she closed her eyes and lay there waiting.

MISS ARMINDA

The people who knew her or, rather, who thought they knew her only because they saw her pass by every morning—always looking very serious and nearly always in a hurry, still pulling on her gloves or her beret—those same people, when they opened the morning paper, all thought that it couldn't possibly be true, that there must be some mistake, or that it was someone with the same name, a photograph of someone very like her. Because what possible connection could there be between that rather sturdy, very punctual woman, with her hair starting to go gray, and who, despite being nearly forty, was still always addressed as *Miss* Arminda, the woman who, every day, at half past nine on the dot, would walk down the street to catch the bus to work and always gave the slightest of nods to the barber standing in the doorway of his shop without actually looking at him and the slightest of smiles to Dona Perpétua standing at her window to keep an eye on passers-by; what possible connection could there be between her and that name, which was her name, and that blank-faced photo, also hers, there in the newspaper, in between a supposed suicide and an armed robbery?

Then again, on second thought, upon further reflection, people came around to the idea that it wasn't as unlikely or as bizarre as it had seemed initially. People do tend to have second thoughts—that is, to correct their positive first impressions of others. And they nearly always find that they were quite right to do so. In this case, for example, they would all agree, or were beginning to agree, even though they didn't know what the others thought and hadn't even exchanged views on the subject, that there had always been something suspicious about that young woman. This was especially true among other women. They enjoyed visiting each other, talking about their children's illnesses and the lives of other people, the ones who weren't there. She didn't. She was always at home. They only saw her when she went to work because, by the time she came back (she only worked in the mornings), the shops were all closed, and families were gathered around the table for lunch. Her maid, an old lady who could barely walk, was as silent as the withered tree trunk she resembled. The nosier neighbors had often offered her a coffee or a little glass of brandy in exchange for answering a question or two. Where did Miss Arminda work? What did she do at home in the afternoons? Was she working? Sewing? Embroidering? The old lady, though, would merely smile a broad, toothless, expressionless smile and say, "That depends."

The truth is that she did absolutely nothing, and this was something that none of those hard-working women could ever comprehend, for they were always cooking, making clothes for their husbands and children, keeping their houses spotlessly clean; they never had any time on their hands, and they were—even those who were unaware of it, and who would be astonished if anyone said as much—extremely happy. They didn't do much thinking, those women, although they usually talked a lot. And it would never enter their heads that Arminda spent her afternoons sitting in a chair, her hands folded in her lap, thinking. And yet this is what she did, and had done for months, ever since her mother died and left her alone in the world. Arminda thought. That is how she spent her afternoons.

Her thoughts, moreover, had undergone an evolution, following a dangerous curve, so dangerous that the end of that curve would lead to the prison gates. After the death of her mother, Dona Laura, Arminda had done a lot of thinking, had grieved for herself, thinking all the while that the tears she shed were for her mother. Then she started mulling over her past life, perhaps in order to feel less lonely and to fill her own thoughts with other things. Inevitably, she began by thinking about *that*. Because *that*, after all, had been the beginning and end of everything, a kind of birth in which the child—herself—had been born dead. There had been nothing before, and there could be nothing afterward. Far ahead, in the distance, at the very end of night, she could make out only a flickering, fleeting light, which she could never reach, a light that was always just ahead of her, and that, later, when she did finally catch hold of it, would burn her up.

When *that* had happened, she was living in a small provincial town, where her mother was a teacher. Her father had died some months before, when she was just fourteen. A child with a woman's body, tall for her age and already quite well developed. She was a happy child and enjoyed playing with the other girls and running about with them in the fields nearby, close to the house where she was living. One afternoon, when she was coming back from school, walking alone along a deserted road, a car drew up alongside her. *Would you like to go for a drive?* asked a soft, persuasive voice. Arminda said Yes. She said Yes because she knew nothing about life, because no one had warned her against it. That man would take care to fill that gap in her knowledge, in his own fashion of course. Not sparing her a single detail. He was a man in a hurry and doubtless had his own reasons and no time to waste on any childish nonsense. They found her later that night, on the highway, some miles from the town, walking along like a sleepwalker with her dress all torn.

Everyone in town talked about what had happened to the teacher's daughter. Arminda, though, was quite oblivious to this because she never again left the house. She was too terrified. It seemed to her that every man she saw from the window was *that man* with his brisk hands, his impatient body, his heavy breathing, which she thought she could still hear months later. She had forgotten his face, as if he never had one. He was just *that man*. Sometimes she would wake up screaming, and then she would climb out of bed and run to embrace her mother or the maid who, even then, was already old and beginning to wither away. This was when they moved to Lisbon, because Arminda's mother couldn't stand the gossip, the inquisitive looks, the lack of sensitivity of people who seemed to think that *that* was the subject she most wanted to talk about and so they never spoke of anything else. For all those reasons, and because she knew that if they stayed there, her daughter would never marry, she decided to retire from teaching and leave the town.

They rented a modest second-story apartment on Rua da Fé. Dona Laura had some stocks and shares, which, together with the small income she made from giving a few private lessons, provided them with enough to live on. Arminda showed no desire to finish her studies, and her mother hadn't even considered finding her a job. She knew that her daughter was a wounded creature and would bear the scars for the rest of her life. If Arminda ever did go out into the street, she walked along with downcast eyes, not looking at anything. At home, she spent all her time devouring novels as if those fictitious worlds gave her some compensation for her otherwise empty existence.

Only one thing, one thing alone, could draw her out of the apathy in which she appeared to be permanently sunk: the children playing in the parks or in the street when they came home from school. She would watch them with wide, greedy eyes, like a poor, hungry child gazing into the window of a cake shop. From when she was very small, she had dreamed of the children she would have. She would have lots, she used to say. Yes, lots. At least five or six. But that sad encounter had destroyed all such hopes. She knew she would never be able to give herself to a man. She had tried, just to show willingness. At the time, she was twenty years old.

In the house of a cousin of her mother's, who also lived in Lisbon, she met a serious young man, a bank clerk, who genuinely loved her. The cousin had told him Arminda's story, and he had been very moved. He wanted to make her forget all that and transform her into a woman like any other woman. He asked her to marry him. Full of hope, Arminda agreed, already looking forward to the child she would have. However, the first time they were alone together, he took her hand in his, and she leaped to her feet, beside herself with fear, raced like a madwoman down the stairs, deaf to the voices calling after her, and only stopped when she reached home. She lay on her bed for hours, sobbing inconsolably. Her mother wept too, in silence, lacking the courage even to take Arminda in her arms, fearing to wound her still more deeply by saying the wrong thing.

The years passed. The children who came into the world in the same year her son might have been born had she married, turned fifteen, then sixteen. Some already had girlfriends. She, however, was still Miss Arminda, and she would be until the day the newspaper called her just plain "Arminda."

Meanwhile, Dona Laura died. Her mother's death gave her life a sudden jolt. Then everything went still again, as still as a lake of stagnant water into which a stone had fallen. The wheelchair in which Dona Laura used to sit remained forever empty and she forever alone.

Without her mother, the house began to feel unbearable. She would have liked to get a job, but she knew this was impossible. She started going out, to the Park, to Campo Grande. She would sit on a bench and watch the children. Fearing that the neighbors or her own maid would think her mad, she invented, for both neighbors and maid, a job to which she went every morning. And every day, so as not to arouse suspicion, she would leave the house at the same time. The first rainy morning of her new life left her at a loss as to what to do. She spent it walking the streets, then returned home at the usual hour. Later, though, she discovered a quiet little café opposite a school in Largo do Intendente, and there she spent any rainy mornings with a cup of coffee and a book, always keeping a watchful eye on the children entering and leaving the school gates.

The light she had glimpsed earlier, and which, at first, was faint and fleeting as a will-o'-the-wisp, gradually grew steadier and one day revealed itself to Arminda so clearly she could even touch it. At first, she recoiled as if she had received an electric shock, but then she reached out her hand and grasped it. She even smiled at the new prospect on offer. Why not? she thought. And she began to devise a plan to kidnap a child, something that seemed to her perfectly straightforward and possible. Adopting an orphaned or abandoned child did not for one moment occur to her. That really would frighten her. Talking to people, answering all those endless questions, visiting government offices. Kidnapping a child would be far simpler.

There followed days of great excitement. Why hadn't she thought of this ages ago? she asked herself. The idea had come to her like a long-delayed dawn after the black night of her life.

Every morning in Parque Eduardo VII, she would see a little boy in a blue stroller. He was blond and pink and would either be waving his plump little hands in the air or sleeping like an angel. His regular nanny called him Joãozinho. Arminda had gone over to him several times, smiled at the nanny, then fearfully touched the child's lovely little face. She now regretted having drawn attention to herself. Even though the nanny spent all her time either reading or flirting with one of the park keepers, she would be sure to remember her when the baby disappeared and might even be able to describe her to the police. Arminda, however, was sure everything would be fine and that she would never be found out. For the first time since *that*, she was filled with hope. Besides, she couldn't possibly give up Joãozinho now. She was in love for the first time, irrationally in love with that pink baby waving his small plump hands in the air. It had to be him.

One day, she told the maid that someone at work had asked her to take care of a child for a while and, that very afternoon, she was going to buy a stroller and some baby's clothes. For the first time in her life, she went into a pawn shop, taking her mother's rings and her gold chain. At lunchtime, she returned home in a taxi with a stroller and a suitcase.

The next day, fate was on her side. The baby and the nanny were in their usual place, and there was no one else around. No, there was someone else, the park keeper, but Arminda knew that his presence would be useful because he would distract the nanny. She moved a little farther off. They had their backs to her and were laughing. The nanny had held out her hand to say goodbye to him but then carried on talking. The little boy was happily asleep. Arminda picked him up very gently so as not to wake him. Then she slipped away without anyone seeing her. No one saw her on Rua da Fé either. It was lunchtime, and all the shops were shut. Only Dona Perpétua, at her window, saw her pass, but she wasn't wearing her glasses and so couldn't quite see what Miss Arminda was carrying, perhaps a kind of package held close to her chest. For the same reason, she didn't see Arminda's bright eyes and the look of utter happiness on her face, a happiness she had never known before.

She wasn't a complete stranger to the child, and so he didn't cry much when he opened his eyes. It was as if he already knew her or somehow sensed that Arminda loved him. He whimpered a little, and she lifted him out of the stroller where she had placed him and very cautiously clasped him to her, rocking him gently. She felt as if her heart would burst, unable to contain so much happiness.

That happiness lasted exactly two days and two nights. She spent those nights awake in a chair, beside the stroller, changing Joãozinho's nappy whenever he wet himself or covering him with a blanket, afraid he might catch cold. The maid would appear now and then and look at her with her old, dull, weary eyes, which could, nonetheless, still see.

The maid's silent gaze made Arminda blush. They understood each other very well. They had lived together for thirty-eight years. How could they not understand each other? Although they spoke very little, the old lady knew many things, among them that Arminda had never had a job and that she had kidnapped Joãozinho in one of the parks where she spent the mornings. She prepared herself for the arrival of the police and wore her best clothes, in order to be decently dressed when they came to arrest them.

And come they did. On the third morning. The neighbor on the first floor had mentioned, while at her sister's house, where she had gone to have supper, that there was now a baby in the apartment above. She had heard it crying at night. Her brother-in-law, who had read about the kidnapping in the paper, asked for more details and then phoned a policeman friend of his. And that's how it happened.

When they knocked on the door, Arminda had just finished giving Joãozinho a bath. She was surrounded by nappies, talcum powder, a basin full of water, and a brand-new towel. Her eyes were shining, and her quick, apparently confident gestures, newly learned, were merely a sad imitation of those of her neighbors who were wives and mothers. The maid tried to stop the policemen at the door but soon gave up. Why bother if, sooner or later, they were sure to come in?

Arminda turned very pale when she saw the two men enter her bedroom, and she clutched Joãozinho to her breast so tightly that he began to cry.

"It was you, wasn't it, Senhora?" asked the taller of the men brusquely, gripping her arm. "You're under arrest. Come on, be quick. And you too!"

Arminda opened her eyes very wide. That iron grip on her arm was suddenly the hand of *that man*, and the harsh, brusque, implacable voice was *his voice*. She put down the baby, who was crying more and more loudly, and fought back, as she had on that other occasion, twenty-four years ago, and the police had a real struggle to handcuff her. The maid's eyes filled with tears. "Poor child," she kept saying, "poor child." But one of the men shook her and said:

"What do you mean, you crazy old bat? If you felt so sorry for the child, why didn't you report her?"

The old woman shrugged and went to fetch Arminda's coat. She herself had been dressed and ready for a long time.

CHRISTMAS EVE

It happened on Christmas Eve. The brother, sister-in-law, and nieces and nephews had just left—she could still hear their cart creaking as it rounded the bend in the road—and Emília, after one last glance at the crib, leaned against the window to peer out at the night. It was the vast, deep night of the open countryside, with no moon and an entire vault of stars. In the distance, the bell on the village church rang out lightly, brightly, in celebration, breaking the silence. From the kitchen, where she was washing the wine glasses, came the weary, monotonous voice of Dores:

"João will miss the beginning of mass."

Emília shivered. She made as if to answer her mother, to at least say something, but the silence of the night had wrapped about her, and she couldn't utter a word. Nor could she think. It was as if she had dissolved into that calm atmosphere and completely ceased to exist. Then her mother coughed, and she remembered that she wouldn't be there for another Christmas. She smiled contentedly at the thought of Joaquim. What was he doing at that moment, far away, lost in the city, without family, without friends, without her... He had sounded rather fed up in his last letter, more so than in his previous ones. He spoke of the barrack as if it were a prison where he was serving a sentence for murder. He asked wistfully about the land, if it had rained lately, if there had been a good olive harvest. He thought the city very ugly, said he couldn't breathe there, and that as soon as he had done his military service, he would leave and never set foot in the city again. It would only be a few months now; next year she would be married, far from her father, her mother, and the lonely country life to which she had never become accustomed. Far away... She smiled again. When Joaquim came back...

"That man will be the death of me!" Dores said, standing in the doorway. "He won't leave that wretched bar, not even tonight, not even on Christmas Eve. And he's sure to make a scene when he gets in. That's if he doesn't fall over in the street like he did before."

"Best not to say anything and just leave him be."

"Oh, gladly. But he'll kick up a huge fuss, don't you worry. You can imagine the state he'll be in. A couple of days ago, he received the money for the olive harvest, so he's a wealthy man. I'm just afraid he might fall in the river."

Emília looked away. The light from the oil lamp lit up Dores' gaunt face, lending it the yellowish tinge of a dying woman, an impression confirmed by her black dress and bony hands. Her burning eyes were almost too deep-set to be seen.

"I'm going to bed," said Emília, yawning. "At least he won't bother me there. Goodnight."

"Goodnight."

Emília lit a candle and closed her bedroom door. She paused for a moment before the plastic-framed mirror that Joaquim had given her when they had first started going out together, then very quickly got undressed because it was so cold. Next Christmas would be different. She imagined a very quiet night, with her and Joaquim sitting by the fire. They would definitely have cakes to eat, because he had a very sweet tooth. She would make *filhoses* like her mother always did… She stopped unbuttoning her top to ponder what it was that always prevented her from loving her mother. Did she really not love her mother? Of course she did, but… Her father was a drunk, and she had always felt afraid of him. As a child, she would tremble like a reed when he came home, his face all flushed, and start blubbering and kissing her. Even now, he would sometimes try and kiss her, but she always ran away from the horrible stink of wine on his breath. Her father would chase after her, determined to plant a kiss on her forehead and run his calloused hand over her head. Emília always avoided looking him in the eye and instead stared down at the floor. His eyes made her feel physically sick. Sometimes, they were so sad, like those of a stray dog, sad and bloodshot. They seemed to beg her to look at them, as if begging her for a little love. And Emília had finally come to realize that she despised him and that, even though he couldn't give up the booze, he couldn't bear to feel that his own daughter despised him. Emília shrugged. It came down to this: He was a hopeless drunk and no one took him seriously. But her mother…why did she not love her mother as she ought to? Was it because she'd never seen her fight back? Was it that waxen complexion; those moist, transparent hands; those dark, sunken, accusing

"Yes, who is it who does all the work around here? You and your daughter, is it? Who's the slave here, the drudge?"

He spoke in fits and starts, swallowing half his words; he was probably about to throw up, thought Emília in disgust.

Her mother said softly, calmly:

"Don't you know what day it is today? João and Maria and the little ones were here, then they went off to mass. João was sorry to miss you."

The man swore.

"I know what he needs...and I'll tell him when I see him. So he couldn't wait for me, eh? He may be quite the gentleman, but I'll tell him."

"We ate *filhoses*," said Dores. "The little ones loved them. I kept some for you in the pantry."

There was a menacing silence.

"So they couldn't even wait for me?" he said slowly, as if he couldn't believe such an injustice. "They ate *filhoses*, but they couldn't wait for me..."

Emília pulled the blankets up over her head. He had almost reached the blubbering stage, she thought. A few moments more and he'd be going on about how he was the unhappiest man in the world and how no one cared about him. But that isn't what happened. Suddenly his furious voice filled the whole house; it must have been audible outside too, because the dogs started barking again.

"You bitch!" he shouted. "You great bitch! You shameless cow. So they filled their bellies, did they? I'm warning you... You won't do that again, I swear you won't do that again!"

Dores screamed:

"Emília! Emília!"

Emília jumped out of bed but couldn't find the candle. She wasted a few seconds feeling her way along the wall in the dark, her heart pounding. Her mother kept screaming, clearly terrified now.

When Emília went into the kitchen, she met her father's eyes, but he didn't seem to see her. He was like a madman. He had his wife firmly in his grip with one hand and in the other he was holding the iron poker.

Dores' eyes were very wide, and she was staring at the poker as if hypnotized. Emília felt her blood run cold. She was too terrified to think.

"Just you wait, you bitch! Just you wait!" And he laughed a smug, imbecilic laugh.

Emília went over to the hearth and picked up a small log that was lying there. With one short, sharp blow, she struck the drunkard on the head. And suddenly, the poker dropped, Dores staggered a little, and the man fell slowly to the floor and lay there full length. Emília couldn't quite grasp what had happened. Dores was staring at her husband in a strange way. Emília then looked down and saw an open mouth and two motionless, glassy pupils. A shudder ran through her, and she realized she was still in her nightgown. This seemed very important, and she felt she really should put on something else because it wasn't decent to stand like that next to her father's body…

Dores murmured in a voice not her own:

"This is bad, very bad… What did you do?"

"I think I've killed him…"

And she started sobbing like a mad thing, resting her head on Dores' cold bosom, and her mother, without a word, held her close.

When, much later, she managed to draw away from her mother, her head felt heavy, her thoughts confused. All she wanted was to go to sleep. She was falling asleep on her feet, her eyelids heavy as lead. Dores crossed the kitchen as if sleepwalking, then returned shortly afterward with a shawl that she placed around Emília's shoulders. She had an anguished expression on her face. Twice she opened her mouth to speak, but gazed instead at Emília's pale face. Emília wanted to speak too—indeed she felt she really must—but still she couldn't open her mouth. Finally, in a faint voice, she said:

"Do you think I should go to the police tomorrow and tell them everything?"

She was standing very erect and didn't want to start crying again. Her mother must decide; she would do whatever her mother told her to do. Dores didn't even move. She was leaning on the table, her face in her hands.

"We haven't checked," she said. "We haven't made sure yet… You're talking as if…"

But neither of them dared to make sure. They stood there, transfixed, neither doing or thinking anything. Emília began to weep softly. Then her mother bent over the body and picked up one lifeless, almost cold hand.

"Is he…?"

"Yes," said Dores with a weary sigh. "He is."

She looked straight at her daughter, and it seemed to Emília that she was no longer the same weak, long-suffering creature she had been a second ago. Her eyes were different, her voice too. She seemed more alive.

"We must hide his body," she said abruptly. "No one needs to know anything."

Emília suddenly felt something opening up inside

her. Hide him, yes, hide him. Why had she not thought of something so simple? And only now that she felt free did she comprehend the terror of those last few moments. No one needs to know anything, her mother had said. No one would know, and she would still see the morning sun and still marry Joaquim. It hadn't been her fault; there was no reason to feel remorse. Suddenly everything was very easy and clear. And yet…

"What if someone passed him on the way here?" she asked fearfully, hoping against hope that her mother would convince her that no one had seen him.

Dores said slightly brusquely:

"It's not very likely, but if someone did see him, too bad. We have to take that risk. The only thing we can do now is hide him in the barn. If they come and search the place and find him, too bad."

Emília felt her eyes filling with tears and had a great desire to kiss her mother. She had said "we," voluntarily throwing in her lot with hers, taking her side without anyone asking her to. And still she stood there stiff and motionless. She hadn't kissed her mother for years. Dores herself would be surprised if she did. She didn't like that kind of thing. Sappy, she would call it…

"You must put some clothes on," said Dores. "Then we'll go to the barn."

"Now?"

Her mother gave her a hard stare.

"What? Do you think we should wait until tomorrow? You may not remember, but Bento's coming to fix the netting on the chicken run tomorrow. We have to work quickly so that everything's ready by sunrise."

They first had to move the cow, then sweep away the

layer of straw on the floor. They dug for two hours, until they were completely exhausted. Emília was eager for it all to be over, but she worked slowly because the thought of going to fetch *him* and pick *him* up filled her with horror. When the moment came, she almost fainted. Dores went over to her and slapped her.

"We have to finish this," she said bluntly. "Then you can faint as much as you like."

Since Emília was the stronger of the two, she picked the dead man up by his armpits, and her mother by his feet. Together they dragged him over to the barn, as if he were a scarecrow. They dropped him into the hole and, still without saying a word, refilled the hole with earth and smoothed it over. It was almost dawn by the time they had covered the spot with straw again and put the cow back. Then they went into the house and lay down in bed together, their arms about each other, eyes wide open.

Bento turned up at eight o'clock, and Dores told him she was very worried, because her husband hadn't come home that night, so she was going into the village to find out what had happened. She wrapped her shawl around her and set off.

That same day, the search began, although they didn't waste much time on it. Various witnesses, the owner of the bar among others, said that Dores' husband had walked through the village drunk as a skunk and singing loudly. Many of them thought he must have fallen in the river, and two policemen spent an afternoon patrolling the banks. Then the matter was forgotten.

Emília lived through several nightmarish days. She didn't eat and could barely sleep. She looked like death, and everyone was surprised at the depth of her grief. Then, when she learned that the police had dropped the case, she fell into a deep melancholy. She spent hours and hours sitting in a chair, staring into space, with some sewing forgotten in her lap. Dores would sometimes shake her out of this torpor with her newly acquired sharpness of tone. Emília would then get up and go to finish making supper or fetch water from the well. They never again talked about *it*. Both women knew, though, that they thought of nothing else. João and Maria came every Sunday. They talked about *him*, recalled things *he* had done or said. Once, Emília jumped to her feet, her lips trembling. Her mother said quickly:

"She gets like this whenever anyone talks about her father. She's still very upset..." And she said nothing more until the visitors had left.

João began to visit less frequently, and his wife, Maria, was glad because she had never liked her sister-in-law or her mother-in-law. In the village, people were starting to say that the two women weren't "quite right in the head." The only time they left the farm was on a Sunday to attend seven o'clock mass, but they never lingered. They now looked more alike too, and no one could say if it was because the mother seemed less downtrodden or because the daughter had lost her youthful freshness. "Joaquim's in for a shock when he comes back!" said the local gossips with a snicker. Emília was also keenly aware of Joaquim's imminent return, and the thought filled her with anxiety.

One day, she sat down at the table, her eyes red from crying. Dores looked at her attentively but said nothing. For a long time, they hadn't felt the need to say anything to each other. At the end of the meal, Emília said in a voice that struggled to sound natural:

"I wrote to him today breaking off our engagement."

Her mother replied simply:

"Quite right. I don't think you had any choice."

And for the first time since that other night, they embraced each other and wept together.

Emília then experienced a few days of great calm. Without the threat of Joaquim's return hanging over her, she felt that her life belonged to her entirely. She stopped doing anything. She would sometimes wander around the farm or sit down on a stone or a bale of hay to think. She almost stopped washing, and her hair was greasy and tangled.

One afternoon, her mother said:

"I'm going to sell the cow."

Emília did not respond. She understood. Dores could not bear going into the barn any more. God knows how she must have suffered during the last months whenever she went in to give the cow its feed.

They sold the cow and closed the barn door. At around that time, they also stopped attending Sunday mass. For lunch they ate boiled potatoes and for supper whatever their very neglected vegetable patch continued to provide. They had both grown very thin, and in the village it was said that they were going hungry so as not to spend any money. Joaquim, fully recovered now from his disappointment, was courting the grocer's daughter and telling his friends that God had clearly been on his side because Emília had turned into a real old crone. He had seen her one day leaving mass with her mother, both of them with their heads swathed in black shawls, and he had barely recognized her. She was thin as a rake, he said. Emília had seen him too. And after that, she never went back to the village.

The year was passing. Dores and her daughter slept in the same bed now. Sometimes, at night, Emília would wake up terrified and shake her mother awake too, then lie staring into the darkness unable to rest until Dores, all atremble, lit the candle. Sometimes, Dores would wake Emília up:

"Did you hear? Someone's at the door...can't you hear it? Can't you hear?"

Emília would break out in a cold sweat and listen tensely, intently. And the two of them, mad with terror, their wide eyes trying to penetrate the blackness, would wait, expecting that, at any moment, the door would open and *something* would enter the room and touch them with its cold, clammy hands. They would only calm down as day began to dawn. Then they would sleep until late and often even forget to eat lunch. They would get up in the late afternoon, always looking at the clock, already thinking about the fast-approaching night.

One day, the two women had a long conversation, as perhaps they never had before. The daughter began by suggesting something to her mother that had long been germinating in her mother's mind too. It was, therefore, easy to reach an agreement, and that night they both slept more easily.

When, many days later, João came to visit the farm, he found it deserted. He called out, but no one answered. He searched the whole house, but found nothing and no one. Noticing that one of the dogs was sitting outside the barn, whining, he put his shoulder to the door and burst in. The two women had hanged themselves.

back on a couch. The pretty, rather serious maid would bring him his breakfast every morning. His mother, always fresh and good-humored and smelling of soap, would appear promptly at half past nine to plant a kiss on his forehead. He would smile at his mother, but not at the maid. This was all part of toeing the line. The atmosphere in the house began to take effect, enfolding him as it had before, so that it felt as if he had never left. A house in which everything and everyone were as they should be and in their proper places. This was precisely what, fifteen or even twenty years earlier, had first aroused in him the desire to run far away, but in his current state of disillusionment he found it rather comforting, almost sweet. His father continued to set off every Saturday to spend the weekend with a widowed sister who had a house in the country. On Sundays, Luísa came to tea, without her mother now, for her mother had died that winter from a heart attack. A habit of many years. How many? He had always avoided habits or had perhaps become used to not having them, he wasn't sure. Now, though, it was as if he had succumbed without a struggle. On the first Sunday, he stayed at home looking at Luísa, whom he found almost interesting, almost pretty, listening to her silences, which were suddenly full of memories. How old would she be, he wondered. Thirty-two, thirty-three? Yes, she must be about thirty-three. Why had she never married? She wasn't ugly, no, not at all… She was rich, which simplified even complicated situations, let alone a simple one such as hers… There must be a reason. But what? A case of unrequited love? Did people still speak of such things? Perhaps it was nothing of the sort; perhaps she was just one of those cold women who has no interest in men, who has no interest in anything, one of those women who simply lives. During his yearly two-week visits to Lisbon, Duarte had barely seen her because he was always in too much of a hurry, with too many things to do, and with his male friends dragging him here, there, and everywhere from morning to night. Only now did he notice how different she was from the seventeen- or eighteen-year-old girl he had known—all makeup and meaningful glances, filling every house she entered with gusts of perfume—and with whom he'd had a brief, inconsequential fling. The woman before him now was nothing like the Luísa that Duarte had known then. There was something very serene about her long face, her tranquil features, her large brown eyes that had the steady glow of a candle flame on a windless night.

His mother asked him the next day:

"Have you never noticed that Luísa is in love with you?"

"What!"

"Sure. Everyone knows; everyone has always known. You're the only one who never noticed. She's felt like that ever since she was a child, a girl. I never said anything to you because I knew you didn't want to get married, but now…"

Duarte looked at her in alarm. What did she mean by that? Was she planning to marry him off to Luísa? Although, when he thought about it, this was not so very surprising. It was just like his mother to come out with the most unexpected ideas, already complete and beautifully constructed by her overly fertile imagination.

"I really don't want to marry," he said coolly, to put an end to any possible and more-than-probable hopes she might have.

"Well, you should. This student life you lead isn't right for a man your age. I mean, having no home, living in hotels... Luísa's a really good girl, almost as if she belonged to a different age. She loves you... She's honest too. As very few women are, believe me."

Duarte, however, didn't want to hear any more. He left the house feeling most disgruntled and wanting to run away, as he had before. This was an old habit of his, getting angry whenever his mother spoke to him about this or that woman's honesty. There were many things hidden away inside him that he judged to be private, and it always upset him when he found them so clearly and concisely expressed by his mother, and realized that he had learned them from her and felt just as she felt, although perhaps less crudely. Hence her lifelong preoccupation with honesty, which had always led her to demand that none of her female friends or her maids "had a past." When his mother's opinions irritated him, Duarte would laugh at them. He would sometimes annoy her by saying that he would prefer a woman with a past to one who proclaimed her honesty from the rooftops. He liked to say a lot of things that he didn't actually believe, because he was and always would be the product of his upbringing. But he didn't realize this. Only the day before, he had said to Luísa that Portuguese women used marriage as a negotiating tool. She had smiled her usual cool, vague smile and said:

"Maybe, yes... There's a lot of truth in that."

His mother had clutched her head and cried:

"Pay no attention to him, Luísa! Honestly, the things he comes out with!"

For the rest of that week, Duarte avoided his friends and stayed at home thinking about Luísa. He recalled episodes from his youth he thought he'd forgotten and in which she had played a role. And he realized that he felt for her a vast tenderness he had never before felt for anyone. On Sunday, he waited for her, but she never came. Duarte then began thinking seriously about the possibility of marrying her. He didn't feel a great love for her, but, rather, a strong, sincere desire to rest in the light of those calm, soothing eyes. Along with that idea came that of staying, of not going away again, of abandoning forever suitcases, trains, hotel rooms. Of having his own home, with two armchairs by the fireside. Was he getting old, he wondered. Perhaps, it was possible. He only knew that he suddenly needed that woman. His mother, in the middle of a conversation, told him where Luísa worked and what time she left the office. Duarte duly turned up to meet her.

"I didn't know you had a job."

"Yes, I took this one almost six years ago. I needed something to help kill time. Do you know what that means, to kill time? Maybe you don't, you lucky man…"

"Since I came back, I do have some idea. Anyway, if you want to kill a little more time, we could go and have a drink somewhere."

"Good idea. I'm thirsty. The department doesn't exactly overwork its employees, but it hasn't yet reached such a degree of perfection that they offer us tea and cakes before we go home. So inconsiderate!"

When he sat down opposite her at a café in the Baixa, for a moment he simply looked at her in silence. Luísa said in her slightly drawling voice.

"I'm sorry if I'm not dressed elegantly enough. If I'd known I would be meeting you, I'd have worn my feathered hat."

"In my honor?"

"In honor of you inviting me to have tea with you. Before, you've always spoken to me as if you could barely remember who I was."

Duarte excused himself on the grounds that he'd been very busy.

"Well, long live idleness, then! I've always been in favor of idleness. That's actually one of the reasons that keeps me coming into the office. Haven't you ever noticed that the people who don't do much work are almost always terribly nice?"

She laughed, then slowly bit into her piece of cake before asking:

"Are you staying or going back to Paris?"

"I'm not sure yet. It all depends on whether or not I get the thing I want!"

"Ah!"

That *ah* was almost a full stop, but Duarte knew that this didn't mean she necessarily wanted it to be taken as a full stop. He remembered that it had always been difficult talking to Luísa because every now and then, she would drift off, lose track of whatever the other person was saying, which, only shortly before, she had appeared to find interesting. Her eyes suddenly seemed to be looking at nothing at all.

This was when Duarte asked her:

"Luísa, would you like to marry me?"

Her gaze once again focused on him.

"I would," she said, "but would you really want to marry me?"

Duarte began speaking. About his past life, but mainly about his future. He hoped to make a success of his career after those long years abroad. There were, of course, plenty of engineers, but not all had his experience. And if he didn't succeed, never mind. He could still live.

Luísa was apparently listening attentively, although she couldn't understand the meaning of the words he uttered with such enthusiasm.

"Do you remember why we stopped going out together when we were seventeen?" she asked when he fell silent.

Duarte was expecting her to say something quite different, so the question left him rather nonplussed.

"For that very reason, because we were only seventeen."

"I was. You were twenty-three."

"It comes to the same thing."

"No, it's very different. You were twenty-three and seemed much older. You'd already been abroad and experienced a lot for a young man of your age. Whereas I had just left school and, unlikely though it might seem, knew nothing about life. No, don't laugh. Of course I knew, in theory at least, how babies are born and even how babies are made. I'd also heard a few scabrous stories from my schoolfriends, but that isn't knowing about life. My ideas about life were very general and completely phoney."

Her voice had lost that slight drawl and was now serene and very calm.

"You didn't want to marry, and now I think you were quite right. You would have jeopardized your career. Anyway, you liked me well enough and were perhaps amused by me in my 'fresh-from-the-oven' phase. I still have photos from then. I used to wear ridiculous amounts of makeup and would look at men as if I were Joan Crawford, because, at a dance once, someone told me

I had eyes like hers. And I believed it too! The things we believe when we're seventeen! I think all girls go through a similar phase. Mine was just a little late. Usually it happens when you're fifteen."

Duarte was looking at her, uncomprehending. Luísa broke off to take a sip of tea, then went on:

"How were you to know that I was full of hopes when I was always adopting movie-star poses and changing my hairstyle every two weeks? You suggested, half-jokingly, that we go to Sintra to stay at the house your parents owned there. The house would, of course, be empty. Then a few days later, you asked me again and got really angry when I said No. I clearly remember you saying I was a 'prude,' and that really hurt me. You said that, fortunately, girls in other countries weren't like me, that I was being ridiculous, still clinging to that stupid virginity complex. I still didn't want to go whatever you said, and that's why we broke up."

"And that's why I came to see you today, Luísa. I've always wanted…"

She ignored him and continued:

"Later on, I often regretted not having gone to Sintra with you that day. Life has taught me that, in the end, doing such things is both of great importance and of no importance at all. I don't think this was what you were expecting me to say, but it's true. I waited for you for years, Duarte. I don't know how long now, but a long time. I would spend months thinking about the two weeks you would come to spend with your parents. Perhaps this time he'll notice me, I would tell myself. But you never did. You came and you left, as if you had walked straight through me without even seeing me. Once, we passed each other on the stairs in your house, and you didn't even recognize me. True, I was looking very different, because I'd been ill. I went to hold out my hand, but you merely nodded to me very formally. I wept buckets that day and spent the night thinking that I'd ruined my life because of you. I was about to turn thirty just two months after that. Thirty is a very sad, disheartening age for women who haven't married… I had stayed single because I was waiting for you and had forgotten I had a right to a husband and children and a normal life. That night, I decided to think about myself and follow a different path and find someone else. Perhaps, for women, love is more flexible and more passive than it is for men. They do the choosing, and we almost always come to like whoever chooses us. I think I really loved Francisco…"

He broke in:

"You *think*?"

"Yes. The years pass and we become less certain about things. That was four years ago now…I can't be sure what I thought or felt. He was married, but separated from his wife. He wanted to divorce her and marry me, and I'm sure he would have. Alas, he died in an accident. We were only together for a year. I was terribly upset and even considered suicide."

She shrugged.

"But here I am drinking tea with you."

There was a silence. Duarte asked:

"And then?"

"Then there was someone else. He was much younger than me. A complicated man with a gift for making life absurdly difficult. That relationship simply ran out of steam really, without either of us making any real decision to end it. I heard later that he married and went to Africa. And that's all. That's what I wanted to tell you. Why are you looking at me like that, Duarte?"

"Listen, I..."

He came to a halt in the middle of the sentence.

Luísa smiled. It was faint, joyless smile that didn't even reach her eyes. Then, still smiling and looking at him, she got to her feet and picked up her handbag.

"I knew this would happen. It's odd, Duarte: I've spent my life knowing what people were going to say before they said it. And I knew that sooner or later this would happen. It's strange, isn't it? Thanks for the tea. I'm so glad I didn't wear my feathered hat. It wouldn't have been worth it..."

"Listen, Luísa..."

But listen to what? Say what? She left with her head held high, almost running past the other tables and vanishing into the crowded street.

Duarte left for Paris that same week.

THE SUNDAY OUTING

When spring arrived on that April morning, slightly late but in all its vigor, it had been many months since Marcelino Ramos, one of the clerks at H. Silva & Co., had had a day off. He spent the week in the small, ill-lit, airless room where the Silvas—first the father, then the son, and now the grandson—had run their modest retail business for more than a century, and where he worked beneath the vigilant, suspicious, and always oblique gaze of the boss, who seemed convinced that his employees were robbing him of whatever was most precious to him and was his alone, be it phone calls, copying paper, or their time, which also belonged to him, because he bought it by the month. Marcelino spent Sundays at home, doing some book-keeping he had taken on "to fill the holes," as he put it, while his wife darned clothes or altered a dress that was so old-fashioned she felt ashamed to wear it when she did her morning shopping—her one diversion. And her eyes, when fixed on her work or, if she had no alternative, on her husband's eyes, were always sad, her voice brusque and very sour.

She never said as much, she may even have thought he didn't know—since she didn't consider him to be very bright—but she blamed him for all her ills and for wrecking any hopes she might have had. She had spent years cursing the day she had placed her life in the hands of this quiet, hardworking man, who was, nonetheless, as ill-equipped for life as the most passive of beasts. His boss was devouring him, as he had been for the last twenty years, paying him the same wage as on the day he started; and she was devouring him with her sad, accusing eyes that made him avert his gaze. He was being devoured a little by everyone: those who laughed, those who suffered, those who struggled to achieve an impossible dream. And this seemed to her intolerable. She felt wounded not *for* him but *through* him. Her husband was the window that allowed in the rays of sun that were making her shrivel up. This is why she was already an old woman at forty-five and why it had been many years—she had lost count—since she'd sung or laughed. She did occasionally smile at someone she met, purely out of politeness. The equivalent of nodding your head or holding out one's hand to be shaken.

You would never think it now, but she had once been a fresh-faced, desirable young woman with many hopes for the future, her heart full of dreams, all of which she felt were achievable because, she thought, they were not too ambitious. Among those dreams were living in a nice house, meeting the love of her life, and having one or two children—two would be her ideal. However, she hadn't had the children she had dreamed of; love had gradually eaten away at time and at all the other wishes that came to nothing; and their apartment, which they lived in because it was rent controlled, was old, damp, and uncomfortable, and in winter the roof leaked. She was a poor woman who had been betrayed by a faithful husband and who, one day—one night—watching him working away at his book-keeping, found herself quite alone in the world, incapable of addressing a single word to him, the kind of word you say to fill the silence. No, all her accumulated resentments had completely dried up her voice, and the only words she had to say were those that were strictly necessary—short and to the point.

He knew all this, although he had never plumbed the depths of her pain. He was a simple man, enough of an optimist to believe that only great suffering brought great pain. He knew she was unhappy but had never thought she was *that* unhappy. He put it down to bad temper and an inability to adapt to circumstances. It was no secret to him that she blamed him for her frustrations. He knew, too, that this was partly true and that, in her own way, she was right, but, on the other hand, he was sure that he could not have done things any differently.

Spring, then, had been almost punctual and had arrived on that April Thursday at around eleven o'clock in the morning. A pleasant sun, warm and comforting, lay on the streets like a light blanket. The atmosphere in the office, though, was most unpleasant, and the sun coming in through the grubby windows felt dirty and dusty, a sun as old as the office itself, as timeworn as the air they breathed there: a mixture of dust, old papers, and cheap brilliantine—the brilliantine that Alberto applied rather too lavishly.

Hermes Silva, perhaps tempted by the sun (well, anything is possible), had gone over to the coat stand to fetch his hat before fixing his two employees with a penetrating gaze and saying, "Gentlemen, I have to go out for a while to speak with Alves & Alves," in a tone of voice that meant, "Gentlemen, no idling around while I'm away." And he slammed the door behind him.

Alberto immediately abandoned his typewriter and ran one plump, stubby-fingered hand over his lustrous hair. Then he said firmly:

"Well, it looks like it's finally arrived. About time too!"

"What? What's arrived?"

Marcelino was so immersed in resolving some complicated debit and credit problem that he hadn't even heard the boss leave and was surprised to find him not at his desk.

"Spring, man!"

"Ah!"

This was a somewhat indifferent response. What was spring to Marcelino, or summer for that matter, or, indeed, winter? The same timetable: long, monotonous days that followed one on the other like beads on a rosary. In summer it was hot and he would take off his coat; in winter it was cold and he would put it on. Of what possible significance could this newborn spring be to him? It was the office during the week, bookkeeping on Sunday accompanied by his wife's accusing glances and the vast solitude of his existence. He shrugged.

Alberto, though, was looking at him and smiling at an idea that had just occurred to him.

"Listen, my friend."

Marcelino looked at him, and Alberto turned nervously toward the door through which the boss had just exited, then said in a low voice:

"I've arranged a bit of a jaunt into the countryside on Sunday. Do you want to come?"

"I can't, old man, I've got that book-keeping to do."

"It's only one day. And we all need a bit of a change now and then."

"My wife wouldn't be keen."

Alberto laughed.

"No, you don't get it. There aren't any women involved, well, not our wives anyway. My wife, for example, is going to spend the day with her sister, because I told her I was going to see a friend of mine who's ill."

"A friend who's ill?"

"Yes, you."

He laughed, pleased at his own cleverness.

"Well, you have been ill on occasion, haven't you, my friend? And always on a Sunday too! And of course you haven't anyone to look after you…"

"But I do…"

"No, my friend; you're a bachelor."

He came closer and said in an even quieter voice:

"You could do the same. You tell your wife that on Saturday you've got to go and see your poor colleague Alberto, who has no family in Lisbon, and that's that. I usually take my girl, Arlete, and a friend of hers, Lurdes, who's a real stunner. My cousin comes too, but he can't this time, because he has to go to Porto to sort out some business about an inheritance or something equally boring, a real drag. We always have lunch, usually sardines, at a bar where I bet you anything you want you'll eat better than you can at the Avis, and then we go for a little stroll. You'll love it, my friend. Quick, make up your mind, Silva will be back soon. I'm telling you, that Lurdes is really something!"

Marcelino did feel tempted. Sorely tempted. That outing into the countryside, which his colleague had presented to him as a possibility, suddenly seemed to him like a return to his youth. That promise of a Sunday jaunt had awoken something in him, something barely visible, hidden somewhere far off in the mists of the past. That mist was gradually lifting though, the image becoming clearer, and he could see a young twenty-something called Marcelino—at least he thought it was him—with a friend and two professionally cheerful women, all of them out on an excursion. They took a picnic, a big bottle of wine, and they ate in the friendly shade of an olive tree. It had been spring then too, and one of the women had started singing a fado. She had a thin little voice, like broken glass, but there, in the open air and after a few glasses of *vinho verde*, it sounded quite marvelous. He could still remember her. She was very thin, had a pale moon-face, dark eyes, a slight squint, and a small, plump mouth, heavily lipsticked. Her name was Ilda, at least that was the name she was known by, and their affair had lasted a few months. Then he'd left her, the day he met a pure, young thing with whom he had fallen in love and who he ended up marrying. Goodness, that was a long time ago!

"Quick, make up your mind; the guy'll be back any minute!"

Alberto wrenched him from his daydream, and Marcelino found himself once again old and tired and sad in the office of H. Silva & Co.

"OK, I'll go."

His words coincided with the sound of the door opening, and as the boss entered the room he shot his two employees a probing glance. Alberto was already back at his typewriter, and Marcelino looked as if he hadn't so much as raised his eyes from his accounts book.

However, Marcelino couldn't now see the figures on the page, which were dancing before him. He was alarmed at his own words, which he had spoken almost without thinking. He was vaguely beginning to understand that he had allowed himself to be drawn in by those ancient images buried deep inside him, which Alberto's unexpected invitation had brought to the surface. He had agreed without a thought for his wife, his work, the money he would spend, his life as a serious, responsible man, all of which were quite incompatible with jaunts into the countryside in the company of two loose women. And now it would be difficult to back out. Did he even want to back out? Did he want to say No to Alberto?

No, he didn't. So much so that when the time came to leave the office, while he was putting on the crocheted scarf his wife had made for him—in her usual silent way—he asked Alberto:

"So when do we set off?"

"Oh, we've got time to think about that," Alberto said, laughing. "Lots of time!"

Alberto might have time, Alberto might have lots of time, with many years ahead of him, but he did not. That's why he was in a hurry, a great hurry. That's why he suddenly wanted Sunday to come quickly and for them to leave early. At home with his wife—who was busy darning socks and suffering the effects of a heavy cold, while he grappled with the book-keeping that had, all of a sudden, become strange and incomprehensible, as well as deeply boring—he was dreaming about the outing and about that "stunner" Lurdes, who, in his imagination, had

Ilda's pale face and shrill little voice. And he was thinking this in silence, but so loudly, so emphatically, that once or twice he looked up, afraid his wife might have actually heard him say, "It's on Sunday, this Sunday."

The next day, though, as he was crossing a street on his way to work, a truck ran him over. He was thinking about Sunday and was so deep in thought that he didn't even see the truck or hear the simultaneous shouts of the people nearby. He didn't hear or see anything. The last image in his mind was that of Ilda's face (the face of a woman he hadn't seen for more than twenty years and to whom he hadn't given a thought in all that time), and the last sound was that of her voice singing an old fado.

Marcelino's body did not go serenely into the ground, as had happened to other people of his acquaintance. It spent some time in the morgue, where it was cut open, and only afterward could he have the decent funeral his wife wanted for him. There were not many people at the funeral. Neither of them had any family, and Marcelino was a glum, silent man who had never made friends easily. The truth is that only two people accompanied him: his wife, all in black, dry-eyed and filled with a dull pain that was something like rage at the man who had died and left her still more alone; and Silva, all black tie and grave demeanor, genuinely and silently regretting the loss of that excellent employee, because, in those wretched times, good employees were few and far between.

Alberto wasn't there. Marcelino was buried on the Sunday, and Alberto had already arranged everything with the girls, and it didn't seem right to postpone it in order to go to a funeral. However, since the cemetery where Marcelino was going to be buried was the Lumiar cemetery, they crossed paths near Campo Grande. Alberto, who was in the tram with Lurdes, Arlete, and a friend he'd invited at the last minute, reverentially doffed his hat. Then he leaned toward one of the girls, a peroxide blonde with an equine face, and said:

"That guy in the coffin, he's the colleague I told you about. What bad luck, eh? Poor devil. I feel sorry for him."

The woman said "Ah!" and drew her coat more closely about her, because a shudder had run through her from head to toe. And so for a few minutes, the tram accompanied Marcelino's funeral, behind his wife and Silva.

THE WORDS LEFT UNSAID

The faded, obsequious, courteous clerk opens the glass door, keeps it open with one foot (it's an automatic door)—"Mind the step, Madame"—and bends slightly to allow her to pass. He is carrying a large round package, clumsily wrapped in brown paper; he has it clutched to his chest with one hairy hand. She notices that he has very long fingernails, one of which, the index finger, is stained yellow with nicotine. In exchange, Graça offers him her static, impersonal, almost invisible smile and finds herself out on the street in the rain—which hasn't stopped since morning—wondering why she always feels obliged to thank people, to reciprocate acts of kindness and acts of rudeness with various kinds of smiles, of which she has so many! The last, most recent smile remains forgotten on her face, frozen, indissoluble in the air. However, the clerk standing next to her doesn't even notice—and would it matter if he did?—the customer smiled at him, and that was kind of her. Not that he's thinking any of this, because he has his back to her, his right arm raised. The taxi, however, doesn't stop. It's already occupied.

"It's always difficult at this time of day: too much traffic, a real nuisance. We just have to be patient… And this rain certainly doesn't help. What weather, eh? A whole two weeks of it we've had… Say what they like, Madame, but I blame those atomic bombs and the rockets they keep sending up to the moon; don't you agree, Madame? They call it progress, but to what end? If they at least made some useful discoveries, a cure for cancer, for example… That's just my personal opinion of course… But we've never had rain like this in October, not on the tenth of October. If there aren't any taxis, we can always phone the taxi stand, because sometimes…" He's speaking slowly in a voice that is neither too loud nor too soft. A quiet, careful, cautious voice that shifts unaltered from subject to subject, without registering the change, always the same, independent of the rest of his body, unrelated to the concave chest in which the great brown paper package appears to have embedded itself, almost penetrated.

"Ah, at last!" cries the man. And this cry is immediately followed by a faint splashing sound, and the man looks anxiously down at the package, studying it with an expression that closely resembles professional concern, then he turns to Graça: "My pleasure, Madame." He opens the taxi door with his free hand and allows her to get in; she holds out her black-gloved hands—everything about her is black, apart from her triangular face with its round, oblique features, incredibly white next to all that blackness, almost luminous in the half-light of the car, rather like certain phosphorescent images that are visible at night.

"Take care, Madame," he says. And to the driver: "Don't drive too fast, please." Then, turning to her again, feeling completely at ease now: "Thank you so much, Madame, always glad to help. Don't forget the pebbles; they're important."

Graça says "Goodbye" and in the same neutral tone, announces the name of the street where she lives and the number of the house, so that she is then free to drift freely—such peace! —over the surface of things and gestures and sounds. And the car sets off, slowly, as the clerk had requested. Too slowly. She half-closes her eyes, which are green or brown depending on the day. Whenever she gets into a taxi (it has to be a taxi, not an ordinary car; a car always has someone driving it, someone who speaks, and to whom you have to listen and respond—not in a taxi though, where the driver doesn't exist, can't be seen, well, he doesn't have a face, just a pair of shoulders, the nape of a neck), whenever she gets into a taxi, she has the feeling, half-pleasure, half-anxiety, that she's setting off with no fixed destination, borne along inside some unknown animal. Or quite simply en route to a new life or even to a gentle, friendly, mysterious death, faceless and painless. At such times, she barely feels, barely sees, merely thinks how sweet and consoling it is. She almost never regrets what she has done or what she has lost. She almost never says to herself, if only I could go back...

But no one can go back, Claude would tell her. Why ruminate about things; why chew over what's already been digested? Graça would talk, would tell him things, always returning to the same spot. Claude would shrug, quite certain he was right. "Why bother, if every night we die a kind of death? The next day is always new: We emerge once more from our mother's womb, are once again thrown to the lions, but everything is different; we see it in a different way, in a different light. Why look back at what's happened when it's lost, irrecoverable, if it can't be fixed?"

This was the voice of Claude, a voice that, despite it all, had not yet begun to decompose, rising up from that ever-present past, flapping its wings and brushing her cold forehead, but lacking the strength to go any farther, any deeper, into her heart. Claude's hesitant, sometimes strident, always monotone voice.

Piedade has a monotone voice too, but hers is a gray voice, so there's no comparison. Claude's voice is the color of verdigris. Graça feels almost irritated with herself, but it's only a very slight, almost insubstantial irritation. Not even irritation really. Perhaps a mere disagreement between the part of her that always disagrees and the other part that usually accepts everything with a wan smile or, rather, pretends to accept out of inertia, too tired to argue.

She cautiously rotates her left wrist, peers at her watch, and sees that it's five to one. Her lunchtime (the time set by her maid Piedade) is half past twelve. This means that Piedade has been sitting for twenty-five minutes, seething and talking to herself, because when she's angry, Piedade talks to herself and refers to Graça in the third-person plural.

Graça likes to enter the apartment without Piedade noticing and then eavesdrop on her muttered complaints: "Where on earth can they have gotten to at this hour? The lunch will be ruined, but what do they expect, it's not my fault." Or is it? For Graça suspects that, on those occasions, Piedade takes her cruel revenge by deliberately to explain that she had been miles away (thinking about Piedade, how ridiculous!); she opens her handbag, takes from her purse the tightly folded twenty escudo note, receives her change, and gives him a one escudo coin as a tip. The driver rather sullenly takes the coin, reaches over, and unlocks the door. Graça carefully places the parcel on the seat, gets out, then turns to pick the parcel up. This is becoming an endless chain, she thinks, but it doesn't end there; it's much longer. There are still a few more links—only a few?—that she knows about, those she can foresee. The others will perhaps only end that night or never. *Jusqu'à ce que mort s'ensuive*... What a stupid idea! She slightly raises her shoulders as she picks up the parcel, or rather she thinks she does. Then it's the mesh elevator door sliding to the right at the same time as the light comes on, and outside, in another world, the engine of the taxi starts up again. The small metal button; the jolt as the lift sets off; the ascent skyward; the sudden, inevitable juddering halt. If only she could carry on going up and up, but no, there's always a terminus, and this is hers. How often as a child did she dream about the fifth floor and gaze enviously at the neighbors who lived up there... But she always had to come down again, to this second floor: The rest doesn't belong to her, and she's never been there; it remains a complete unknown. She rings the bell (her hands too occupied for her to get the key out of her handbag); hears the slow, reluctant steps of Piedade, who silently opens the door and lets her in; then she very cautiously puts everything down on the table in the hallway, gives a weary sigh, takes off her scarf, takes off her gloves, breathes in the new smell of the apartment—what does it smell of?—and says in her quiet, implacable voice, before turning her back on Piedade:

"The rice smells burned."

The fish is swimming around and around in its small translucent planet. "You can put some sand in the bottom along with a few colored pebbles," said the man in the shop. As if she didn't know that… For the moment, though, the bowl is empty, and the fish has it all to itself and is dancing about, occasionally stopping to stare at her in surprise, opening and closing its fat round lips. She really must do something about it; that complete absence of any scenery is terribly sad, almost painful. It's cold.

"Lunch is on the table. If you want…"

To eat. But that censorious sentence is even more truncated than usual: It stops right there, overwhelmed by the force of the image, and Piedade abandons her position in the doorway, from where she usually hurls her hard, well-aimed words at Graça. She takes two steps forward and stares, unable to understand what that fishbowl is doing there. She doesn't speak; she merely looks at Graça, at the fish, and then back at Graça.

"What's that?" she says at last, without the slightest rise in intonation. It's not so much a question as a demand for a response.

Graça smiles. Another of her many smiles. This is the false-trail kind of smile, which always points the wrong way and never to the easiest path, the one that will lead straight out into open countryside. This one is in subterranean communication with her eyes, which are suddenly larger and brighter. A smile that confuses Piedade.

"I've always liked animals. And now that I have my own apartment…"

She stops and, for a moment, ponders her own words. Her own apartment… Was the other one not hers? The other one, with its pale furniture; colored formica countertops, curtains, and armchairs, all with an abstract design; and a big poster for a Jean Lurçat exhibition on the wall? Wasn't that hers? She asks the question three times, but doesn't wait for an answer; she runs away, turns her back on Piedade, thinks it's not worth the bother, no, she doesn't even think that. She returns to the room.

"…and I'm going to get a cat too."

She isn't going to get a cat. This is just a simple, last-minute excuse. And of course she doesn't know (how could she?) that Piedade cannot stand cats, can't even look at them: All the hairs on her large body stand on end. She fears both their volatility and their stillness, but most of all she fears that fixed gaze of theirs (like the gaze of a snake, she says); a cat only has to arch its back slightly for her to feel she's about to be attacked, mauled, possibly have her eyes scratched out, and definitely end up covered in blood. That's all it takes for her to utter terrified screams, completely absurd in that tall, sturdy, fifty-something woman with a gruff, almost masculine voice. Graça knows nothing about this. Piedade first hints at it, then tells her straight out, giving her a kind of ultimatum:

"The day you bring one of those creatures in here, I'll be leaving on that very same day."

Graça accepts this statement, ponders it gravely, and reserves it for later consideration. In fact, she only heard what Piedade said very vaguely, in passing. Equally vaguely, she saw Piedade turn and go back into the kitchen, her world and her refuge. We all have one. Hers… Hers what? What was she thinking about? About the fishbowl of course. About the fishbowl and where she was going to put it. Where else, but in the living room? Isn't that why she bought it, to put it in the living room? That's where Leda used to keep her goldfish, on the shelf next to the record player. But the record player has gone; what could have happened to it? Did it stop working? Had her father removed it because it brought back too many painful memories? Yet the shelf is still the best place. She again picks up the fishbowl, goes into the living room, and looks around. The same furniture in the same places: She hadn't wanted to move anything. She's always had a horror of moving things and, if she ever does, she just can't get used to it: The furniture becomes somehow aggressive, too real; she keeps bumping into it and always ends up restoring it to its previous location. To the comfortable absences of their former positions. Opposite her is the big glass cabinet full of leatherbound books; to the right, the velvet-upholstered divan; and opposite that, the two armchairs and the low table with the pink cut-glass ashtray on one corner. To the left, the console table on which sits the bust of her father, chin raised, eyes vacant. Beside it, the small bookshelf, empty now, where he kept his favorite books: Cronin, Maugham, Pierre Benoit. Opposite that, the large drafting table, where he always worked standing up. Sad and empty. On the wall, a single painting—why that one?—the peasant woman wrapped in a black shawl, holding a basket in her large, red hands, swollen with the cold.

She used to suffer from chilblains, horrible things. Her fingers resembled suspiciously pink sausages, almost bursting out of their skins, possibly going off. She couldn't even bend them. Claude would clasp her always-icy hands and try to warm them with his. Even when he had just come in from the street, his hands would be warm with quick, lively blood. Then, though, she would get a terrible itching and bite her fingers to stop the itch, leaving deep, white marks on her taut skin that would then, slowly, disappear.

The worst thing was having to wash her clothes when there was no hot water, which was most of the day. The water was only really hot until half past nine in the morning. After that, it was always cold, no matter how long Graça let the water run. Only sometimes, purely by chance, would it come warm from the spring.

Washing clothes first thing in the morning was even more unpleasant. At around midday, someone would come to clean the room—*je ne dérange pas ces messieurs dames*—and that daily interruption of their relative privacy was intensely annoying! She couldn't drape her handkerchiefs over the wardrobe door to dry or hang her underwear on the heater. She preferred to do this only when she was sure no one would come in. By then, though, the water was already cold. It was so irritating!

ooooo

She had never before noticed how flat the painting was, how crude the drawing. She sits down in order to study it more closely and because she feels tired. Looking at it now, the woman's hands appear to be made not of skin, but rubber; the basket has no substance to it; her face lacks all expression. A mannequin wrapped in a shawl. What was he trying to paint? Despair? Weariness? His ignorance of a weariness that nonetheless exists? Vasco always had plenty of ideas but was incapable of transferring them to his paintings. That is why he couldn't sell them and why the art critics ignored him. He would shrug and say he didn't give two hoots, he really didn't… "What kind of hoots?" Clotilde-my-love had asked once. "Loud or soft?" But no one had laughed, apart, that is, from Clotilde's husband of course.

It was Vasco who had taught her how to wash and dry handkerchiefs, a memory from his days as a penniless student. Graça hadn't believed him—no, really, it was perfectly possible; he would show her—and in one of his bursts of childish enthusiasm, he had rushed into the bathroom, taken his white handkerchief out of his pocket, run it under the tap, carefully wrung it out, then placed it perfectly flat on the surface of the mirror. There were a few small wrinkles, some bigger than others, Great Walls of China that wouldn't stick to the glass, but Vasco had used his large, bony hand to eradicate those so that the now-almost-transparent fabric, with its satiny edge, became as smooth as the mirror. She was so thrilled she even climbed onto a chair to get a better look.

"When will it be dry, Vasco? In an hour?"

"Yes, in an hour, sweetie."

He had then turned around, put his hands on her waist, and lifted her bodily into the air. Graça could still remember how she had started kicking and protesting, albeit softly, so that only he would hear:

"Let me go. You're hurting me. Let me go, you hear! Let…me…go!"

Her eyes welled up with tears, but she drew them back in with all her might.

"What's wrong? Are you mad? What's gotten into you?"

He finally put her down. He was standing in the middle of the bathroom, his long arms hanging by his sides; his pale eyebrows furrowed, confused; his upper lip drawn back slightly, almost scornfully, to reveal his white teeth. She could see him now, and yet that image was so ancient, so fleeting, caught on the wing. Back in her bedroom, before she could close the door, she heard him explaining what had happened, and thus the incident didn't remain just between the two of them: Everyone knew.

"...All I did was pick her up, but anyone would think I was going to kill her. She's a strange child!"

And then her father's voice saying very slowly, but not so softly that she couldn't hear, "You must remember, Vasco, she's a motherless child."

Graça had closed the door, not wanting to hear any more, but she did this very quietly so as not to be heard. So that they would forget all about her, so that not even the sound of the door closing would remind them of her existence. She wished she could dissolve into the air, go to sleep and wake up another person—wouldn't that be wonderful? To wake up as Antoninha Lima, who was so happy; or Glória, who was so pretty; or Armanda. What was so special about Armanda that she should want to be her? She didn't know—perhaps there was no particular reason—but she would have liked to wake up in Armanda's skin or in that of any of her school friends, although not in Meneses' skin, because Meneses stammered. Or even in the skin of a complete stranger: Yes, that would be the ideal. What a surprise to wake up with a new face, in a house she had never seen before, and with a mother... Yes, with a mother. Of course that was it; she had never known anything else. With a mother—like Armanda and Glória and Antoninha and everyone else. Why couldn't something like that happen?

She was standing before the mirror taking a long, searching look at herself, as if waiting for something that had not yet been born, that wasn't there, that didn't exist. That was her face, the face she saw every day, how tedious. Was she ugly? She had no idea. That didn't even interest her. She hadn't yet reached the stage where that problem would be waiting for her. Without realizing it, she was starting at the end, at the top. She was looking at the mirror feeling weary of that still-incomplete face—the face of a fourteen-year-old girl!—feeling thoroughly fed up with it. A strange child. "You must remember, Vasco, she's a motherless child."

Those were such terrible words. They had often kept her awake at night and would end up bringing her to tears that would finally lull her to sleep. But on that day, it wasn't the words or, by association of ideas, Leda that wounded and hurt her. She couldn't get away from those other words, the first words. She's a strange child. It wasn't just her father who spoke of her as a child, *he* had done that. *He* had called her a child. The pronouns that, to Graça's way of thinking, belonged solely to him. *Him.* But this was a secret, one of those big secrets that she kept hidden from herself as jealously as she did from the others, possibly more so. Vasco, *he*, often came into her thoughts, caught her by surprise, ambushed her, but Graça didn't stop; she fled far away, anywhere. He, however, was still present, despite all. And deep inside her, Graça preserved a sediment of unsuspected pride: the thought that Vasco was a man and she was hopelessly in love with him, which made her interesting in her own closed eyes.

Vasco was just gorgeous. He had lovely, pale, porcelain blue eyes; a straight nose; a mouth that lifted at the corners in a smile even when he wasn't smiling. When she looked at him, she felt the same as she had one day when, from a tram window, she saw a vast beige car belonging to the Diplomatic Corps with, at the wheel, an imposing man wearing a uniform replete with gold braid. She felt diminished, humiliated, pleasantly relegated to a much lower rung, full of pure, flawless admiration. Vasco was that beige car. Beside him, other people felt ugly and awkward.

From her room, Graça could hear them in the corridor, then in the dining room. "Sit where you usually sit, Vasco." The voice of her stepmother. "The little one's not here, though. I'll go and call her."

She just had time to lie down on the bed and press her hand to her head, which, as she only then realized, was actually aching.

"What's the matter? Are you ill? Go on, come to supper. Your father will get annoyed, and poor Vasco thinks you're angry with him. Come on, make an effort; don't be a spoilsport. Clotilde and Emília are coming after supper."

She, however, declared:

"No, I won't, I'm ill."

Leda's light hand on her forehead.

"You do have a bit of a fever."

She had a temperature of 100. The doctor came that same evening and, after examining her closely, diagnosed a kidney infection.

Illness makes everyone forget any other upsets, and

Vasco, even though he must have known this was a diplomatic illness, came to say he hoped she would get better soon.

"And don't go thinking I'm angry. We're still friends, sweetie. Always will be."

"I want that handkerchief."

"What handkerchief?"

"The one you left on the mirror to dry."

That night, she slept with the still-damp handkerchief under her pillow, and the following morning, she put it away in the little silver box where she kept all her secrets, and then locked it. It must still be there. But the key is lost.

The fishbowl looks great there; it couldn't be better. It's in its rightful place, thinks Graça, when she takes the time to think about it. Just as a rectangle of wall from which a painting has been removed will always belong to that painting. The wallpaper grows darker or paler (fading over time or getting scorched) and looks horribly bare and empty. There had been too much space on the wall above that shelf. Now, everything is as it should be. Serene, almost at peace.

The fishbowl draws her along secret paths to the Dupont and then, by a familiar route, to the trout at the Royal. The Brazilian man punching the waiter so hard he was hurled against the fish tank, which immediately shattered, leaving the trout free—free at last—the trout leaping around on the floor.

She had been sitting at a table with Claude but had merely glanced at that *fait-divers*, which was, at least, original and that on another occasion she might possibly have found amusing. On the wall beside her is a large mirror that now and then offers her fleeting images of herself, blurred, green, aquatic.

She always avoided sitting near a mirror. Mirrors, she thought, were made so that people could study themselves intently, full-face or three-quarter-face, for just a few seconds, and then cease to exist. However, she was troubled by mirrors that reflected dozens, hundreds, thousands of images of her in motion. She could see them even without looking. A hand raised slowly to a mouth, the ashtray into which the ash (hers?) was slowly falling. Expressions she didn't recognize as hers were thrown treacherously in her face. A film to be viewed by the whole room. Her self being offered up to the world without her knowledge.

"What are you looking at?"

Claude was looking at the mirror (it was opposite him), or perhaps he wasn't looking at anything and was simply drinking his coffee. The cup was raised into the air; his slender lips were already half-open.

"Nothing. At the mirror. Why?"

But the cup made the return journey without having reached its destination, and Claude, still holding the handle, was looking at her attentively.

"What's wrong?" he asked at last. "You look strange. Don't you feel well? If you like, we can leave."

What, and go back to the hotel? To the hotel room? To the room with all the lights off? To lie down and go to sleep or to lie down and not go to sleep? No, no, not that. At least here, despite all the mirrors, there were people; there was light. Fluorescent light, strangers… It was the best she could do...

Three policemen, and the waiter pointing at the

Brazilian who was calmly finishing his *demi*. "*Il aurait pu me tuer, monsieur l'agent*." And he kept feeling the back of his neck, all bloody from the broken glass. "*Il aurait pu me tuer...*" The thought of that possible death, so important to him—well, it *was* his death! —was so all-absorbing that he couldn't think of anything else to say. His brain was in shock. "*Il aurait pu...*"

"My father has died, Claude. I've just received a telegram."

Anyone else would have asked "When?" and then "Why didn't you say something? Why are you only telling me now? Why choose this moment to tell me?" And then, "What did your father die of? Who sent you the telegram?" These were, after all, the obvious questions to ask. But with Claude everything was easy, all too desolatingly straightforward, with no possibility of a detour, of a shortcut through tall vegetation that would hide her from his gaze. With him, the path was always broad and the visibility excellent. He understood everything, and he knew her so well that she sometimes found it troubling. Like now. He was looking at her, reaching out his hands to her across the table, and Graça could see on his face what he was thinking. He was of course thinking that she had only been able to speak now and to share with someone else the grief she had kept inside her for hours, hers alone. What could be more natural? There was a kind of hope in that silence. Now she had spoken and suddenly her father really had died, and she could cry.

Graça raised her hands to her face and felt her palms become wet. As she always mechanically did, she pressed them to her mouth, half-opened her lips, and touched them with her tongue.

The rice is burned as usual and over-salted too. Inedible. Piedade has outdone herself.

This is where she always stands, with her back to the door. Her father would be to the right and, opposite her, Leda. Behind her, almost leaning on the back of her chair, the maid serving at table. Right now, it is Piedade who she can neither see nor hear, but whose presence she can feel: stiff, resentful, suspicious, her eyes fixed on the pile of burned rice that remains uneaten on her plate. And Graça tries to think of something that will take her away from there, from the solitude of that day (and of many other days), that will carry her off somewhere, but she can't because she's waiting intensely, almost eagerly for Piedade to say what she has to say.

"Would you like some eggs? There's ham in the fridge..."

A sigh. There it is. She feels liberated and almost grateful. "No, there's no need," she replies meekly. "I'm not hungry. You can serve the coffee." And then, as if she had only just remembered something of no importance: "Ah, yes, a lady is coming to see me. Show her into the living room."

The coffee is dreadful. Piedade is hopeless at making coffee, and Graça still hasn't got around to buying a machine. Piedade's coffee is either like dark, insipid water or a thick, bitter, disgusting brew. At least this time it doesn't taste of anything, which is preferable... At the Royal...

"What I find hardest is that he hadn't forgiven me," she had said.

"I know."

And suddenly she felt welling up inside her an invisible fountain that flowed through her veins and into her heart, something very familiar and very painful.

"No, you don't know!" she cried. How could he know if she had never told him? That serene gaze and those calm hands clasping hers irritated her. She felt a sudden desire to hurt him, to ruffle the smooth surface of the waters, to throw in a pebble just to see that surface dimple and wrinkle with little waves. "It was much more complicated than you think. I was fourteen…"

She was fourteen then, and now she's thirty-four. Could it be that the images are still intact and that she's spent twenty years playing a game of chess with herself, moving the pieces, then taking them only to put them back, oblivious to life passing her by? Where have those twenty years of long, long days that took such an age to pass, where have they gone, and how is it possible that she already has a few gray hairs—not many, but some?

She realized all this only because the days were so long and difficult, and not only for her, but for many other people: a day, or, to be more precise, a night. She was in her apartment—the other one, the one furnished American style—that had been hers only episodically, although that particular episode had lasted a good twelve years. They'd had guests to supper, a married couple of a certain age—the husband was an engineer and worked in the factory owned by Claude's uncle. After the meal, coffee, and liqueurs, they had set up the card table. Purely out of politeness. They knew that the engineer named Van-something-or-other loved to play poker. His wife wasn't so keen and played badly. She was a fine, fat bourgeois woman with a high color, lots of children, and already quite a number of grandchildren, and her handbag was always full of photographs of children. "Aren't they lovely?"

she would ask. They weren't the slightest bit lovely, but the touching way in which she asked was more a desire for confirmation than a question: a need for everyone to agree that they really were adorable, irresistible. As it turned out, that evening, Mrs. Van-something-or-other really got into the poker game, and her unexpected enthusiasm meant that they didn't finish playing until nearly three in the morning. No one lost or won very much. They pretty much broke even. And as she was leaving, after saying her goodbyes, the woman said:

"I enjoyed it so much that I'm going to become a proper gambler, because it's such a good way of passing the time."

Passing the time: That was the real solution, or, rather, the real problem. Passing the time. By gambling, according to the Belgian lady's new theory. Chewing over the past, according to Graça. Time was so long for a lot of people, even for a good bourgeois lady with lots of grandchildren. And yet how natural it sounded: "It's such a good way of passing the time." That was all. She had discovered the medicine and would perhaps use it from now on. But what about Graça? She was fed up with moving the pieces about on the board, fed up with the pieces and with the hands moving them and the board she was moving them on. But she couldn't do anything else.

She gets up from the table. A clock somewhere outside strikes two. A few moments later, an eternity later, she will get up from the table again. And tomorrow. And the next day. And for years to come. Everything dies at night, Claude would say. But that wasn't true: Life is long; it slips and slithers seamlessly past. A succession of events, an endless stream of words said and left unsaid. Especially the latter. She had been fourteen that winter, and now she's thirty-four. Twenty years during which nothing died, nothing, not even Claude, and during which, in the mornings when she woke, everything was always as painfully the same as it was when she went to sleep. And here she is in the same place.

It was an almost miraculous age, and she hadn't noticed. The bird had taken flight, but hadn't yet reached the mountain top; it was hovering in the air, wings spread wide, but it lacked the strength to make it to the top. She was always being reminded by people with serious, frowning faces, that she said and did things that were inappropriate, ridiculous—hadn't she realized that she had grown up, that she was a woman? Then they would say, sometimes almost immediately afterward, depending on the time and the day, that she was still too young to adopt certain "modern," "independent" attitudes. Two words, so tightly wrapped in sarcasm that you couldn't even see their original meaning, as if they had just been invented. Her father would pronounce them in a very grave tone of voice, heavy with dark foreboding.

All this happened before her illness. Then, of course, all such values were overturned. Endless, endless time, once of only secondary importance, went straight to the top of the first page, ahead even of Vasco, ahead of Leda.

The winter dragged by, sad, monotonous, and very rainy, but very cold too. The vast, dank days were followed by gray, dry days, when the sun did not shine even for a moment. After this, there had perhaps been worse winters, sadder or more beautiful (the Paris winters drawn in pen and ink, the Brussels winters heavy and white), but they had slipped past her, or she had slipped past them—at any rate she barely noticed them, her eyes and mind occupied with more important matters going on around her or inside her. The actors are always more important than the stage set, and the text is always far more important than the actors. Apart, of course, from the main character, who dominates everything, or, in this case, who dominated everything, because she was the main character. That winter, however, there had been an almost radical schism between her mind and her body, and her body had won by losing. And she had ceased to be the main character and become instead inert matter.

Sometimes, with her lips pressed together and eyes screwed so tightly shut that they hurt, she would hear Leda's light, airy footsteps as she crossed the bedroom, putting everything in order, closing the wooden shutters, so she wouldn't be woken by the grayish, color-of-the-wall-opposite light, and pausing by her bed to listen to her breathing. She would even touch her forehead very lightly to check that she wasn't feverish. Then she would tiptoe out (she had a talent for silent gestures), and Graça would no longer feel the unbearable weight of her presence. She found her stepmother's tender care offensive; she would have preferred her to mistreat or at least neglect her so that she would be free to loathe her with an easy conscience, without remorse. But, no, she wasn't even allowed that. She would then summon up her mother's face, an increasingly difficult task, as if that image would be enough to neutralize the existence of that other woman's face. Alas, this was not the case. Her mother took ever longer to arrive. Her image had, over time, become extremely fluid and slippery, and a moment's distraction on her part was all it took for the image to escape; she would catch it just as it was about to disappear, but the shadow (because eventually it was no more than a shadow) always ended up slipping down into a deep dark hole and the effort involved in retrieving it became simply too exhausting. In the end, she would give up, open hands and eyes, and let it go. She would relax completely then and be filled by a great sense of calm and great bitterness too.

How many winters had passed since then, and inside her, even today, there are moments and sounds, and smells too, bequeathed to her by that winter. She had become incredibly attentive and sensitive to so many things: To the cold, for example, which, even when she was tucked up in bed under several woolen blankets, covered her meager flesh with goosebumps; or to the rain that wept at her window for whole afternoons, for endless days and weeks. Her senses became keener inside the new, more restricted, and therefore much clearer world that had become hers. The bedroom. The fragment of street she could see from the window. The perfume her stepmother was using that winter (Vasco had brought it for her from Tangiers), an "oriental essence of lotus blossom"—that, at least, was what it said on the label in English—coarse and sickly, heavy and persistent. It wasn't a normal, invisible, modestly airy perfume like others she had known. It was shaped like Leda. And sounded like her too. It had lasted all that winter until the day they found the bottle broken, the house left horribly steeped in *Lotus Blossom*, a smell that would become indissolubly linked to everything else: the cold, the rain, the doctor's visits, Vasco's visits, and so many other things. The voices she would hear coming from the living room on the rare evenings they had visitors. Clotilde's rippling laughter. Clotilde, who had been her mother's friend, but who had accepted Leda unconditionally. Vasco's concise, audible comments. The voice of Clotilde's husband, a vast, placid, vegetable of a man, who was in the habit of agreeing with everyone, even if their opinions were entirely contradictory, and who always called his wife Clotilde-my-love. Her father's long, slow, categorical statements. Even Leda's silences, for she could imagine Leda sipping a glass of Chartreuse and lighting endless Camel cigarettes, which she would stub out having smoked only half of them, or sometimes without even raising them to her lips. The people who walked down the quiet street at night and told her, just by the sound their feet made on the paving stones, if it was raining or dry. The tree opposite, the top of which she could see from her bed. What kind of tree was it? She didn't know and never had. For her, they were all just trees and had never been anything more than that. They had no other name; nothing distinguished one from the other. She remembers how the wind would furiously flail the leaves with a kind of gentle, serene, implacable loathing, and how they would surrender slowly, softly and without a struggle, then hover for an instant in the air like small frozen hands, sometimes tapping at her window pane asking for refuge, before drifting down to the street below. Watching them detach themselves then fall became a painful game for Graça, and she would think, "If that one on the left, the big one, falls in the next five minutes, it means I'll get better soon." Once though, it occurred to her to think: "… it means that she'll leave, that something will make her leave." And the leaf had fallen.

She could also hear the noises of the house, familiar sounds that formed part of the habitual silence or an amalgam of sounds so unworthy of attention that they touched her ears too lightly even to be noticed. The maids talking in the kitchen when no one else was home. The faucet in the sink out on the veranda. The clink of glasses when the table was being laid, quite different from the sound they made when the table was being cleared. The shrill sound of the doorbell. That record—what was it called?—that Leda would play in the afternoons when her father wasn't there, the volume turned right down so as not to bother her. An irritating pianola java, the notes endlessly circling and entangling, so that she sometimes had to cover her ears in order not to scream, but to which her stepmother listened, placidly seated in her usual chair. At first, Graça thought, What is it she likes about that music? Then she wondered, What memories does it summon up for her?

Claude was listening, uncomprehending. "Do you honestly think all this is necessary?" And he glanced at his watch. "It's almost half past midnight; couldn't we talk on our way back to the hotel?"

No, they couldn't. She needed his face, his unfurrowed brow in order to talk. She needed to shape her words, to see them, to offer them to him in her hand. She didn't want to lose them in the dark, in the streets of Paris.

It was a Thursday in February, Claude. A day like any other, like those that have been and gone and those still to come. Another day spent in the cramped bunk onboard the sailing ship, which, when things became difficult, went back to being her bedroom. Now and then she would cheat time and sleep for a couple of hours in the afternoon. She would wake at the sweet, brief, maternal hour as dusk was falling. Then night would come, and that was always pleasant. Not that she had a particular predilection for the night, but it was like a door closing on yet another day, another day that had passed, one day less. Sometimes, she would pick up her alarm clock and make the hands spin. One day, eight days, thirty days… But when she stopped, only two or three minutes had passed, five at most, and there she was in the same place still holding the clock. She did jigsaw puzzles and read a lot, but reading always tired her. She would close her eyes and, after her own fashion, reimagine the stories she had read. She would enter into them and would, of course, become the main character, even if only in her imagination. These were her best moments, when she descended to the center of the Earth with Axel and Professor Lidenbrock or fearlessly went down into King Solomon's mines. Then that too would weary her, and she would once again find herself alone with herself, an encounter that had nothing new about it and always bored her.

Just be patient for a little while longer, Claude. She was telling him all this so that he would understand, so that he would see how lonely she had been. Why? Because she wanted to be? Because she wanted to keep Leda at a distance? Because she refused to speak to her? Yes, perhaps that was it. But none of that made her any less lonely or prevented everything, even contemptible things, from expanding and growing inside her. As for the other things, they seemed equally vast to her then.

And Vasco? Didn't Vasco keep her company sometimes? Strangely enough, she couldn't remember… What was Vasco doing at the time? Where was he? Ah, that's right, he had gone to spend a month with a friend on an estate he had in the North. Vasco? No, his friend. His name was Ferreira. A very ordinary name that died as soon as it was spoken. Which is why she could remember it. Vasco would mention his friend and repeat something he had said, and there would be a silence finally broken by her father or by Leda, who would *always* change the subject. But going back to that winter, Claude.

Sometimes, her friend Antoninha Lima, who shared a desk at school with her, would come and visit her. At first, she would come every Friday, and she always came bearing news, things that had happened during the week, minor intrigues. However, the visits, which she had initially greeted with excitement, had begun to bore her. Everything her friend told her felt as if it had happened in another life to which she no longer had a ticket. And Antoninha's visits grew less frequent, perhaps because she realized she was no longer greeted with that initial enthusiasm and consequently felt her own enthusiasm waning—a praiseworthy enthusiasm, like that of a budding nun doing her Christian duty by visiting the sick and those in prison. Then she stopped coming altogether. Graça had found this perfectly natural and had even smiled at her stepmother's childish questions. "What's become of Antoninha? Is she ill too? Would you like me to phone and ask?" She had told her No, she certainly didn't want that, and did her best not to think about her ex-friend. She had never felt capable of doing much for other people, and so she wasn't surprised when they did little or nothing for her. Besides, since she had never gone back to school, she had never seen her again.

She opens the door of what has always been her bedroom. The other rooms where she had lived with Claude, even their bedroom in Brussels, had been merely temporary, with no glass in the windows, with no windows, open to everyone's gaze. This room is her fortress, and she has never known another. It's dangerous outside: The phone's always ringing and you have to answer it; someone comes knocking at the door and you have to speak to them; even the maid's silent presence was still a presence, and she might, at any moment, appear at her side. For Piedade is very fond of making those sudden random appearances, just to say that there's no bacalhau or that the cleaner who comes once a week (and whom she recommended) has a reputation as a thief. A high-class thief, to use her words. The things she comes to tell her, though, are almost never true, mere gossip she's heard when out and about in the morning. And Piedade knows them to be false or, at the very least, suspects that they might be. If that weren't the case, she would say nothing and would instead wait until disaster was imminent or had actually occurred, so that she could announce, "There's no bacalhau at the shop." Or better still, wait in total silence until Graça said, "One of my petticoats has gone missing." Or a ring. Or money. So that she could then declare in triumphant tones, "Everyone knows the cleaner is a high-class thief."

There needs to be a wall and a locked door between Graça and Piedade. And the only guarantee of her safety was the locked door.

None of the furniture has changed: The very grand bed her grandmother gave her before she died; the little dressing table with its tarnished mirror cracked in one corner (Vasco broke it one day when he was playing ball with her); the two chairs with their faded blue upholstery; the rug her mother embroidered with its border of birds, also in blue. Blue birds and pink anemones. Next to the door stood the desk where she did her homework, which used to be adorned by a tall bronze candlestick. So many things heard and stored away forever while she was mechanically memorizing the rivers of Asia and the conjugation of the verb *to have.*

The room is on one side of the corridor. On the other, almost opposite, but farther to the right, is the living room.

ooooo

The coffee had gone cold. Her cigarette had burned out alone in the ashtray, but the ash had not yet crumbled into nothing. Claude was staring at the room reflected in the mirror, dark and tinged with green like a giant aquarium, and he was asking "So what happened then?" in a dull, impersonal tone, not because he was interested, but merely to be polite.

Her father had come into her room as he did every morning. He always kissed her on her left cheek—not because this was on the same side as her heart, but because it was closest to the door. "Did you have a good night?" he would ask, and then he was gone, even if his body remained there for a few more moments. She only saw him again at night, when he would come to say goodnight. "Goodnight, Maria da Graça." It was as if he cared only about the night. However, this wasn't the reason. Her father cultivated to perfection those polite bourgeois, or perhaps even petit-bourgeois, formulae that, according to him, shaped a person's character. Graça thought he was quite right. Or perhaps she didn't even think that, because it was only later, when she was living with Claude, that she began to regard her father in a slightly critical light, an ability she had suddenly and unexpectedly discovered she possessed.

Later, she couldn't recall the date or even the month—only that it was winter—but she could recall less significant things. For example, Leda coming into her room long after her father had left. "Good morning, Graça." She had adapted very quickly to the household rituals; you might almost say she had embraced them with the overenthusiasm of all recent converts. "How are you feeling today?" A question with a prepaid answer. Naturally, what she ought to say, with one of those prefabricated little smiles she always had on hand, was "Better, thank you," or "Much the same, thank you for asking." And all of it was utterly meaningless, given that everyone knew she wasn't in pain or feverish. What continued to trouble her most were her chilblains.

She didn't know now what answer she had given. Another of her memory lapses. She was too impractical, her father would say. And he would then launch into one of his rather didactic little speeches, sprinkled with proverbs, clichés, and quotes from Father Vieira or Dom Francisco Manuel or the wisdom of the people. He usually chose as an example (not to be followed) Uncle Rafael, his brother, who lived in Africa, but that is another story.

On that day, contrary to custom, she must have told Leda that she was feeling ill or bored, because Leda had answered "Poor thing, and who can blame you?" and sat down at the foot of the bed, looking at her. Did they say anything more? She couldn't remember. She knew only that Leda had given a quick little smile that was more like a nervous tic, one that occurred whenever she was feeling ill at ease and that she couldn't control. Graça had watched her fidgeting awkwardly and crossing her thin legs. Then she had looked away.

That image would also stay with her like a photograph taken at point-blank range and carefully stowed away in her personal album—just in case. This was a new pose that Leda was adopting for the first time along with the black dress, which made her look younger and more elegant and that Graça had never seen before. The camera had failed to capture her face with its very regular but unlovely features, her clear, hesitant, slightly squinting eyes, which remained forever blurred. What shape was her nose? And her eyes? Were they really blue or just faded, colorless?

Graça could no longer remember. What she could remember was that her store of weariness was fuller than usual that day, and several times she had opened and closed the book by A. J. Cronin that her father had so kindly lent her along with many words of advice: "Now don't turn down the corners of the pages. And be sure not to stain them." Concluding with a moral lesson: "Never forget, books are our best friends."

Vasco had arrived in the early afternoon, having returned from the North a week before. Why had he come then, when he knew her father was never at home at that hour? He usually came into her bedroom, pushing open the door without even knocking. Not on that day though. He had walked past her and past her door and gone straight to the living room. He had already been there for a quarter of an hour. A murmur of muffled voices reached Graça's sharp ears along with a wave, then another—or was that just her imagination?—of perfume. She had slipped out of bed then, though she was never quite sure why. And yet...on second thought...when she thought about it… Her suspicious subconscious—pricked by a little apparently unprovoked laughter that was immediately suppressed, again for no apparent reason, and by what she imagined might be a longer-than-usual handshake and a few long, lingering looks—told her she was right and set her legs in motion. She almost collapsed in the middle of the room, not having taken so much as a step for two months. She had opened the door very slowly and peered over toward the kitchen. However, all that reached her was a distant voice coming from the garden, singing some fado or other. She had advanced then, barefoot and in her flannel nightdress (decorated with little blue flowers), prepared to face whatever dangers might arise from this "raid." When she reached the living room door, she very, very gently drew aside the curtain, and a slender ribbon of truth appeared before her nonetheless astonished eyes. A bright, vertical ribbon on which were painted two static figures, glued together in an embrace. On one of the armchairs, spliced in two by the edge of the ribbon, lay a bunch of yellow carnations (Leda's favorite flower) wrapped in cellophane. She had then loosened her grip on the velvet curtain and slowly made the return journey from that brief incursion into the mysterious, brutal, incomprehensible world of adults.

Claude is perched on the dressing table, imprisoned in his window frame of red leather and golden thread and from which he gazes out at nothing at all. In a moment of enthusiasm, she'd had an enlargement made of a small passport photo, the only one she had, and locked him up in there forever.

"It's one o'clock, Graça; we'd better go. I have to get

up early tomorrow, and I can't miss the first class. It's really important to me. We have time, don't we? All the time in the world. Tomorrow, or the day after, whenever you want, whenever you feel like it, you can tell me the rest of the story. Although, when I think about it, Graça, why tell me? It can only bring you pain. Your stepmother was having an affair with Vasco, who you were in love with... What could be more natural? That you should love him, I mean. Fourteen-year-old girls are easily dazzled by older men. And it was only natural that your stepmother should be his lover. He was a good-looking young man, with nothing to do—and women adore men with nothing to do and who, therefore, have time to spend with them (as long as they have a husband who earns the money, of course). Besides, your father was a difficult man, wasn't he? *Garçon, les deux cafés!*"

"But it's important. I wanted to tell you; I needed you to understand, to try and understand..."

"But I have understood, Graça. One day, when you were chatting with someone, you told them what you'd seen, and your father found out... Am I right?"

"Yes."

But he wasn't right. That would be too simple. Above all, there was the bitter or perhaps insipid sense that she had spoiled things—which were perhaps already spoiled—that her mere presence had somehow curdled the milk. The trout from the shattered fish tank had all disappeared (when did that happen?), and the floor had been carefully mopped clean. Only the tank itself and the stain on the rug bore witness to that recent epic scene. And the back of the waiter's head of course. "*Il aurait pu me tuer, monsieur l'agent.*" He, however, was no longer there.

He had left. It was a warm spring night, so sweet. There was an indefinable scent in the air, but what was it? Then something like cotton wool touched her face, sending a shudder through her. The repellent touch of a cobweb. But, no, it was only the petals from the horse chestnut blossoms, which had been fluttering over the city all day, wafted along on the breeze.

The nightwatchman opened the door to them. They had gone up to their room in silence. They had lain down in silence. Then Claude turned out the light and felt for her hand, which was cold and suddenly hard and absent.

"Try not to think about it, my love. Do you promise?"

"I promise."

Was that so difficult?

"I'm here!" she says in response to Piedade's unnecessary question: "Are you there, Senhora?" Where else would she be?

The door slowly opens, and Piedade tiptoes over to her and almost whispers in her ear in a mysterious manner:

"That lady has just arrived. She's in the living room."

For a moment, Graça feels lost and reaches for something to hold onto and steady herself, but looking around she can find nothing. Everything is fragile and insubstantial. She's filled with a desire to run far away, to put on her coat and creep down the stairs. Piedade could easily go into the living room and say, "I'm afraid my mistress has gone out. I thought she was here, but she's gone." She's not prepared and has never been any good at improvising. She needs to concentrate, to summon up her courage and then think slowly and calmly, telling herself there's nothing to worry about, that she can simply rehearse everything she's going to say, or at least, everything she'd like to say but that, as she well knows, she won't. Because she never has said what she wants to say, but always other different, irrelevant things that had taken shape inside her without her realizing and that are often completely inappropriate...

Piedade is looking at her in alarm—or is it scorn? (it's hard to read Piedade's feelings; she's remarkably inscrutable)—and Graça is beginning to think that it can't possibly be "that woman," the one she's expecting, whom she had told to come. It's too early. She had said on the phone, "Would six o'clock be all right?" And Graça: "Yes, six will be fine." But it's only twenty to three.

"What she's like, the lady in the living room?"

"Short, fat, and dark. She's wearing glasses and has a weird-looking nose."

Piedade never ceases to surprise her. With just five strokes of the pen, she's drawn a portrait that is Clotilde-my-love to a T. Graça takes a deep breath, feeling vastly relieved. She gets up, smooths her very creased skirt, and goes out into the corridor. At the door of the living room, she places her hand lightly on the velvet curtain, as she had on that now-distant afternoon. And she stands there, looking.

There, she had said it. At last. Not very well, admittedly, but it had at last fluttered out of her and into someone else's ears, and that was what mattered. She had thought about it for years, had stuffed it away in the bottom of a drawer (she didn't know what to do with that uncomfortable, unnecessary thing); she had forgotten it—the words that is, not the image, which had been photographed and hung forever on a wall in her memory. She had come across the words—intact—a few days before. "Don't throw anything away; you never know when it will come in handy," her father used to say. "Don't be like your Uncle Rafael." He was right. About that and many other things.

She had just turned twenty-two and was visiting Clotilde. In the big room that Clotilde always referred to in English as "the living-dining room." Clotilde was sitting across from her in that living-dining room, next to a low table with a glass top (on which lay a detective novel, a glass of water, and a small brass bell); she had one huge leg encased in plaster, and her plump mouth was hanging open.

"Are you absolutely sure, my dear?"

Her voice sounded different, no longer rising up and down like a rollercoaster, and Graça had seen and heard her swallowing hard. Yes, her mouth was positively watering. Graça had smiled. Her of-course-I'm-sure smile. Who did she take her for? Why would she say it if she wasn't absolutely sure? Really.

Clotilde had muttered, "Yes, but something like that…although, of course, anything's possible!"

It is, but not something so obvious, so blatant. You might feel a vague suspicion, a moment's doubt…but don't you think, Clotilde… Clotilde, don't you find it strange… Or something like that. And then that bold statement of fact… I saw them. Clotilde had shifted in her chair, and her leg no longer seemed to hurt her.

Now Graça can hear again her own words, what she had said—how many years ago was it now?—in Clotilde-my-love's living-dining room, words that come ricocheting back at her, sounding as false as Judas. She had thought about them for so long, had shaped them… It was as if she had dreamed it and believed the dream was true—it can happen to anyone—and then told someone her dream. Or as if she had given false testimony, for which she could be put on trial.

Clotilde was looking at her, speechless. "Is that really true? I mean if it were…if it were…"

"If it were?"

"It would be terribly funny!"

So she didn't believe her. And when she heard her own words, she too found them strange, almost ridiculous. She had been practicing for such a long time, admittedly after a long interval, but lately she had been furiously studying as if on the eve of a difficult exam, just to come out with that hesitant, feeble phrase.

Perhaps, when she had gone down the stairs, even before she stepped out into the street, Clotilde had gone straight to the phone, dragging her enormous leg, and called Leda. "Do you know who was just here? I'll give you a clue. Your lovely stepdaughter. And do you know why she came? To see me, of course, to visit the poor invalid—well, that was her excuse. But the real reason? You'll die laughing when I tell you, but I just wanted you to be warned." But, no, something in Clotilde's anxious (or was it smug?) expression reassured her. Imagining Clotilde-my-love doing such a thing was most unfair, did not do her justice. She would have to tell someone, to whisper it, but not to Leda. And she would demand total secrecy. "Now don't get me into trouble, because if anyone found out…well, it doesn't bear thinking about…" That was more her style.

"How old were you?" she had asked at last. "Thirteen, fourteen?"

"Fourteen."

"You were still a child. You could have been mistaken. Children often do exaggerate the facts, without even realizing it. You saw them kissing, fine. But it may have gone no further than that. You know Vasco…"

She had interrupted her at that point, quite why she didn't know, or rather she did, yes, perhaps she did, but she preferred not to think about it. She had interrupted her.

"I'm not exaggerating. Besides, if I did get out of bed that afternoon…"

Clotilde-my-love had also tried to get up but had fallen back with a cry and a grimace of pain. "That wretched banana peel!" Then, returning to the matter in hand: "Basically, all you can be sure of is that you saw them kissing, which isn't really much to go on. Saying that Leda was Vasco's lover seems a leap too far. Especially since Vasco…"

Graça had then abruptly changed the subject and asked her about her fall. People really shouldn't drop banana peels in the middle of the Chiado. It was dangerous enough as it was. It had happened at the top of Rua Garrett, hadn't it?

Clotilde answered her questions and chatted, but she wasn't really there. She returned only after a silence that proved hard to fill, so hard that Graça had actually stood up to leave. And there was a sly smile on Clotilde's wrinkled lips.

"Listen, why come and tell me this now, after all these years? It's because they hurt you, isn't it? Because they don't like your beloved. And you thought it would be a good trick to play on them and thought I would be your dupe. The king's messenger, the town crier. The scandal-monger. A splendid way of having your revenge. Didn't you know that I'm your stepmother's friend? Oh dear, my poor little Graça, I'm afraid you came knocking at the wrong door!"

"My poor little Graça..."

Clotilde is there before her now, arms flung wide, her grizzled, tousled hair wet with rain, and somehow or other, Graça finds herself clasped in those two strong arms and pressed against that plump bosom by two equally plump hands, which then, still gripping her shoulders, push her away so as to get a good look at her.

"My poor little Graça..."

What can she say, what is there to say? She had never seen Clotilde again after the day she went to visit her, ostensibly because she had slipped and broken her leg. Was that the reason? No, of course not.

"...how you've changed!"

Has she? Possibly, it's only natural that she would. But has she really changed that much? The remark is classic Clotilde.

"I only found out yesterday, completely by chance, when I was talking to someone...goodness, it's a small world. Imagine, you and I go to the same dressmaker, Virgínia. I went to see her yesterday, and she was telling me how busy she was and so on and that she had to make some dresses for a widow who lives in Campo Grande and who has just returned from Belgium. Campo Grande, Belgium, well, my heart turned over. 'What's the lady's name?' I asked. And when she told me, well, I was all set to give you a call, but you know what I'm like; you remember, don't you?"

Graça doesn't remember, but she nods anyway.

"Exactly. The telephone and me have never got along. To be able to talk on the phone, you need a kind of mysticism I lack. So I said to myself, I'll just turn up. It'll be a surprise."

"A very pleasant surprise. Do sit down, Clotilde."

Clotilde-my-love takes two steps. She's limping (the result of that fall) and has grown extraordinarily fat. She has a neglected air about her too and isn't wearing any makeup. What with her dark, shiny skin, the little moustache above her top lip that she has given up tweezering, and her receding chin, she looks uncannily like a seal.

"How's your husband?"

"He's fine, as always. He's thinner, though, whereas I, as you see, am fatter, by a good thirty pounds. Time passes."

"It does."

She doesn't know what to say. What can they possibly talk about apart from Leda? She's there now; Graça can feel her presence. She's there between them. And they're both thinking about her. Her two executioners. That's why they decide to escape down other paths, even the most painful ones. Clotilde asks:

"When did your husband die?"

"Six months ago. Six months ago yesterday."

She had never told Claude the rest of the story. He hadn't been interested that night (he had an important class the next day), and once that ideal moment passed, Graça could never bring herself to tell him the end, even if she had wanted to. Never again.

Besides, Claude had felt it was all over and done with. Sometimes, if he saw her looking sad or if she seemed irritable, he would tell her that there was no point mulling over what was done and dusted. "What's the point, Graça? We die each night and wake each day anew." And that was that. Perhaps he didn't want to ruffle the tranquil waters of his own lake. Perhaps he had simply forgotten what she had said to him as well as what she hadn't said.

After those two years in Paris, living in modest hotel rooms and eating in self-service restaurants, they had settled in his hometown of Brussels, where his uncle found him a good job in one of his factories. There, years later, years with no history, he fell ill and died in one short week that, even now, was wrapped in a thick mist; whether that mist hung over the city or existed only inside herself, Graça never knew.

She had grieved, of course she had, but how much and why? For him, for herself? It was all too recent for her to know. Perhaps one day, later on, she would see the movie pass before her eyes. For the moment, that was impossible. She had done so much for him: She had gambled and lost so much for his sake, even her own father, and she was unable to gauge the intensity or the quality of her grief. She knew, though—although she preferred not to think about it, even though it was one of those secrets she kept to herself—that she had felt somehow liberated, troublingly herself, and this was such an ill-defined feeling that she didn't know whether to file it away among the sweet things or the bitter things.

She had closed the apartment (the one with the pale furniture and abstract-patterned curtains). It was just another hotel really, where instead of one tiny room, they'd had several tiny rooms. She had never felt at ease there; she had never felt she owned that furniture—she found the colors hostile, and they screamed their presence and blotted out hers. It wasn't the right backdrop for her. And she had suffered with the cold, her hands swollen with chilblains, and spent her days beside the stove. How different from Paris, where she had never felt the lack of the sun. The mist irritated her, the snow forced her to stay at home, and she didn't like the Belgians.

"But, Graça, *I'm* Belgian."

Yes, he was. How strange. But before, in Lisbon, and later, in Paris, she had never registered this.

"Six months ago yesterday."

"Fancy that. Life's so strange. You've never had much luck either, have you, poor dear?"

Who was that "either" intended for? Her or Clotilde?

Clotilde-my-love was always a rather sour person; she always enjoyed hearing about other people's misfortunes, especially any that affected those closest to her. Was this because she was unhappy, and their bad luck served as a balm? But why was she unhappy? Her husband adored her (Clotilde-my-love), she had no money worries, and she was in good health. But who knows? Everything is possible in life, even the strangest things, the least likely... Clotilde is unhappy, and why shouldn't she be? And so she takes her revenge with sour words wrapped in the honey of her voice: "How you've changed!" Or with anonymous letters full of declarations of friendship and devotion...

But perhaps Clotilde isn't referring to herself when she says that Graça hasn't had much luck *either*. She could be thinking of many other people: Leda, her father, even Emília.

Clotilde and Emilia sometimes came to tea, and when she came home from school, she would hear them talking in the living room. She would sometimes go and speak to them, presenting her pink cheek—pink either with cold or with heat—to Emília's condescending kiss and to Clotilde's overly affectionate one. However, she usually went straight to her room, took her schoolbooks out of her bag, and sat down to do her homework for the next day. Leda would then ask, "Is that you, Graça?" and she would say Yes, and the voices would grow lower and more muffled. Talking like that proved tiring, though, and gradually they would return to their normal volume. One of them would say, "Ssh, the child might hear." And the voices would again grow quieter. Emília spoke slowly, dragging the words after her. She would say, for example, that she wished she could do something useful or even useless, one of the useless things people feel obliged to do, like writing bad books or painting bad paintings. "Like a message in a bottle," Leda would say. And Emília would go on: "I'm sure most women who write or paint do so in the same way my mother would embroider tea towels, just to feel they were somehow useful, femininely useful. So that they wouldn't feel they were redundant, that they were, in short, paying their way." And everything she said seemed extremely important, even profound.

At other times, Leda would meet up with her friends in a café downtown, or they would go to a matinee together. When she returned, her eyes would always seem brighter and she would have lots to say; she would often open her mouth only to close it again without having said anything. Sometimes she couldn't help herself, and she would struggle against the insurmountable wall of silence that Graça's father usually built around him and would end up saying something entirely insignificant about someone she had met, or about someone who had married or had died. Graça's father would look up from his work and utter the entirely meaningless "Oh, really?" of someone who hasn't the slightest interest in what he has just heard, and then he would continue drawing mysterious lines on a sheet of white drawing paper. Leda would blush deeply, and at such moments, her shoulders would droop a little more and her eyelids would close over her eyes like blinds she had chosen to draw because there was nothing outside worth looking at. She would sometimes stand in front of the fishbowl, as if lost in thought, but what would she be thinking?

When her friends came to the apartment, she was quite different. She would become almost cheerful; she would talk and laugh. From the privacy of her room, Graça began to penetrate the lives of Clotilde and Emília, especially when the latter turned up alone. From her deep voice Graça learned a great deal about life in general and about Emília in particular. She had learned about Clotilde too. "Knowledge doesn't take up any room," her father used to say. And again he was right.

Among other things, she learned that Emília had just taken the plunge and begun what Clotilde referred to euphemistically (she was always very careful about the terminology she used) as a belated extramarital experience. Her lover (Clotilde didn't use that word; she called him simply *he*—*he*, how sad, because for Graça, *he* was and continued to be Vasco and no one else), anyway, Emília's lover or *he* was Bernardo de Melo, and he was an obscure but ambitious lawyer who would go on to make a remarkable career for himself and would appear at least once a week (having since acquired another "l"—Mello—to look classier) on the front page of the papers where he would be described as "well known," having for a while been only "up and coming." Emília had belonged to Bernardo's prehistoric period. "Don't you find it all rather indecent?" Clotilde-my-love would ask. "I don't know, I still find it shocking. Not that I'm a puritan, well, you know I'm not, but deep down I'm just a poor bourgeois woman with liberal ideas, liberal bourgeois ideas, if you see what I mean. And doesn't it all seem a bit late in the day to you? When you're forty, no, forty-two..." Graça heard someone whisper her name, and everything concluded in a murmur of voices or a torrent of music.

Emília wasn't old, although, at the time, sixteen- or seventeen-year-old Graça found it hard to believe that anyone would give her a second glance. Now, though, viewed through her distance glasses, Emília wasn't old at all, far from it, although there was in her something that was not yet visible, but that Emília herself was beginning to feel and others were beginning to sense. A shift as invisible as time itself—one experienced by all bodies that have reached their apogee and, having lingered there for as long as possible, set off earthward, toward the earth that will one day open up and devour them. This was the case with Emília's tall, white body: her complexion slightly duller; the skin beneath her eyes beginning, very discreetly, to sag; the first gray hairs making an appearance, only to be immediately disguised. "Such bad luck," said Clotilde, "and just when she's found love!" She then went on to say that Emília was doing the rounds of the beauticians, covering herself in masks from head to toe, mud masks—"Life as a mudbath, eh, Leda!"—and had even started going to exercise classes. "I mean, exercise classes, really!" And she snorted with sheer pleasure.

Sometimes, when the two of them came, Graça would hear Clotilde say tenderly, "You poor dear, you look so tired. Did you go to bed late? You look positively ancient…" Leda would break in rather too quickly, "Not at all. Emília's in wonderful shape. The years may pass, but she always looks the same."

According to Clotilde-my-love, no one, apart from her and Leda, knew about Emília's "affair." "Besides, if she didn't have at least two people in the know, what would be the point of all these complications?" she said once. Leda risked a cautiously critical comment. She was very fond of Emília, but…

"I don't understand such duplicity. If she loves Bernardo de Melo, why doesn't she leave her husband?"

Clotilde laughed and mentally jigged up and down, guffawing loudly. Graça was astonished. Her stepmother had said, "If she loves Bernardo de Melo…" Had she heard right?

But Clotilde-my-love interrupted her thoughts and launched into a determined defense of her friend. A defense of sorts, of course, from which her "friend" emerged covered in scratch marks. According to her, Emília genuinely loved Bernardo—"With a passion, my dear." (But hadn't she just said that there would really be no point in Emília having a lover if there weren't at least two people in the know?) First and foremost, however, she went on, first and foremost there was her son, João, a bright young fellow who was going to study engineering. Emília believed—and quite rightly too—that the family home should remain unsullied. "Have you considered how many people would suffer if Emília was actually to leave home and live with *him*? Let's start with her husband, poor man; we mustn't forget him (he's a real saint, but, between you and me, terribly dull), who just adores her. Yes, *ad-o-res* her. Then there's João, such a sensitive boy. He even writes poetry... How he would suffer if he ever found out that his mother, well, you know what I mean... And then there's *him*. What would become of an ambitious young man like that with a golden future ahead of him if he had a married woman of forty-two in tow?" No, the fact is that Emília was proceeding in the best possible way and with great tact and intelligence. Although of course—and here she giggled—while this was the best possible way to proceed given the situation, the best of all things would be if there were no "situation." However, one must be understanding and accept people as they are, with their good and bad qualities. "Because Emília has lots of good qualities, Leda." The truth is that not all women were capable of making sacrifices and resisting the temptations that life placed in their path, but this didn't mean they were worse than anyone else.

On the other side of the corridor, Graça was holding her breath. She wondered what the look on her stepmother's face would be at that moment? Especially her mouth. But the monologue continued. Now Clotilde was singing the praises of her friend's purity. Graça couldn't now remember the reasons she gave, but she knows they were very convincing.

Graça shrugs and tells Clotilde that life is like that. She feels like using an expletive—and she hates expletives—to provide a more accurate definition of life, the only one that occurs to her just then. Clotilde, though, would react badly. She would say in shocked tones, "Oh, Graça!" And so instead she says that life is like that, a suitably vague definition that embraces everything she wants to include, from her father's death to her own widowhood, including, inevitably, Leda. And that could embrace—and does embrace—many more things.

There is now a faint smile on those dark features. It had been there for some time, but Graça hadn't noticed.

"Oh, my dear…"

Clotilde is looking at one particular place in the room, opposite her and a little to the left.

"…you still have the goldfish."

Graça gives a nervous little laugh.

"It's part of the décor. I've always had a goldfish."

"No, you haven't, Leda always had one…" says Clotilde.

"Leda? Possibly…"

They can finally look at the image that has been there since the start. Now that their ramblings about Claude and Emília are over, they can look at that image full on. Clotilde sits back in her chair; crosses her plump or, rather, sturdy legs, sturdy as tree trunks; and blows her nose. She has only just remembered that she has a horrible cold. Graça asks:

"Have you seen Leda? I haven't heard from her since…" Not since yesterday, she thinks.

"Only very rarely. Sometimes whole months go by. I get most of my news from Emília because she lives near Leda, on the same street, and they often see each other. Besides, Leda doesn't have much free time, and, as you know, I live in the boonies… Anyway, life does drive people apart…"

She says this so nonchalantly. Graça is afraid that, at any moment, she will hear her say, "…even the very best of friends" or "even close friends like us." Or something of the sort. But Clotilde-my-love prudently stops before she goes too far, and says only:

"Did you know that Leda's working now?"

No, she didn't. Working where? Did she have any qualifications?

"Don't you remember, she speaks excellent English. And some German."

There were so many things she didn't remember! There were some images that were too big (and too vivid), powerful memories whose presence had devoured and dazzled and obscured other memories, had consigned them forever to oblivion. No, of course she didn't remember. Always assuming she had ever known.

"She was a teacher before she married, living with some very wealthy family and teaching the kids English. That's where your father met her."

"Ah!" She had thought (the things young girls think!) that her father had come across her in some much seedier place. Antoninha had told her about certain women and certain establishments occupied by Arletes, Carlas, and Rosas…so why not Ledas too? Only some shameless woman, coming from who knows where, would deceive a husband who happened to be Graça's father. Even if she was deceiving him with Vasco. The idea had stuck. She had never managed to get rid of it entirely. Where did Leda come from?

"Otherwise," (this is Clotilde speaking), "I really don't

know what would have become of her, poor thing, if she hadn't found that job—if *I* hadn't found it for her, because I was the one who got her the job—but, as I say, I don't know what would have become of her. Your father, may he rest in peace and I hate to speak ill of the dead, but the fact is he treated her very badly indeed. He split up with her without a word of explanation and left her without a penny."

"Was there never any explanation as to why they split up?"

"No one ever knew why, nor did she. The fact is, she suspects you, because it all coincided with you leaving home… But she has no idea what you could have told your father."

"Me? Really?" Graça smooths her skirt and doesn't know quite what to say. "Me?" she says again.

She tries to change the subject, to ask about someone else, Vasco for example, yes, why not? She carries inside her the faint hope that Clotilde will tell her that he's back, that he sometimes mentions her, that he hasn't forgotten her, or simply to know that he's all right. However, she doesn't have the courage. She feels a sudden desire, which she struggles to suppress, to get up, drag Clotilde over to the front door, and throw her out, possibly even push her down the stairs. She can't stand her, she never could, but now she's even worse. With age, Clotilde must have prospered and increased her stock of bitterness. Or perhaps she, Graça, is the one who has grown more impatient and lost what little sense of humor she had. Clotilde used to amuse her or at the very least, shock her. Now she merely irritates her. "Poor girl…"; "I was the one who got her the job…" What a load of nonsense.

"Today is clearly my day for visitors..."

Clotilde takes off her thick-lensed glasses and polishes them carefully. Her eyes suddenly shrink and become two tremulous, naked, anxious cracks. Then she puts her glasses back on and is herself again.

"I'm expecting Leda. She phoned me yesterday, saying she wants to speak to me. To clear up a number of things she has never understood. That's what she said. So I'm just waiting to see what she wants to know."

She watches Clotilde, expecting her to react. Will Clotilde-my-love leap out of her chair, scream, turn pale? No. She simply says very calmly and imperturbably:

"That will be an interesting encounter. I'd certainly like to be a fly on the wall for that. Anyway, I'll be on my way and leave you two alone. Your conversation won't do my heart any good. Did you know I have heart problems? Nor did I! They've only just found out... Anyway, stay in touch. We could even arrange to meet one Saturday afternoon. Leda and Emília could come too. I'm sure Emília would love to see you. She often speaks of you... You knew about that business with Bernardo de Melo..." (and she makes a horizontal movement with her hand across her plump throat.) "What am I saying? Of course you do, that was long before you left home."

It was. Two years perhaps, or more. She remembers it vividly. One day, Bernardo de Mello (now with two *l*s) had appeared for the first time by himself on the front page of the newspapers. He had been appointed director-general of some organization or other, or perhaps he had been made chairman of some board, and almost at the same time, he had written the words *The End* on his love affair with Emília. Shortly afterward, he had married a girl from a good family, a family with a good deal of money too, which was equally important for an ambitious man like him, keen to rise to the top quickly, and he hadn't hesitated for one moment to place his sacrifice at the feet of his new bride all in white, and that sacrifice was Emília.

For some time, Emília had talked of killing herself and had even gone so far as to take a massive overdose of some sedative or other, but, after having her stomach pumped, she survived, albeit mortally wounded. Or so it seemed.

Enlivened by the memory of her friend's misfortune, Clotilde tells her that Bernardo is very happy, and his wife's about to have their eighth child. Emília, though, is a changed woman—("Poor Graça, how you've changed!")—an old crock.

"Yes, a real old crock; you'd hardly recognize her."

And from behind the thick round lenses of her glasses, Clotilde-my-love's eyes glinted in all their shameless splendor.

She sets off down the stairs. Graça keeps the latch drawn back as she very slowly and carefully closes the door, gradually letting the latch return to its original position. Out in the corridor, she can still hear Clotilde's slow, heavy, fearful footsteps. Ever since that fall, which had left her permanently lame (yet another reason for her to hate other people, the ones who were not lame), ever since that day, Clotilde has had to keep an even more watchful eye on the ground she treads, afraid she might fall over again. One of her feet makes a lopsided noise as she walks. Why did she choose not to go down in the elevator? Ah, now she remembers. Clotilde has never liked elevators.

Nor did Uncle Rafael. Little Graça used to laugh out loud at that inexplicable phobia of his, which seemed utterly ridiculous in such a strong, cheerful man. "But why, Uncle, why?" He would shrug and then smile that almost childlike smile, which revealed his small teeth and made his plump cheeks tremble. He was both the saving grace and the black sheep of the family, qualities (or defects, depending on your point of view) that often exist side by side. A poet, and this was something Graça would only understand later on, who had never written any poems and on whom life had played a dastardly trick (because life doesn't like poets, or as her father would say: Because that idler never applied himself) by finding him a job in the Commissioning Department of Faria Benavente & Co. on Rua dos Fanqueiros, where, it's true, he rarely put in an appearance. He never had any money and was always accumulating debts, and her father had never forgiven him for his complete lack of common sense. They were constantly embroiled in rather bitter arguments. If Leda or Graça spoke well of him, praised his qualities, Graça's father would get very annoyed. "And what exactly are these qualities; can you tell me that?" Leda would open her mouth to speak, unsure how to separate out the qualities from what made her declare simply that he was "an excellent fellow." Graça's father would respond bluntly, "Most of the world's imbeciles are 'excellent fellows.'"

One day, though, Uncle Rafael, having had enough of the Commissioning Department and, doubtless, having had more than enough of those endless arguments with his brother, had decided to head off to Luanda as a tourist—on an adventure with no job lined up and waiting for him. And so off he went on that huge gray-and-white

doctor and, over supper, explained that he had a bad heart and must avoid any stressful situations.

ooooo

Graça goes back into the living room. The image of Clotilde and her voice had departed along with her, and, fortunately, nothing of her remained. Memories are sometimes more potent than any actual presence, and for a moment, Uncle Rafael is sitting there before her, legs crossed, savoring the thin cigarette he himself has just rolled. Then he leaves as well, and as she feels him going and makes not the slightest effort to stop him, Graça sits down on the rounded arm of Vasco's armchair. Uncle Rafael is gone. She is left alone with the armchair that will, for all eternity, be Vasco's armchair. She reaches out her right arm, and her hand remains open, in mid-air, as if it really was encircling someone's shoulder.

Where will Vasco be now? Will he have put on weight? Will he have gone gray? What will he be like?

The night brought with it his fine, serene, perfect profile, his beautifully cut gray suit, his green suede vest. Graça threw back her head and saw his thick two-toned brown hair that curled almost down to his neck.

"How are things, sweetie. How's school? Is Antoninha all right?"

Graça shrank back. School. Antoninha. He was talking down to her now. Why didn't he just go ahead and ask to look at her school books?...

"I got 12 in Portuguese, 13 in French, 8 in Math..."

"Amazing!"

Vasco was holding up his hands in pretend astonishment. His large, bony hands were carefully manicured. Her father had raised his eyes from his drawing board:

"You should be ashamed of yourself. Fancy boasting about such bad marks. Go to your room and study. You're almost fourteen and in the third year now. Don't you realize you're a grown-up now, a young woman? People should be aware of their responsibilities. Go on, go and study. And then straight to bed." He had glanced at his wristwatch. "It's nearly eleven o'clock. You're still too young to be going to bed so late."

She had slouched across the room, her blue pleated skirt swinging, the skirt that was beginning to be too short for her.

"Don't I get a goodnight kiss, sweetie?"

No, she wasn't going to give him a kiss. But what if she did? She had stopped at the door, hesitating. But the others had already forgotten all about her. Especially Vasco. He had set aside the gentle voice he adopted to speak to her, and it was now almost excessively normal.

"Do you want anything from Tangiers?"

"Are you going to Tangiers?" asked Leda, taken aback.

"Yes, tomorrow. I'm going with a friend who has a car. We're driving through Spain. Just for a week."

She heard the faint click of his lighter. Graça had stopped on her way out of the room and was standing still and expectant behind the curtain, surrounded by a pleasant, protective penumbra. What was she going to do in her room? Study? She was, in fact, really sleepy. It's nearly eleven o'clock. You're still too young to be going to bed so late. She crossed the corridor, dragging her feet.

"Are you going with Ferreira?"

"Yes."

A silence. The sound of an eraser rubbing something out.

"You shouldn't see so much of that Ferreira fellow."

How odd her stepmother's voice sounded, and what an odd thing to say. "Why shouldn't Vasco go around with whoever he wants?" her father said. "That's taking your maternal instincts too far…"

"My frustrated maternal instincts, you mean."

"Well, frustrated or not, don't exaggerate. Vasco knows perfectly well, or at least he should, who he should go around with, whether A or B. It's none of our business. So, Vasco, you're off to Tangiers? Good. *Il faut que jeunesse se passe*. Would you like Vasco to bring you something, Leda? I might have a few pesetas somewhere…"

Her stepmother said only, "No, I don't want anything."

"Well, I'm going to bring you a present anyway. How about a bottle of perfume?"

Graça had gone into her room, locked the door, thrown herself down on the bed, and wept.

She had arisen from her illness looking terribly thin and so weak she could barely stand. At the same time, though, she felt extraordinarily powerful. She would often find herself thinking, "One day, tomorrow or the day after, whenever I choose, that'll be the end of Leda. An end to the good life and to little tea parties with her female friends." This, however, was a purely abstract desire. She thought, Whenever I choose, but never properly considered the manner of her choosing. And her revenge—her sad, pathetic revenge—was limited to breaking the bottle of Lotus Blossom perfume that Vasco had brought back from his trip to Tangiers. Only much later, when she was with Claude, would she look at the problem head on. And Clotilde's sudden reappearance would provide her only way out.

One Sunday afternoon, the telephone rang, and Leda had answered, then held the receiver out to Graça's father.

"It's someone asking for you."

"Who is it?"

"He didn't say…"

"You should have asked. You know perfectly well that I hate answering the phone when I don't… Hello? Yes, yes, of course I remember you. How are you?"

There was a long silence. The voice on the other end talked on and on. Finally, her father was able to respond: "My dear fellow, what you're asking me is really most unpleasant… He and I are really not that close. He's the cousin of my first wife. Is there no other solution? Is it really necessary?'

Again there came that disembodied voice talking about Vasco. What was he saying? Leda was sitting rigid, empty, and had, it seemed, completely forgotten how to breathe.

"All right, fine. I'll come immediately, although I don't honestly know what I can say. It doesn't matter, you say? Come now. All right, my friend, goodbye."

He had disconnected the phone with his left hand, while still keeping the receiver held to his ear, as he always did when he was very annoyed.

"Vasco has been arrested. Hardly a surprise really. However, I never imagined I would have to get involved. Apparently, I must tell his family because his brother-in-law has influence in high places. I just wish I knew what precisely I'm expected to say—tell them he's been arrested, I suppose."

"Arrested?"

Leda had turned very pale, and Graça could see her mouth moving, grimacing, quite independent of her will. "But why?" her stepmother had asked at last, in a breathless, fearful voice. She had said this not intending to be heard and then turned away, pressing her hand to her lips.

Graça's father had said sharply, "Please, don't ask stupid questions. I'm up to here with it."

Then he'd said that this could only ever happen to Vasco, that he attracted trouble like a magnet, yes, that was it, like a magnet. He then rammed his hat on his head and angrily pulled on his coat, so hastily that a coat button fell off and rolled onto the mat. Then he left, slamming all the doors: the apartment door, the elevator door, and the street door. And the echoes had lingered, as if glued one to the other, until they finally dissolved into the air.

Another door banging. This time it's the kitchen door, and Piedade suddenly appears before Graça—"Oh, I didn't know you were in here, Senhora, I thought you were in your bedroom"—thus catches Piedade in fraternal flagrante delicto, holding a saucer of breadcrumbs for the fish. Graça pretends not to notice and leaves the room.

"I'm still expecting that lady," she says on her way to the door, but without turning around. "The one who just left was someone else."

Piedade mumbles affirmatively, and Graça hears the faint sound of breadcrumbs being scattered from on high, while the fish, presumably unaware of the kindness of humans, must be descending to its deepest submarine depths.

Graça walks past the dressing-table mirror and sees,

without even looking, the shadow of her profile. She loathes that unknown profile, which she has only ever been able to see with great difficulty by sitting before a mirror and holding another mirror in her hand, the profile that belongs not to her, but only to other people. Even when alone, she feels embarrassed by that momentary image, which is hers, after all, and that floats into view only to vanish at once, leaving the stage empty. "Poor Graça, how you've changed!" The image of that Graça, of that one or another, it really doesn't matter. "You've never had much luck either, have you, poor dear." No she hadn't. Or had she, but simply never noticed? At first, it had all been so marvelous, just amazing. But had it really been so very amazing? Wasn't it just that she had wanted it to be amazing, had wanted to be amazed, to embrace with the desperation of a drowning woman the first illusory hope that hove into view?

She was phoning a university friend and had gotten two of the numbers the wrong way around. Instead of a two and a five, she had dialed a five and a two. Because of this mistake her life had taken a completely different route—and not only her life, but also the lives of her father and of Leda. A voice had answered, the voice of a man who spoke very bad Portuguese.

"Hello."

"Oh, I'm sorry, I think I must have made a mistake. What number is this?"

"We spend our lives making mistakes. Don't you?"

It was a cheerful, slightly sharp voice, with a pleasantly foreign accent. She had said, "Me? I'm not sure… It's hard to say…"

But she hadn't put the phone down. The voice at the

other end was waiting too. It was one of those vast, dense silences that occurs when we're waiting for nothing at all, while clasping a receiver in one hand.

"Aren't you going to hang up?" he had asked.

"I hate hanging up. It means taking responsibility for something, and I hate doing that."

"Yes, I know, the responsibility of cutting the fragile thread that, just for a moment, joins us together. If you hang up, it's all over; you'll have killed me forever. And I might have been something important. Is that what you mean?"

"More or less."

This is how things had been born. How they had died, or, rather, withered away, was harder to say. The fact is that she couldn't pinpoint the exact moment when she had begun to view Claude through those lenses that make everything so clear, so frighteningly real, like seeing ourselves reflected in one of those mirrors used to study imperfections of the skin. Blackheads, huge craters; the hairs above the upper lip like bushes leaning over into the abyss. With him, with Claude, there were no imaginary lenses, no blurred images, no comforting, soothing crepuscular atmospheres. Why was that? She had no idea…

And yet, the beginning had been quite different. They had met after that chance telephone conversation, and he had not arrived as other people arrive. Or was it perhaps that she had not waited for him as people usually wait… But why think about that? Her lingering impression was of him arriving, not of her waiting, of him arriving not as other men did, with a smile, a witty remark, a glance, a presence. No, that wasn't him. He had erupted into her life, emptying out everything she had kept safely stashed in drawers, filed away all neatly labeled or, quite simply, things she had been quite unaware of and that were brought to light by the sheer force of those storm winds. She was surrounded by wreckage, the key to all secrets bobbing about on the crest of the waves (it had not bobbed for long, for she had managed to retrieve it), fragments of ideas she had inherited and dreams that were actually hers. Or were they? Here and there, she spotted bits of her father, scattered remnants of that venerable image, unwittingly shattered by the iconoclast. And she regarded it all quite serenely, because she suddenly realized that none of it was of any value. Such a relief.

Claude understood everything. Wasn't that extraordinary? She would begin a sentence, then pause, and he would finish it for her. It was as if he knew her father and Leda. He spoke of them as if nothing about them were unknown to him. And Graça felt that this, at last, was love. Finding a person you could tell everything to. Everything? No, that would be impossible. But as much as she could tell him: The tears she had shed for the dog that had been run over; how she missed her mother; how she hated Leda…

Life could at last be different, and it lay before her like a broad green sea, upon which she could set off in any direction. Was it green? On that point, she recalled, she had hesitated. Was it green or some other color, or no color at all, and later on how would it be? Anyway, regardless of color, it was a sea. And that was what mattered.

The journey began in the streets of the city, either crowded with people or deserted, far from the people who walked past them and who weren't even there…far, too, from the rusty old machines repeating the same thing every day of every year. "Did you sleep well?"—"Your grandmother, may she rest in peace…"—"Let that be an example to you, Graça… Work…"

With him, though, everything was new, even when the same thing was repeated, because she hadn't yet understood it or become accustomed to it, finding it normal and commonplace and growing tired of it. A little as if the air she breathed hadn't had time to leave her lungs. And this was how—holding her breath, her chest still full of air, and lightly, lightly hovering above everything and everyone—she visited the places Claude had already discovered in the few months he had lived in Lisbon, but that she still didn't know because she had been born in Estrela, just up the hill from the town center. These were places he had cut out from the landscape for his own personal use in order to stick them in his album of memories and, of course, so he could show them to her. He had an unusual technique. To obtain the best shot he required five square feet of ground (that particular spot and no other: neither the one that lay to the right or the left, behind or in front), and from there he would gaze to the south or the east or even the southwest and at a particular time of day, down to the very minute and sometimes even down to the very second. And the shot came out precisely as he wanted it. In Cascais (they had gone there on purpose) there were two boats among many others. She had never known quite why they were the chosen ones and had perhaps never bothered to find out, but they were the ones. They would sit and wait, he with not a trace of anxiety on his face, only a look of expectation. The sun would be about to sink below the horizon, sometimes still aglow, at others like a punctured balloon letting out air, lighting up, or already lit, falling into the blood-red water. Then, as if he had suddenly lost all interest, he would say, "Right, shall we go?"

But what she took for imagination, enthusiasm, a love of beautiful things, turned out to be merely the passing interest of a tourist. Claude did not own a camera and had perhaps never even considered owning one. He photographed things with his eyes, then put the photo away in his album of memories and closed the book. Did he really do that, Graça wondered later on. But he did. He remembered those images in every tiny detail. All of them. He had an amazing visual memory. Like Vasco.

Vasco. Where would he and his perfect profile be now? She could have asked Clotilde, who knows everything, and who's always up to speed on the lives of everyone, but her courage had failed her. Leda is about to arrive, but she won't ask her either. She wouldn't be able to; she wouldn't want to. Leda will talk about Vasco, but about the old Vasco they had both known, whom they had both loved. Perhaps not about the other one. Graça, though, is afraid this might not be the case, and her stepmother will bring her more recent news, news she doesn't want to receive. Anything she said about him would be bad news, regardless of whether he's alive or dead. The vague atmosphere of childhood in which he was so at ease, and in which he was *he*, is infinitely preferable to any harsh, wounding, explanatory words. He would have no place in the present, which is all too real and transparent. The once-beautiful hands of the peasant woman (Vasco's work) now look as if they were made of rubber and, just a while ago, had reminded her of the terrible chilblains she used to suffer from (but no longer does). Vasco at fifty, with white hair or almost bald. Old. Dead. Rotting. Why would she want *him*?

No, the Vasco she wanted was the one who would arrive and sit down in Vasco's armchair opposite Vasco's painting. Sometimes when he arrived early and her stepmother had not yet come home, she would go and keep him company. Those were the best moments of her life, the ones she spent sitting opposite him. Dazzled by his face, by his hands, by the words he said. She would talk then and tell him all the unimportant things as well, sometimes, as the really important things she needed to tell someone, but that she couldn't tell her father or Leda. What she was thinking. Her mother's death. How much she missed her. Vasco would smile and say:

"These aren't things you need to worry about at your age, sweetie. Nor at my age either for that matter. I'm not saying don't think about your mother, of course not, but leave old graybeards and devout old ladies to worry about death. You should be thinking about life, looking to the future, going to the cinema, learning to swim, never missing a class..."

"It's nearly two o'clock, Papa. I mustn't miss my class."

Her father, grave-faced, chin lifted, was standing very stiffly by the bookshelf next to the bust of his head.

"Well, you're going to have to miss it, not, I imagine, for the first time. You've been spotted by my friends at some time or other either down by the river or in a park. Even in Cascais, watching the boats... And on a weekday too, if I'm not mistaken. When you should have been in class."

"I was watching the sunset, Papa," said Graça with her discreet little smile.

"I'm not joking."

"Nor am I, Papa. But I like to tell things as they are. It wasn't the boats we were looking at, but the sunset."

Her father gave her a heavy, meaningful stare, but Graça didn't waver and withstood the weight of his eyes.

"Why didn't you tell me all this earlier?"

"I suppose because I wasn't sure."

"And now you are?"

"Yes."

"I see."

Two such simple words, so laden with irony. Her father had left his place beside his own private pedestal and taken a few steps around the room, around the table where the pink cut-glass ashtray already bloomed. Then he came to an abrupt halt in front of Graça and stuck his thumbs in the armholes of his vest, ready to attack.

"What does he do?"

"He's a student of course. In Paris. He's in the final year of his Engineering degree."

"Which he clearly failed."

"No, his uncle lives here and wanted him to come and work with him for a while. Besides, it was a unique opportunity."

More pacing up and down. Another sudden halt next to the bust, and then one important sentence was followed by other, equally grave, sentences.

"Well, you must stop seeing him. I say this, as you must realize, because I have good reason to do so. And obviously I've made my enquiries."

"What, like getting references for a maid? It looks like they were pretty bad…"

"They were. Your Claude, my poor Graça—his name is Claude, isn't it?—doesn't have a penny to his name. He was brought up by that uncle who, while he does have a bit of money, also has three legitimate children. It's not worth leaving your country in order to live a modest, even poor, existence abroad."

"And what if I think it is worth it?"

"That's your affair. At twenty-two, you're a grown-up. Marry if you want to, but be aware that you can't count on me for help of any kind."

Graça then lifted her chin defiantly, or perhaps she had already; she wasn't sure. That had been the moment, though, when the first cracks had begun to appear in her father's image, so small as to be almost invisible—not cracks exactly, but the kind of crazing that appears on poor-quality porcelain when it's been used for a while. Or rather, that had been the moment when Graça's eyes were keen enough to see them.

"May I leave now, or was there something else you wanted to say?"

He was probably expecting some reaction, tears perhaps, and then he would console her, and after that, who knows: She would perhaps gradually come to understand why he was so upset. Graça, however, was standing before him, not moving, just waiting. Not a sign of tears, and she appeared to be perfectly calm. Was this really his daughter, or some stranger? Was the man looking at Graça and saying, "Yes, you can leave; I've nothing more to say," was he a stranger? Was her father a stranger? His image shattered.

Only later on did Graça try to piece it together again, but it was always a difficult job, a far more complicated puzzle than that letter from Luanda. Some of the pieces she never even found and never would. They were lost in the maelstrom, borne away on the current. That image would remain forever incomplete, not to be discarded, but kept in a corner of the attic of memories.

She looks at the small wristwatch that Claude gave her as birthday present one year. It's almost six o'clock. Leda should be arriving soon.

She had phoned the previous evening. Graça had heard her low, slow voice, which sometimes seemed on the point of disappearing altogether: "Is that you, Graça?" As naturally as that, as if they had parted the best of friends only the day before. "Is that you, Graça?" No, it couldn't be, it couldn't possibly be Leda. What could she have to say to her or to ask her after all those years?

"Yes," she had replied. "Who's speaking?"

"Don't you recognize my voice?"

A silence. She could not, for the moment, find the right words. It was as if they had all fled far away, leaving her empty, alone, with no chance of salvation. Everything seemed to her so false, so absurd... Leda talking to her after all those years and speaking to her like that. "Is that you, Graça? Don't you recognize my voice?" What should she do? Allow herself to take the easy way out and say, "Sorry, I don't know who's speaking..."? But Leda had a unique voice, and there could be no mistaking it.

"Leda!" she had exclaimed at last.

A simple, overenthusiastic exclamation, which had nothing to do with what she was actually feeling or had felt in the past. Then silence. As if the shock had left her speechless. It fell to the other person to continue the conversation, to say something that revealed why she was phoning, whether she was on the attack or came with good intentions.

"I found out this morning from Emília that you were in Lisbon. Clotilde told her. I'd like to talk to you. Are you home tomorrow?"

That could mean anything…

"Yes, I am, Leda. All afternoon. You can come whenever you like."

"I'll be there around six o'clock…"

"Great. I'll be waiting."

Waiting for love, waiting for her father to understand, waiting for Clotilde to speak, waiting for a forgiveness that would never come, waiting, unconsciously waiting to be free, waiting to return to a place where nothing awaited her, waiting for Leda… And what else?

"Is my husband's illness terminal, doctor?"

Even before she asked the question, she knew very well that Claude would not survive. She had always known about things before they happened. She had always known that Leda would leave the family home, ever since that now-distant day when a leaf had fallen from a tree.

"We must never lose hope. Where would we be without hope?"

It was the doctor speaking, already with his mind on other matters.

"I understand, doctor."

She was pale and disheveled and so profoundly exhausted that she could serenely face the idea of Claude's death. All that mattered was having a bed and being able to sleep for many hours.

"You need to rest," the doctor had said. "Why make yourself suffer like this, what good does it do your husband? Why spend every night in the waiting room if you can't even see him?"

"I know, doctor."

But she stayed sitting in an uncomfortable chair, leafing through dog-eared copies of *Paris-Match*, allowing herself to be lulled to sleep by the light of the solitary bulb in the ceiling. Sometimes her head would droop and she would awake with a start. Claude was going to die, and he was calling her; she could hear his voice clearly. She would leave the room and go to reception.

"How is the patient in room 90?"

"He's slightly better."

He remained slightly better until the very last moment.

"How is the patient in room 90?"

"You're going to have to be brave…"

She had been brave. She was even filled by a strange feeling of serenity. As if after swimming for a long time against the current she found herself adrift in the calm waters of a lake, with no need to move her arms. Claude had been a nice dream that had lasted long into the morning, one of those dreams in which we are never entirely present, in which there is always some part of us absent, listening for footsteps in the corridor outside.

Now she had opened her eyes. What would Vasco be like now? And Leda? How old would she be? She must be, what, fifty or more? Would her hair have turned white, and would she have false teeth? What would her face and her mouth be like now?

In the days that followed the winter afternoon when she had surprised Vasco and Leda, she felt almost bent beneath the weight of that enormous secret, far too heavy a weight for her young shoulders. Then she had gradually grown used to the idea and contented herself with savoring words that were hers alone, and she eventually came to enjoy the pleasure she felt would be lost completely if, one day, she were to reveal those words to someone else. Later, it took some external force for her to free herself from the words she had stored away, indeed, almost forgotten. And she would choose Clotilde as a bridge. She had kept for herself the modest role of instrument of fate acting from a distance. Unfortunately, instruments of fate are never popular. They are the intermediaries of evil. The enemy chooses such intermediaries either because they are weak or else very strong. And understandably enough, both types are universally disliked.

One day, a letter arrived. Graça had seen it on the silver tray and would always remember the blueish envelope it came in and the cheap paper on which the words were scrawled in red ink. There was no return address. Her father had opened it in the evening, when he came home for supper, opening it very carefully with the brass letter-opener as he always did. Slowly, so as not to tear any of the corners. He read it once, twice, just as he had read that other letter many years before, and again he turned very pale, but this time he put it in his pocket without looking at anyone. Not even at Graça or at Leda. They ate supper just as they had on other days, and just as on those other days, his father asked Leda to please pass him the salt and told the maid, in his usual voice, to tell the cook that there wasn't enough salt in the soup.

Then, when they were all about to leave the table, he turned to his wife and said:

"Will you excuse me? I need to have a word with Graça."

Leda left, closing the door slowly behind her. Graça's father was once again holding the letter, which he threw down on the table.

"Read it."

Graça never finished reading it. There was a strange magnetic current between her eyes and that cheap piece of paper spattered with the occasional ink blot.

"You wrote this, didn't you?"

Graça was still transfixed, unable to look up, unable to speak. Her face remained calm and unruffled and not a sound emerged from her lips.

"You wrote it. This is what it says: 'Someone who saw them in the living room. That someone cannot be wrong.' Someone. Who, eight years later, would write that? A maid? That would be handy, wouldn't it? But no maid ever grew old in this household. How many have passed through here in the last eight years? No…only you could have written this, to avenge yourself for the cool reception we gave to that friend of yours. Come on, speak. Why did you write this wretched thing? An anonymous letter… How base… My own daughter! I'm right, aren't I?"

Graça remained obstinately still, her eyes lowered, the letter gripped firmly in one hand. She heard a slap, then another and another. On her face? Possibly. It might have been her face, but she wasn't sure. It was a strange, muffled sound. Then she nearly lost her balance and was thrown against the wall. So someone *was* slapping her face.

"Papa…"

"So it's true?"

Graça nodded.

"Listen, Papa…"

He snatched the letter from her, opened the living room door and went out into the corridor. For a long while, Graça stayed where she was, not moving, not thinking. Then she picked up the phone and dialed Claude's number.

"I have to leave here tonight," she said.

ooooo

Her father had died without ever forgiving her. And what about Leda? And Vasco? Not that he had anything to forgive her for—he might know nothing about it, that was possible; yes, he almost certainly knew nothing about it. Vasco disappeared immediately after the day of his arrest. She had never seen him again.

One day, her father left home earlier than usual. That evening he said:

"I've just come from the station, goodness, what a rabble… Anyway, *noblesse oblige*."

Graça had felt as if her heart had suddenly shriveled up, like a small hard pebble in her chest—such a strange sensation.

"Who did you go there to see off, Papa?

"Vasco. Didn't you know? I thought Leda would have told you."

"So he didn't even come to say goodbye. Where has he gone, Papa?"

But her father had responded angrily, unfeelingly: "To the devil for all I care. No, to Paris. Now, please, don't ask me any more questions. I'm up to here with it."

Those last words were so unlike her father. Nevertheless, she had persisted: "Will he write? Did you ask him to write?"

"He'll write if he wants to, Graça." This was her stepmother speaking, very gently, even more gently than usual. "You should never ask people to write to you. It's rather like asking them for alms, do you see?"

It was a day of horrors. Graça gazed at Leda uncomprehendingly. How could she speak so calmly about Vasco's departure, about the possibility that he would never write to them? She would never forget him. Never, never, never. She fled to her bedroom. Her face was wet with tears.

She opens the window. It gets dark early in October, on this, the tenth of October. It has rained all afternoon, but now there's a lull, and beneath the streetlamp on the pavement opposite, a few yards from the tree—what kind is it?—there is a round, still, luminous puddle. Graça half-closes her eyes and sees the light form flickering golden darts around the lamp-turned-star.

It's exactly twenty past six, and Leda has still not arrived. Graça peers up and down the street, but sees only a fat man in a raincoat carrying a large umbrella over his arm. Then the man disappears, and the street is once more deserted. It feels like a Sunday.

Why is Leda coming to see her? What's she going to say, to ask? What is she expecting to hear? Will she arrive full of explanations, to tell her that there never was anything between her and Vasco apart from what Graça saw that one day? Will she come to tell her about her life as an almost-abandoned wife, about the brief illusory hope of love that Vasco had given her? Will she come in an accusatory mood, accusing her of destroying a home, of having killed her father with the shock, of having killed her? Or is she simply coming to see her, unaware that Graça was the guilty party, the real criminal? And what will Graça say to her if she mentions the letter? That she didn't write it? What difference would that make? And what if she does speak and explain everything, what would happen then?

But nothing is going to happen. Everything will stay irremediably, irreparably the same. Because what could be spoiled has been spoiled. It died one night, never to return.

Suddenly, almost seamlessly, she opens the wardrobe, takes out her coat—the heaviest one, the camelhair one she had dyed black. She picks up her handbag, glances at the dressing-table mirror with the crack in one corner. She sees that her face is paler than usual and that her hazel eyes are almost green, as they always are when the tide is coming in, bringing with it seaweed and slime.

She's standing at the door, holding the handle, when she sees Piedade staring at her in astonishment, bewildered.

"What about that lady? Weren't you waiting for some lady to call?"

Graça's response is quick, hasty, and her slippery eyes choose not to look at Piedade; they slither past her and are gone. Where?

"If the lady does come, tell her I've left, that…that I've left Lisbon and that you don't know when I'll be back.

Tell her anything."

"All right..."

Piedade doesn't like obscure situations, and this one strikes her as pretty murky. She shakes her head and tut-tuts.

"All right... I suppose you know what you're doing."

No, Graça doesn't know. She races down the stairs, deliberately avoiding the elevator, afraid she might meet Leda when she gets out down below.

Her stepmother could easily be downstairs, waiting to take the elevator. They're less likely to meet on the stairs.

She stops at the front door and looks cautiously right and left, but the street is still deserted. In the distance to the right, she sees a skinny woman with white hair walking along in the rain that has just started again, but she isn't hurrying, as if she weren't even aware of the rain. Graça pulls her scarf over her head and turns left. Could that be Leda? She doesn't know and prefers not to.

A large gray car speeds past, splattering her with mud. Graça feels the thick, cold substance on her legs, and, at the same time, she's conscious of a lump in her throat ready to turn into tears. But she refuses to cry. She summons the tears back inside; she drowns them, masters them. Instead, with a handkerchief, she quickly wipes away the mud on her black silk stockings.

It's raining harder now. A taxi with a green light slows to a halt next to her. Graça opens the door and hurls herself inside, where she huddles in a corner.

"Where do you want to go?"

But Graça doesn't want to go anywhere; she just wants to be. Just be. Not feel hungry or thirsty or sleepy, not feel the stupid anxiety that has never left her. Not think about Leda or about her father, or about Claude or Vasco or herself.

"Carry on down the avenue," is all she says.

If only she could always carry on down—or up—without stopping, yes, carry straight on without looking to either side, without any sides to look at. With nothing at the end of the road except the end of the road. Impossible. At some point, in five or ten minutes at most, she will have to rematerialize, to open her mouth and say "I'll get out here" or "Drop me at the end of this street" or "Drive around the square." She'll have no alternative.

Meanwhile, though, she will simply carry on down the avenue, which means she can close her eyes. A sweet moment of respite.

A LOVE STORY

Did anyone admire or envy them; could anyone look at them without smirking? Was there anyone who would have given anything to be like them? You must be joking! People laughed when they saw them. I did too. I know I was very young then, and, at that age, we do tend to make fun of everything, even the most serious things, even those most deserving of our respect. As I well know.

They, and this is the absolute truth—and not at all to their credit—had no notion of how ridiculous they were. None at all. They would walk down the street hand in hand, laughing and whispering to each other like lovers out for a Sunday morning stroll, and the way they dressed...especially her. I can still remember a particular black woolen dress that she wore with various scarlet accessories—she was very into accessories. She looked, how can I put it, diabolical, although she was far from being diabolical. Imagine a woman no longer in the first flush of youth; somewhat on the buxom side; with an ample, motherly bosom; and wearing hat, shoes, gloves, and handbag, all of them a bright blood red... She also tended to combine colors that no one would ever dream of putting together: orange and purple, for example; canary yellow and peacock blue. And she never wore makeup, apart from a light dusting of face powder, and then there were the thick, almost brown, lisle stockings she wore. All these things—the garish colors, the pouter-pigeon breast, the thick stockings, and the face powder—were strangely at odds with each other. They simply didn't go somehow.

As for him, he made rather less of an impact, although he, too, was far from ordinary looking. He was short and skinny. A poor excuse for a man, as people say, with a large, snub nose, very round nostrils, thick glasses, and a tie. Ties were his one great extravagance. And although he was noted for wearing very light-colored suits in winter and summer, with over-long jackets and bell-bottom pants, it was his ties that marked him out. He had them in every color and every fabric, from wool to taffeta, all of them adorned with polka dots.

We lived in the same building: they on the third floor and we on the second. I remember my mother coming home one day, looking rather flustered and saying, "I just met our upstairs neighbor. Goodness, she looked as if she was wearing a blanket. I mean it. Broad vertical stripes from top to bottom and in green and yellow! You'd think her husband would say something." My father replied placidly, "Of course he won't. You and me and, yes, a lot of other people, we're the malicious ones. We, in short, suffer from a disease of the mind. *They* are the healthy ones, God bless them."

I doubt if God did bestow many blessings on them, but that's beside the point. This is all about a recent discovery I made, because the fact is, I hadn't really thought about them once we moved.

I think all streets have their unwitting clowns, just as they have their villains, their heroes, and their idiots. They were the clowns of our street. We talked about them and we smiled; we couldn't help but smile. Did they know that they kept the whole street amused? That's one mystery I never fathomed. Now, though, I'm convinced that even had they known, they wouldn't have cared. The truth is that they were the truly wealthy ones, because they didn't need anyone else. And yet there we were—the real imbeciles—laughing at them!

I went to their apartment only once. Our phone wasn't working, and someone who, at the time, needed to speak to me urgently had called their number instead. She came to fetch me because her husband wasn't home at that hour. I was just about to say thank you and leave, when she asked me to stay a while. "We sometimes talk about you. We've watched you grow up and become a young woman… People can become fond of other people even if they don't know them, don't you agree? Perhaps especially those they don't know." She talked about when I was a child and about a lovely white lace dress I used to wear. Whenever we met on the stairs, she would pat me on the head, and I would run away, I was so shy! Silva—that was her husband's name—always liked me too. He would sometimes say, "If only we'd had a little girl like her…" But God chose otherwise.

They had an extraordinary living room, full of figurines and faded, moth-eaten dolls, vases of flowers, leather pouffes, bead-embroidered cushions, doilies, and, on the flock wallpaper, family photos all with dedications written in the righthand corner. This was her sister—you've probably seen her visiting sometimes—that was her sister-in-law, and that was her cousin Rui: He was in the merchant navy, and was the one who had given them that ship in a bottle. Because one of the many objects was a bottle with a ship inside it. However, she spoke of these people indifferently, with little enthusiasm, rather as if she were a bored museum guard explaining an exhibit. She only waxed enthusiastic when she spoke about her husband. "We're very happy together. Even now, when he's away, I feel a strange unease, as if I were lacking something. Then, when he comes home and closes the door, everything is right again, in its proper place, peace restored! It's so consoling, the sound of the door closing behind him when he gets home... The two of us snug in our apartment. That's all we want, nothing more. But you're still too young to understand."

I told her that I did understand, which wasn't true. Yes, if she were young or pretty, I could understand that, but given the way she looked and dressed... Then she asked me—not that she wanted to pry—about the boy who had just phoned me. Did he really like me? And did I like him? Because this was what mattered, and it was very easy to deceive yourself... If both parties were equally deceived, that was fine, but if only one of them was... "People are born with wings, and suddenly someone clips them. They become like chickens, poor things, with only the remnants of wings that won't let them fly. If anyone clipped my wings, I might do something completely crazy... Yes, I think I would."

She remained thoughtful for a while, and I took advantage of that pause to make my escape. From then on, we always exchanged a few words whenever we met on the stairs, but I was convinced she wasn't quite right in the head.

No, no one envied them, no one would give up everything just to be like them. And yet—at the time—they were possibly the most enviable creatures in the street, so much so that they could become fond of people they didn't even know or need. Me, for example.

I was only seventeen, though, and all I brought back from that visit was the troubling idea that she had wings. Wings…

Then my father died, we changed both our apartment and our lives, and the world turned on its axis many times.

ooooo

On one of those turns, I found myself teaching at a school in the Estrela district of Lisbon. I would get off the tram and walk part of the way, taking a shortcut down my old street. I enjoyed doing this, but often it troubled me to see, standing at the same door or window or coming out of the same shop, the very same people I had left behind there ten years before. It was as if I alone had moved through time and that, for those other people, time was something static. One day, purely out of curiosity and to see if I was right, I went into the tobacconist's on the corner and saw the same owner chatting to the same man, as they doubtless had on some day in my youth, about a football match that probably wasn't the same one, but was almost certainly not very different. It was as if the people there hadn't grown older or as if time had forgotten them.

Meanwhile, I had lived, yes, really lived! I had blossomed, and the wind had carried off my dead leaves. But spring always returned. For how much longer though? I preferred not to ask myself that question. I simply let life happen.

ooooo

A crowd of people were gathered outside my old house. I stopped and asked what was going on. "A murder," I was told. "On the third floor." I wanted to run away, to be far from there, but somehow or other, for reasons I don't understand, I found myself right at the front of that agitated group of people, who were all pushing and shoving in order to see nothing at all. A policeman was preventing anyone from going in. I considered saying, "I used to live here ten years ago. Can't I go in?" but quickly realized that this was pure madness and that policemen are not noted for their sense of humor. Nor, for that matter, am I. At least not then. The truth is that I wanted to run away, to get as far from there as possible, but it was as if my will and my actions had suddenly become separated, breaking their ancient bond. I wanted to do one thing and found myself doing exactly the opposite. I wanted to distance myself, but there I was, elbowing my way through the crowd and, like everyone else, trying to get a place at the front, where, with bruised shoulders and wide eyes, I waited for who knows what.

"Who'd have thought it, eh? Well, I certainly wouldn't want to be in her shoes!" came the shrill voice of a woman dressed all in black who was standing beside me. Even without turning around, without even moving my eyes—which the incident had somehow rendered immobile—I saw a tall, thin creature with a sallow, bird-like profile. I could have asked, "So what happened?" but it was too late now. I had been there for so long, motionless and vacant... What would the others think? Besides, there was no point asking questions. I had already been given the answer: "A murder. On the third floor."

"Why did she do it?" I asked fearfully. The others looked at me in alarm. "Did you know them then?" "Just a minute," said someone, "didn't you used to live here, in this very building, on the second floor?" Yes, I said, and asked again, "What happened?"

They shrugged and exchanged glances. No one knew for sure. They had their ideas, but they didn't actually know... Meanwhile, a blonde woman, who lived on the top floor (I could still remember her) declared roundly that, lately, the couple hadn't been getting along; there were fights and screams and tears. She leaned closer and said softly, "He wanted to leave her."

Leave her? Was that possible? But why? Who for?

There it was. Who for? The blonde woman gave an arch, knowing smile. "Well, she was getting on a bit, wasn't she? Fifty, although she looked even older, and she had no fashion sense, poor woman. No, what am I saying, poor *man*, since he's the one who's dead. But she had no fashion sense at all. Men age more slowly, don't they? Some other woman must have turned his head. And she killed him."

"How? How?" I asked eagerly. The woman said coldly, "With a kitchen knife."

I broke away from that magnetic circle then and walked on up the street. I didn't go to school that day. I couldn't. I returned to my cold apartment, where nothing was waiting for me. An empty apartment, with no kitsch objects, no kitsch feelings. And I thought about her—a lot.

"Perhaps she did do something crazy…" What will the men appointed to judge her think? An ugly old woman committing a crime of passion and who will perhaps turn up at the trial dressed in green and yellow… How grotesque, and, above all, ridiculous. But as I think I said earlier, the two of them never did have any sense of how ridiculous they were.

A BALCONY WITH FLOWERS

The little old lady leaned very slightly to the right and ran one wrinkled hand—dark, tremulous, with ridged fingernails—over the cat's soft, furry back. The cat uttered a brief purr of pleasure—or was it merely world-weary gratitude?—and she gave the very faintest of smiles. She was someone whom age had clearly rendered both slow and also, perhaps, indifferent to the world around her, with a few, very few, possible exceptions, things that others deemed almost worthless, but that to her, were still important despite everything: the cat, the warm sun, her hot water bottle, her afternoon cup of tea, the lace she sometimes made, the flowers on the balcony... Her whole being seemed imbued with a great languor or, possibly, a complete absence of enthusiasm or even will. She had time: She always had plenty of time; nothing was urgent. Her colorless, wizened lips blended in with her equally wizened face, and they took their time before beginning to smile, as if they needed to think about it first, like a rehearsal before the final performance. And it was as if all this happened without her knowledge, without her noticing. Then, equally slowly and gradually, the smile would vanish from her face. Time was vast and far from fleeting. Time never flees except when people are afraid. And she was no longer afraid of anything. What was there to fear? Death? But the tides had eaten away at all the mooring ropes. Nothing bound her to life now. This is why, for years, she had drifted around in that third-floor apartment in the crumbling building where she lived with that cat and a maid almost as old as her. And each day, she woke feeling a little closer. Closer to what? She didn't know.

The armchair she was sitting in had very slender, carved legs and ball feet. On the floor, the faded, foot-worn rug was more canvas than wool. A pillar, a begonia in a cracked and yellowing ceramic pot, and, in one corner, an old piano with, on the lid, a photograph of her when she was twenty: her ample bosom filling out her high-necked white blouse, her fair hair framing her plump, contented face. A ray of sunlight entered from the balcony, penetrating the net curtains she herself had once made and embroidered with two cupids at play, and the light cast a checkered shadow on the floor and ended up on the satin cushion on which the cat had once again fallen asleep—assuming it had actually woken up—next to the hot water bottle and the old lady's feet, horribly swollen with rheumatism. Beyond the curtains, a large bluebottle beat against that invisible but brightly lit wall, then skittered down the glass with a wild beating of metallic wings, and the cat, suddenly interested, twitched its small gray ears. The old lady said in a soft, slow, slightly quavery voice:

"Now then, pussy cat, now then… It's not worth

getting up for a fly, a mere fly. You just stay where you are…"

Then the noise stopped. The fly, having flitted across the floor, had doubtless alighted on a piece of furniture or somewhere on the dark floral wallpaper. And everything was once again sunk in silence.

The other woman, dressed all in black, her eyes red from crying, sat perched right on the edge of her chair, right on the very edge as if she too were about to take flight. Feeling that she had been forgotten, she tentatively cleared her throat because she was sure she would startle the old lady if she abruptly broke the silence and began to speak without first announcing her presence. This is why she coughed, a short, dry, very artificial cough. The old lady looked up, blinking, and said slowly:

"Oh, you're still here… I'd quite forgotten. Yes, I'd completely forgotten. Oh dear, my poor head… I thought… You will forgive me, won't you. I'm so sorry!"

The visitor opened her handbag and produced a handkerchief with which she dabbed at her eyes. Please don't worry; think no more about it. It was only natural. It had happened to her as well on occasions, and she was much younger…

"But do try and remember. It's so important to me, how can I put it…it's really vital!"

She had started out speaking in the gentle, drawling, wheedling voice of a child asking for a cake, but now her voice had grown firmer, harsher, as if she were demanding something that was her due, something that was hers and that she had come looking for. The old lady, however, didn't appear to take offense, as though the visitor's tone of voice were a matter of complete indifference to her, as if she hadn't even noticed:

"I really don't remember. It's hard at my age, you know. I'll be eighty-five next month. Or am I eighty-six? I've never had a good memory, not even when I was young, and it's a lot worse now...and yet..."

"And yet?"

The woman almost sprang from her chair. The old lady was about to remember something; the veil was about to be torn asunder and the light would come pouring in. What light? For her, there would never again be any light. Never. The gloom of dusk or black night were all she could hope for. But the old lady had stopped, poised on the edge of an abyss full of clouds, unable to go any further.

"And yet, there was something," she said at last. "Something that might be important to you and that, at the time, made a real impression on me. But I just don't know what it was. If you had come right away, I would definitely have remembered. But it happened two weeks ago... I think whatever it was is lost. I am eighty-five, you know."

"No, I couldn't have come then. I came as soon as I could. I've been ill. I was..."

No, it was impossible. The woman had seen everything, and had said as much the moment the visitor entered the room: "You're the lady who lives across from her, aren't you? The mother of that poor child. I saw everything, I was standing at the window..." She had seen everything. She had been the sole witness to the accident. If it was an accident? Theirs was a narrow street; their two buildings were directly opposite each other, and they both lived on the third floor. But hers was a new building, with an elevator, whereas this was an old, only partially inhabited building, with graffiti scrawled on the broken windowpanes, a building just waiting for the old lady to die to be demolished. The mother of the present owner had been a friend of the old lady's and had promised she would never be forcibly evicted. Everyone knew this; the whole neighborhood knew. She alone had seen the child, who, at the time, was on the balcony watering the flowers. The others had merely seen the broken doll lying where it fell in the street. "Lost," said the old lady calmly. "Lost a long way back, at the end of a white road I can't recall ever having walked along."

"But you must remember. Wouldn't you have told your maid?"

The old lady shook her head, and the woman suddenly noticed her sparse, white hair, neatly combed over her pink scalp. No, she hadn't told the maid anything. She was so deaf, the poor thing—"and she's younger than me too, only seventy!"—so deaf that she had to write down anything she needed her to do. And she couldn't bear to shout; she'd never been able to shout. Now...

"You're absolutely sure..."

"Oh, yes, absolutely. I didn't tell her or anyone else. I haven't had any visitors for nearly a month. It's still rather cold, don't you think? And none of my friends—my few remaining friends—are exactly young..."

The woman moved her chair closer to the armchair where the old lady was once again lost in her own thoughts, a smile on her face.

"Senhora...forgive me, I don't know your name."

"My name's Cristina, Cristina Rita, at your service."

"Senhora Dona Cristina, I'm going to tell you everything, and God knows how hard that is for me."

"But I'm not interested, my dear, not interested at all.

I live here in my apartment and know almost no one. The friends who come to see me, to keep me amused they say, to keep me company, well, all they do is tire me out. I'm eighty-five now… If I could, I would tell you everything you want to know, really I would. But I can't. However much I want to draw those memories up from the well, they refuse to come to the surface. They have drowned in the depths. So why bother telling me painful things? What do you gain by that? The poor child died, and that's all there is to it."

The woman sat back in her chair and sighed.

"You saw my daughter fall, didn't you? You were looking at her, weren't you? Did you see her…throw herself off…"

And at this, she burst into tears.

"There, there…" The old lady's voice was gentle and persuasive. "You must calm yourself. What can you do about it now? She was an angel, and now she's in Heaven."

"She was. She should be. If there is a Heaven, then she should be there." She spoke these stark words angrily. "If she hadn't been an angel, she would be alive now."

"But who told you it wasn't an accident, that she didn't just lean over and fall? I don't know, I can't remember, but it's possible."

"And who's to say that it didn't happen the other way, the way I fear it did? I didn't bring her up properly: I let her be an angel, and that doesn't work in this life. Life wasn't made for angels. It's an unhealthy air we breathe, and we need a good dose of microbes inside us to fight off those coming from outside. Gininha was defenseless. And I was foolish."

"Be brave. It's too late now, isn't it?"

"Is it? Yes, you're right, it is."

She sat silent and thoughtful for a long while. Then she spoke again, this time very quickly.

"She was all I had, I swear she was all I had: I lived only for her, I worked only for her. I was widowed four years ago. I'm thirty-five. That afternoon, a friend came to visit, a man. I thought Gininha had gone out; I completely forgot it was a holiday and that she had no classes that morning. At one point, we heard a dull thud, like a huge hand striking a table, calling for silence. Then there was a scream, a lot of screams all at once. I went to the window, and I saw her. *I saw her*, do you understand?"

She covered her face with her hands, unable to speak for a moment. The old lady said:

"It must have been terrible for you."

"It was terrible. She was my only child, and she was only eleven. He didn't mean anything to me, or not very much. I told him I never wanted to see him again, and I never do want to see him again. She was eleven years old, Senhora. She knew nothing of life, nothing. And I was proud of that, imagine…"

The old lady frowned and said:

"There was something, I know there was, but what?"

"A look of horror perhaps? Tears? Did she look very pale? She always turned really pale whenever she'd had a big shock. She was a nervous child, very sensitive. You perhaps saw her jump into the street or just lean out very slowly… Do you think perhaps she saw something interesting, one of those acrobats who sometimes turns up and puts down a mat and performs tricks?" she asked with sudden urgency. "At the time, I didn't notice anything else… I only saw you; in fact, I think I saw you even before I looked down. She was still holding the watering can. Think, please, try and remember…"

The woman was standing up now; she held out one cold hand to her. No, she needn't get up—she knew where the front door was.

"But promise me that you'll make a note if you do remember anything, all right? And, if you don't mind, if it wouldn't be too much bother, I'll come back tomorrow."

"Come back whenever you like, my dear. I never go out. But I really do feel that it's lost forever."

The street door banged lightly, and the old lady shivered. The bluebottle started buzzing again, beating against the window before skittering down. The cat stretched and yawned, gave the insect a dismissive glance, and closed its yellow eyes. The old lady closed her eyes too, her head dropped onto her chest and she fell into a doze.

IT RAINED THIS AFTERNOON

It was at the end of the intermission, when the bell was ringing and people had started returning to their seats, that she heard the voice behind her. "No, what nonsense, how could it possibly be by Fellini!" A slightly irritated, angry voice, oozing exasperation, as if everything around him were, always had been, and always would be *in saecula saeculorum*, a perpetual source of annoyance. He said this while thinking of something else—yes, he was clearly thinking of something else. Perhaps about taking flight but without knowing quite where to land. Or even if he should land. But this wasn't because he felt superior, just weary. She knew it was weariness. How could she not know?

Because when you think about it, time passes and all that's left of people are old fossilized images. Images that no longer exist. Did they ever exist as we see them now? Everything is constantly dying. The man sitting behind her was not the same man; she didn't know him…not now. How many different men would he have been in the last twenty years! And how many deaths had she died! Despite this…

Then, as now, his voice had also come out of nowhere. "What a lovely night! It's such a shame it should end so soon. What kind of day will it be tomorrow?" She had replied without looking at him; she didn't need to, for she had heard only him since the moment he arrived: "Why, it'll be just another day, of course." But those were mere words. She knew that tomorrow would be different because he would still be there in that tomorrow. She could think about him, dream about him. But who can hold on to their dreams?

She was standing at the window in Aninha's living room, the windows open onto the garden, and she could smell the spring. She really could. Why had she never been able to smell it like that since? It was a mixture of… oh, she had no idea! She had never been any good at distinguishing different smells. She had a terrible sense of smell! But that day… Not that she could summon it up again now. And yet at the time…

"But who gave you the idea that it was by Fellini?"

"I don't know…I really don't…Perhaps it was Manuel… I can't quite recall, but, yes, I think it was Manuel…"

The voice was faint and timid, timorous and tiny. A voice apologizing for its very existence. Or perhaps contrite.

There's nothing you can do, my dear, nothing at all, she thought. You just have to wait. You're not strong enough; you don't have the necessary courage; you can't just stand there on the edge of the abyss, waiting for who knows what. Is that how it is? Well, so much the worse for you.

"By Fellini? But didn't you see that a complete and utter dud like this couldn't possibly be by him… Only someone with not the slightest inkling…"

The dud recommenced. And it really was a dud, and she closed her eyes, pleased that he and she were still in agreement (an invisible link of which he was quite oblivious), and she again allowed herself to be drawn along deserted paths to that living room. She had been wearing her best dress, turquoise silk, new patent leather shoes worn specially for the occasion, the three-stranded necklace a university colleague had lent her. Baroque pearls. Oh, how she loved that necklace. She had spent the afternoon stroking the pearls with the tips of her fingers, cautiously, as if they were made of flesh, and when she put the necklace on, something happened, and she was suddenly no longer herself, but someone else. Her usual dull, timid self? No, she was strangely sure of herself and even came up with the perfect response to the famous pianist, saying that the next day would be the same as all the others: "Why, it'll be just another day of course."

How foolish to look back! To seek out memories that had ended up collecting dust in the lost corners of time. Or not even that. Memories at which time had eaten away. What would his face be like? She would still be capable of giving a detailed, literary description. But to see his face, to actually see it?

On the screen, the star of the movie was adjusting her garters while sitting on the edge of a miserable bed, and everyone knew she was thinking about the man she would meet a few moments later. Meanwhile, *she* was thinking about him, about the face she could no longer quite summon up, the face of the man sitting behind her, right behind her.

He always used to get her a free ticket whenever he

was giving a concert and would sometimes look at her from the stage and smile discreetly. A smile that was just between them and that no one else would notice, because she would never smile back; that was their tacit agreement. A slightly acidic, weary smile, a teeny-tiny bit (but only a teeny-tiny bit) happy.

And what about her, she thought. Had she been happy? In the early days, yes, she really had, no doubt about it. Alone in the vast city where she had gone to study, she had grown drunk on a freedom she didn't make use of because she didn't know how. But then he arrived, and it was a revelation, swiftly followed by anguish and pain.

Then one day, that slightly irritated, sulky tone had appeared in his voice. "No, what nonsense, of course it's not by Fellini..." Or something along those lines. That poor woman with her frightened little voice. No, that relationship wasn't going to last very long, not long at all. She knew. Who better than she?

One evening when they were together, she asked him, "You seem miles away. Where were you?" He had started laughing. "Do I have to be somewhere? Is that absolutely necessary?" "Yes, it is." "The fact is, I wasn't here, but in Copacabana. Did I mention that I might be going to Brazil? I've received an interesting invitation." "When would you go?" "This month." "Will you stay long?" "I don't know."

The quay, and the ship moving off as slowly and inexorably as time. She had gone to say goodbye, despite it all. Despite knowing that this was the last line on the last page. Despite having seen the end in his eyes, in his weary voice.

What if she left before the lights came up? But then she wouldn't see him. Not that she still loved him. Twenty years are twenty years, and many days had raced by since. Now she was a placid middle-aged lady, very attached to her worldly goods and with a daughter about to get married. At seventeen… Well, the boy in question seemed a decent fellow and had his own money. And he was clearly very fond of her daughter. And, fortunately, he wasn't an artist. He had his feet firmly on the ground. As had her husband for that matter. A highly respected businessman. Say what you like, but this did give you a sense of security… It was, how could she put it, reassuring, a source of peace.

No, she may no longer love that man, but she still wanted to see him. To see her youth in his face. Inside her there was also a slight, unacknowledged curiosity to see "her" too, the woman with the fearful voice, whom he would one day leave.

She waited until the end. Then, when the lights came up, she got quickly, hastily, to her feet. He had stood up too, and he was still just as handsome, more so if that was possible, and beside him, a young but rather faded woman was looking at him anxiously, asking in a tremulous voice, "Were you very bored? If I'd known it was going to be that bad, I would never have suggested coming. Really."

Then, for one brief, fleeting moment, he looked at *her*. Quite naturally and without even seeing her, yes, her.

No, he hadn't recognized her. Twenty years, dyed-blonde hair, not to mention the ravages of time. As well as the extra twenty-two pounds she had put on.

How sad it all was. All what? Everything.

Over supper, she hardly spoke. She had a terrible

headache, she said. She'd take a paracetamol and go to bed. She'd been to see a dreadful movie. A real dud, she said almost savoring the word.

"Really? What was it?" asked her husband purely out of politeness.

"I don't even know. I just went in out of the rain. It rained this afternoon, did you notice? Anyway, it definitely wasn't by Fellini…"

"Who said it was?"

She laughed awkwardly.

"I don't know. I can't remember, but someone did."

She almost said: "It was Manuel." Madness. She gave another nervous laugh, then went to bed. She wept a little before falling asleep. The following morning, though, she woke in an excellent mood and recalled that encounter almost without emotion. And during the busy day that followed, full of things to do, she thought no more about it.

THE SHADOW OF THE TREE

However long and hard he thought about it, he could never have pinpointed the exact day on which the wind deposited inside him that tiny grain of pollen. Nor had he noticed—he was convinced of this, although again he couldn't be absolutely sure—when, precisely, germination began. Something, though, had slowly and gradually put down invisible but energetic, roots, which had grown and, with each passing day, taken an ever firmer hold. Meanwhile, he still couldn't see the plant, or perhaps he simply wasn't looking. Only when there was nothing else around him, and it stood silhouetted against the sky as tall as a tree, plunging everything into darkness (or, who knows, perhaps protecting everything with the guarantee of its shadow), only then did old Alves Firmino face it full on. And he felt neither surprise nor fear, only a certain bitterness. The bitterness of one who is allowed to take shelter somewhere, but does so because he has no alternative, since, outside, there is only either scalding sun or freezing cold.

None of this was his fault. At sixty-five, Alves Firmino

was a robust old man, his skin coarsened by fair weather and foul, especially the latter, because, for some people, the winter always lasts longer than the summer. He dreaded the bad weather but was able to withstand it nonetheless. His wife, however, had been an invalid for six years and would now never be able to leave her bed. This was the most important thing. Indeed, it went from being important to disastrous on the day he had his first heart attack, which left him poised between life and death.

"Be careful, my friend; these are treacherous illnesses," the doctor told him when he declared him out of danger. And he had clapped him on the back with that phoney air of human sympathy, a kind of superficial vertical closeness that always keeps a safe distance, a useful way of disguising the gulf between your two situations. "Don't tire yourself; that's the best treatment. And come and see me again in a month."

Don't tire yourself. Firmino felt like laughing or possibly crying, a desire to turn his back on life and carry on regardless. But he couldn't carry on regardless. He had to keep looking back at his bedridden wife endlessly making the crocheted lace that the seamstress who lived upstairs bought from her by the yard; gazing at him with those sad, meek eyes of hers, so terribly fearful and sometimes downright terrified. She had been like that for six years now. With her right leg bent, her left leg straight, and her upper body supported by two pillows. She was small and frail and as wrinkled as a dry, frightened leaf, her eyes fixed on the clock if he was even a quarter of an hour late arriving home from the shop where he worked as an accounts clerk in the afternoons. When he came through the door feeling tired (lately, he did get very tired), the home help would immediately stop work, leaving him to serve supper to the patient, get her ready for the night, and wash the dishes. He also had to talk to her, although that was rather a pleasant task, a kind of diary in which he gave her an account of the day's events. She would listen with the troubling intensity of someone cut off from the world, eager to know everything, seizing hold of the most insignificant details, like the physical description of some person he had spoken to, their age, or the exact time something happened.

How could he, Firmino, rest? How could he take good care of himself if he had to care for her? And what if he were to die first, leaving her alone? What would happen then?

When he went to see the doctor a month later and explained his situation, the doctor listened to him first attentively, then wearily, and finally with evident irritation. Firmino had no family; he and his wife were quite alone, with no siblings and no children. The doctor nodded, occasionally saying "yes, yes," or interrupting him—one moment, my friend—to answer the phone. "Go on, go on, but I am in a bit of a hurry, you know. Carry on though..." And he made a great show of looking at his watch. His waiting room was full of other patients, and he wanted to have an early supper so that he could get to the cinema in time to watch a documentary he was excited to see. His wife had called a short time before to remind him, "You've done it before, haven't you? I mean, frankly, you do have a right to a private life. It's really too much." She was right, poor thing; it really was too much. They never went anywhere together... The case of the man sitting opposite him, eyes downcast, was indeed very sad, but what could he do? He was only a doctor… He could put in a word with a colleague to see if the wife could be moved into a residential home? "Ah, you don't want that…have you never considered it?" Sorry, he had misunderstood; he thought this was precisely what he did want. In that case…

Firmino's monotonous voice droned on, listing all his woes, all his worries. It seemed to him that there must be some solution, quite what he didn't know, but surely the doctor must know…

"I'm afraid I don't understand… I mentioned the possibility of putting your wife in a home—which won't be easy, of course, but we could try—and you tell me you don't want that. In that case, there's nothing more I can do for you. I'm genuinely sorry, but I can't. My job is to prescribe, not to get involved in the lives of my patients. Keep taking the pills and watching your diet… And I hope you feel better soon. Alda, send in the next patient!"

"Goodbye, Doctor, and forgive me…"

But the doctor didn't hear him. He had closed the door.

Firmino made his slow, grim way back down the stairs. He had probably explained himself badly. Because there must be a solution. Put her in a home, the doctor had said. Put her in a home?

It was perhaps on that day or on one of the following days that the grain of pollen began to germinate. Meanwhile, he said he was feeling much better and studied every other possible solution, apart from *that* one. No, he didn't study them, he looked for them, but found none, which was quite a different matter. He systematically set *that* solution to one side. He didn't want to think about it.

Perhaps because he knew it was the only one available and felt afraid. Yes, perhaps that was why.

If he were to die suddenly—and the doctor hadn't held out much hope, especially given the life he led—what would become of his wife, alone in bed, with her only source of income her crocheted lace? There had to be a solution, there must be. There were plenty of other men and women around them… People who, years before, had called themselves their friends… "Look, my friend, if I can ever be of any help, just let me know…" But when he went looking for them, as he had on several occasions, none of them were there. Time was tight, life was hard, their children, their grandchildren, sickness…the usual spiel. And then total silence. "Senhor A is away… Senhor B has just this minute gone out… Senhor C won't be here for supper…" A city so full of people, people who issue orders and others who receive orders and issue them in turn; people he knew and others he had never seen; people who go to mass and are good people; people who don't go to church because they, too, are good people, the ones who don't go at all; so many identical men, his brothers. His brothers! Was it really possible that no one would make an effort to understand, that no one would lend him a hand? "Lie down and die, old man, and do so safe in the knowledge that she won't starve, won't be left alone, won't be sent to a home…" That was all he wanted, so little, but no one would come to him and say this, and he knew it. People walked along, eyes front, never looking to right or left, colliding with other people also walking straight ahead. They bumped into each other, became squashed together, but they never paused to look. This was what life was like. Life as people understood it. They all had somewhere to go and that was where they were going, striding down the street at top speed. Only he felt lost, only he couldn't find the way home to his street, only he didn't know which street it was, only he had no street.

A sudden, unexpected thought occurred to him: Why didn't they leave together, side by side? That was the solution, the only one, and so easy too. The tree was beginning to cast its shadow, and, from a distance, that shadow looked like an irresistible patch of peace and coolness.

He continued to resist though. He kept postponing it. Next week, it was always next week. There's time; there was always time. Why rush things? Now that he had looked it in the eye, it felt to him like a close, quiet, almost friendly presence. It wouldn't avoid him, it wouldn't offer any excuses, it wouldn't walk straight past him. It was standing there, waiting for him.

His wife thought he seemed somehow different. She was so accustomed to seeing him and only him that she immediately noticed any change. What was wrong? Was he feeling worse? And he knew she was worried, terrified of being left alone; of him being the first to leave; of her missing the train and being left at the station, with no one to help her, alone and abandoned like an old, forgotten suitcase.

That morning, Firmino woke to find his feet badly swollen and his heartbeat irregular. He could wait no longer; it had to be today. He was a simple man, ill-prepared for such desperate measures, and yet life was obliging him to take such measures without giving him time to prepare himself and get used to the idea. It had to be today. Tomorrow it might be too late.

He stayed at home that day, claiming he had a headache. Now and then, he would press his hand to his forehead to show he was telling the truth, but she kept eyeing him suspiciously. "You swear that's all it is?" "Of course, what else would it be?"

He spent the afternoon slouching around in his slippers, tidying drawers, trying to bring a little order to everything. Then he warmed up the evening soup, made a dish of tomato rice, poured his wife a little more wine than usual. She said, "That's too much, my dear, you'll get me tipsy…" "Just a drop more to cheer you up…" He was sure that, after supper, she would fall into a deep sleep, as she usually did. When he saw her eyelids droop, her scrawny chin sinking onto her chest, he sat and looked at her. Poor old thing. She would forgive him, wouldn't she? This was the only way out, there was no other…

He stood up and went into the kitchen to fetch the portable stove he had just filled with coal. Then he closed the bedroom door, sealed it as best he could, and waited.

It was eight in the morning when the seamstress from upstairs rang the doorbell. She had some urgent work for his wife to do and needed to give it to her before she went shopping. When no one answered, she rang again, and again. She found this odd, because both husband and wife were light sleepers and usually awake by seven. She then phoned the police.

Firmino and his wife were taken to hospital.

The old man was dead on arrival. His heart had given out. The tree had cast too brief a shadow, only long enough to reach him. His invalid wife survived.

THE INCONSOLABLE FIANCÉE

Both women had kissed and embraced her and offered their sincere condolences in tremulous, tearful, deeply felt words: "You poor thing, what dreadful luck!" "When I found out, my dear, I was just speechless, I couldn't believe it..." "How is such a thing possible, how is it possible?" They asked for details. How had it happened? What exactly *had* happened? The newspaper had explained things so badly, been so unclear... And Joana repeated the same story over and over, in the same flat, weary voice. He had called her the evening before and told her that the next day—yesterday—he was going to the beach with some friends after work. "We're going to nip over to Carcavelos for a swim." It was as if she'd had a presentiment, because she'd done her very best to dissuade him. He had insisted though: it was all arranged, etc. etc. And so, he had gone to the beach. That's all she knew. No one knew any more than that.

"It was death calling him."

"Yes..."

"We can't avoid our fate, my dear, whatever people

might say. If he hadn't gone for a swim at Carcavelos, something else would have happened to him. He might have been run over, for example. Yesterday was simply his day to die."

"Yes, yesterday was his day, and who knows when our own will be?"

There was a brief silence, full of unspoken questions. Elsa, a dark-haired woman wearing a lot of makeup, got to her feet and said with a sigh:

"I have to go. I just wanted to see you and give you a hug, but now I really have to go. I have a dentist appointment at half past five, so I'd better get a move on."

The other woman, who was sitting near the window, asked if her dentist was downtown. If so, she would go with her, because she needed to buy some buttons. "You don't mind, do you, it's just that I really do need some!"

More loud kisses and pleas or, rather, exhortations for her to accept her fate. There was nothing she could do about it now. She must be brave and simply face up to the facts. Elsa was just about to add that there was no point in shedding tears, but stopped herself in time when she realized that Joana wasn't actually crying, but was looking straight at them, with not a tear in her eye and wearing her usual expression. Her usual expression? No, perhaps not. Her expression wasn't her usual one at all, but a very new one, different from all her other expressions. However, neither Guida nor Elsa could grasp its meaning. They were simple souls, who rarely peered beneath the surface of things.

The door closed slowly behind them, and they began going down the stairs. The late afternoon sun, grubby and yellow, barely penetrated the skylight.

"Poor thing," said Guida, opening her handbag to look at herself in the mirror. "She hasn't exactly had much luck. It took her ages to find a man, and then he goes and dies just like that. Death by drowning too—horrible!"

"I've always had a terrible fear of drowning," said Elsa. "I mean, I know how to swim…but then so did he. I don't know what it is, but out at sea you get those hideous creatures, don't you? Eels, I mean, those things that look like snakes. I remember seeing two eels at the aquarium in Algés. They had very bright eyes, and they were fixed on me. It gave me nightmares every time I went there. When I was a child, of course. I haven't been back since. They're probably dead by now. How long does the average eel live?"

The other woman laughed.

"I have no idea! Anyway, I doubt there are many eels in the sea at Carcavelos. But yes…you're right… We don't know where he is—where his body is, I mean. It hasn't been found. It hasn't been washed ashore yet. In that case, he must be… Yuck. I'm not going to eat any fish for a very long time."

She shuddered. "Poor Joana, she'll never meet anyone else. Not with her looks. Do you think he really was going to marry her?"

"It certainly seemed like it. They had even bought some bedroom furniture… So…"

"Yes, but it's odd, don't you think?"

"Well, there are plenty of odd things in this world. Look at me, for example, I don't have a dental appointment at all. Zé will be waiting for me at the bus stop."

The other woman burst out laughing.

"And I'm not going downtown to buy buttons. I'm

going to the second showing at the Tivoli. And I'd better hail a cab; otherwise I'll be late."

They parted gaily. Deep down, they were nice enough girls and hadn't wanted to talk about boyfriends or movies because they did at least have a sense of what was appropriate and what was not.

ooooo

Joana was alone again. Her friends had just left, and her brother had not yet arrived. Her mother wouldn't be long though; she had gone out to buy her a black blouse and stockings. She hadn't even kissed her or offered a single consoling word. She was never aggressive, never; that was one advantage she had over the others. She remained stiff and unmoving, as if enclosed inside her own narrow, hermetic world. She was a good wife and a good mother—the nights she had spent and still spent at their bedside if one of them was ill!—and they couldn't really ask her for more than that, nor did they. Her brother came and went and was never at home. But that's boys for you. Boys will be boys. As for her father, he considered anything that wasn't entirely transparent, anything that seemed to him even slightly obscure, as mere complications dreamed up by a load of hysterics. And he always spoke with the confident air of someone who has a right to offer an opinion on everything because he knows everything.

Was she really their daughter? Was she her brother's sister? Whenever she thought this, it felt to her as if she had given birth to herself and that no ties bound her to anyone else. And yet, how she needed those ties now! A seed blown in from who knows where that the wind just happened to drop here. She felt distant from her family, from their petty ambitions, from their mean-minded envy. "As Rebelo's righthand man," her brother would say, "I'm going to really clean up. Rebelo, poor thing, is a good fellow, but not exactly the sharpest knife in the drawer, and he's allowed that rabble to get away with things for far too long. Everything's going to get back on track now, though, you just wait. They know me, and they know I always play fair." When the post of deputy chief of staff was given to that waste of space, that illiterate, Silva, her father had said, "That post was intended for me; everyone said so." Her brother had smiled a superior smile, which their mother silently applauded: "Dad's such an innocent. The job was there for the taking, but he failed to seize the opportunity. Do you remember that afternoon when he found out Felismino had had his hand in the till? He missed his chance, and now, of course, it's too late. That's why I..."

In her head, Joana referred to them by their proper names, responded to them with her silence, with the book she would read during mealtimes so as not to be obliged to hear them, to refuse to hear them. She didn't hate them, no: They simply didn't interest her. She felt far away, alone in the world, alone in a kind of no man's land. That was all.

She and her small plain rabbit face, her thick glasses, her heavy, graceless figure. These were not the only barriers that kept her isolated from the outside world, barring the door to anyone who came, not that anyone tried. She was so alone, poor thing. She would look at herself in the mirror, study her new hairstyle à la Farah Diba, try out a face cream raved about in the latest issue of *Elle*, but that little rabbit face of hers proved stronger than all those things. It was always too center stage somehow.

Then one day, *he* had appeared. A handsome young man and very pleasant too. She had never bothered to ask herself whether she really loved him. All she needed were those eyes of his looking at her, those words she had never heard before that he was saying to her, the promise of his hands.

When her mother learned that they were courting, she was quite worried. It was as if she were looking everywhere for a reason—because there must be one—why that man, the first ever, should be attracted to Joana. Her father, without even looking up from his newspaper, merely commented that it was about time, asking in the same indifferent tone of voice if anyone knew how much he earned. As for her brother, he had regarded her with an almost insulting air of astonishment and advised her to be sure to hang on to him and to get married as quickly as possible.

At first, he had wanted to do just that, and they had even bought some furniture with their joint savings. Then he had begun talking about an excellent job he had been offered in Africa. In the end, he had avoided mentioning either of those things. He rarely came to visit her, and whenever he called, he was always in a hurry, always had some urgent piece of work to do: "You will forgive me, won't you? I'll explain tomorrow." He never did explain, because he never came to see her tomorrow, only days later, and, by then, he'd forgotten all about it, as was only natural, given all the many things he had to think about. And it reached the point where it would have seemed strange to her to remind him of what was now a thing of the past.

Gradually, the barriers that had fallen away months before began to rise up around her. She rediscovered things once lost and found again: Her small, now thirty-year-old rabbit face, for example; her awkward body; and she heard her own voice asking herself questions she refused to answer. She felt a great desire to weep, and every morning she would wake in terror, wondering if today would be the day.

The day before, he had called to give her that message about going to the beach. Joana had begged him not to go. Why didn't he come and see her instead? They had so much to talk about! He hadn't been to visit her for nearly a week. "A week? You're kidding…" She wasn't. A week. "Goodness, how time flies!" he had declared. Goodness, how time drags, she was thinking. How slowly time passes!

Then, that morning, she had read the news in the paper. It was accompanied by a photo of him, an old one she didn't know, but then there were so many things and so many people she knew nothing about… People talking and her listening and responding and expressing opinions. What opinions? What had she said? Her actual thoughts were adrift somewhere in a very gentle atmosphere, lightly beating their wings, brushing over the surface of things. All her anxiety had vanished. She was no longer filled with dread; she would no longer wake each morning thinking that it would all be over before the day was out. Even though she couldn't see it, she felt that same great calm on her face, in her still hands, in the voice that emerged confidently, almost sternly. It was the serenity he had bequeathed her! She felt like smiling even though she wasn't happy, but precisely because she was sad. Smiling at her mother when she arrived bearing the black clothes she

certificate, the glass of which had cracked, and where some clearly very competent person declared (in fine Gothic script) that Dr. Raul Heleno Boaventura had graduated from such and such a university in such and such a year. And yet people would still say they didn't believe a word of it. The truth is that all wills and large bequests automatically bypassed him and ended up in the wise hands of his friend, neighbor, and rival, Margarido. He was given only insignificant documents to witness. Anyway, the certificate confirmed that Dr. Boaventura was a notary. As for Silvano being his assistant… In what way did he assist him? There was really very little that required any assistance.

It was only when Dr. Boaventura reached the age of fifty—or more precisely the exact day on which he turned fifty—that he finally understood that he was doing nothing in this world; or still worse, that he had *never* done anything in this world. This, it must be said, is something that happens to many people, although only a few go to the trouble of finding it out. Having too much time on his hands certainly contributed, because Dr. Boaventura decided to devote that day—for want of anything better to do and because of Reis's memory lapse—to examining his conscience, a task to which people rarely devote themselves and one to which they really never should devote themselves. It couldn't be called a bad habit exactly, but it is nonetheless extremely dangerous and, if one can put it like this, unhealthy. Because there is such a thing as being too clean, which can bring on a bad bout of double pneumonia.

When Dr. Boaventura arrived at the office, he already, all unknowing, carried within him the germ of that examination. He had felt a slight twinge as he was coming up the stairs. For some reason he had thought, "What am I doing in this world?" perhaps because his fiftieth birthday brought with it a certain feeling of melancholy. "Why haven't I been as successful as Margarido?" he thought. And at the same time: "Why can't I be like Silvano? Life is such a hard thing to explain," he had added as he went up the final flight of stairs. "Still, there's no point worrying about these things, and asking why something turned out this way and not that. That's life, and that's all there is to it." And he shrugged, the equivalent of drawing a line under something.

As he went into the office, though, Reis immediately informed him—once he had said his usual "Good morning, sir, how are you?"—that Silvano had gone to Senhora Dona Amélia's house. This, among other things, meant—for Boaventura was feeling extremely sensitive that morning—that Reis had forgotten it was his birthday. This, to Dr. Boaventura, was a gross lapse of memory. Reis may have been profoundly stupid, but he had a prodigious memory for dates, addresses, food prices, and telephone numbers. He also knew where to find all the files, which were in less-than-perfect order, as were their contents. On every 17th of March in the past, Reis had always greeted his boss with a broad smile that revealed his rotten teeth and with a few words especially reserved for the occasion: "A very happy birthday, sir, and many happy returns." And Boaventura would reply, "Thank you, Reis, how very kind of you to remember. I had quite forgotten, and if it wasn't for you… Of course, when one gets to my age…" Reis would then say that Dr. Boaventura was in fine form, really top notch, and looked much younger than his years. If he, Reis, hadn't known how old he was… But he did. Reis knew everyone's age.

On that day, however, nothing like this happened, and Boaventura glanced anxiously around him, as if he suspected that someone had stolen his wallet or pinned a donkey's tail on his coat. There was something wrong, but he couldn't put his finger on what it was. Things weren't right, and he felt uneasy. Reis was, as usual, sweeping the office floor, and, just in case, Boaventura opened the drawer in his desk, the top one on the right, and slyly took out a bottle of nasal spray. A quick squirt up each nostril and he would be immune. Who knows what diseases the dust might cause! Reis continued his sweeping and, as was his custom, talked as he did so:

"What weather, eh? What *is* going on? I mean, it's March for heaven's sake…"

Dr. Boaventura took a risk and said:

"It's not just March, it's the 17th of March…"

This was Reis's cue to spin around, possibly drop his broom, and exclaim in great embarrassment, "Oh, sir, many congratulations!" But he didn't. He carried on sweeping and merely commented, as he stooped to pick up a paper clip, that he was convinced that the blame lay squarely with the Americans and the Russians. "You just have to look at what's happening with football…" This change of subject was skillfully done, but not unexpected. Dr. Boaventura knew that any conversation involving Reis, even as a mere onlooker, always ended up, in word or thought, at football, the one area where his ideas could move around with relative ease.

Boaventura stopped him, though, saying that he had some very urgent work to do, and so Reis took his broom out into the corridor, where he sat down to ponder whether the new player Sporting had just bought really would turn out to be as valuable an acquisition as people said.

It was a rainy morning, one of winter's final tantrums, which needed to be gotten out of the way before spring arrived. Sitting at his desk underneath his framed degree certificate, and opposite the wicker chair—the client's chair—Dr. Boaventura involuntarily began his examination of conscience.

There wasn't really much to examine. What can one see in an empty glass except what lies behind it? But what did lie behind his life? His parents' lives? The endless arguments, that life of constant battles, which had, even then, made him want to withdraw into his shell? He could see his mother, driven to distraction by the slightest sign of fever in him, as if she had no one else but him in the world. Nights spent at his bedside, the wide, anxious gaze he found so troubling. And her words of advice when he set off to school: "Be sure to put your hat on at playtime, because this sun can be very treacherous. And be careful when crossing the road; always look both ways..."

And when he was a child, there had hardly been much traffic in the provincial town where he was born and grew up. Even now, there were still not that many cars. Dona Arminda Guerreiro's Citroën, the Costa Pais's Ford, and the one owned by the Vasques family...theirs was the biggest. They were, after all, the richest and most influential family in the town. Property, land, a large factory, a cousin who was a monsignor, an uncle who was a judge... When he was twenty-five, Boaventura had fallen in love with the Vasques' youngest daughter, Amélia. She had been a slender girl, very fair, with large blue eyes. It was said that she wrote poetry and had a weak chest. When that final detail reached his ears, Boaventura was just about to send her a declaration of love. He had been encouraged to do so by a few glances she had sent his way during the last dance at the local social club. A weak chest. He hesitated. This was not something to be taken lightly. He asked his mother's advice, and she thought it best to go no further. "You might catch something, Raulinho, and what about your children? You need to think about the children."

She was right. And so he never said a word to Amélia, who, only yesterday—now a widow and a grandmother—had come to the office to witness a document. And the wicker chair had creaked under her weight. Life! He had stayed a bachelor because of that large woman, now verging on plump, and all that remained of the little Amélia of yesteryear were her sweet, ingenuous blue eyes.

Then his father had died, and he had continued to live with his mother. "Take good care of yourself, Raulinho; you might catch cold, so wrap up warm…" He was Raulinho, and his life was like an old bottle of medicine that had formed a sediment at the bottom. Shake before use, says the label. No, he couldn't do that. Not now. Was he happy like that? Happy? Well, at least he had no problems to speak of. And why get married? And to whom? Then time passed, and he was already forty, forty-five, forty-nine. Today he was fifty.

He could have had a "nice" career, as his mother used to say. But he hadn't even managed that. Why? Because he was incapable or just unlucky? He would say it was down to a lack of will. It wasn't worth it. Why bother? For the same reason, because it wasn't worth it, he had almost lost touch with his friends. Were they really friends though? Acquaintances more like, yes, acquaintances. Margarido, who proclaimed from the rooftops that Boaventura was utterly useless; Costa Pais, whom he hadn't seen for more than two months; Silvano...

Silvano was his bête noire. He was everything that Boaventura wasn't. He was a handsome fellow ("Silvano always looks the same, the years don't seem to pass for him, he must have made a pact with the Devil," Amélia had said only yesterday), and he was very bright and totally at ease with himself, something that never failed to astonish Boaventura. Silvano wasn't always careful (in fact he rarely was), but if Silvano did make some major error, he just had to say a few words, smile sweetly as only he knew how, and people would come and apologize to *him*. I'm so sorry, sir, so sorry. And as for women, it was positively sickening. Boaventura couldn't stand his fatuous air, grand gestures that he always made at just the right moment, but the truth was, he had to put up with him, because ten years earlier, he had made him a partner, urged on by his mother, who adored "poor Silvano." Yes, even his mother. Even her.

And all these thoughts arose because no one had wished him Happy Birthday. Not Reis, not his mother, although she, poor thing, had now squashed all her ideas into a ball, and from that coagulated mass a single idea would occasionally emerge and be repeated obsessively for a while before returning to the ball. His mother had no idea it was his birthday. His mother didn't even know people had birthdays.

Silvano arrived at around eleven, complete with his calf-leather briefcase, his manicured nails, and a delicate waft of lavender. How did he manage to look so prosperous? True, he was much sought after, people liked him and asked him to collect rents, to deal with demanding tenants, to sell property. And the word was that he was involved with a rich widow.

Amélia! The idea entered his head with the force of an axe striking the trunk of an old tree. Of course, the rich widow must be Amélia. And he was so stupid that it had never once occurred to him. He had mentally run through all the town's wealthy widows, wondering who it could be… Amélia. No, it was impossible. He could hear her saying yesterday, without a flicker of embarrassment, "That Silvano always looks the same…" He couldn't believe that she would behave so contemptibly…no he couldn't.

He picked up the mail just in order to do something, to look as if he were busy. A letter from Lisbon of no importance, the catalog from a bookshop in Porto, another from a manufacturer of sewing machines (why would he want a sewing machine?), an advertisement for a new detergent. Underneath all this the narrow envelope made of cheap paper, crumpled and grubby, that had been laboriously sealed with someone's spit, then pressed down with their fingers, the way people do who are not in the habit of writing letters. The seal was not properly stuck down, some parts of it not at all. The writing was clumsy; even the address had several spelling errors in it, as well as two ink blots. A letter asking for money or even, who knows, a poison-pen letter.

Boaventura nervously tore open the envelope, all the while thinking of Amélia. The words formed a tangled heap on the cheap paper and were so poorly written as to be almost illegible. There were more inkblots too. The notary began reading in the spirit of someone piecing together a jigsaw puzzle or solving a crossword: to pass the time and to avoid having to think about anything else. Suddenly, though, he gave a yelp, and the piece of paper he had in his right hand and the envelope he was still holding in his left were both hurled into the air, where they hovered briefly before landing near the door. Silvano raised his dark, velvety eyes. Reis ran in, looking distressed and clutching the sports page.

Boaventura was pointing at the letter and saying:

"Quick, Reis, pick it up and flush it down the toilet. It's a letter from a...leper."

Reis was already bending down and about to do as he was told. However, he immediately straightened up.

"But I might catch it too, sir."

"Sweep it up then, man, do whatever you like, but get rid of it!"

Silvano got slowly to his feet. He took a few steps, pushed Reis to one side, picked up the letter, and read it attentively.

"He's going to come by this afternoon to know what your answer is. Listen, Reis, tell him to go to Senhora Dona Amélia's house; give him her address. He can say I sent him. She has lots of useful contacts in Lisbon, and I'm sure she'll find something for him."

Reis said faintly, reluctantly:

"But will I have to speak to him?"

Silvano laughed and clapped him on the back.

"Don't be such a coward, man. Don't worry, you can't catch leprosy that easily."

Boaventura felt even more alone and more wretched than ever. What did he want? Even he didn't know. Perhaps, above all, he wanted it not to be his birthday.

THE WAKE

The slow, weary silence, already thirteen hours old, composed of whispers with the occasional sigh or sob punctuating the long, interminable night, that same difficult silence against which no one dared rebel was suddenly torn apart, shattered, by Genoveva's unreasonably loud, strident voice: "Oh, dear God, how dreadful! How is it possible!"

It was possible, however, and for the moment, nothing could be more real or more palpable, they all thought in unison with the exception perhaps of Sara, the oldest sister, who was stone deaf and tended not to think, but to vegetate, smiling or pondering prayers. And then the murmuring suddenly stopped, as if entirely absorbed by that one idea, just as the sobbing and, naturally enough, the subsequent sniffling, grew faster and more intense.

Standing motionless at the sacristy door, Genoveva, all in black, still elegant despite her slightly careless, disheveled appearance, and giving off a strong smell of naphthalene, was looking around her, stunned, as if waiting for someone to tell her that it really was impossible.

There it was, though, in the middle of the large, cold sacristy full of long shadows (which sometimes, as if stirred by an invisible breath, moved very slowly, licking the grubby walls) and damp, musty corners where the light didn't reach. Where, one might say, the light had never reached.

A short, very thin woman, old before her time, her eyes red and febrile, suddenly started to her feet and went stumbling and tottering over to the new arrival, whom she clasped convulsively to her. "Genoveva, Genoveva… Our António, your brother, is dead…" And she held Genoveva close, then studied her face with wide, wild eyes. Then she went over to the coffin—adorned with ornate needle lace and pink gladioli—fearfully drew back the linen cloth covering the dead man's face, and burst into tears. "It's Genoveva, António. She came at once, the poor thing. It's Genoveva…"

Everyone automatically looked at the stiff body lying in its final resting place. Extraordinarily big, bigger than ever, and imposing in his definitive immobility. Genoveva knelt down, rapidly crossed herself, then went to look at him for the last time and run her hand over his cold, smooth brow.

It was the face of a recumbent statue, serene, at rest, happy. All suffering, past and future, expunged. Or was this now merely the redundant shell the creature had sloughed off? Where could he have gone; where was he? Was he there, all of him, preparing to rot? No, no, that was impossible. Now, in the face of death, she refused to believe in what she had always believed to be natural and sensible. She felt tears trembling on her fair eyelashes. Why such grief, such suffering for that thing? Was it possible?

António looked so serene. Him serene? Yes, serene. Him, the man lying there. That thing. Oh, what did it matter? He was smiling...or was he? No, perhaps he wasn't. It was the knowing expression he would adopt sometimes when looking at other people, all the while thinking that he was so much cleverer than them, and that no one would ever get the better of him. The man hasn't been born yet, he would say. Or perhaps he didn't; no, she had never heard him say such a thing. But those words were so visible on his face that it was as if she had heard him say it a million times. The man hasn't been born yet... That was her brother... She was getting used to the idea; people always do get used to ideas, even the most unexpected, the hardest to accept. Yes, it was possible. Everything was possible. That was her brother.

That was my father, thought Jaime, hunched at one end of the bench, leaning against the huge closet containing the priest's vestments. His father. So terrifyingly still and silent. The same father who, only the night before, had yelled at the maid because there wasn't enough salt in the food and at him that morning because he had spent too long in the bathroom. So many unnecessary things. We live and die surrounded by unnecessary things, worrying and battling... He stood up to go over and put his arm around the bowed shoulders of his mother, who was still staring at her husband's face and weeping, her handkerchief in her hand. Was that a necessary gesture, he wondered. No, it wasn't, but he had to do it.

"You've got to be brave, Mama. It's horrible, I know, we all know it's horrible, but what can we do? Dad was ill; we were expecting this to happen, weren't we? The doctor had said as much..." Then he kissed his Aunt Genoveva, indicated the place where he had been sitting and said, "Go and sit down; you must be very tired after your journey."

Genoveva went to greet Sara and the women friends who were also there, then slumped down on the bench, and the silence closed in again, deeper and heavier.

"This solves everything; now there won't be any more complications," Júlio had said to her a few hours earlier, when he had seen her off at the station. "That's at least some consolation. If there can be any."

And she had felt inside her a faint glimmer of pleasure, which she immediately rejected, brushing it aside with her hand in a tremulous, troubled, remorseful gesture. That heavy silence, though, proved useful for clarifying the very sketchy ideas that came to her unbidden, unwanted, spiraling around her until they fixed on one point, on *the* point, from where, so to speak, they eyed her boldly. Don't you see, Genoveva? Now, everything is simple; all the windows have been flung open; you can finally enjoy the sun... The sun, Genoveva, just imagine that.

Her brother, poor thing, had consigned her to the night or, at the very least, to darkness. For six years. "Do whatever you like; you're a grownup and it's none of my business. But I won't open my door to you, you hear. I won't have you shame me." "António, don't you understand; I can't get a divorce. I'm still a young woman, and I love Júlio." "All I understand is that I don't want people pointing at my sister in the street. That's all I understand. All right?"

These were sterile conversations that led nowhere, only to the usual cul-de-sac. And she continued living alone in the town in the north where Júlio lived (this had been

António's one concession) and to have him visit her when no one was looking and to otherwise feign complete indifference whenever they met in public. "Hello, how have you been? Long time, no see... How are things?" She even began to hate herself for agreeing so easily, even eagerly, to playing that game. She didn't hate her brother; she loved him too much. He was a very upright man who placed honesty above all else. What could be more natural?

Where were her brother's honesty and intransigence now? They had died. All that remained was that empty body covered in silence and pink gladioli.

Then came the faint, reticent morning light and the sound of solemn footsteps approaching down the aisle. It was the sacristan. Her thoughts stopped, the thread broke, and Genoveva was once again simply there in the sacristy, watching the sacristan change the burned-out candles for tall, yellowish ones. The widow blew her nose, then, turning to her son, said in a tearful voice:

"Go home, my dear. Remember, you have an exam in a couple of days. Go and rest a little."

"Don't worry, Mama. There's time."

Now, suddenly—how long had the idea been germinating inside him?—Jaime knew he wouldn't be taking that exam the day after tomorrow, that he wasn't going to go through that door beyond which lay a life that wasn't his, a life he rejected. Now he would be able to fight; it's so easy to fight a weaker opponent... It would never have been possible with his father. His loud voice drowning out all other voices, smothering them, killing them, and abandoning them once they had fallen silent. He had never been able to talk to his father, to discuss a problem. Besides, his father didn't like discussing problems.

He always had a solution, and his certainties were so unshakeable that there had never been any need to put them to the test. He, Jaime, had to study law because it was only logical that he should take over his father's practice and his clientele. There was no question about this, was there? None at all. Becoming an artist… But what did that mean, becoming an artist? Mere childishness. A pastime worthy only of life's failures.

No, he could never have fought his father, but his mother was a different matter. Not right away: that would be difficult, his father would still be a presence, and his giving up a career in law would seem to her, poor woman, a betrayal. How can you, my son, with your father barely cold in his grave… Or something of the sort. But he had to do it. Perhaps he would pretend he had taken the exam, because it was still too soon for her to be able to listen to him calmly. Yes, he would tell her he had taken the exam…

"Isn't that right, Jaime?"

He nodded a response to his Aunt Genoveva, with no idea what he was responding to. He only knew that they were, of course, talking about his father, and that his mother had again begun to cry, and one of her friends was urging her to accept his death and think of her son.

"Yes, you still have your son," said Genoveva.

"Yes, I do; I still have Jaime, poor love. He's such a good boy. But it's not enough. I'm going to be left so alone. I already feel so alone… He was so strong, he knew everything, he always had a solution to everything. I always had him to lean on. It was all so simple, Genoveva. That's how it always was, right from the beginning. Nineteen years we were married."

"There, there..."

"You have to be brave, my dear..."

"These are misfortunes we all have to face at some point..."

"That's life, and there's nothing to be done about it..."

There's nothing to be done about it... That's what she had always thought, which is why she had never done anything. She had allowed herself to be carried along, saying nothing, pretending. She had spent her whole life pretending. What else could someone like her do, someone so terrified of life? He would have supper out and neglect to tell her where—she had found that monogrammed handkerchief in his pocket, an M and an A intertwined—and he would arrive home late one night or even on two or three consecutive nights or, indeed, every night and offer vague excuses no one had asked him for, and for which she no longer bothered to ask because she was afraid of what she might hear. It was so large, the heart inside her breast, overflowing with tears, and then it had gradually grown so small, so shriveled, so hard. And she said nothing that might bring comfort to that heart... What would happen if she spoke? It might be a trap. But that uncertainty slowly wore away at her, and she became lined and wrinkled before her time. Old, yes, she was growing older by the day... His voice came back to her; it was there in her head, clear and robust and certain. "I won't be home for supper tonight. I told you that already, didn't I?" No, he hadn't. "Oh, I thought I had. A meeting with a client, a real bore, but I can't not go. I'll be back late, but don't wait up for me. It irritates me when I see you've been waiting up for me. Whatever for?" Yes, whatever for?

The voice fell silent, to be replaced by sobs. Her sobs.

It was then that Sara broke the silence with a question, an awkward question as her rare questions usually were, and almost always peculiar to her.

"What if he isn't dead? There are such cases. I read about it in the paper. *Ca-ta-lep-si-a*!"

The widow let out a scream, and Genoveva said very loudly to Sara, "Don't be such a fool!" Then she got up and again went over to the large, motionless body beneath the flowers. She lifted up the white cloth and gazed eagerly and fixedly at the face of her imminent freedom. Jaime felt his heart beating very fast and didn't dare to move. Genoveva returned to her place and said in a trembling voice:

"No, poor António is well and truly dead. There are already some purplish patches on his face, poor man. Didn't anyone bring some camphor?"

The widow gave a faint sigh and huddled down on the bench between her sister and her sister-in-law. Jaime offered to go to the nearby pharmacy, not realizing that this helpful gesture was, after all, a contribution to the definitive death of his father.

JOURNEY

Neither earth nor sky. Outside, always the same dark, dull, dizzyingly still night, which had been like that for nearly three hours. An abstract, unreal night, impossible to fill with ordinary, everyday images. Or so at least he thought. Frighteningly pure. Intangible. And so solitary.

He had always liked solitary places: vast deserted beaches where his were the only footprints—such a sense of ownership!—the long horizons of empty plains, cities at that same late hour, gentle and yet slightly angst ridden too, in which people sleep or toss and turn calling out for a sleep that refuses to come. Now, however, those glimpses of old scenes seemed crude, terrestrial imitations of this unsullied solitude, so large and perfect, through which he was traveling. Beyond the double panes of the window everything was possible, even the soft, white hand of a protective God reaching out to him. Even a little wandering ectoplasm. Even the angel of death, yes, even that. But nothing vulgar or probable.

If, as the flight progressed, a screw—a tiny but important, not to say, vital, screw—were to break or gradually come loose and fall into space, or if a needle were suddenly to go crazy, and the plane begin to rise and rise until it disintegrated (wasn't that the word the newspapers used about the satellite, that it had disintegrated?), or if the pilot suddenly died—which was perfectly possible—what would happen or, rather, how would it be?

He found himself repeating an old definition lost, he thought, in the dark night of time. "We give the name 'celestial sphere' to the majestic vault whose center appears to be occupied by the Earth and on whose inner surface we see the stars." And at that moment, he was a speck of dust traveling through that celestial sphere, albeit very low down. But did that actually count as the celestial sphere? Of course, that's what the definition said: "whose center appears to be occupied by the Earth..." That's the advantage of definitions... There is always something to be found in the midst of all the rubbish. Lavoisier's law, Archimedes' principle, Mendel's laws...

"Do you know where we are?" he asked the woman. "In the celestial sphere."

She jumped, slightly embarrassed:

"*Where*?"

Ramiro laughed softly, that rather arrogant laugh of his, the laugh of someone older than his years, and he took her small hand, with its stubby fingers (her stupid hand, he thought). Then he shrugged and said:

"It's really of no importance, none whatsoever. What were you thinking about?"

Branca smiled at him with genuine fondness and, after a moment's thought (she always paused to think before opening her small round flower of a mouth), said gravely that she was thinking about their luggage. What if it hadn't all been put on the plane? What if the blue suitcase had been left behind? It was so small; that could easily happen...

The same could be said of her. She was full of such homely thoughts, and the last idea she had was always the most important. As for the others, where did they go? He placed his other hand on the warm, round knee revealed by her skirt and reassured her as he would a child:

"It'll all be there, don't you worry. I hate to see you upset; it makes you look ugly..."

She pulled a funny face and brushed her cheek against his shoulder.

"Ugly? Do I really? You cruel thing..."

Ramiro turned abruptly away and gazed out of the window again, where the night was still uniformly black, with no moon and no stars. A square of black cloth, an empty square. He slowly, gradually released the woman's hand. Her hand was left, forgotten and unhappy, slightly open and slightly pink on her green tweed thigh, as if it didn't know where to go or what it had done to be banished like that.

He was looking out at the night and thinking that the woman, who had been his since yesterday—and who would be his for who knows how long—filled him with disgust. Disgust. She had taken so long to accept him, saying she wasn't sure she loved him, that she was still very young, and so on and so forth, and then there were the copious tears she had shed during the ceremony and the way she had clung to her mother as if he were intending to kill her, and now she was like a cat in heat. A stupid cat in heat. With certain fixed ideas. A cat's ideas of course. And after just one night. She was quite simply disgusting.

If such a thing happened… The screw coming loose, the needle going crazy, the pilot dying… That would be a good joke… He had nothing to lose—how long would he last with that heart of his?—but she, she had her whole life ahead of her, and what a life! Given how pretty she was, how attractive, and once he died, she would be both free and rich, and stupid too (an essential quality if one is to be entirely happy), yes, her future was full of possibilities. And full of other men too, of course. Not that he minded—what did he care—but, on the other hand, it wasn't nice to think that she would stay here having a high old time while he would be rotting in some cemetery with a wreath of flowers on top of him. Because she was very dutiful. She would be sure to take him flowers every week or at least every two. Initially, that is. Before he died completely.

If the plane was suddenly to burst into flames… He hadn't thought of that as a hypothesis. And yet a fire… All it took was for someone to hold a lighter to one of the curtains… Or drop a cigarette butt… Or not, because cigarettes only work when you don't want them to. You can't count on them. They have no sense of solidarity at all.

He hadn't spoken to the woman about his illness nor to his doctor about the marriage. He hadn't told his friends either. He had demanded a simple ceremony: just her parents, the best man, and a maid of honor. He had made it appear that the idea came not from him, but from Branca. She was so easily influenced, poor love!

His friends…but what friends? He had always been a sickly child, and children don't like ill people, especially those who stay ill for a long time. They get bored, irritated. And they are extremely cruel. That's why he loathed them all. All of them. From his bedroom window he would watch them playing football in the street, and what he felt then was hatred. Hatred. What if that boy slipped and broke his leg? What if that other one broke his spine? What if a car passed and…? He had only to walk more quickly or speak more loudly for his mother to say, "Now don't wear yourself out, Ramiro. Don't overdo it, Ramiro. Remember your heart…"

But his mother was dead now, and yesterday he had married. Was it yesterday or much longer ago? He was twenty-three and she was eighteen. Eighteen healthy years. She was perfectly at liberty to get married and overdo things. She had firm flesh and a fireproof heart.

If the plane were to burst into flames… He began imagining the disaster in all its details. Everyone dead, no survivors. Branca's lovely body forever still, silent, useless. The man he had seen sit down in the seat behind him, a man wearing an English-style overcoat and a diplomat's hat, the sort of man you don't see much these days, but who was clearly convinced of his importance in the world. A banker on a business trip? A well-known politician (he could be; he didn't know any well-known politicians) going abroad to sign some treaty? And suddenly, farewell treaty and farewell business deal. Perhaps all that would remain—as a symbol of ridiculous mediocrity—would be that diplomatic hat. Nothing else. Otherwise, just bits and pieces scattered all over the place. Mortal remains was the phrase. Including the very blonde stewardess, with her very blue eyes and very white teeth… "My name is Marina Vaz." Poor Marina Vaz!

He started laughing, forgetting that the woman next to him could hear. Only when the sound of his own laughter resounded in his ears did he shoot her a sideways glance, grown suddenly serious again. Branca, though, was absorbed in studying the cracked nail polish on the index finger of her left hand. "What dreadful nail polish," she must be thinking. Indeed, she was so taken up with this that she clearly found it a fascinating subject.

How stupid of him to get married! But he was in a hurry; he couldn't wait. Besides, what is life but a series of increasingly stupid incidents? Why not marry if she wanted to and this was the only way he could get her? She knew he was ugly, boring, and disagreeable. No woman had ever taken any interest in him. His one quality, which he had always made use of, was his money. He had always bought women. Those others had been bought by the hour; this one was for life. And he had spent his entire fortune on Branca. For her, it was, after all, a very good deal. Because his life would not be a long one.

Again he thought of the needle going crazy, the screw coming loose, the fire, the pilot dying... What would happen? The floor would shake violently. Then the plane would doubtless plummet earthward or perhaps flip over. It would certainly be interesting. Branca wouldn't be able to cope with such a situation. The poor girl wasn't born to be a heroine. When she married again...

"When you marry again, Branca..."

He was going to talk to her about death, to tell her he was a hopeless case, to ruin her journey completely and, more importantly, crush any illusions she might have of present happiness. That would be a plus. He saw, though, that she had fallen peacefully asleep, her dark head turned slightly toward the window. The effects of the motion-sickness pill she had insisted on taking.

Outside, the velvet-black night had lost its former purity. Its atmosphere seemed dense and difficult to penetrate, suffocating. "We're flying through clouds," he thought. "I am flying through clouds."

Suddenly the plane shook violently, and Ramiro thought it was about to nosedive. He had often dreamed of such a thing. It wasn't a nightmare exactly nor was it part of a story. Just a sensation. He and a precipice. He couldn't see it, but he knew it was a precipice. And he would plummet vertically downward in small, repeated impulses. He never reached the end of the dream, so he didn't know what the end would be like. Or he would wake up or simply forget the rest or change dreams. But he had never found out what it was like down below.

Nor did he now. Were they flying over the sea or the land? He wasn't going to ask the stewardess or the flight attendant; they might think he was afraid. If only the woman would wake up, then he could explain that it was all because of her... He looked at Branca again, but she was still deep in the same peaceful, almost childlike sleep that made her small, round chest rise and fall. The sleep of the blessed. Or of the simpleminded?

An air pocket, then another and another. The worthy gentleman behind him yelled out loud enough to be heard above the noise of the engines. Then Ramiro saw a bright flash light up the darkness outside, but all that brief flash showed him was the darkness itself. Where were the clouds they had just flown through? He looked in the other direction but saw only a brilliant line of light zigzagging across the dark backdrop. The plane was ascending, fleeing from the storm, then descending again and shaking in the angry air, battered by contrary winds.

Just as Ramiro was about to wake the woman, he felt a sharp pain in his chest that wouldn't let him breathe. The lightning flashes continued to illuminate the squares of night, but the engines drowned out the thunder. Was the storm near or far?

At this point, and this coincided with a still more intense pain, unbearable now, he saw some little fluttering fingers tapping on the glass. He reached out to them with his heavy hands and suddenly he was outside, falling down and down as he did in that familiar dream. He felt cold and thought vaguely about people who'd had a leg amputated and remembered too that he had left something behind on a seat somewhere, beside someone, something that was part of his daily existence. Probably nothing of any importance.

occasional "fancy that," "well, what do you know," and "who'd have thought it," but these were merely phrases utterly devoid of meaning whose sole aim was to prove that she was still there and continuing, more or less attentively, to follow the thread—which she wasn't always. She did sometimes have the depressing feeling that she was at a lecture where she had gone in search of self-improvement, and she would feel bored, almost angry, and her interjections would suddenly take on an almost aggressive edge, and she would feel tempted to end the call. She never did though. She invariably waited for Paula to do that.

When she was speaking on the phone to Paula, she liked to imagine her sitting on that velvet sofa because this was a useful image from which she could, if she wanted, free herself. Lately, she found people very tiring, perhaps, among other reasons, because of the bad weather, and yet she could talk to them—to their voices that is—for hours. What chiefly wore her out were people's eyes, whether bright and lively or dull and distracted, always fixed on hers, intent on drawing her in and holding her captive for some unspecified length of time. On the phone it was different. Paula would talk, and Jô could choose whether or not to imagine the stage set and the principal actor. The shelves of books, mostly unread, lining the walls, except, here and there, for an occasional rectangle, in the largest of which a small pink Pierrot smiled a sad, sweet smile (Paula's Picasso, her famous Picasso lit by a fluorescent light), the lichen-green sofa, the imposing armchairs, and, last of all, Paula's own face. The *voice* chose its words carefully, rejecting some, considering others, hesitating before making a final choice, then enthusiastically—or at least confidently—adopting one. That word—the one she needed—sometimes mischievously eluded her, hiding away in the innermost folds of her memory, or, more prosaically, under her tongue. Paula could sometimes be very prosaic; yes, she could—she allowed herself that luxury, and would even sometimes come straight out with some word that would grate on Jô's sensitive ears. On her lips, however, that word would sound witty, and anyone hearing it would find it simple and fresh. Natural.

Jô would sometimes help her find the elusive word—a way of passing the time like any other. "Meticulous? Perfect?" she would suggest. But, no, what Paula meant was "scrupulous." That word and that word alone. "Francisco is very scrupulous about everything he does. At the factory, everything goes like clockwork."

And then, suddenly, as unexpectedly as ever, even though this had long since become a habit, she would bring the conversation to an abrupt close, as she did on that night (and on other subsequent nights), with nothing to announce or prepare her listener for that ending with no epilogue.

"Right, goodbye then. And come and see us one day, make an effort, don't be difficult. I have things I want to show you."

"I'll do my best!"

"It really is no way to live, Jô, I'm tired of telling you that. When will you make a decision? What are you waiting for? It's no kind of life, Jô."

"No, it isn't, but there's no alternative."

She would put down the phone, and the usual light tinkling sound of the receiver returning to the rest would be followed by a huge, heavy, devastating silence that would invade the apartment like a wave. It always took Jô a moment to grow accustomed to not hearing Paula's voice. A slow process. Thanks to her naturally gregarious spirit, Paula, her childhood friend and frequent enemy, brought Jô very different images from those that usually filled her day-to-day life. On some nights it was irritating; on others it had a sedative, but, almost always, diverting effect: So-and-so, that blonde who was a member of the Braganza family, albeit the bastard branch…welcomed into the fold, of course, despite a divorce, a registry office wedding, and a lot of gossip… Some other Tom, Dick, or Harry, our man in Karachi (where exactly is Karachi? In which country? What exactly is a minister plenipotentiary? Or is this all nonsense?). And some other fellow, a playboy and a winner of car races, who was best buddies with the Aga Khan. Sometimes, one of these fairy-tale people orbiting Paula—a planet with the right to satellites—would disappear, and she would never know where they went or why they had enjoyed such a brief existence. She would ask, "How's Tom? What's happened to Dick? And what about Harry?" Paula would then give a vague, suddenly offhand explanation, and her lips (Jô could sense it) wore the grimace of someone immersed in an atmosphere stinking of boiled cabbage. Tom (or Dick or Harry) had long ago plunged into the pool of oblivion into which she usually threw people past their sell-by date. Casually tossing them over her shoulder.

On the worst days—or nights—the ones when she found Paula's chatter most bruising—not that this stopped her listening attentively and ending the call when Paula decided to—she would put down the phone and, with that unlocatable pain gone, would immediately return with a bump to the cul-de-sac that was her life, where she found problems aplenty, but no plans and no hopes. Paula talked to her about many things, far too many for someone in her state of mind. But how could Paula, sitting on her velvet sofa, possibly know what state of mind she was in? She did go too far sometimes, talking about *her* trips, *her* clothes, *her* friendships, the pearls that Francisco had given *her* for *her* birthday. "He's such a love, Francisco. I really can't complain, although few people can consider themselves to be completely happy. Isn't that so, Jô?"

Every night, in the small hours, a cock would crow in the garden of the naval captain who lived in the ground-floor apartment. The fine, sturdy, white cockerel with his triumphant red crest was the master of ten Orpington hens. Jô liked to hear him as she lay in the dark, her eyes wide, because he gave her a real impression of strength, of spontaneous joie de vivre. When the cock crowed at dawn—when Jô heard him crow—she had a feeling of peace and, more than that, of invulnerability. He didn't wake her up completely. She would open her eyes with a slight shiver, and yet many things inside her continued to sleep, only to be woken later by her luminous alarm clock, as implacable as the eye of God. The sense of invulnerability came from feeling that she was still protected by a remnant, however tenuous, of the night. These were very pleasant moments. When she woke like that, and could hear—and did hear—the cock crowing and the other cocks answering him from far off beyond the other garden walls, these sounds and the cold were just vague sensations happening only on the surface. The rest of her continued to sleep and would sleep for a few more hours until the alarm clock summoned her brutally back to life.

four corners of the city or else sitting at home, waiting for the ever-present possibility of a phone call or a visit, killing time and ingloriously pacing up and down, engaged in a constant battle with objects: the objects that gradually accumulated somehow or other—even the furniture itself, which was full of life, especially at night, before she went to bed, before she took the second sleeping pill she always ended up taking, because until she did, she could think of nothing else, like an obsession. The chest of drawers on the left, under the window, would sometimes creak because a tiny bit of inert matter had suddenly sprung into life. And she would always turn on the light, initially out of shock, but afterward because she couldn't stand to be alone in the dark with that unbearable presence, the near certainty that something or someone was spying on her through an invisible crack. She would then turn out the light, feeling calmer, her eyes filled by the totally unenigmatic image of an old chest of drawers piled high with books and almost-empty perfume bottles and ashtrays full of hairpins and lipsticks, and a three-quarter photo of her when she was seventeen, wearing a sky-blue taffeta dress with a high neck and puff sleeves, which, at the time, she thought very pretty.

This was the worst time, the most difficult, because it required her to remain utterly impassive before the parade of images from past and future. During the day, she could move, escape, set off along other paths, but not at that hour. The nets she had unwittingly cast into the sea dredged up those who had drowned, some of whom were so old and worn she could barely recognize them, others dangerously new. Her grandparents; her father, poor thing; her mother as she used to be, still skinny and with brown hair (now she was blonde); Paula in pigtails (people called her little Paula even though she was rather fat); Mário…am I going senile? she thought, addressing Artur, who was waiting for her there in the darkness, stiff and inexpressive.

When she left for school in the morning, she would sometimes meet the captain who lived on the ground floor. They would happen to open their respective doors at the same time, or would meet in the hallway, with her racing down the stairs and him walking very slowly, dragging his feet, which, in the last few months, had seemed to weigh like lead. He would always stand aside to let her pass, which would have seemed perfectly natural if he hadn't made such a point of it. He was an extremely polite man, but in a slightly old-fashioned way, always addressing her formally as "Senhora." "How have you been, Senhora? I haven't had the pleasure of seeing you for a while. I even wondered if you were ill." She would thank him and say she was fine, then cast a diplomatic eye at her watch and another at the bus stop, ready for a quick escape. Sometimes, though, the captain would catch the same number five bus into town to deal with some pressing business ("pressing" was a word he used a lot), and he liked to be there early. When there were seats, a rare occurrence at that hour, he would sit beside her and insist on paying her fare. "Please, Senhora, don't even think about it, it's such a small thing." Yes, such a small thing.

Not that long ago, as she left the house, she had met the captain and spoken to him about his garden and his hens. About the white cockerel too, of course. She had never before told him that she sometimes sat at her window to watch the hens pecking around on the ground or counting the eggs that his old servant collected for some dish or other.

"It's just a hobby," said the captain apologetically.

"Yes, and a very useful one," she said.

"Some people," he went on, wrinkling his bushy, grizzled eyebrows, "some people think it's hardly an appropriate pastime for a naval officer, even an officer in the merchant navy or a reservist. But what is a naval officer-now-landlubber supposed to do? I could read perhaps, but I've never been a great reader. I've always led a very active life, you see. I was, if you like, the main protagonist in the story—in my story. I've never been much interested in other people's stories, or, rather, in the stories that some people go to the trouble of inventing, because they've never actually lived them themselves, to be read by other people who have also never lived those stories. So, what am I supposed to do? Sail paper boats on the lake? But what lake? It's difficult, you know… Fortunately, I'm a bachelor; otherwise I would make a most undesirable husband or father."

"We all have our little obsessions," she said, and hesitated, afraid that this remark might have offended him. "I know someone, a friend, who reads the *Times*. I wouldn't say he reads it from first page to last; that would be impracticable. But he certainly reads it every day. He spends hours hidden behind his newspaper."

"But that's a very fine pastime. That way, he knows what's going on in the world, which for most people is important, I would almost say pressing. Among the more evolved in society, that is. And the *Times* is a serious paper;

it doesn't tell lies or commit sins of omission. Generally speaking, that is. There are always exceptions—I won't deny it—but, still, it's a serious newspaper. Anyway, that's the way it is. When I stopped being a naval officer, when they decided I was too old to command my own ship, I also ceased to take any interest in important matters, grave matters like space travel, politics, the possibility of war, and so on. At first, I found it hard, but I eventually got used to it. We can get used to anything, Senhora, even to being unnecessary. Up until then, I was passionately interested in such things and, like most people, had some pretty firm opinions. Opinions that would have saved the world. Now it all seems very remote or, more than that, infantile. If I were to start taking an interest again, I would have to change my whole culture, relearn what I had forgotten, start putting things in their proper places. But why? And what *is* the proper place for current events? But please forgive this bit of homespun philosophy," he concluded with a smile.

"Sometimes I spend quite a long time watching the hens, and it's really restful," she said. "I think if I had a garden, I would have some hens too."

The captain said slowly:

"We all need something to do. The sea is very tiresome when it's too calm."

"So are the plains when they're too solitary."

He looked at her curiously and smiled a little.

Sometimes, the days lay before her flat and calm, but fortunately not often. Mostly they were already planned out, full of straight lines or curves, sometimes so tangled it was hard to disentangle them, but nevertheless easier to deal with. She remembered, as a little girl, holding a ball of thread and a crochet needle, her eyes filled with tears. The needlework teacher, a dark, oily woman named Aurora, would say, "Joana, untangle that awful mess!" And she would set about undoing the knots, which only grew in number because, far from undoing them, she was creating them. She would decide then to carry on regardless, but the other girls would laugh at her because what she was making didn't even resemble crochetwork, and she would always end the class in tears and would sometimes be punished by being made to stand on the bench. Such ignominy!

That day, however—which had promised to be very tangled, with two written tests, two private lessons, some homework to grade, and a meeting later in the day with Artur—suddenly turned into one of those solitary plains when the phone rang and she was told that all classes were canceled because the head teacher's mother had just died. Jô was getting dressed and looking out at the gray day beyond the veiled rectangle of the window. The fact that it was a gray day was not, in itself, of great importance. What mattered was the fact that this was the first in a long, long series of gray days that would last throughout a long, long winter. Dark days with no sun, or only a damp, hesitant sun. Short days, as if shriveled up by the cold. "It'll be a long haul," she would think or say. It would be a long haul until the sun was once again high in the sky and the days stretched out endlessly. It's true that the long haul would gradually grow shorter, and, at some point, the summer would arrive along with summer dresses and the pool where she sometimes went to swim; and the month at the beach, alone in some hotel or other; and the tan that neither suited nor didn't suit her, but which she liked because, for a time, it made her another person. The circumference was very slowly being drawn, though, and was about to close. She was once more standing at the door of winter. And this time, she was thirty-eight, which certainly didn't help.

She put on her blue woolen sweater, carefully combed her hair and pinned it up neatly at the back of her head, then paused for a moment to regard herself objectively in the closet mirror. She still didn't look old, thanks to her slender face and prominent cheekbones. She studied her high, domed, almost medieval forehead; her pale eyes; her all-important mouth, as exactly drawn as that of a black woman. That mouth rarely smiled, but when it did, it smiled broadly, showing very regular white teeth, slightly on the large size.

When she had finished getting dressed, she wondered how she was going to spend that long day, with so much free time in which to think. Lately, she had grown to dread such days. Then it occurred to her: Why not go to the bank?

She is reverently leaning on the counter, but, so that no one will sense her troubled state of mind, she adopts a relaxed, nonchalant pose. She places her red handbag on the glass top, beneath which there is a display of reports full of numbers and a few tourist brochures (a commercial map of the city; a stylized sunflower above a blue stripe on which sits a white sail without a boat—false, distant promises of April in Portugal), and then casts her eye over the dark or bald heads, bent and intent.

Then he comes over to her, taking advantage of the

walk from the door he emerged from to the counter where she is waiting for him to issue a few important orders, pausing, head bowed, before this or that clerk. He is a very sober man. He moves unhurriedly—not only now, but almost always—and he thinks slowly and speaks very deliberately. It's as if there's a little hydraulic elevator that, when necessary, descends from his brain to his mouth, carrying inside it words that then serenely enter the world. Thoughtful words. Sometimes, he is stopped just a few feet away from her by an aromatic gentleman (English lavender and American tobacco) who has just arrived and is doubtless a good customer and who wants to know, in his busy capitalist way, if it would still be possible to arrange a few more of those useful little bonds they talked about a few days ago. Artur replies in the same attentive way as he does to everyone, in the low, mild-mannered voice of a repentant ecclesiastic—his *s*'s simultaneously sibilant and soft, or perhaps "gentle" would be a better word. He doesn't even look at her, or only afterward, once the important gentleman has taken his leave: "So I can rest easy, then, my friend. You reckon that by next week…"

"Yes, they should be here next week. If you come in on Thursday…"

He looks at her then as if he has only just seen her. What are you doing here, his eyes ask. He discreetly holds out his hand, and for a second she thinks, or rather fears, that he is going to address her as the captain does: "How have you been, Senhora?" He doesn't though. He merely asks her quietly if anything has happened.

So many things happen, she thinks. So many. At every moment and every hour. And yet we don't even notice.

"The head teacher's mother has died."

He nods, the purely external nod of a puppet on a string.

"Well, that's life, I suppose. On the one hand…"

"Yes, on the one hand… But even so…"

"Of course, of course. Had she been ill?"

"Yes, she had. Old age, I suppose. The head teacher must be nearly sixty herself, and her mother was still teaching too. Ethics."

"I see."

His eyes—which once were blue but have, over time, been watered down to a murky blueish blur, thus losing their original all-important blueness—linger on his wristwatch, Swiss-made and self-winding, of which he is very proud because it neither loses nor gains, a particularly precious quality for him, for whom time is money. His large, bony right hand, with its carefully manicured nails, plays a few simple scales on the map of downtown Lisbon. *Do re mi fa so la ti do.* His thumb beats hard three times on the Rossio square. *Do do do.* Meanwhile, he turns slightly to glance over at the clerks, afraid they might be observing him, criticizing him.

"Anyway, yes, the head teacher's mother…"

He interrupts her:

"Fine, but you presumably didn't come here just to deliver this death notice. You must agree…"

"Yes, I did, no, no, I didn't, of course, that isn't the only reason I came, but…"

She couldn't tell him that she had suddenly felt terribly alone in the middle of that empty day. He wouldn't understand and might even smile ironically: "If you had as much work to do as me, you wouldn't mind a day off…" Jô thinks suddenly: Is he an estimable person or isn't he?

Well, he wouldn't hurt a fly and would certainly never spill blood. If anyone spilled blood on his behalf, though, he would simply walk away. He just isn't capable of seeing other people's minor problems.

She says nothing and waits, then sees him shake his head.

"You have to understand," he says at last. "I was in the middle of a meeting with the director and left halfway through, having first asked his permission of course… I have a truly hellish day ahead of me, with tons to do. It's lovely to see you, but you don't seem to appreciate…"

"…the heavy responsibility I bear."

"Exactly," he says gravely. "Exactly. I thought it must be something serious."

"Well, I'm sorry it wasn't."

She smiles. So does Artur. Purely out of politeness.

"Will you be going to the head teacher's house?" he asks, just to make conversation.

"Certainly not!" says Jô. "I can't bear the sight of dead bodies, absolutely not. Some people can… But don't you find that rather morbid? They go to the cemetery laden down with flowers, but who are the flowers for, *what* are they for? The soul, if there was one, has departed, and the body is being devoured by worms."

He says, "That depends on your point of view." Then: "Since you don't have any classes, make the most of the day, and relax. And just this once, cancel your private lessons. Listen, why don't you call your friend Paula and arrange to meet up? She's always asking you to go and see her, isn't she?" He must think that word, *Listen*, redeems him. Spoken in a tone of voice that was simultaneously concerned, insistent, interested, and slightly anxious.

Listen. "She might be at home. It would be a change. Or else go to the cinema; there's nothing better for soothing the mind. The movies they show are always so stupid that there's no temptation to actually think."

"That's your opinion."

"It is, but since you're of the opposite opinion, then go to the cinema precisely in order to think since, according to you, the movies they show are always so intelligent."

"Well, some are, then again…"

He suggests something else. He is suddenly full of ideas, all of them urgent, requiring immediate action. A clerk approaches and stops about six feet away to deal with a very old lady who, in one tremulous hand, is holding a small bundle of coupons held together with a rubber band. Then Artur says loudly, well, more loudly anyway, loud enough for the clerk to hear:

"A pleasure to see you Senhora Dona Joana. And hold on to those bills of exchange; they're solid stuff. Best wishes to your family."

She didn't, in fact, go to the bank that morning. To do so would involve an entirely unnecessary walk that would lead her—as it always did lately—to the bitter palace of disenchantments. It was cold in the bank, and she always left it with her collar turned up and her arms covered in goosebumps. Why insist? Besides, she had long since realized—without entirely admitting it to herself—that there was no point in insisting; it was best just to go with the flow and be borne along on the current that carries us to the place where, for some reason, we are fated to arrive. You could flail around as much as you liked, but what was the point? You just floundered around and got out of breath and arrived either a little too early or a little too late. Always at the wrong time.

The trip to the bank was just an idea, but when it vanished, Jô realized that a lot of other things vanished too, and she could see their absence, or, rather, was obliged to see it (because she really didn't want to). They were old things, precious in their day, that she kept safely stored away inside herself because even one glance from other people could bruise or upset them. And now where were they? The dissolution had started long ago, and she knew this very well, even if she had only now allowed herself to make this discovery.

A discovery that brought her such serenity. Standing nose in the air like a tourist with all the time in the world, she could finally properly observe things that she knew only glancingly. There had been images that had touched some retina or other, or ideas or even mere tones of voice. She, however, had always carried on, had chosen to hurry on ahead, as if too distressed to stop. Now, however, she could see it all, and the sight did not make her heart beat any faster.

When had he ceased to be him? He had been lost along the way, and all that remained as a reminder for posterity was his immutable wax effigy. A speaking effigy, it was true, but then why shouldn't wax effigies be able to speak, given that the words they spoke were also made of wax? There was something about him... She didn't know how to explain; suddenly she didn't know how to explain anything, not even to herself. She needed to study him closely, to set aside all subjectivity, to look at him for a few moments with a cold critical eye. The watery, once-blue eyes behind the tortoiseshell glasses; the straight nose; the large, slender, almost lipless mouth with deep lines on either side; the strong jaw; the perfect hands; the well-tailored suit. What else? Not much really, because with time he had been transformed into an effigy—of himself. Inside, like a kind of alloy, there were various secret layers, superimposed, hidden away. Jô had known about these layers, but she didn't know if some of them still existed or if they had been suffocated by the outer shell. Now, she thought, she never would. It was too late.

Sometimes—and she knew this was madness—she fancied playing a trick and giving the mannequin a shove, for example, or painting a mustache on him or shouting right in his ear. It was irresistible. She would wait until there was no one else in the museum, no guards and no visitors—which was easy enough—and then she would go over to him. However hard she pushed, though, the mannequin wouldn't fall: It would merely rock gently, just for a moment, like a tumbler toy, then return to its vertical position. The ink she was using, the only sort she had to hand, didn't stay on the wax, which remained smooth and impeccable. As for shouting, that had no effect whatsoever. The mannequin knew how to turn a deaf ear when convenient.

That all-too-familiar feeling of unease, which always came out of nowhere, as it did right now, at this very moment—but why?—or a faint bitterness rising up from within, then spilling over or unfurling, and ultimately overwhelming her, a cloud suddenly dissolving (opaque air inside translucent air, nothing inside nothing). Her lips tasted salty, and she realized she was crying. After her own fashion, with no fuss. Two tears running calmly, obliquely, down her motionless cheeks, as far as her neck. She wiped them away with her hands and picked up the phone. She needed to talk to someone. With her mother perhaps. Or with Paula. But her mother had gone out, and Paula was asleep. "She got in very late last night," she was told. "She's resting."

Perhaps Paula would phone later to tell her about her day. "I'm her personal diary," Jô thought suddenly, in order to think about something else. "She can't be bothered to set things down in writing, but she needs to make a report. So, she dials a number, mine, and dictates to me all the important events of the day." They weren't what you would call close friends, although they had always been friends. They talked, but nothing they said was particularly meaningful or even personal. She, in turn, told Paula about school matters, about a good movie she had seen, and occasionally, in passing, she would mention Artur. "Artur went to..." "Artur said..." "Artur and I..." Casually, but discreetly. And Paula, for her part, never asked any questions, something for which Jô was grateful. Lately, though, she had begun urging her to make a decision, telling her that "that" was no kind of a life, although without specifying what decision she should make or what kind of life "that" was. Sometimes she would describe the people she hobnobbed with, or tell her about their trips abroad, the presents her husband gave her ("He's such a sweetheart, Francisco"), the fashion shows she attended, the charity teas she organized in December (or was it earlier?) so that the poor could enjoy a decent Christmas meal, about the latest opera at the Teatro São Carlos or the latest reception held at the Palácio de São Bento, always splendid affairs held in one of those two very fancy "saints." Jô would pick up the phone, and the teller of tales would launch into one of her stories. Sometimes these were third-person narratives involving one of her friends or acquaintances; other times, it was some matter of great importance that had happened to her; at still other times, they took the form of a sudden, unexpected return to the past. Then Jô's heart would always beat a little faster, out of fear or anxiety.

Sitting on her big velvet sofa, Paula always really enjoyed those oral forays into old times, which, while not exactly hard, had been far from wonderful. Jô was the only person with whom she could recall the past, their days at school, the café where they would go to for a glass of hot milk that they would drink along with the bread roll they would bring from home because that worked out cheaper. She doubtless thought how nice it was to remember these things out loud and to have someone with her, at the end of a telephone line, someone who could add the odd forgotten detail that had vanished over time... And to have that someone as audience: that was the main advantage. Paula would talk. In the first-person singular of course. These memories were hers; she was the one who used to go and drink a glass of hot milk at that café: "You know the one, Pastelaria Chique." "You mean, Pâtisserie," Jô would say. "Patisserie Chique!" "Oh, that's right, Pâtisserie, Pâtisserie Chique. Of course!"

She would sometimes forget that Jô had been there too and say how delicious it had been, that bread roll—"Just marvelous, you've no idea." Like the great man talking to journalists about his modest beginnings, thought Jô. John Ford or Steve Rockefeller remembering, with a touch of nostalgia, the bread roll they would gobble down while sitting at some drugstore counter. Marilyn Monroe harkening back to her years in the orphanage. But she had fought back and triumphed, right? And now she was someone. The journalists would take notes, or perhaps not. Perhaps they had eaten at the same drugstore as Ford or Rockefeller or lived in the same orphanage as Marilyn. But they had not triumphed.

"Those were great times," Paula would say. "I miss them. Not that I'd want to go back, mind you. We get used to a certain way of life, don't we? Going back is always difficult. And why would you, even if you could? More years to be lived and you might perhaps end up doing the same thing over and over—too boring. Besides, it wasn't all positive. Money problems and so on. Yes, that was the main thing, money problems. But at the same time… Expectation is so delightful though, or how can I put, so fruitful. Nothing had yet happened, and anything could happen…"

Then she would suddenly, unexpectedly stop:

"I'd better go; it's getting late. I have to be in good form tomorrow. We're having supper with an English guy, a business colleague of Francisco's, and his wife. All he ever talks about are horses and hunting dogs, and she's a real snob and has absolutely nothing interesting to say. Absolutely nothing. I'll tell you all about it."

ooooo

Artur was a mere profile, and those once-blue eyes seemed quite innocuous. On the steering wheel, his white hands, faintly luminous in the dark, so still and almost unnecessary, seemed suddenly timeless. Ten minutes ago (or was it ten hours?) he had asked if she wanted the window open. After which the dense, heavy silence had reinstalled itself between them.

She starts talking then, but without making a sound, talking silently, telling him everything that's going on inside her. She even talks to him about something she rarely dares to think about, a taboo subject: the children she didn't have and won't have now. Yes, she even mentions them. She accuses him of wanting to be a free man. He, however, stares fixedly at the road ahead, and his eyes are all innocence. If the expression on his face were any different, then the scales would balance evenly, but he is all serenity and purity of soul. And Jô's dish on the scales is dropping lower and lower, while his rises, growing lighter and lighter. Not a flicker of a frown. At her final thought, "I feel betrayed," the two dishes stop: one low down, the other high up.

I have neither a past nor a future, and sometimes I refuse to have a present. The lives of people are so gray, so empty. An amalgam of tedious, meaningless events. What did she think at any given moment? What did she feel? She no longer knows. Time passes and passed, never stopping—it can't—and things become covered in successive layers of dust. Old dust, venerable dust. It's like some kind of conjuring trick, and the rabbit and the doves and the string of multicolored handkerchiefs disappear into the top hat. And the top hat is turned this way and that for the respectable audience to see, and it's completely empty. I refuse to have a present.

"I was just thinking..." she began cautiously.

"What about?"

She stopped, because anything she said was bound

to seem overly significant after that long silence, and she felt intimidated by the words she was about to say. It was difficult, though, to stop halfway.

"Go on," said Artur encouragingly.

"Well, among other things, I was thinking that our lives, yours and mine, are stuck in a cul-de-sac. In our different ways, we are both heading for the same wall. You happily and me feeling well and truly fed up. But perhaps it's not even the same wall. The plaster on yours will at least be in better condition than mine; that would only be fair."

"This isn't like you."

"It's just that..."

"What?"

"I would like to have had a child," she said shyly, taking a risk. "That's all, a child. It's not much to ask, is it? It's easy enough and usually happens by chance. An accident. Well, I would like to have had such an accident."

"It wasn't possible, Jô," he said.

"No, it wasn't," she said, "but I feel, how can I put it..."

"Frustrated?" suggested Artur, ever helpful.

"No, more than that, betrayed."

"By me?"

"No, no, you never promised me anything. I really have no right to complain. No, I feel betrayed by life, by circumstances. I sometimes wonder if this is just a total lack of humility on my part. Anyway... Anyway," she said glancing at him, "don't go thinking I'm about to ask for your hand in marriage."

Artur laughed quietly.

"I know you're not. You're too timid to do that. And

too sensible."

"Yes, I think I am both those things, but just imagine, yes, imagine for a moment that I am asking you to marry me. This is a hypothetical question of a purely experimental nature. What would you say?"

He didn't even pause.

"You know the answer already. We've talked about this so often…"

"But not for ages!"

"Yes, it was ages ago, but the problem remains the same. My daughter has not yet married. She's seventeen. We discussed this right at the start."

"I remember," she said. "And I remember what I thought too: 'He's an honest fellow, and I like honest fellows.' It was all very clear from the start. I really have no grounds for complaint."

Artur nodded, and for a long time they said nothing. Then she asked:

"Have you never felt that you didn't know yourself—have you never had the feeling that you were a stranger to yourself?"

"You're in a funny mood today."

"It's the weather, I think. I always find the beginning of winter difficult. It's like the beginning of old age, the beginning of death, the beginning of many things that imply the end of other things. I get all lucid and clear-sighted. On the other hand, I find the spring exciting. Ah, the spring…"

Artur said:

"Yes, give me the spring any time."

And she agreed:

"Of course."

"Do you want to go back?" he said.

"Yes, I'm feeling tired."

The Lancia made a U-turn in the middle of the road, and they set off back to Lisbon. Again in silence.

She was just coming in the front door when the phone began to ring loudly. It was her mother. At that hour, she would be in her dressing gown and phoning from Benfica, where she lived, and her face would be smeared with anti-wrinkle cream and hope, and she'd have curlers in her Venetian-gold hair.

"How are you? I've been calling for ages, but no one answered," she bellowed because she was deaf.

"I went out. I just got back this minute."

"Did you go to the cinema? What did you see?"

"What did I see?"

"Yes, what movie?"

"None. I didn't go to the cinema."

"Ah, I understand."

Silence. Then her mother's voice grew louder, as if she had lost control. "I understand!" she yelled. "I UNDERSTAND!"

"I sometimes ask myself how often I've heard that word in the last few years, how often you have 'understood.' Because you always act as if you've understood everything."

Her mother said, "Things change, and people do too; that's only normal. You, for example…"

"Me?"

"What do you intend to do?"

Jô shrugged off the question.

"I don't know. I'm waiting for something that will

come either from outside me or from inside. For the time being, there's nothing. A vacuum. And who can have thoughts in a vacuum?"

"My poor Jô," her mother said theatrically. And Jô could imagine her at the other end of the line, pursing her lips and shaking her head like someone who can't believe what she's just heard, and gesticulating with the hand on which her emerald ring glitters in the light of the lamp. "My poor Jô."

"Don't feel sorry for me; you know I hate that. Besides, I don't feel unhappy exactly, just a bit lost. It's as if everyone else is sitting in their seats and suddenly, I don't have a seat, do you see? Obviously sometimes… But anyway, it comes and goes. I think I've only just realized that today… Look, I'd prefer it if you didn't say anything more about that now. As I said, I have no real thoughts at the moment. They're sure to come back eventually, and when they do, I'll let you know, don't worry."

"May I ask one last question?" her mother said. "Why don't you marry? He's free and so are you."

"You said it: he's free. And he wants to stay free. Some business about his daughter… Anyway, how many times have you asked me that same question?"

"Good grief, Jô, you have a strange way of looking at things. And you speak so objectively about your own life…"

"I do my best. And, believe me, it goes against my nature. I'd like to complain and find someone to blame, to shift responsibility. That always makes life so much easier."

"Perhaps," said her mother. "Perhaps." Then she talked about other things, among them the organized bus tour she would be going on in October, that she always went on in October. "Why don't you come with me?" she asked. "It's really not that expensive. Shall I send you the brochure? If you're interested..."

Jô interrupted her. She wasn't interested. If she *were* to go on holiday one day, it wouldn't be in a group. Besides, in October she would be teaching.

"I could always go in September."

Jô closed her eyes and went looking for her mother. She found her after a few fruitless attempts, and there she was: wearing a light-colored suit and dark glasses, smiling at the passing photographer and surrounded by white doves fluttering in St Mark's Square. Unaware then that she had a bad heart. She would write to her often when she went traveling. Postcards with pictures of Stratford-upon-Avon or Madrid or Venice, and on which she never said very much. They were more like circulars. "Still dazzled. Italy (or France or England or Spain) is an absolute dream. You can't imagine the fun I've had. *Unforgettable*. I often think of you. Are you very busy? See you soon, *cara* (or *ma chérie* or *darling*)." The prodigal mother, thought Jô with a smile, with her little organized madnesses, always within reason of course.

"If you need money, I can lend you some," said her mother. "A change of air would do you good. Believe me, there's nothing like a little trip somewhere to help you see things in a new light."

Her mother thought she had a monopoly on ideas that she felt were real discoveries: the secret of being happy. This is good, she would say, or that. Believe me.

"I'll think about it. You may be right."

This was the best way to deal with her. Her memory

was getting worse, and she would probably have forgotten their conversation by the next day.

She was sitting in one corner of the staff room, in the middle of which was a round table and a few dog-eared copies of *Paris-Match*, as if it was a doctor's waiting room, and she was laboriously pondering her life while listening to the history teacher, whose name was Lucrécia, going on and on about her many ailments. She was a short, skinny woman who always wore rather long pleated skirts and off-white blouses. In winter, the skirts and blouses were made of wool, and in summer of cotton or silk.

"I've been to the ophthalmologist," the teacher was saying. "He prescribed some new lenses, but to be honest, nothing has changed. I still get the most appalling headaches."

"Terrible."

"It is. Only someone who's had them can know. Do you get many headaches?"

She said she didn't, and her colleague looked at her with a mixture of superiority and envy. Envy won out, though, and she remarked, "You don't know how lucky you are. The number of doctors I've seen, the money I've spent! I've even wondered if it might be some kind of allergy."

Jô thought about Paula, who also suffered from allergies, and would sometimes phone her just to say, "I've got one of my allergies; it's just dreadful, you can't imagine. No, really, you can't..."

"I have a friend..." she began to say.

The telephone interrupted her, though, and she stayed where she was, watching the history teacher's arm reaching for the phone. "Hello?" she said, adding, yes, she was here. She would pass her over, one moment. She then handed Jô the phone and explained that it was for her—a man, but he hadn't given his name. Then she got up and went over to the window where she stood, apparently absorbed in watching what was going on out in the street.

Artur. But what could have happened for him to call her at school, something he had never done in all those years…

"Is that you, Jô?" asked a voice that wasn't Artur's. "Don't you recognize me? Have a think…" No need to think. She was dumbstruck, could barely breathe, suddenly unable to speak or find the words. Deathly pale. When she did speak, it was in a strained, unfamiliar voice.

"Is it you? Good heavens, where did you spring from?"

Laughing, the man said that he had arrived some time ago, visiting old haunts, and had asked various people where he could find her. They all told him, however, that she had disappeared, that they'd completely lost sight of her. He finally found out—well, there are always ways. Persistence, eh? He then said he hoped she didn't mind him phoning her at school, but it was the only possible way to make contact with her. All he had been told was that she taught at that school. "What do you teach, Jô?"

"Physics and chemistry."

"Well, who would have thought it?"

"I know."

They both laughed at the same time, and all the while she was staring at the history teacher's tense, intent, motionless back.

"I hope you won't get into trouble because of me."

She said that she hoped so too, but there was no

reason why she should, although you never knew. Her words had suddenly returned, and she could once again think and put her thoughts into words. Mário—his name was Mário—then asked what time she got out of school, which was a difficult question to answer when the history teacher was standing so close and was clearly listening. She pretended not to have heard the question and asked if he was going to be in Lisbon for long.

"I'm not sure yet," he said. "I thought I'd stay for six months, but I don't honestly think I'll last that long, and will probably leave earlier. I feel as if I didn't belong here anymore, but I'll definitely come back now and then. I've even rented a house."

"Seriously?"

"Yes, imagine that. What time do you finish work? Can I meet you outside the school?"

The history teacher's back and shoulders stirred beneath her cream blouse, and then Jô told Mário yes, he could, she'd be leaving at a quarter past five, and all the while she was saying this, she kept her eyes fixed on the figure standing by the window, silhouetted against the light.

"Splendid," he said. "See you later then."

Her putting the phone down coincided with the history teacher's sudden return to life. She breathed, moved slightly, and when Jô saw her eyes fix on her so inquisitively, she determined not to tell her anything. "Splendid," Mário had said, and that meaningless word had somehow given her new life, like a kind of stimulating injection. She suddenly felt cheerful, eager to live. This, she thought, is how he always used to be, and she would let herself be carried along on his enthusiasm, unable to resist, even though it sometimes filled her with fear. That enthusiasm had been useful even when nothing came of it but a bitter future. That vaguely—only vaguely—plaintive tone of voice, which didn't wait for an answer. Lack of time perhaps, or because there was no point in waiting, since he had achieved the result he wanted.

Lucrécia walked over to the door.

"See you later," she said. "It's almost time for class."

She didn't rehearse what she would say, the right words, nor did she reject those that weren't right—she didn't even summon them up, preferring to forget them altogether: Don't say this or this, and don't even think of saying that. She felt empty of any ideas that would be of immediate interest and made her way down the stairs very cautiously, like someone afraid the ground might play a trick on her and treacherously slip from under her. She scrutinized each step, measuring it, as if she were calculating its width in relation to the weight of her body and the speed acquired as it descended from the floor above. When she reached the street, she spotted him immediately, sitting at the wheel of a pale green car.

"My reputation is going to be ruined," she said, just to say something, as she slid into the passenger seat beside him. "I hope I wasn't seen by too many people."

"I doubt it. But do you really care what they might think?" he asked, smiling.

"Somewhat, even if only because my daily bread depends on it. But yes, I do care about what other people think. Everyone's different, and that's the way I am. So, yes, I hope no one saw me."

"I was expecting that you would have changed more," said Mário. "How many years has it been?"

"Haven't I changed then? You are sweet. But then you haven't either."

"Haven't what?"

"Haven't changed much. I mean, you look different, but you're not visibly in decline. Forty is a dangerous age, they say. For men, of course."

"You don't look more than thirty," said Mário. "And you're now..."

"Thirty-eight."

"That's right, thirty-eight." There was a silence, then he said, "I'm going to show you my house, if that's all right with you."

"Of course."

They drove around the Bairro Alto, finally stopping outside a large two-story house with a tiny garden surrounded by railings, behind which she could see two palm trees.

"This is it," said Mário. "It has a lovely view, though you'd never think it, would you? You can see the river and everything. It's the house I've always dreamed of having."

He opened the car door to let her out, then opened the door that led into the garden and then the door to the house.

"These two doors always remind me of that toy we all had when we were kids. A small box inside a bigger one inside an even bigger one. Do you remember?"

"I never had a toy like that."

He thought for a moment.

"Really? Are you sure? Perhaps I didn't have one either; that's quite possible, and yet I do remember that toy. I found the house by chance. I was just passing by and saw a notice pinned to the door. At first, I thought it was a demolition notice, since they seem intent on demolishing most of the city, but it turned out it was for rent. And I rented it then and there. I would have bought it if it had been for sale."

They went into a small hallway where there was a rather ancient oil painting, an old table, and two chairs. Mário opened a glass door on the right and smiled broadly as if silently asking: How do you like it? What do you think? Tell me.

She entered a large room and turned slowly around. Where could she find words to express her astonishment, eyes wide with delight, eyebrows raised? How long should she remain silent? It was lovely, really lovely, she said at last. Just gorgeous, Mário. Such exquisite taste. That chest over there was wonderful. And where had he found that tapestry? Those rich autumn colors. And the sofa? It was Venetian, wasn't it? She could tell at once. From the second half of the eighteenth century perhaps? She joined in the game enthusiastically, passionately.

"First half," he said. "Do you remember there was a big auction held in Sintra last month? Well, I had just arrived and, at the time, I still didn't have a house. I bought a few things with the intention of taking them back to Brazil with me. Then I changed my mind… They weren't that expensive. This chest, for example: How much do you think it cost me? No, no, nothing like that. It cost me twelve contos. You can pick up some real bargains at auctions sometimes. That's how I furnished my apartment in Rio. Of course, you need a combination of luck and judgement. You need to be a connoisseur. Otherwise, you can easily miss a real gem and get palmed off with some worthless imitation. Look at that picture, for example."

She sat down before a large, very dark painting of flowers, positioning herself so that the glare from the window didn't blot out the colors completely. Seen like that, almost all you could make out was a blood-red stain in the middle of a dark, glossy, cracked surface, but it was nevertheless very imposing. A museum piece. Very old, no, not just old, an antique.

"Artist unknown," said Mário, opening the door to the liquor cabinet.

"It's really beautiful," said Jô, standing up to take a closer look. "Very beautiful."

"It is, isn't it? Now, what would you like to drink? A whiskey?"

"I never drink whiskey during the day. Only at night, and even then, the conditions have to be just right. Actually, I don't really like the taste; I find it rather unpleasant, but don't tell anyone."

He gazed at her sadly.

"And there I was convinced you were a good drinking companion. Before…"

People have this obsession with connecting facts, with building bridges, or, as also happened, opening the floodgates onto rivers with no bridges or boats, rivers that create borders never to be crossed. She broke in:

"Oh, before! When we were that age, we liked pretty much anything that was forbidden. The thrill of smoking a clandestine cigarette! And as for drinking, well! We thought we were so grown up, didn't we? Then, as time passes, everything takes on its normal proportions and becomes merely an occasional pleasure or even just plain boring."

"Well, I love whiskey," he said very seriously.

Jô realized that, despite all she had said, she did want a drink. However, she preferred not to; it wasn't the moment.

The only important moments were those she spent alone. All the others were pure fiction and, only later, when she was alone, did they acquire a certain density and a relative reality. Sometimes, when she came home from school or when she said goodbye to Artur, it would occur to her to think, "Was I really me? The real me? The me who is here now, complete and always absorbed in myself?" It was only when she got home in the evening, or at night when she turned out the light, that those images acquired some substance, stereophonic sound, a more-or-less concrete meaning. Right now, in this unfamiliar setting, she was leafing through a few pages of a book she had put down many years ago, when she had barely begun reading it (she had been forced to put it down), and which she had just now opened by chance. A man named Mário, newly arrived from Brazil, was showing his house to a woman named Jô, who was exclaiming enthusiastically as she looked at various works of art. Enthusiastic exclamations and admiring words, which had so little to do with her that she even ended up glancing around her in search of someone else to attribute them to. They were, however, alone. So alone that he had opened the door with a key and not a sound was to be heard inside. Was there no maid? She thought. The situation suddenly struck her as somewhat compromising, but she reminded herself that she was, alas, no longer eighteen, but thirty-eight. Twenty years older.

"What are you thinking about?" he asked, now holding a glass of whiskey.

"I'm meditating," she said, "but don't ask me on what. My meditations have always been private and untransmissible."

"Always. That's what is so extraordinary about you. And so restful too!"

"What do you mean 'restful,' Mário?"

"All this. You being here and being just the same. And after twenty years have passed,"

She sighed and said:

"I suppose I am the same, but I've changed a lot too." And it seemed to her that she really had changed. She had loved Mário, and then she had loved Artur, but now she was dried up inside, and any feelings of love had dried up too.

Nevertheless, she wanted to feel happy like she had before, and she tried to return to the past, insofar as that was possible of course, and in a way that would hurt no one's feelings. To feel happy to be with Mário, alone with him, but it was difficult, not to say impossible, to return to one's youth. And yet she would like to run her hand over his smooth, thick hair and ask him for the *n*th time that day if he loved her. And to hear him say Yes. Simply because this would bring back what had happened then, at that time, her time. The question and the answer and the situation had long since expired.

"...and this room is pure Queen Maria," said Mário, concluding a sentence she hadn't heard. "But you must drink something. A Grand Marnier? A Marie Brizzard?"

She accepted a liqueur, hoping to find the courage to speak of a certain matter, as soon as she saw the way ahead was clear. Ever since she had entered the house—or, rather, ever since she had heard his voice—she had known that she had to speak about that. Mário, however, seemed to be wallowing in the present. He talked about Rio, his house in Rio, how he had often thought about coming back to Portugal.

"So, you're a rich man," she said, for want of anything better to say.

He pulled the contrite face, half proud, half embarrassed, of all rich men in this world. "Not rich exactly," he said. "Well, I have enough to live comfortably and not worry about tomorrow."

He made a point of saying this with an impersonal and, at the same time, disinterested air—and she laughed, because this was something new in him.

"It's funny," she said. "My cleaning lady thinks I'm rich because I earn more than she does. You don't consider yourself to be rich because above you rises a long ladder at the top of which sits who knows who, the Shah of Persia perhaps?" She laughed, then grew serious and turned to face him. "It's been ages since I laughed, you know. You have no idea how happy I am, how happy I was when I found out, I don't remember when or who from, that you were rich. You have no idea. It was, you might say, a liberation. I felt so guilty."

"There was no reason to feel guilty." He got to his feet, picked up a lovely ornate silver box, offered her a cigarette that she refused, then came and sat beside her on the Venetian sofa. Jô was wearing her usual placid face; her heart, though, was far from placid. "There was no reason," he went on. "If anyone should feel guilty, I should, because I never once wrote to you. But what can you expect? I remade my life, isn't that what people say? I tried to remake it. To be born again. It was enjoyable too. I was about to say thrilling if that word wasn't…"

She murmured, "Quite."

"I was a new man. I severed all links with the past: I changed scene, found new cast members, but, most important of all, I changed plays. And I was lucky of course. My uncle was just great. He pretended to know nothing about the whole affair, and neither of us ever mentioned it. I really loved him for that."

"And did he love you?"

"He had no one else. We bonded. It's good to bond with someone, even with an uncle you've never even met before."

She said:

"Yes, that must be good." Then she asked him for a whiskey. "But only a very small one. And even if I ask you for more, don't give it to me."

"Tell me about you," he said. "I assume you didn't marry."

"No, but why do you assume that?"

"I don't know. Perhaps because you haven't mentioned it yet. Or because someone else told me."

Tell me about you. When would he ask her if she was happy? She got it in before him.

"Are you happy?

"I think so," he said. "Not that I've ever examined the matter closely; I've never felt the need. Perhaps because I *am* happy. You must be thinking…"

"What?"

"That I've clung too tightly to the things of this world, and if so, you're right. But what are we to cling to in this world if not to them? Fortunately, I think I understood this early on."

"Yes, it's good that you did understand that so early. Tell me how it happened; what's it like?" She had always felt a great admiration for people who understand things early on, who don't have to wait until the end of their life or, at least, until they reach old age.

He stood up and started talking and gesticulating, as he used to do, pacing up and down and sometimes tripping on the rug.

"Well, it's this: Comfort, good food (I have the best cook in Rio, an amazing mulatto woman), a few women friends—none of whom I'm in love with, or just enough to deceive my heart. Before, I used to speak scornfully of 'the things of this world,' didn't I? Even that plan of ours was only intended to get us through to adulthood, wasn't it? But you know, it's important to be healthy, my dear, and that's what being healthy is. I don't know if you're following me... I mean, having good things, enjoying them, and thinking how extremely lucky you are because many people don't have them."

"Giving thanks to God."

"In a way."

Jô smiled contentedly, throwing herself, as she used to do, into one of these conversations they both loved and in which nothing much was said.

"There's your liver to consider, of course," she said. "A nice house, or two in your case, has never done anyone any harm, but good food, Mário, and made by the best cook in Rio, isn't that what you said? And then there's the drinking, of course. Don't forget about your liver. As for those lady friends, an excess of lady friends..."

"I'm a careful man. The occasional lady friend, the occasional lavish supper... In between, a chaste life, a little grilled fish, and a sip of whiskey, which never killed anyone. I'm a cautious fellow."

She again laughed gaily. Their love had been a happy one, however surrounded it was by the barbed wire of obstacles. Had Mário been different it would have been a love full of sadness and lamentations. With him, though, this was impossible. She remembered him as a discreet young man. Quiet and solitary sometimes, but at others, really happy, almost alarmingly exuberant and communicative. Impatient too, and changeable. His need for change, though, was purely physical, in revolt against static people and static landscapes. He was first here, then there. And she was the only one who understood that he was really always in the same place.

He was a nice boy, the Mário she had known. Was he any more than that? Was he? Everyone liked him, and he liked everyone; he was, if you like, an omnivore. And Jô had often wondered if there was much merit in the love he felt for her. He liked everyone equally and equally indulgently, almost, one might say, like a professional Christian. But she thought all this later on, when he had left, after he had been forced to leave.

"Anyway, I've told you about me," he said.

Now tell me about you, he must be thinking. About your life and loves, your problems. Why did you never marry? Because you didn't want to or because the right man never appeared?

She said quickly:

"You've really told me very little, Mário, and only briefly. I know you have a lovely home in Rio and now another—this one—in Lisbon. That you eat and drink well, that you have a few lady friends. All that is fairly obvious.

What about the rest?"

"No, it's too soon for that. We'll meet again I hope. What about you? You still haven't told me about you. I was told that you were or are in a relationship."

"Yes, but that didn't happen right away. I needed time to think."

"About me?"

"Not about you so much as about the fallibility of things, even the best-laid plans. They fall apart and nothing is left."

"Nothing at all?"

She wanted to say, "Nothing, absolutely nothing," which, two hours ago, would have been easy enough to say, but it was now much less so, and she said instead that sometimes something did remain, something imponderable or inexplicable, and she felt suddenly glad to have said it. Lighter, almost freer, but sad too, sad and happy at the same time. Mário was looking at her, unblinking, and it occurred to Jô that perhaps he was thinking something else and that there was still time to make a U-turn without a great squealing of brakes. This is what she imagined or understood, or at least suspected, and she laughed even though she didn't really want to, because she saw that he was about to speak and feared hearing unwanted words. She laughed then, but in a disciplined manner. A little light laugh, as if to herself, but also out of politeness.

"I don't think I should have come," she said with an exaggerated degree of nonchalance. "I should have told you that it looked bad and so on. Or simply that I was too busy, but I wanted to see you and talk to you. A battle between me and propriety!"

"I was thinking that I ruined your life."

Ah, so that was it. Jô lost all the combative spirit she had started to feel and all moderation too. She shrugged and held out her empty glass, which he silently refilled.

"I think we both did that, Mário. I'm talking about my life, not yours, because you've only gained by leaving. My life though… Well, if it hadn't been for that idea of mine… I was more to blame; that's the truth of the matter, and that's what I've always thought. It's true that you never did write…deep down, though, I think you did the right thing, I mean, the logical thing. We are all made to take care of ourselves; I'm more and more convinced of that. Of our own beloved bodies and minds. As for others, regardless of whether they're the love of our life or the grocer on the corner… We're the pits really!"

"Oh, come on!"

"Why? You would say the same or, rather, think it. Or at least feel it. We don't feel another person's headache; we don't die instead of them. We are, how can I put it, impervious. Why should such things be shared? It's impossible. You were and still are right. Having those 'lady friends' is a good idea. Excellent. You were born again, isn't that what you said? You were, of course. Tell me what you felt."

"Do you really want to know?"

"I do, yes."

"Well, I felt a great desire to be a different person, to do a lot of things and do them well, of course, and to be able to return one day as that different person."

"Purified."

"I wouldn't go that far. Something more modest. Cleansed if you like. At most, disinfected. There was nothing particularly lofty in that ambition."

"And you did return a different person, so you must

be very pleased."

"Yes, I am."

She stood up then and said goodbye because it was getting late and she had to meet someone. Mário asked if he could call her again at the school.

"Best not to," she said. "It could cause problems. Call me at home. I assume you can still remember my full name."

The dying day—the dying light—brought with it a bitterly cold wind. Mário offered to drive her home, but she declined. "I like walking, as you know." He did know and so did not insist. Jô set off down the street as if she had no particular goal, taking irregular steps, now long and slow, now very short and almost hasty, following the edge of the sidewalk, keeping a careful eye on the paving stones, worried she might stub her toe on a raised edge, barely visible in the nocturnal light of the streetlamps. She felt rather excited, with no sense of sadness or bitterness. It was a new feeling or, rather, a rediscovered one that she had not felt for a long time and that filled her whole being, spilling over into a faint smile she didn't even know was there.

Mário Sena: That is what her smooth, white hand used to write slowly, carefully, like someone painting a miniature. Beside it she wrote Joana Sena, but she didn't like that and corrected it to read Joana de Sena. A lovely name. It sounded good. She liked the sound of it. Later, there had been another possibility, albeit remote, and she had written Artur Fraga on the blank piece of paper, and after that, Joana Fraga. Poor Joana Fraga. Fraga, imagine!

In the darkness of her bedroom, with her head under

the covers, Jô was thinking about Joana de Sena and Joana Fraga, and about just plain Joana, about Jô, and she felt like weeping for all of them.

That night, the captain's cockerel crowed even more loudly than usual, extinguishing all of those images at a stroke with the sheer strident force of his call. In the distance, like lost echoes, other cockerels responded, first one, then another, and another. A chair creaked and she turned on the light and took a sleeping pill.

The temptation to shout in the mannequin's ear. The irresistible temptation to punish that diluted gaze, those sealed lips. Besides, she felt that people should speak during mealtimes, even if they had nothing to say; otherwise, there was something ignoble about their self-absorbed chewing. Even if they had nothing to say, which was not her case.

"Mário's here."

"Mário who?"

"Mário Sena."

"Sena…let me think…"

"He arrived from Brazil a month or so ago."

He understood then who she meant and let out a brief cry:

"Ah, your old boyfriend. Why didn't you say so? I know so many people. Mário… Mário Sena… How was I to know?"

Jô said nothing, and he asked:

"Who told you?"

"He called me at school. I went to his house."

"To Mário Sena's house."

"To Mário Sena's house."

He didn't even look up. He was occupied, even preoccupied, with liberating a bone from the fish on the plate before him, a fish with a golden skin and a creamy sauce, adorned with a single prawn. He raised the fork to his mouth, chewed, swallowed, discreetly wiped his lips, took a sip of white wine, called the waiter over to tell him the wine was warm. Then he looked at her, but his face expressed no feeling at all, not even surprise. A weary face, no, not even that, indifferent.

"And?" he asked.

"He insisted on showing me his house," said Jô. "He's very proud of it. It's his dream house and so on. He's been buying furniture at auctions."

"Is it a nice house?" he asked, showing a polite interest.

"Not bad. Too museum-like for my taste. Cold too. Furniture with a past, you know the kind of thing. The sort that makes you feel uncomfortable, awkward."

Artur ate a piece of bread.

"I find that shocking," he said.

"What?"

"The enthusiasm certain men have for décor. It has a whiff of the new bride in her new home or the homosexual in his bijou residence, if you know what I mean. Aren't you eating your fish?"

She realized that she had forgotten about the fish on her plate, and she found this as exasperating as his impassivity. The shout hadn't worked, she thought as she chewed laboriously. The mannequin hadn't even wobbled, not even a tremor. A twitch of the mouth perhaps, almost imperceptible. No, that was just her imagination. Artur's mouth didn't twitch, and she felt embarrassed because she had failed, and he knew—she was sure of this—he knew she had failed.

"Aren't you drinking?"

"The wine isn't chilled."

"I know, it's very annoying."

He again summoned the waiter, asked him urgently to bring another bottle. "Did you only talk about furniture?" he asked.

"No, of course not, although it was one of the main subjects of conversation. Furniture, paintings, auctions. All very concrete stuff. Mário has become very much the materialist."

"What did you expect?"

"Nothing, I suppose, which left me with all paths open. I hadn't seen him for twenty years, and in twenty years…well, it's only natural that people would change. Evolution and all that."

Artur said, "Quite." He handed her the menu. "Do you want dessert? Peach melba? And would you mind if I just glance at the newspaper? I haven't had a moment today…"

And the *Times* opened up between them.

ooooo

Jô turned out the light, and the room seemed suddenly small, poor, almost squalid. From the ceiling hung a bare lightbulb, and the curtains at the window were threadbare. On that day—why did she remember that day and not some other day?—they had been feeling sad, hopeless, and full of rebellious feelings. At least she was. But perhaps she had infected him, too, because Mário was frowning and staring into space. Lying side by side and yet so separate that not even their hands were touching. Two parallel rays of sunlight, once so warm, now ice cold.

"But why wouldn't they understand?" she asked when she could find the words. "It seems so simple. It *is* so simple."

"Perhaps not for them. They're old, remember. And they may not recall how it was for them. We've already forgotten what we did and said as children."

"And they haven't."

"And they haven't."

"When will they realize that their children have their own lives to live, that their lives belong to them and no one else? That they were once the way their children are now?"

"But they don't know that anymore, Jô. Don't you see, they've forgotten."

"Yes, you're right."

There was another silence, which she tried to end several times. It was, however, too dense a silence, made up of all the questions they were asking and that were churning around inside them. And every time Jô opened her mouth to speak, she wished she hadn't because nothing she might say was worth saying.

"What are you thinking?" Mário asked at last.

"Nothing."

"Tell me."

"It's not important."

"It might be."

"No, really, it's not important."

"They insist on seeing us as if we were children," he said. "They make me sick. They say I can only get married when I'm older; no, more than that, when I can earn enough to keep myself without having to go hat in hand to them for money. It's always about money. If only we could live without the stuff."

"Apparently we can't; it's just not possible."

"If there were some way..."

She still did not move, a recumbent statue, arms by its sides, blind eyes gazing up at the ceiling.

"There is a way," she said. "But I wouldn't advise you to take that route."

"What's that?"

He propped himself up on one elbow, waiting. "What?" he said again.

"Like I said, it's not advisable. Since we have to have money, we'll try and get some somehow, then hide away in some remote village until we're old enough. Where no one will know us. I love the countryside. It must be lovely in the spring."

"But how do we find the money?"

Another silence, filled with all kinds of answers. He, however, heard none of them and insisted, "Have you got an idea, then? Go on, tell me." Then more softly, "Unless you're thinking that I might... But I can't do that... My father..."

"If we hid ourselves away..."

Nothing more was said. They were afraid of their own thoughts, but they felt drawn to them too, seduced, and allowed themselves to be seduced. The two of them alone and without her mother's distrustful, accusing eyes on her whenever she came home late. "What time do you call this to be coming home? And don't tell me you're just back from school. I'm not a fool, you know." Without his father shouting at him whenever he mentioned getting married. "You're not getting married: I mean, you're barely out of diapers and already you're causing me problems, as if I didn't have enough to deal with… Marry? Grow up first, and then we'll talk again. You need to acquire a bit of common sense, no, what am I saying, a lot, if not it's Brazil for you, and there'll be no studying there, no, you'll work for your Uncle Ernesto!" Without having to see or hear them. Without the clock continually shouting out the hours that separated them. Alone and sole masters of their time. They gradually grew accustomed to the idea, and now that she had shared it with Mário, she felt less bitter and less alone. His father wasn't exactly rich, but he earned a good salary. What difference would a few *contos de réis* make to him?

Mário broke the silence, saying tentatively:

"It would have to be on the day he gets paid."

"Yes," said Jô quietly. "It's the twenty-fifth today, isn't it?"

"Twenty-sixth."

"Ah."

They left the room. Jô spent the next few days secretly packing a small suitcase with her most precious possessions and hid the case in her closet. At the bottom, she put the few bits of jewelery she owned: the ring, the gold chain and medallion, the little sapphire cross, the charm bracelet. Much later, she would often think how selfish she had been to encourage Mário to commit an act in which she herself would take no active part. She had only her own possessions in the suitcase.

Her mother never knew anything about it. She never found the suitcase hidden in the closet and never noticed that, one day, it had returned to its former place, along with the other suitcases, in the storage room. The one thing she did find strange was that Jô started coming home earlier in the evening and that the phone suddenly fell silent. None of this worried her overmuch, though, because she thought they were both too young, and, in her opinion, their relationship wasn't going to last anyway. That's a relief, she had probably thought. And despite Jô's concealed and unexplained tears, she felt content. "Sometimes people cry only to laugh later on," she would say. And she prayed to all the saints that Mário would not return.

Beaten, insulted, and alone, Mário, the inept and shamefaced thief, was at that point on his way to Brazil.

ooooo

"I thought my life was over, you know, had reached its inglorious end," he told her a few days later, in a café downtown. "I really did. Everything we had thought and felt. I've never been so unhappy or felt so grubby. I was a complete wreck. Oh, yes, I missed you, but even more important than that was the shame I felt just to exist, to be me, unable to escape myself. There I was on the ship, in first class (my father always cared about appearances), in the midst of all those kindly people who smiled at me and tried to strike up conversations. There was even a lady in her fifties, which seemed positively ancient to me then, who decided to be my protector. I fled, and avoided her like the plague. Then, one day, when I was feeling even more alone and abandoned than usual, I let her talk to me, and she told me then that she'd had a son whom I resembled, and that he had died in an accident. She had a photo of him in her handbag, and he did look like me, a really striking resemblance. I told her everything, imagine! And to my amazement, she smiled. 'Believe me, it's not that bad,' she said. 'The only question is whether your uncle will prove more understanding than your father. You're truly sorry for what you did, and that's the main thing. We've all done similar things in thought, word, or deed. Or worse things. You've never killed anyone? You're a saint! The number of people I've killed… The number of times I wished I had a magic lamp!' I remember saying to her that words were of little importance and thoughts even less so, but she didn't agree and gave me her reasons. Good reasons too. She spoke to me again—and at length—about the people she had, as she loved to say, murdered. And she persuaded me of course. I really wanted to believe it. Then when I arrived in Rio and was welcomed with open arms, the world seemed to me a marvelous place. I was walking on roses even if I did sometimes fear their thorns. Then, over time, I decided that there really were very few thorns."

"All this makes me think…"

"What?"

"That woman, your uncle, your father, especially him, whatever can they have thought of me? You did point your father out to me once, do you remember? He was walking up the Chiado on the righthand side, and we were walking down on the left. I would sometimes say to myself, If I ever meet him, I'll run away. And I would pray to God that he had never recognized my face."

"There was no reason to feel afraid, Jô; he never mentioned you," said Mário, slightly taken aback. "As far as he was concerned, you knew nothing about it, you never did. And when I think about it now, I didn't keep silent out of loyalty, but out of egotism. Yes, it was egotism. Basically, I felt proud—well, a residue of pride at least—about an act that was simultaneously shameful and regrettable. If I placed all the responsibility on your shoulders, my love, I would be in the sad position of a young kid blaming a cleverer one for leading him astray."

"Cleverer, are you sure?"

He said that, no, he wasn't sure, but that everyone would think so and that was what mattered. Then he spoke about his first few weeks in Rio and about the time, ten years later, when Uncle Ernesto had died, and, from one day to the next, he had become a man with money. With money. He still didn't use the word "rich." Jô listened and looked at him, and she had an odd feeling, which wasn't a new feeling, but one that had dissolved in time and was now being restored: the feeling that she had always known Mário. Not just since the day of her seventeenth birthday, when they had met at a dance at the Clube Brasileiro, to which she had worn her sky-blue taffeta dress, but before that, in another existence, where they had both lived, even though they had no memory of it. After all those years, he was again becoming a person who was important in her life. More than that, he may never have ceased to be important, despite her falling in love with Artur with an enthusiasm bordering on affectation. And despite her loving neither one nor the other now. Mário was far away, on the far shore, beyond all that sea and mist and days and nights of traveling, so faint and futile and lost somewhere over the horizon that most of the time she wasn't even conscious of his absent presence.

"What are you thinking about so deeply that you can't even hear me?"

"Nothing."

"You said that once before."

Jô shrugged and made as if to laugh, but immediately stopped because laughter seemed inappropriate. She always used to say that she wasn't thinking about anything, and Mário had remembered. Contented but serious, almost somber.

"It's impossible to say. I've never been able to explain my thoughts. It's as if you were to ask me to separate out the ingredients of a cake once I'd mixed them all up. My thoughts are a cake, and there comes a point when I can't remember what I put in the pan. I was thinking about you, of course. And about me. But what? Where were we?"

"Were you thinking bad things about me?"

"As if I could! And why would I? Oh, there was a time, and I expect I've already told you about that. I thought a lot of things about you, but I never wished you dead, I swear. They were bitter, but placid, thoughts. Mere cogitations on the absurdity of eternal loves. Then it all passed."

"Everything passes," he said.

"Yes, almost everything. Except…"

The waiter came over and asked what she wanted. Tea? Cakes?

"Yes, some of those very buttery ones with chocolate on top. What are they called?"

"Do you mean *londrinos*?" said the waiter. "I think that's what you want. Square ones, right?"

"Yes, square. Londrinos, that's what I want."

"Aren't you worried about putting on weight?" Mário asked once the waiter had left.

"If only! Fat women have such a smug look about them, as if everything in their life was hunky-dory… Say what you like about the sin of gluttony, but I would love to be one of those women whose skirt rides up a lot when they sit down, and who spend all their time tugging it down. Do you know the sort?"

He did, and asked after Paula, who used to be so fat. That was then, said Jô. If he saw her now… She never went above 120 pounds; she refused to.

They spoke about Paula for the rest of the afternoon.

"We talked about you, Paula," she said when Paula called her that night.

"And how is he?"

"Fine. Twenty years older, but then so am I. And so are you. I went to his house. He wanted to show me. He's so proud of it. He says he's going to come and stay here every now and then. *His* house. It was quite a shock, you know, to see him in *his* house. Artur says…"

Paula interrupted.

"Why a shock?" she asked.

"Because it was him, of course. He used to be so, oh, I don't know, such a free spirit… Tables were there for him to put his feet up on them. Now the tables are covered with bibelots, antique clocks inside glass domes. Things like that. He's so settled, so contented…"

Paula laughed out loud on the other end of the line.

"That's not so very extraordinary."

"No, you're right, it isn't. You must think I'm being a bit ridiculous."

"Not at all. Anyway, how did he seem to you?"

Jô thought for a moment.

"I don't know," she said at last. "I don't know yet. I'm a bit slow on the uptake; I always have been. It takes me a while to assimilate things, and occasionally, by the time I do, I've lost interest. That's the way I am, I'm afraid. Anyway…I definitely enjoyed seeing him. Besides, after twenty years, there was something we needed to clear up, or rather, talk through. Things left unsaid leave an unpleasant sense of unfinished business. That's why I was pleased to see him."

Paula did not pursue the matter, perhaps because she had played no part in it.

"I'm having one of my allergic reactions," she said. "It's ghastly. It happened just now. I suddenly had a weird feeling, as if my face no longer belonged to me. I stood up and went over to the mirror…" A suspense movie, pure Hitchcock, thought Jô. The music rising to a crescendo, loud enough to set your ears ringing. She stood up, went over to the mirror and what did she see? "You can't imagine what it's like. I very nearly screamed, which would have alarmed everyone, of course. Anyway, I managed to control myself. I came that close though. It has to be seen to be believed." The music was fading away now, until it vanished almost completely, leaving only the sound of fluttering wings. "It's happened before, but never like this. My lips swell up a little, and I know what to do: I take an antihistamine, watch what I eat, and the swelling goes down. This time I'm not so sure. I'm in a real state… It was something I ate at that cocktail party, but what?"

What? thought Jô. What? she thought again.

Her mother's heart condition had worsened, and she had gone to the doctor that afternoon. She called Jô as soon as Paula hung up, and her voice was quiet and fearful.

"I didn't even dare mention going on vacation. You know there comes a moment," she whispered as if it were a secret, "there comes a moment, and I know you won't understand this, but there comes a time when you feel you're beginning to decay, yes, decay, Jô. Your eyesight isn't as good as it was, you start having problems digesting food, your hearing gets worse, your heart begins to fail, not to mention your memory. Do you remember what a good memory I had? If anyone ever needed someone's phone number and didn't have the phonebook on hand, or a date or a name lost in the mists of time, they would come to me."

Jô said she thought her mother had a pretty reasonable memory, perhaps not as good as it used to be, but she would say it was still "effective," in that it only really retained what her heart deemed to be important.

"Ah, my heart, dear… I'm warning you, at thirty, we all start to decay. We take endless medications and smear ourselves with unguents to stave off total decay, but it never stops its inevitable advance," said her mother in her rather recondite language. "Day by day. Hour by hour. I don't want to die!" she screamed almost hysterically.

"Who's talking about dying?"

"I could live another five or six years, ten at the most. I know I can. I take Quinicardine at mealtimes, fill myself up with vitamins, take it slow on the stairs, eat sensibly. Then there are other worries, but we all have them, don't we? After a time, death is inevitable, but there are so many things I haven't done, Jô, and that I won't do now!"

"That's what everyone must think," Jô said wearily. "No one has done everything they wanted to do; everyone gets lost along the way."

"Yes, but we all worry about our own death. And this is my death, you understand."

It was five o'clock, and both students and teachers were getting ready to leave, when the head teacher asked Jô to go and see her. Jô had just spent three hours looking out over three different groups of small gleaming faces, all pink and white in the afternoon light, afloat in an odorless atmosphere. She found the head teacher sitting as usual behind her baroque desk with its twisted columns and heavy moldings. She was a dark-haired woman in her sixties, entirely dressed in black, but with a deceptively kind expression. She smiled when Jô entered the room and indicated the chair usually reserved for the mother of the student.

"I'm sorry to delay you, but I needed to talk to you, and this is the only time when there's any peace and quiet. In the breaks between classes, there are constant interruptions and it's almost impossible to exchange more than a few words. I hope I'm not inconveniencing you too much."

Firstly, she asked if she was still happy with her work. She was? Excellent. She felt it was important that all the teachers should enjoy working there. The school was like a big family, at least that's how she had always seen it. "That's what my mother—may she rest in peace—intended when she set up the school."

"I certainly have no complaints," said Jô.

"Good, and how about the girls?"

For about half an hour, they talked about the students, the good and the mediocre, those who might pass, and those who definitely wouldn't. They also discussed a private pupil that the head teacher would like her to take on. The girl's mother was a relative of hers.

Where was she heading with this? Jô felt that behind this conversation lay larger or at least more important issues that would soon take center stage, leaving any others to fade into the background. The head teacher was very skillfully skirting around the subject, drawing spirals that coiled, then uncoiled, circles and occasional straight lines. She tended to avoid the latter, though, perhaps considering them too easy and commonplace, something anyone could draw, the easiest of shortcuts available to anyone. Sometimes, she would linger over a particular point, then abandon it to follow long, convoluted paths only to return to the same place, where no one was now expecting her.

She rambled on about some pedagogue she had once read, about something her father used to say…then about her mother, poor thing, who had worked right until the end because she felt everything was so important. We are like stupid, imbecilic bees, she commented pensively. Then she hurriedly returned to the subject:

"The girl's mother has no illusions, because the child is nothing…special, shall we say, rather ordinary?" Jô smiled discreetly. As did the head teacher. The kind of regretful smile one would bestow on an inconsolable daughter and an illustrious relative bemoaning such ordinariness in their family. Ordinary. The casual, very slightly, just sufficiently, disdainful way in which she said the word "ordinary." No, nothing very special. However, she wanted to please the mother, who had asked her to find her a good tutor.

"That's all really. I won't keep you any longer."

Jô stood up, feeling disappointed. Would the head teacher leave it there? She proffered her hand, and the head teacher held on to it longer than usual.

"Well, I'm very glad to know that you're still happy working with us. I was afraid you might be thinking of leaving."

"Why?"

"When you marry, I mean."

"I have no intention of marrying."

She would like to have rephrased that answer, but it was too late. It had been said and was lost, launched into the world and now in the head teacher's possession. Someone had obviously seen her with Artur. Perhaps someone had told her about their affair.

"Ah, I thought..." began the head teacher raising her very dark eyebrows. "I was told that a few days ago, someone called and then came to pick you up in their car... If you have no intention of marrying, I assume this will not happen again; otherwise, I would have to ask you to avoid such phone calls and being picked up outside school. That would set a bad example, as I'm sure you understand. The little ones..."

"You can be quite sure that such a thing won't happen again. It was perhaps rashness on my part, but it was a friend I hadn't seen for twenty years and who had just returned from abroad."

"Of course, of course. I thought it must be something like that. But we must consider the little ones...and some families are very particular."

Jô realized that no one even suspected that Artur existed, and for a moment, this thought filled her mind. She was mechanically putting on her soft new gloves, which were the subtle, uncertain, slightly melancholy color of a dried leaf. They were hard to put on, and she had to ease them on over each finger, slowly, patiently. She concentrated on this task with great patience and attention, as if her whole life depended on how she put on those gloves. She wasn't looking at anything else, only at her small hands with their slender fingers, now almost chestnut brown and almost smooth. No, she wasn't looking at anything else, but she was a long way from there, a very long way.

The night was sometimes vast. And dense. So dense that the white cockerel could scarcely pierce it with his crowing. The air was no longer air, but an interval between things, empty space; it was made up of a thicker material, larger and more present and almost unbreathable. A room-sized muzzle was slowly approaching and about to cover her mouth. The furniture wasn't creaking either, or perhaps it was, but she couldn't hear it. On such nights, she would fling back the bedclothes and get up, regardless of the cold, and go into the living room at the other end of the apartment. There she would turn on the light; sit in her armchair; take up the first detective novel she found on the shelf; and drink one or two, sometimes three whiskies, making a face as she did so. It was alarming how light and easy and pleasant everything became, as if it took on a different tonality. She would gaze almost tenderly at the wet ring the glass left on the marble table top. And she would end up falling asleep.

So it was on that night. Except that instead of reading, she thought. And while thinking, she resolved a number of things. The alcohol was helping her to think and to resolve matters.

Artur is sitting there either beside her or in front of her, and the radio is broadcasting a concert.

"Will it last much longer?" she asks.

Artur tells her to be quiet and then, about twenty minutes later, when the mellow-voiced presenter tells the esteemed listeners that they have just heard Max Bruch's Violin Concerto No. 1 in G Minor, he crosses his legs and declares that not liking music shows a deplorable lack of sensitivity, an ugly defect that was nothing to be proud of.

"But I'm not proud of it; I'm just saying what I feel."

"You think it makes you more 'interesting' if you dislike something everyone else likes."

"No, you're quite wrong. I deeply regret not liking it. I loathe being 'interesting.'"

"Deeply regret. Loathe. What on earth has happened to you, Jô? Why are you being so over the top?"

She shrugs.

"Maybe I am, but I can assure you that I genuinely have no wish to appear 'interesting.' I insist on that."

"I'm sorry if I offended you. Far be it from me..."

She isn't in the least offended, but, rather, filled with despair. As if this conversation were terribly important. And she is annoyed that he doesn't finish what he was about to say, and wishes he would. She needs an argument, not an apology.

"A deplorable lack of sensitivity...fine, I agree. But it's hardly a grave matter, is it? It doesn't harm anyone, does it? Who is going to suffer because I don't like music? What does it matter if I am not to be seen at concerts or sitting by the radio? On the other hand, there are people whose deplorable lack of sensitivity can cause a great deal of suffering. Isn't that so, Artur?"

"Sorry?"

"I said, 'Isn't that so, Artur?'"

"What?"

"Oh, I don't know, Artur, I don't know, but I do know that it's all over between us."

He stares at her, uncomprehending. Then he asks her why. The expression on his face is almost pathetic. His mouth is slightly open, his gaze uneasy. For a moment, a very brief moment, he ceases to be a mannequin.

"Why, Jô? Is it because of Mário Sena?"

She shakes her head. That all ended a long time ago. And she hadn't even thought about Mário for years.

He says again:

"Why then?"

Why? She doesn't know. Perhaps because she hasn't achieved what she wanted, because that got lost along the way. Perhaps because their life together was always too sterile, with no roots and no flowers. No fruit, she thought. Perhaps because she had grown tired, simply that.

"I'm fed up with living in the shadows," she says. "No, 'fed up' isn't really the right expression—that implies some kind of strong feeling, even if only an unspoken one. Tired is closer to the truth. Exhausted. So deep in the shadows, Artur, that no one knows anything about our relationship. Not even at the bank where you work or at the school where I teach. And yet, the head teacher has already asked about Mário."

"And did you find that useful, Jô?"

"Yes, I did."

"Can you explain why, Jô?"

"No, I can't. I myself don't know. I haven't really thought about it. But I know it was useful. Mário is going to leave at some point, and he won't be back for a long time."

"He has a house here now, so perhaps he'll be back sooner."

"Possibly, but that really doesn't matter."

"I'm going," he says. "It's late."

"Yes, it is," says Jô.

She opens her eyes, then closes them and falls asleep, right there, curled up in the armchair.

Mário called and he sounded anxious and in a hurry. Or perhaps the anxiety and haste weren't just in his voice, but in him, and found expression in his rushed words.

"I'm leaving tomorrow. Just as I was thinking of having a quiet holiday, a day or so in Paris… I have to go. I've just received an urgent telegram. A complication, Jô. A really serious complication."

She asked:

"To do with business?"

"No, no, as I say, it's a really serious problem." He fell silent for a moment, then went on: "I think I just have to make the best of it and face it head on. It's a problem that, it turns out, I can solve with a single word."

"It's always good, feeling sure that you can do something, isn't it?" she said in a worldly-wise way.

Mário agreed, although he would have preferred not to feel under pressure to do it. "I think this is the moment," he said. "I think this time I'll have to get married."

"Good heavens, you're getting married?" And her ideas ceased being images and became small personal nebulae. "Married?"

"Given the circumstances…"

"Ah."

He asked her to forgive him, but it was highly unlikely

that he would be able to come by her apartment and say goodbye. He had various things to do, a few last-minute complications with the consulate. He hoped that on the next occasion they would have more time:

"We haven't even been anywhere together."

"No."

"It's just one of those things, but I'm planning to come back in the spring. Then it will be different."

"In the spring?"

"In April or May. It might be my honeymoon."

"That would be a good time to show your wife Europe."

"Yes, the weather should be good by then."

"And not too hot."

"Warm enough to swim in the sea."

"For some people, yes."

"Or for a trip into the countryside."

"Impossible though it might seem, I've never been to the countryside, or only very briefly. I was once all set to go and spend some time there. In the spring. But it came to nothing."

"Life."

"Yes, life. I always go to the beach in the summer, though. I'm usually the only single woman in the hotel. There's always one, I suppose. Like the village idiot or the street drunk."

"When I come…"

"When you and your wife come…"

"Yes, when we come."

"You and your wife."

"Me and her. We'll have to make a little trip into the countryside, the three of us."

"Yes, why not?"

"It's agreed, then."

"Agreed."

There was a silence, then he said:

"Don't think this is some kind of tragedy for me. She's pretty, she's eighteen, and I have to marry her. That's the way it is. But it's not a tragedy."

"I know it isn't."

"Goodbye, Jô. I'll write as soon as I arrive in Rio."

"Sure," she said, not that she believed him, but she spoke as if she did. "And I'll write back."

Mário hung up, and she sat there quietly, not thinking, the phone still in her hand.

That night, Paula's voice again told her that "that" wasn't a life. She first talked about other things and other people. And about herself of course. Such a busy life, Jô, so full of obligations. Some people never have enough time, and she was one of them. "Is that the time? Is it already the twentieth? How did that happen?" She never had enough time; it was dreadful. Francisco was different, he was amazing, he had time for everything and was never in a hurry. Her father had been the same. She went back many years and spoke about her father. She took short cuts, leaped over ditches and climbed walls. By that stage, poor man—by what stage, Jô wondered because she hadn't been following her—by that stage, he was having problems with his heart, but she didn't know, nor did anyone else. He must have known though. All the men on his side of the family had bad hearts, and that was what took them to their graves. Peaceful deaths. One night, her father had gone to sleep and never woken up. It was a family disease. Jô found herself thinking that Paula must find that "family disease" elegant and therefore worth milking. Something like the Habsburg jaw or the hemophilia found in Queen Victoria's descendants.

Jô gave some random answer, and it seemed to her that Paula was a happy woman and always had been. She had been at school too, except then she was more warily, cautiously happy. Happiness, though, was in her chromosomes. As it was in Mário's. Even if things appeared not to be going well for him, they would always turn out for the best. They were both clever at looking for happiness and finding it. The doors always stood open for them: Before they even knocked, or, at the very least, the first time they rang the bell, the doors would be flung wide. And people would receive them with open arms. They already had a place for them; they were expecting them to come. How so? "Why," the people would laugh, "we had a sixth sense, a feeling in our bones." Two or three such welcomes create a great sense of confidence and drive away any complexes, thought Jô. And even if other doors were opened with less enthusiasm, less quickly, the individuals in question still felt confident and invulnerable. They knocked or rang in a certain way and smiled loftily. And in they went. They pushed past other people, forged paths, obliging those others, by their mere presence, to leave their seats if necessary, so that they could sit where it best suited them.

"…and we'll probably spend Christmas in Paris. The Royers are very insistent, and Francisco is almost convinced."

"Really!"

"Can I bring you anything?"

"A pack of Gauloises."

"Goodness, you're easy to please."

"I am, aren't I?"

"You know, sometimes I really don't understand you."

"I'm an island, Paula." Yes, a small island, with no archipelago, surrounded by an unknown ocean and a mist so thick you couldn't see the ships, if there were any. But it would be only natural that there were. There are always ships around islands. She had visited an island like that once...

In her living room, seated on her sofa, Paula's voice was laughing. "Well, we're all islands; you're not alone in that."

"Yes, but I'm this particular island."

Small and with pebbly, rather unlovely, east-facing beaches. The sun abandoned them halfway through the afternoon, and then it was cold, and the water, which had been pleasantly warm until then, turned icy, opaque, full of life and death and mysteries. There was only one thing to do: go higher and higher in search of a little sun. However, the western side of the island was the realm of seagulls and steep cliffs. Things to be looked at. Noises that were silence. And she always ended up going back to the tent where she was camping with friends. Tired. Fed up. Wanting to leave and not leaving.

"But it's your life that's an island, not you."

"Yes, it's my life," Jô said. "But what am I without my life; what are any of us without our lives?"

"It's getting late, I'm off to bed," said Paula. "And your situation, has it changed at all?"

She closed her eyes or opened them. Tomorrow, she thought, I have classes, two private lessons, and a meeting in the evening with Artur. We'll go and have a coffee in Cascais or to Guincho beach, if it's not raining of course, and, at a certain point, he'll open the *Times* and read out the most important bits of news, because he's always up to speed on what's going on in the world, which is important, even pressing—now who used to use that word? As for me, I will wait patiently, or apparently patiently, for his daughter, one day, to marry.

Then all of this seemed to her unbearable, and she decided that the next day she would have a conversation with him, perhaps that one, perhaps another, but a definitive one in any case. Her mother was right. Paula was right. Tomorrow. She would phone him on purpose, she would ask him to meet her, she might even go to the bank. Tomorrow.

She was still thinking this when she fell asleep, and she did so peacefully. The night, though, was long, one of those very solid nights, so heavy they stop you from breathing and almost suffocate you. One of those nights. She woke up, took her sleeping pills, and dreamed of the father she had barely known, about her ancient mother, about fat Paula with her hair in braids, but she didn't dream about Mário. It wasn't a dream; it was a patchwork quilt. In the morning, the surface of the water was slightly ruffled—a mere shudder, a shiver—by the strident sound and by its echoes. She, though, had not quite come to, and only a part of herself, a very small part, heard those echoes. The rest, the most important part, was still hidden or forgotten deep down, possibly lost, in that place where no shadow fish slithered past. Among seaweed, empty seashells, and the skeletons of ships.

EVERYTHING IS GOING TO CHANGE

Freeze everything—things, people, moments—then rip off their veils one by one in order to take a long, hard look at them, and keep looking until your eyes hurt and your eyelids close from sheer exhaustion. Do this just so you can summon up enough courage. Scrutinize everything you're leaving behind, everything; see it properly and fearlessly for the first time, simply to confirm that you really don't have any regrets about leaving. No running away, no escaping down side streets, no ducking into the first open doorway. No dreaming. Above all, no dreaming.

He has lived—for how many years now?—on hopes built in the air with no foundations, no supporting walls, no roof, only open windows he never actually looks out of because he doesn't even dare to, or, at most, he takes a peep; besides, the windows all open onto an impossibility that he is gradually, fearfully beginning to absorb. He could not have survived without those hopes.

Suddenly, though, for some unknown reason, his dreams are not enough. Now there is always a broad, white swath of anxiety that coils around his chest like a serpent, squeezing him until it hurts and stopping him from breathing. And now it's not just his chest; the whole of him is being squeezed and squashed by multiple invisible rings.

In his dreams, his boss, Senhor Valdemar, would frequently heap praise on him and promote him, and Fausto would leave his office and stride back through the main office, past his colleagues' desks, as if he were walking down the aisle of a church. Everyone would look at him admiringly and respectfully, and trailing behind him would be the long, heavy mantle of his new post, that of office manager. This, of course, would have major consequences. His daughter could fulfill her dream of having piano lessons; his wife could afford to rest a little (they might even hire a maid); and, after twenty years of waiting, despairing and hoping in shared houses or in rented rooms, they would finally be able to move to an apartment all to themselves. And he, Fausto, could have a new suit made. How many years had it been since he had done that?

In other dreams, prosperity would arrive not through him, but through his daughter, who would marry—not the pale, scrawny boyfriend who planned to marry her and came each night to talk to her outside in the street (the landlady would not allow such shameless behavior in the house), and who earned a measly six hundred escudos a month, but a rich man with a car, a man who smoked American cigarettes like Senhor Valdemar. Or why not Senhor Valdemar himself? He wasn't that old, and he had plenty of money. Then, of course, they would immediately move, and he would get his new suit. The suit is one of his main preoccupations and has been for some time. The one he wears has been darned and patched from top to bottom. His wife has added patches inside to make it more resistant, but every day the cloth around the patches frays a little more, and she spends most nights darning.

Needless to say, he had a few supplementary dreams too. For example, finding a wallet in the street, which went unclaimed by its owner; or his Uncle Bento, who had left for Brazil when he was a boy, suddenly resurfacing after a nearly forty-year silence as an old man, on his last legs and stinking rich. And with him as sole heir. This, however, is an almost frighteningly lavish dream, and Fausto is a modest man. What would he do with Uncle Bento's millions? This is why he prefers the dream of being promoted—quite rightly—to the post of office manager or the one about Isaura getting married, which is, after all, perfectly possible. You hear such stories on the radio every day.

That would have been his preference. Now, though, he can no longer dream, and he wouldn't, even if he had the chance, even if that thing, whatever it is, didn't keep tightening its grip around his chest. What he wants is to look at things frankly, lucidly, and to see them clearly outlined against the backdrop of his empty life. Suddenly, his wife is that old woman, old and flaccid, worn out before her time, and it is all his fault. Is it? If it wasn't for him, if it wasn't for his dead-end office job, if that wasn't the only job he was capable of doing, they could both have had a very different life, in the village where they still had family. Their daughter could even have married a farmer with a little land of his own, who would have been delighted to marry a delicate beauty like her from the big city. A delicate beauty? The moment of truth has arrived. Isaura is ugly, like him; she has the same sharp nose, the same weak mouth, the same deep-set eyes. He no longer wants to delude himself, to dream. No, absolutely not. The dark room—the only room—with no sun, no view, no fresh air coming in through the window. No window. Not even a crack letting in the gray weather from the hallway. The paper-thin wall separating them from their daughter. The bathroom and the smell of the bathroom. The arguments in the kitchen when the wives are preparing the meals, and the smell of the rancid oil in which the typographer's wife fries potatoes. The shabby shoes with holes in them that they can never afford to get mended. Perhaps at the beginning of the month… But at the beginning of the month, there's never enough money to get the shoes mended, unless they do without something else: bus fare, for example. And for a few days—eight, ten, fifteen days—Fausto leaves home earlier than usual to arrive at work in time to sign on. His daughter spending all day sewing. His wife's lined face and her legs so swollen she can barely walk. The sharp-tongued landlady, who always demands that the rent be paid on the first day of the month and who is always hinting that, if they don't like it, they can leave. And if that hypothetical marriage did take place, well, there's no reason why it shouldn't—after all, he got married and so did his wife—his daughter would move into a room identical to theirs, possibly worse, possibly without even a narrow transom window giving onto the hallway, where she would live to the end of her days.

Dreams are no longer enough, because everything has become too big, too sad. And Fausto wishes he could die. Death seems to him the only solution. It would bring calm and serenity. And God? Gradually, without even realizing it, he has completely lost sight of God, ever since the day he and his wife got married in the village church full of white roses. The fact is that God had never again made his presence felt, and Fausto has never been good at asking favors of others, or asking for their love, be they gods or men. And now he's all alone.

Despite not feeling hungry (his stomach hurts, he says), he has just finished his evening meal of tomato rice and fried fish. He leaves the table and puts on his hat. He's going for a walk, he says, he won't be long, see you later. His wife stares at him in bewilderment, and says, yes, all right, see you later; and Isaura says nothing because she has noticed nothing and is concentrating on finishing the dress she has to deliver tomorrow afternoon.

Fausto looks around, taking in, in that one glance, his wife, his daughter, and the rickety furniture that grows frailer with each change of address. Not that he waxes sentimental—he is not a sentimentalist. He doesn't kiss either of the women goodbye; he doesn't say a word that they might be able to interpret later on. He has made his decision: He is going to be the victim of an accident.

He starts walking, and his footsteps echo strangely in the night. He walks down Rua das Pretas and finds himself on the Avenida. He crosses it carefully, looking right and left (the moment has not yet arrived), and then continues walking slowly along, keeping very close to the edge of the sidewalk, near the road itself. There are not many cars at that hour; he has not chosen a good time. But he can't go home now. He feels that to do so would be an act of cowardice, and Fausto doesn't want to be a coward, anything but that. He hears the long, slow steps of other passers-by, people out for a post-supper walk. A black car is approaching fast, and Fausto feels that he must seize the opportunity. He waits for the right moment, closes his eyes, then launches himself into the road.

ooooo

However, he steps back as quickly as he stepped forward. There is a strange noise, as if something inside him had torn, perhaps his heart, which feels suddenly larger, and the black car whisks past his feet, leaving him untouched. Fausto struggles, but the hand gripping his right arm is strong, or perhaps stubborn, and won't give an inch. He stops struggling and surrenders, then turns cautiously round.

"What were you about to do?" someone asks.

Fausto gives a faint smile, but that suggestion of a smile didn't have its origins within him; it's quite independent of him, meaningless. It simply appeared.

"I was about to cross the Avenida," he says at last. "I was going home..."

"You were about to throw yourself under that car. I could see that you were about to step forward. I was watching you, just in case, and I saw what you were going to do. Fortunately, I have good reflexes."

In a dull, foolish voice, Fausto repeats, "Fortunately... good reflexes..." but he doesn't know what he's saying. He has still not quite understood what has just happened. He is in a state of utter incomprehension, and even the sounds he makes seem somehow different. Slowly, though, normality is returning, and Fausto is standing on the edge of the sidewalk beside a man who still has a firm grip on his arm, as if he were afraid Fausto might try to throw himself under another car.

Fausto delicately tries to free himself. Life has taught him to be delicate, even with busybodies, or especially with them. This is why, with an effortless bow of his head, he says:

"Thank you."

A happy smile appears on his companion's young face. Young? Perhaps he isn't so very young. An unlined face anyway, with youthful, unfinished features. They begin to walk along together in silence. Then the stranger starts talking, quickly, about fate, chance, and God, carefully measuring out each concept and placing them in separate compartments. Sometimes the ideas overflow and intermingle a little, and God and chance find themselves face to face. This, however, is a brief, fortuitous encounter, and one of them is immediately obliged to withdraw and make way for the other, and this happens so quickly, and the man's voice is so convincing, that Fausto doesn't even notice and, even if he had, he might perhaps have found such an encounter perfectly natural.

He tries to leave. Once and then again. He is straying too far from the dark, malodorous room to which he will, ultimately, return. He has spent all his courage, squandered all possibilities in that one failed attempt. He tries to pull away. The other man, however, continues to grip his arm, and, as Fausto now realizes, he is drawing him along with him.

"Let's go to my house. You need a drink. Then you'll feel better."

"It's getting late…my family…"

"For someone who had no intention of going back home, my friend, it's still early."

Yes, it's still early. And Fausto listlessly allows himself

to be led who knows where. They turn to the left, cross the tram line, walk up another street, stop, get into an elevator full of mirrors.

"I wouldn't want to inconvenience anyone..."

"I live alone."

"Yes, but isn't it getting late?"

A small hall with lights on the wall and curtains covering the doors; a living room where two of the walls are lined with books, paintings, and trinkets that seem quite marvelous to Fausto; the deep, soft, welcoming armchair into which he allows himself respectfully to fall.

Now he has a glass in his hand, and a golden liquid he had believed lost in the mists of time—How long has it been since he drank a good cognac? How many has he drunk in his entire life?—is filling him with a strange feeling of wellbeing, a light, gently euphoric state. He has a vague memory of trying to throw himself under a black car, but he doesn't know exactly why or where this happened or if it was a long time ago or right now.

"You may not appreciate what this means to me."

It's the other man speaking. He has an odd face, a very fixed gaze. Fausto finds himself smiling wryly, as if he found the situation amusing.

"Perhaps not."

Suddenly, he is waiting, almost eagerly, for the other man's response. However, the man says only that it's hardly surprising that Fausto should feel confused and offers him a Chesterfield cigarette. Fausto has seen such cigarettes in Senhor Valdemar's office but has never smoked one. Besides, it's many years since he smoked anything, since he lost that expensive habit. Now though... Today is different... Today perhaps...

The man uses a lovely golden lighter to light his cigarette and looks in his direction, but not at him. His gaze is so intense that it goes straight through him, is lost—more sword than gaze.

"I turned thirty-nine a week ago, and so far nothing has ever happened to me. *Nothing*. And yet here I am, having saved someone's life. Your life. I didn't choose to; I just happened to be there, close enough to reach out a hand. But it was so important to me, my friend, do you understand?"

"Not many important things do happen in people's lives," says Fausto, not knowing what else to say.

"True. And that's true of anyone's life. But people don't realize this and believe that important things do happen. I was waiting for something…I've always been waiting. For what? I don't know… To make someone happy perhaps. Completely happy, I mean. To give them everything I have, for example, although that's impossible. I did actually try to do that once, but without success. She didn't understand; she never understood anything. She thought it all rather vulgar… And, when I think about it now, I'm not sure I even loved her. Ridiculous, eh? The stuff of a cheap novel, don't you agree?"

No, Fausto doesn't agree. He understands, he corroborates, even while disagreeing. Does he openly disagree? No. The truth is that he has already drunk his cognac and is gazing absently at his empty glass. He is no longer in the room he first entered, but in an atmosphere into which he has slowly dissolved. He is studying, with neither wonder nor admiration, the large multi-colored painting to his left.

"That's an abstract painting, isn't it?"

The other man looks at him, surprised at this sudden leap in space, and follows his gaze.

"Yes, it is. Don't you like abstract painting?"

Fausto shakes his head, and the other man starts talking about Braque. Who's Braque? thinks Fausto fleetingly as he begins his second drink.

"I must go," he says. "It's getting late."

Late, late, LATE! says the echo inside his head. How often has he uttered the same meaningless words?

The other man makes a gesture that prevents him from standing up. From a distance, without a word. Or perhaps all Fausto saw was that one white hand, and the words were lost in his incipient drunkenness. Whatever the truth, the gesture immobilizes him; he remains motionless, pinned to the spines of the books on the shelves.

"I would like to do something for you, to help you, insofar as I can. Why did you want to die? Lack of money?"

Fausto opens his mouth, but cannot find any words. In that room, holding that glass, he can't explain to the man that he wanted to die because of the bad smell in the house where he lives; because of the dark, sunless room; because of his daughter's marriage and his shabby shoes and his threadbare suit and so much else, so much else... He can't, it's too complicated.

"It's too complicated," he murmurs. "We reach a certain stage in life and discover that... how can I put it... that we..."

His sentence remains hanging in the air, and no one takes it up in order to continue it, not even him. There is no way of continuing.

He stands up and only then does he notice that his right sleeve is ripped from wrist to elbow. This leaves him feeling so distraught that he cannot even hear what is being said to him, the explanation. He knows only that his sleeve is ripped and that tomorrow he won't be able to go to the office. And, of course, he has to go to the office tomorrow. That is the natural order of things, the very order he has so signally failed to escape from. The man says:

"That was my fault. I must have done it when I grabbed your arm."

As if this admission of guilt could console him. As if the fact that the other man had done it, and not him or the cloth itself, could be of any help.

Why did that man have to be there at precisely that moment, why there and not a few feet behind or ahead or to one side? Why?

If he had been a few feet away, or even a few inches, he wouldn't have been able to reach out his hand, and Fausto wouldn't be sitting in this apartment or anywhere else. He raises his eyes from his empty glass, once again empty, and which he doesn't recall having emptied, but the other man is no longer there—he has run out of the room only to return at once carrying a brown suit.

"Put it on and see if it fits. I'm sure it will. We seem to be about the same size or similar. You're thinner, but that might help, because I may be a little shorter. Go on, put it on. The tailor sent it to me yesterday. It's brand new, never been worn. It's lambswool, feel it."

Faust feels it, puts it on, buttons it up, bends down, turns around, and he's surprised. The suit fits him well, like a glove. Should he thank the man? Should he accept it as a perfectly natural gift? The other man, however, is pressing a visiting card into his hand.

"Come and see me tomorrow at this address. I'll see

what I can do to help you. Really. Tomorrow."

Fausto steps out into the cold street. He feels happy.

The effects of the alcohol? Possibly, but largely it's that brand-new suit that has never been worn before and that is made to last ten years or more; and it's also the visiting card in his pocket, the card that his fingers are holding and stroking. He can't wait to get home and tell his wife and daughter everything. But tell them what? He can't tell them he tried to kill himself. He could say he met a friend he hadn't seen for years. Maybe… He feels happy. He has forgotten all about the bad smell, the rancid oil, even the boyfriend who only earns 600 escudos a month and wants to marry his daughter. Everything seems suddenly possible, as if he had regained the ability to believe in his dreams again. Tomorrow, he would go to that address… Yes, now he knows that something is going to happen; he is quite sure of this. Things can't go on as they are, not now he has that lambswool suit. Yes, it would be strange, almost ridiculous, now that he has that brand-new, never-before-worn lambswool suit and that visiting card in his pocket: with those two things and his wife… and his daughter…and the house… No, no, it's impossible. Everything is going to change.

It was at precisely this moment, as he was crossing the Avenida to walk back up Rua das Pretas, that Fausto was struck by a car. He died on the way to hospital. And that brown lambswool suit remained an indecipherable mystery to Isaura and her mother.

ROSA AT A SEASIDE GUESTHOUSE

She turned around slightly, discreetly (or was it just her custom to turn around like that?), and her large greenish-yellow eyes, the color of a dried leaf, very lightly brushed his, only to withdraw at once, perhaps surprised or summoned by other more interesting things, fluttering here and there, lingering over a passing hat, before alighting once more on his eyes as if still uncertain: Was it or wasn't it him; could it be? It could. He felt like cupping his mouth with his hands like a megaphone and bellowing: It's me, it's me, or else getting up and running over to the table where she was sitting sipping her drink through a straw, and holding out his hand to her, just like that, frankly and openly. How have you been since that dreadful day, that dreadful hour? How are you, Rosa?

Her name was Rosa. Rosa. It couldn't be anything else. Could she possibly be called Maria or Berta or Ana? No, it had to be Rosa! He enjoyed slowly turning the name over in his mind, and sometimes, when he was alone, murmuring it to himself, savouring it in leisurely fashion, whispering that name in duple time, Ro-sa. A name of which she was sole owner, that belonged to no one and nothing else. She was Rosa, and the word, even in the middle of a sentence—any sentence that referred to rose blossoms—would immediately evoke her image as rose-woman.

And there were, of course, endless images of Rosa. Rosa swimming in the tranquil, almost-blue waters. Rosa asking at reception if there was a letter for her, a letter that never arrived. Rosa having lunch in her corner of the dining room, looking serious, almost absent. But the image that appeared most often on his private screen was not, alas, one of the best, even if it was definitely the clearest, simply because he had focused on it for longest. In that image, he was free to observe Rosa because she was utterly defenseless, lying, eyes closed, on a faux rustic bed, with, to her right, on the bedside table next to the lamp with the round yellow shade, an empty glass and a tube containing some sedative or other with a name suggestive of belladonna.

He had been the first to enter the room, since he had priority—he had after all deserved it—pushing aside the very nervous owner of the guesthouse, and the chambermaid, who had set down on the carpet in the corridor a tray of empty bottles in order to open the door with her pass key.

"I knew it! You can see now that I was right. See? See?"

Of course they could see—they could see nothing else—but neither of them said, yes, he had been quite right, because they had more urgent things to do: most important of all, calling for the doctor. Or perhaps the Red Cross. This was why the owner had gone clattering down the stairs, closely followed by the chambermaid, who had now picked up her tray and urged him, amid all the excitement, to stay there and keep an eye on Rosa.

At that point, he still didn't know her name was Rosa, nor, in retrospect, that he loved her. He had been discreetly courting her, with meaningful glances and the occasional vague murmured "Good morning," but as for loving her… He knew only what everyone else knew about her, and he wasn't particularly impatient to know more. He knew that she had been alone for nearly two weeks at the small guesthouse, that she appeared not to know a soul, spent all her time swimming or lying in the sun, and had lovely pale eyes. No, that wasn't all. He knew too—and this was the most important thing of all—that on that same morning she had gone into a drugstore—where he happened to be buying some toothpaste—and, in a soft, embarrassed voice that seemed to stumble over invisible obstacles, she had asked for a tube of Veronal.

"You can only get that on prescription."

He had seen her hesitate, like someone who hadn't been expecting to find the road ahead blocked and cannot immediately think of an alternative route. She could perhaps have asked for something to help her sleep or an ordinary painkiller like Saridon, just to do something. Instead, she had turned and left without saying another word.

The pharmacist was the one who had sown the seed of doubt in his mind when, as he was wrapping up his toothpaste, he muttered something along the lines of:

"I wouldn't be at all surprised if she was planning to do something foolish."

"Not necessarily…but why do you say that?"

"Because she asked for Veronal. There are other equally strong substances, of course, but she specifically asked for that, which makes one think... Then there was the look on her face..."

"What look?"

He had only been aware of her voice. He had seen from the side, seen her flattering outfit—flowery slacks and black blouse—and nothing else.

Apart, that is, from what the pharmacist said. And this was why he noticed when Rosa (who wasn't yet Rosa) failed to come down to supper. He had eaten his meal with some difficulty, his eyes fixed on her empty table. The guesthouse steak, like all beef steaks, had rolled up into a ball in his mouth and, when he tried to swallow it, had become a hard, dry lump, which, for some reason, his saliva refused to soften into something edible. He had left his table before coffee was served and gone over to the door where Senhor Costa was sitting in a wicker chair whistling to himself as he gazed out, enraptured, at the night.

"Has the lady who usually sits at the table in the corner already left?"

"No, she asked not to be called. She's not feeling well and doesn't want any supper."

He told Senhor Costa about the scene in the drugstore, but Costa's response had been an outright refusal to believe that anyone could possibly do a thing like that to him, Costa. That anyone could be so inconsiderate as to cause such trouble for a poor man who relied on the guesthouse for his living. Especially with the sea so conveniently close.

"Besides, given that he didn't sell her the stuff..." he had concluded in a feeble, semi-acquiescent voice.

But couldn't she have bought it elsewhere? It wasn't far into town. Or perhaps she had thought it through, as would seem logical, and bought something else, even aspirin. Or even slit her wrists…

The idea of a room spattered with blood made Senhor Costa leap up. He still hesitated though. What if she were simply sleeping?

"Then she probably wouldn't even notice you going into the room."

And she hadn't. She was lying across the bed, still in the same slacks and black blouse she'd been wearing that morning. Between her lips, from which all trace of lipstick appeared to have fled, was a very unpleasant bubble of saliva. Her breathing was labored and she was moaning softly.

He had been left alone with her—to keep an eye out—and he was wondering what could have led to that situation. Loneliness, of course.

It was always loneliness. Almost always. She looked healthy enough.

Only once they had taken her away had he discovered her name. Rosa Lima. He had discovered, too, that he loved her, but this knowledge arrived more slowly, little by little, so very slowly that, by the time he realized it, he had already lost track of her. She had gone home, the hospital told him, but they didn't know—or didn't want to tell him—where she lived or even in which city. Besides, when he thought about it, what was the point of him knowing where to find her? He couldn't just turn up at her house and say, "It's me, the man who saved your life on such and such a date…" Who knows, she might curse the person who had saved her.

It was a problem that could lead to many questions, and he didn't shy away from them. Now that he loved Rosa, he welcomed everything that this brought with it, even the—perfectly plausible—idea that occurred to him from time to time that she would have come to hate the person who had thought to open the door of her hotel room. For, by saving her, he had implicitly become the person responsible for her death, not the one she herself had sought, but the other death that would inevitably arrive one day. What would that death be like? When? The sad death from old age of a poor woman grown senile or paralyzed? Cancer? A car accident? Heart disease? Whatever it was, even another suicide attempt, *he* was responsible, he was to blame, as he was for all the sorrows and all the pain she might one day feel, for those moments of loneliness too, those very difficult moments that (as she well knew) make us almost cry out, perhaps simply in order to have someone look at us and actually see us and think about us, just for a moment. Yes, he was the person responsible.

And now, months later, exactly eight months later, there she was sitting outside a café in the Avenida, where he happened to stop for a beer, and her eyes lingered pensively on his. Someone must have told her what had happened. It didn't matter who.

Somehow or other, he found himself standing beside her table, his glass of beer in his hand.

"You probably don't remember me..."

She smiled and responded immediately, unhesitatingly, that of course she remembered him, remembered very clearly... He always had a book with him, didn't he? On the beach, he was always reading. In her mind, he was the young man with the book. It was poetry, wasn't it? No? She had thought… It had seemed to her… She asked him to join her, and she spoke about the weather. He, however, wasn't listening. He was still thinking about something she had said earlier. "In my mind…" He had been in Rosa's mind.

Her eyes—her hazel eyes, no, what was he saying, they were as green as the leaves on the trees—would touch him fleetingly then glance away as if afraid. Rosa opened her handbag and took out a pack of cigarettes. With nervous, incoherent gestures she lit one—he was too busy gazing at her face to offer to light it for her—raised it to her lips, put it down, then looked vainly for an ashtray, before tapping the end of the cigarette so that the as-yet non-existent ash fell to the ground.

"Did you stay for much longer?" she asked suddenly.

"Only two or three days—yes, I think it was three."

He felt himself blush, which was most disagreeable, like being a child. Rosa would laugh at him. No, perhaps she wouldn't: she wasn't, she couldn't be the sort of person who would do such a thing. Nevertheless, it annoyed him that she might notice his confusion.

"You were the one…yes, I think you were the one…"

The one who had found her, making it possible for her to be there now, in that muslin dress, sipping a honey-colored drink; or the one who had obliged her to go on suffering, to continue her lonely life, smiling wanly, saying words she didn't mean, pretending, existing? For which of those things had he been responsible by saving her from death?

"Yes, that was me. I saw you in the drugstore, you see, asking for a tube of Veronal…"

She sat very still, slightly stunned. Then she gave a short, unnaturally nonchalant laugh, only to immediately grow serious again.

"Such strange things happen to people," she said then. "You mean you were in the drugstore...fancy that! I didn't see you. I have absolutely no recollection of your being there. I was having a very difficult time. Too much work, I think. I couldn't sleep, even on vacation, even at the beach. It's terrible not being able to sleep. Do you sleep well? You can't know what it's like then... I managed to buy something else in town, but I think I took too much of it. I can't remember now how many pills I took. It seems that the dose wasn't fatal, though, far from it, but I slept for hours and, when I woke up, I was in the hospital. It was all most unpleasant..."

She shuddered like someone who has just made some terrible blunder and then started talking very quickly:

"Please don't think, though, that I'm not grateful, on the contrary. You were just amazing. It's so rare for someone to feel any concern for other people, for someone they don't even know... I even tried to find your address so that I could thank you, but Senhor Costa had lost it."

"He seems to lose everyone's address. I tried to get in touch with you through the hospital..."

She gave another brief laugh:

"How lucky, then, that we should meet now. I wasn't sure, but it did seem to me that..."

There was a silence, during which Rosa eyed him anxiously, but he was too absorbed in his own thoughts to notice that look.

"You mean that it wasn't...that you weren't attempting...?" he asked at last.

"No, of course not. Is that what you thought? Did you really? Why would I have done that? There was no reason... Really, there was no reason. I just wanted to sleep. Please, believe me, I'm telling you the truth. Why would I lie to you?"

Yes, why? And yet he still found it hard to believe her.

"You mean...you mean..."

He was standing up now, without even realizing that he was, and then she, still a tad anxious, held out her hand, clasped his hand tightly, and, without the flicker of a smile, suddenly strangely serious, suddenly older too (where had all those lines on her face come from?) asked him to drop by and see her one day, so that they could have a more leisurely talk. They were old acquaintances after all...

"I'm in the phone book. Under Rosa Lima."

Her voice was again soft and uncertain, stumbling, falling, then getting up again, as it had been on that morning when she went into the drugstore.

"I'm at home most afternoons."

He bowed slightly, then looked at her without really seeing her, feeling suddenly weary:

"See you again soon then, Rosa."

He spoke her name, and it was a perfectly ordinary name—no, worse than that, it was positively banal (he remembered that, when he was a child, their cook had been named Rosa), and it left no lingering taste in his mouth. Then he walked away between the other tables, unaware that her large, anxious eyes were following him, once again disillusioned and bewildered. He didn't see her eyes because he didn't look back. It didn't even occur to him to do so, what was the point? He remembered then that he hadn't introduced himself, and this fact bothered him because it seemed so rude. But perhaps it didn't really matter. A faint, distant thought was making its slow approach: He never would go and visit Rosa; indeed, she had, at that very moment, already begun to fade in his heart.

ANICA, AS SHE WAS CALLED THEN

Seated on one end of the sofa, his eyes vacant, half-closed, the major was thinking laboriously and intensely about nothing at all. Because inside his head, behind that ample forehead, slightly domed and very pale (the pallor of a soldier with no war to fight), the major could find only a high, smooth, white wall, desolatingly impossible to climb—the wall separating the present from the lost past, which had left nothing behind, not even a brief, fugitive memory.

True, there was the face of that woman sitting opposite him and slightly to the right, and that seemed terribly important among so many other faces of no importance whatsoever. There were her pale, slightly squinting eyes, her sparse eyelashes that trembled in the light, fluttering like those moths so fragile they barely exist, the sort that feed on wool and crumble into dust if you touch them. Her voice, at once hesitant and serious. A placid voice, without the hint of a smile. And those slightly raised eyebrows, naturally high and thin, as perfect as if they had been drawn in pencil. Old-fashioned, even antiquated, eyebrows, and quite different from other eyebrows. There was an expectant air about them, or perhaps a touch of incredulity: "Really? Is that true? Are you sure?" Or something along those lines. And what about her hands? It was as if they, too, were familiar to the major: large but slender, with long, bony fingers and unvarnished nails. He noticed this because all the other women present had painted their nails blood red or shocking pink. Luísa, who wasn't there, and who had left one day without a farewell note, used a mother-of-pearl shade of varnish. That other woman's hands were naked and very still: serene, modest, and averse to any exhibitionism, but not at all shy, definitely not. They were simply there, not retreating or advancing one millimeter. The major studied them intently where they rested on her round knees, one on top of the other. She didn't need them to talk. Nor did she need them to pick up a cigarette (she didn't smoke) or a glass. She had just said that she never drank alcohol. "Does it not agree with you?" someone had asked, feigning interest. "No, I just don't like it," she had replied as if it was a matter of no importance. Even then, though, she hadn't smiled to apologize for this strange dislike. The major felt that it would be only natural to smile and that, in the same situation, he would definitely have smiled at such a clear-cut declaration of abstinence, a slightly embarrassed and apologetic smile. However, despite all this information, the major could still not climb that wall.

The woman had returned to Lisbon from abroad a few days earlier, and from the conversation he'd overheard, but in which he took no part (because he was listening and watching too hard), he gathered that she was married and that her husband was a diplomat. Her name was Adriana, again a suitably serious, rather old-fashioned name. Adriana Moura. That name, however, either in part or whole, meant nothing to the major. It was a new name, newborn, unattached, which set off no echoes in his memory. He had never known an Adriana, and the only Moura he could recall had been his math teacher. Besides, the major was not a man to connect names with the people they belonged to. He remembered the people and remembered the names, but separately. He was certain, though, that he had never heard that particular name.

"Never staying in one place for long becomes very tiring eventually," he heard her voice say rather solemnly, as if the wearisome business of never staying in one place for long were a matter of grave importance.

"Absolutely," said the fat, jewel-laden woman with whom she was talking. "Absolutely."

"It takes a while to get used to a place, and just when you're beginning to feel comfortable and at home, almost as if you belong, off you go again to the other side of the world."

"It must be very tedious, and yet..."

"Yes, there are positive aspects to it. The boys are already fluent in three languages. The youngest can even understand Flemish, which is a real nightmare of a language. And there's never time for us to get tired of the people or the cities. There's never time for us to get tired of anything."

The fat lady then said that she had no gift for languages herself, which, she thought, was a great pity. Her accent was appalling, even in English, which she had spoken since she was a child. She had no ear for it, that was the problem; she had a terrible ear for languages.

The major decided to break free—what was he doing there anyway?—so he left the sofa and made his way over to join a group of men standing near the window who might perhaps be discussing politics. "Excuse me. Sorry, may I get past?" All around him were lights of different tonalities, from pale café crême to an almost dazzling white, from a sandy yellow to a soft pearly glow. Coming from four different lampshades, the tones interpenetrated and finally fused into a single color that made the women's skin and arms and shoulders a uniformly unreal white. Too white to be ordinary skin. Some people were sitting down, others standing up, and one young woman with red hair had sat down on the floor with her glass beside her. He had, as usual, remembered the names he had been given, but had no idea who they belonged to. They were abstract, incorporeal, mysterious names. Maud Navarro. Afonso Nobre the writer. And still more. But which one was Maud Navarro and which one Afonso Nobre the writer? Who were all the others? He had fixed only on Adriana Moura, her face, her hands, her name. Where did he know her from? Where had he met her? When?

The major had great faith in the Common Market, as he declared to Fontes, the party's host, a huge, fat, greasy man, who had no faith in it at all—"None at all, my dear Aníbal, and I'll tell you why…"—and at the same time the major was thinking, still thinking, that he had met that woman before, had perhaps spoken to her, at least seen her flutter those pale eyelashes. Fontes was preparing to launch into an exposition on the problems with customs regulations, and the major, who had heard these slow, detailed, almost scientific expositions before, discreetly moved away again, saying he needed to find an ashtray where he could stub out his cigarette. Very slowly, because every loss was a gain. People talk and talk, he thought. Life is one long monologue repeated a million times that ends in death. Meanwhile, everyone carried on talking and not listening to the others, not a word, so focused were they on their own voices. Always making the same points, always arguing (With the others? With themselves?) about the same subjects. What was his personal monologue like? He had never noticed, but he must have one, he must.

The young woman who had been sitting on the floor came over to him, holding her empty glass in her right hand. She was holding it delicately as if it were a flower whose perfume you could smell from some way away. She had drunk too much, and her large green eyes, heavily edged with black eyeliner, were as choppy as the sea after a storm. She had a knowing smile on her full lips, and her disheveled hair kept falling over her face.

"Major," she said. "Tell me about your last battle." She sat down on the empty ottoman just outside the smoking room and patted the seat next to her. "Come on, Major. I won't eat you. Would you be very kind and pour me another whiskey? It's there, on that table. My legs are a bit wobbly; why do you think that might be? Major…"

"Yes…"

"Tell me something interesting, something that, oh, how can I put it…"

"I'm not really a soldier, just a pencil-pusher. What's your name?"

"Maud. Maud Navarro."

"Well, Maud, Maud Navarro, as I say, I'm really

just a pencil-pusher. No wars for me. Haven't you read the newspapers? An oasis of peace: Isn't that how they used to describe Portugal? An oasis of peace in a troubled world. That was then, of course. Now it's too late. I stopped trying. The only hand-to-hand combat I engage in is with bureaucracy. Those are my unsung battles. I get through several pens a month; they are my munitions. I've never killed anyone, Maud Navarro. I am by nature a peace-loving man."

Her eyes were growing ever stormier, and she was looking at him, fascinated.

"I don't believe you," she said. "Nor do I want to. You're very modest, Major, and it suits you. Yes, it really does. You don't want people to know that you're a hero and killed dozens of the enemy. Dozens! No, what am I saying? Hundreds! Wait, I know. You won the battle of Cannae, didn't you? That's where you got that scar on your face." She was laughing so much that tears were rolling down her cheeks, and that rain of tears washed away the bad weather, leaving the sea green and almost transparent. "Major, I'm proud of you," she said ecstatically. "One day, when I'm an old lady, I will tell my grandchildren that I once sat next to Hannibal on an ottoman the color of... What *is* this color anyway?"

"And that you had drunk too much."

She paused. "Perhaps I won't tell them that," she said. "Perhaps that's not really necessary."

"Perhaps. Although I would say it was obvious."

"Besides, I'm talking nonsense!" she cried. "I have no intention of having any grandchildren!"

She was looking at him. A long uncivilized look that attached itself to his eyes and from which he wouldn't have been able to detach himself even if he had wanted to. Would he want to, though? "Major..." However, just at that moment, he had looked away, because something demanded his presence elsewhere. He turned just in time to see that woman, Adriana, studying him intently, almost scrutinizing him. Her lips were pursed, her brows slightly furrowed. As soon as the major met her gaze, she turned and continued her interrupted conversation with the fat woman who, while she may have lots of diamonds, had a terrible ear for languages; well, one can't have everything.

Adriana clearly knew him too, but where from? He stood up without saying a word to Maud Navarro, who, besides, seemed oblivious to everything going on around her, and he again went over to the group of men—now reduced to two, Fontes and Aires—who were exchanging whispered anecdotes, then roaring with laughter, and turning bright red with the effort, because both men were fat, the proud owners of many pounds of the kind of abundant, flaccid flesh that afflicts the wealthy and comes from lavish suppers, a sedentary lifestyle, and the alcohol they consumed in the evening—on every evening of every year—in their favorite bars. The major was thinking all this as he watched them glorying in their laughter, not even stopping for the inevitable coughing fit that followed.

"Listen, my friend, you simply must hear the story Aires just told me," said Fontes, once he had finished coughing. "Go on, Aires, tell him."

They put their heads together; Aires' voice, leaning in close, whispered, became a mere murmur, almost a mumble. Manuela, the hostess, said out loud and with a natural ease of manner that exuded class:

"There they are with their silly stories, but why do they have to keep them to themselves? There aren't any young innocents among us." She smiled at Maud. "Apart from you, my love. But I reckon you could tell a few good stories of your own, eh?"

"Where would you like me to start?" Maud asked wearily. Then she returned to her whiskey, and the other guests returned to the conversations they had interrupted in order to smile at this exchange. It was Fontes' turn to tell a story. The major, however, didn't hear it, even though he appeared to be listening and laughed politely at the end. Aires became positively apoplectic, and another man who had joined them (Afonso Nobre the writer?) laughed in the moderate fashion befitting an intellectual. "Yes, very amusing," he said distractedly. "Very amusing."

The major was still laughing, although with no idea what he was laughing at. He laughed simply because the others were laughing, out of sheer conformity. Out of fear that he would be seen not to be joining in. I'm just a wimp, he thought sadly. I always have been. What would have become of me in a war? Or in an occupied country? What would I have done if I'd actually had to do something and leave the flock? He was feeling thoroughly fed up and longed to be alone at home again. This is what almost always happened when he made a foray into society. It was clear that everyone around him had been given some important or secondary role and that he alone was marring the play by strolling around among the other actors with no makeup on and without a proper costume, with no witty line to come out with at just the right moment; he alone was ruining the show, just as one day, as a boy during a school play, he had raced across the stage whooping like a Sioux Indian while a little moon-faced girl was declaiming tremulously, "Dear friends and family, I am a poor widow, whom God has deprived of all strength and shelter in this world." Everyone had applauded him then—it was so unexpected—while the little girl, a would-be actress, burst into loud sobs. No one was applauding him now. They doubtless thought him unpopular and talked about him behind his back, and spoke, needless to say, about Luísa, adding perhaps that they could quite understand her position.

That feeling came from way back, and always resurfaced at these so-called society happenings. The major had never felt at ease in those situations, never felt part of it. He had always remained on the outside, looking in. The ladies went to the hairdresser, wore low-cut dresses, carefully painted their faces, and were charming and brimming with wit. The ideal woman! As for the men, they wore beautifully cut, rather dark suits and smelled of lavender in a discreet, very masculine way, and they were all either very intelligent or very rich or very funny. Each of these styles had their supporters and their fans. He, though, was always the soldier and continued to be despite everything, even though he was visibly dressed in civvies, wearing any old tie and any old suit made by any old tailor, and always his same old self. He didn't have much money and wasn't particularly intelligent or witty. He wasn't particularly anything.

He thought about Luísa, whom he had resolved not to think about. And this happened because of the total silence surrounding her name. He had thought of her several times since he arrived at the party, perhaps precisely because no one had mentioned her or asked him about her. And yet that would have been perfectly normal. There was no reason why they should all know, but they did. Manuela, Fontes, Aires…others. All of them perhaps. Even drunk Maud Navarro, even Adriana Moura, who had returned from abroad only a few days ago. Luísa knew so many people; she had so many friends of whom he knew nothing… She was so nice, so kind.

"What are you thinking about, Major?"

He started, then turned, and found himself looking at her with no idea what to say, like a boy caught by the teacher reading an obscene book. Without even realizing it, he had moved away from the group of men and hadn't seen her coming toward him and stopping right there by his side. She was waiting, and she gave the impression that she needed his answer urgently and that not just any answer would do. And she was studying him intently. What are you thinking about, Major?

She had remembered his rank, just as he had remembered her name. Where did he know her from? He was even about to ask her straight out, with no beating around the bush, but he stopped because she was still waiting. After all, what *was* he thinking about?

Since he couldn't mention Luísa, he went back in time a little and ended up saying rather plaintively:

"I was thinking that here we are, the only ones not wearing masks at a masked ball where no one is dancing."

He waited, expecting her to arch her eyebrows in a gesture of incomprehension or scorn, but instead she merely asked:

"Why is that? Why do you assume I share your feelings?"

The major looked at her, perplexed, or, rather, he

continued to look at her much as he had before, but with just a touch of perplexity. He found her answer rather awkward and felt that this new conversation was already beginning to resemble a bout of drawing-room swordplay, a form of conversational dueling he detested and for which he had no natural talent.

"Perhaps because you don't appear to me to be wearing a mask," he said at last, in a modest attempt to join in the game.

She broke in:

"Oh, nonsense," she declared. "And don't go making assumptions. Besides, I'm useless at metaphors—for me, words always mean exactly what they mean."

Given her response, he decided that this was the right moment to ask her where they had met before. He didn't though. His wretched timidity got the better of him. He merely asked if she would like to sit down and then took a seat opposite her. Adriana was waiting. She had her legs pressed together, her feet together, and her hands placed one on top of the other on her knees, like a sensible young lady. She wasn't wearing any rings or bracelets. Not even a wedding ring. The major knew, however—from eavesdropping on her conversation—that she was married and had children. And that her husband was a diplomat somewhere.

"You arrived a few days ago, I understand," he said, just to say something.

"Yes, a week ago. I'm always either leaving or arriving. I seem fated to be eternally packing suitcases and unpacking them. I must have spent whole years of my life filling and emptying suitcases."

"Some women spend years dusting their own little

patch of world, or waxing its floor, enthusiastically and despite terrible back pain. Some even get TB from all that work. Others spend their life looking in shop windows or in the mirror."

"Yes," she said. "Yes, a life within a life. My mother, poor thing, spent her life darning socks. Sometimes they were socks no one would wear anymore and that she knew no one was ever going to put on. But she darned them with all the passion of an artist, all the time complaining. 'I'm a victim,' she would say. 'I've never had a moment's rest. Everyone goes out and has fun, everyone except me.' When the socks were ready, she would put them away in a drawer. What was that about? I really don't know."

"Perhaps she was obeying some order from above," said the major. "Perhaps she really had to do that."

"My situation is different," she said. "I don't do the choosing. It just happens that I'm the one who has to pack the cases and then unpack them. A pointless task, but necessary. It's become second nature to me now, and I'm getting better by the day. It's a speciality like any other. What's best placed at the bottom, what's best on top, what you can stuff down the sides. And the art of filling empty spaces, Major... There comes a point when it's not a suitcase anymore; it's a rectangle of very compact matter." There was a silence. "I'm only ever anywhere for a short while," she went on. "For example, I'm here in Lisbon for just two weeks. Five years is the maximum I've stayed in any one place, and I spent them in Cape Town. Now I live in Amsterdam, but I hate the weather and miss the sun terribly. In fact, I came here just to have a few days in the sun."

"Yes, the weather's very pleasant in May."

"Especially when you live in the north. It's paradise."

"Where do I know you from?" the major asked then. "I've never been to Cape Town, and I've never visited Holland. To tell you the truth, I've only once crossed the Portuguese border, and that was to go to Madrid for a football match. We must have met here, but where?"

She smiled for the first time. It wasn't a happy smile, nor was it a smile indicating amusement, nor even the smile of someone who needed to smile. It was a smile of relief. "Finally!" that smile was saying. He heard her sigh softly and saw the wings of her eyelids flutter twice, covering her pale or, rather, colorless eyes, which had laugh lines around them.

"That's what you've been thinking since the first moment you saw me, isn't it?"

"Yes, it is."

"And you can't remember…"

"And I can't remember."

Her smile went out like a light, and her face once again grew serious. "I, on the other hand," she said as if she were thinking this to herself, "have never forgotten you. I only saw you once, Major, only once. And for just a few minutes. It was a long time ago. You were possibly a lieutenant at the time, or a second lieutenant."

"It was that long ago?"

"Some twenty-five years ago. I was fifteen at the time. Or fourteen. I'm thirty-nine now. Yes, I must have been fourteen."

The major lit a cigarette and put the pack away in his pocket, all very slowly, not hurrying in the least, like a man who has all the time in the world now that he's on the right track. He glanced at his watch, but only to check that it was still early and there was no need to rush.

"Where was that? Where did we meet, I mean?" he asked. He still could not remember, but he was no longer bumping up against the white wall of forgetting. He was simply waiting. The wall was still as high and smooth as before, but there was now a very small crack in it, and that gave him hope. In a few moments, the wall would crumble, and he would be able to see through to the other side. "Where was it? Twenty-five years ago, you say? Well, twenty-five years ago, I was in Elvas, I think..."

"My name is Adriana," she said suddenly.

"Yes, I know. I made a note of your name, and I suppose you did the same with mine."

"I didn't need to. An unnecessary task. You were a second lieutenant—I remember now—Second Lieutenant Aníbal Morais. I didn't know you were a major now or that your hair had gone so gray."

"Time."

"Yes, time."

There was no point in hurrying her. She would tell him, but only when she chose to. Not a minute sooner. She was a woman who knew what she wanted. But what did she want?"

"I sometimes thought you must be dead. Well, that's possible, isn't it?"

"Perfectly possible," he agreed patiently. "Two years ago, I had pleurisy, and five years ago, I was involved in a very serious car crash. I was in the passenger seat."

She said, "I hope you've made a full recovery."

"Yes, fortunately I have. A few scars, but that's all. They look rather good on a soldier." He indicated a deep white line on his left cheek. "See?" he asked.

"I do."

"And ten years ago, I had to have an urgent operation. According to the surgeon who operated on me, they caught me at the very last second of the very last minute. So, as you see, I could easily have been dead."

"When was that?" asked Manuela, who happened to be passing. "I didn't know anything about that, Aníbal."

He laughed.

"Oh, that was ten years ago, possibly eleven. We were just talking…now what was it we were talking about?"

He turned to Adriana, who laughed and made room on the sofa for Manuela.

"Sit down," she said. "The two of us were drawing up a catalog of memories. Ten years ago, five years ago, two… Do you want to join in?"

The major looked at his watch, and it occurred to him that it was getting late, almost a quarter past one.

"Are you in a hurry to leave?"

"No, not at all…"

He became aware that the two women were chatting away enthusiastically—Manuela waving her white arms, Adriana quite serene—about someone he didn't know named Ventura. The major looked around. Here and there, he caught stray, random sentences. "Everyone who meets him dies suddenly, it's a fact." "Ramiro only survives because he's strong as an ox."; "Last year, when I was in Sweden…" "You were in Sweden?" "Yes, a wonderful country and a fine people, the Swedes. When you visit a country like that, it makes you realize that our country, that we're basically…"; "Yes, he's interested in space travel now, which I find odd in someone like him. Doesn't it smack a little of denying the existence of God…" "Denying… I don't understand…" "Perhaps you don't believe in God…" "Of course I do. If Hell and all that didn't exist, this life would be too immoral."

It was Maud who was speaking, no longer holding a glass and considerably more sober. He looked at her and smiled. She abandoned the short, fat, pink gentleman (Afonso Nobre the writer?) and came over to him. The major reluctantly stood up.

"Are you feeling better?" he asked.

"Why? Was I ill? Ah, I see. Yes, you're right, I was a little merry. I still am, but so what? Come here, I want to tell you something…"

She drew him over to a less crowded spot. "I find this kind of party deadly dull," she said softly. "It's only when I drink that I can enjoy myself a little. If I was in my normal state, I might not have noticed you or that old-fashioned lady, the one talking to Manuela now, and who you were getting on so well with. No, I would have been slumped somewhere like a useless lump." He said, "She and I know each other, that's all, but I can't remember where we met."

Maud, however, wasn't listening. "When I drink, I like everyone," she said. "Nice people, admirable people. If I don't drink, everything seems almost unbearable."

"You're exaggerating," said the major.

"Possibly."

"Why do you come to these parties, then?"

"That is the question. Why do I come? I never miss a party, Major. Everyone knows they can count on me. There's never any question of my not coming. I always come."

"Yes, but why?" he asked, purely for the sake of asking.

"Because they would find it odd if I didn't. She's

depressed, they would say, and that's a bad sign. They would start to uncover things about me and invent I don't know what. After spending two months in hospital with nervous exhaustion, I have to keep a close eye on my reputation. I mustn't dye my hair another color because I didn't do that *before*. I must enjoy parties as much as I did *before*. I have to be exactly as I used to be *before*. Do you understand, Major?"

"And did you used to drink a lot *before*, Maud Navarro?" he asked gently.

"Major, you must be psychic. No, *before*, I didn't drink. I started drinking the day when... On a very bad day. A very bitter day. After that... Well, things never did get back to normal, at least not enough for me to stop drinking..."

She fell silent and looked at him with a suddenly detached air:

"I'll see you later," she said. "They're calling you. Off you go."

He turned and saw that Adriana was once again alone and waiting expectantly. He didn't want to rush back. He poured himself a whiskey, raised the glass to his lips, and said to Maud, "I do have to go. It's a matter of life and death. Finding out where I know her from."

"She's a funny little thing," Adriana said when he returned to his seat opposite her. "A little unstable, unfortunately. She's spent time in the hospital. And she drinks like a fish."

"I know, she told me about that, but she seems normal enough. Well, reasonably normal, like the rest of us."

"Possibly," said Adriana, her mind elsewhere.

Then the major said quietly, "I'm waiting." He no

longer felt in the least bit shy with this woman. This old-fashioned lady, as Maud had called her. And the major had to admit that Adriana did resemble a wax figure placed among the public to confuse them.

"Yes, I have to tell you everything now," she said. "I've started, and I can't stop now. I've been putting off the moment for a long time, prolonging the period during which I could justifiably allow myself to remain silent. Why speak about past events? What do we gain by that? But there it is, I've started. I spoke to you when it seemed to me that you were wondering who I was, and that's when I asked what you were thinking about. I don't even have to apologize for the apparent informality."

She was looking down at her right hand, with which she was slowly smoothing a crease in the black silk on her thigh.

"I'm Teresa's sister," she said, without looking up.

"Teresa..."

For a moment, he didn't know who she was referring to. That name thrown out like that, with no place or face to attach it to, meant nothing to him. Teresa... Then suddenly, everything became clear, and Adriana herself emerged from behind the now-ruined wall, seated primly in a wicker chair, having opened the door to him, her hair in braids and sitting, as now, with her hands resting on her round knees, her restless gaze submerged beneath all that apparent serenity.

Off in the distance, Teresa's voice. A different voice, now constrained, now too free, now static, now too fast. Invisible obstacles seemed to break up the sound, distorting it or holding it back, apart from the occasional piece of open ground that made it dangerously loud. Where had it gone, that voice, so easy and clear, the young voice that she would throw out like a red streamer? Teresa was very pale like her sister, and her eyes seemed to rock back and forth as if she were in a small boat battered by the storm and abandoned to the fury of the elements. "The fury of the elements," he could almost swear that he had thought those very words. For a moment, he was afraid she might fall, dragged under by her vague, fluctuating eyes, and he even took two steps forward to catch her in his arms in case she did. However, it was as if she suspected or feared or even foresaw his thoughts and intentions. She recovered quickly, almost abruptly, and held out one damp, slightly tremulous hand to him. Her arm, though, pushed him harshly away. "Hello, what are you doing here?" said the voice that came and went. "Not again. Go away, I asked you not to come to the house. At least my sister is here today; otherwise, what would people think…the neighbors I mean? You have no idea what these provincial folk are like. These women with nothing to do, forever curtain-twitching, gossiping, and inventing stories." She had turned right around and was talking with young Adriana, who was staring at him uncomprehendingly, with those pale, slightly squinting eyes. "Imagine, Anica: Second Lieutenant Aníbal Morais has fallen in love with Alicinha and wants me to talk to her about him. You know what Alicinha is like… I'm not going to get involved in such things…"

"Who was Alicinha?" the major asked Adriana, there in that large room with aquarium-green walls, bathed in the bright light from those four lamps.

"A cousin of ours. A nice girl. Dead now."

"Ah."

The other Adriana, the one with eyes wide with astonishment—Anica as she was then—in her pleated skirt and with her hair in braids, was staring past her sister at Second Lieutenant Aníbal Morais, who that year was the most handsome officer at the Elvas barracks.

"Don't say a word about this at home," Teresa was saying to her. "It's all so stupid." Then she turned to him again, where he stood motionless in the middle of the room, not knowing what to do or say. "And now you'd better leave; yes, that really would be the best thing to do." Her voice was now her voice again. That game of hide-and-seek in the hills was over, and her voice was once more clear, almost cheerful. "Let's see. I would like to help, I really would. No, don't thank me, best not to. I might not be able to do anything. Alicinha is such a funny creature, isn't she, Anica? If I'm to do this, though, you must promise never to come back to my house. If José were to hear about it…isn't that right, Anica? If he ever heard about it… So, we're in agreement, then. You won't come back here, and I'll do what I can. Let me think. I might come up with some brilliant idea, you never know."

Anica's cool, calm little voice made itself heard for the first time. It wasn't a distrustful voice, but helpful, encouraging.

"Why not write to Alicinha or call her? That would be simpler."

She wasn't addressing the visitor, but her sister—although the unspoken subject of the verb "write" was clearly *him*—and her suggestion was too logical to be rejected out of hand. Teresa hesitated for a second. She must have thought that she could carry on regardless. She sounded suddenly irritated. "But I already told you that he doesn't want to speak to her until he can be sure he'll be welcome."

She hadn't said anything of the sort, but that didn't matter. And while she was speaking, Teresa walked very slowly over to the door and opened it wide. He had shaken Anica's hand. "Pleased to meet you," he had said. Then he had shaken Teresa's hand, which was less stiff now, but still cautious, and she had somehow managed to say to him, so that her sister wouldn't hear, so quietly that even he barely heard, that she would expect him the next day at the same time.

"I saw you once, Major," said Adriana. "That time you were there for just five minutes, and my sister, poor thing, dreamed up that whole story for my benefit. I didn't understand at the time, but Alicinha...she had such bad luck, poor thing. She had been in love with José, my brother-in-law. Then Teresa appeared on the scene... She died, did I mention that?"

"Who, Teresa?"

"No, Alicinha. When she was thirty-five and still single. I think she died from lack of love, but the doctors gave some complicated name to the illness that carried her off."

"Poor thing."

"Yes, poor thing."

She paused, then said:

"I thought you were a prince, you know."

"Me?"

"Yes, you."

He, however, had barely noticed little Adriana, or Anica as she was called then, and as he had slouched angrily back down the stairs, he had even called her a rather rude name. He was disappointed and still very young.

And he loved Teresa. Oh, how he loved her! Did he love her? Yes, perhaps he did. At the time. And the presence of her sister had annoyed him. What was she doing there?

"I'd gone there to take Teresa some groceries," Adriana said casually. "Jam, sugar, that sort of thing, which our mother always sent her at the beginning of the month. Teresa was having quite a hard time of it, because her husband didn't earn much and, worse still, never would, as she well knew. Like my own marriage later on, it wasn't a marriage between equals, but whereas I went up a rung, she had gone down one. My brother-in-law was a good man, but that was all. And being a good man wasn't enough, especially not for the woman he married."

"Yes, she told me…"

She broke in, "Yes, of course she did, forgive me. I'm not thinking clearly. I was trying to give you a general idea of the situation, forgetting that you must have known it all in detail. A good man. A serious man. He believed in people, and that was what killed him eventually. Thinking about it now, I find his belief in people almost moving. Did you know him, Major? I mean, did you ever meet him?"

No, he said, he had never seen him, then asked slightly warily if the husband had been caught embezzling money. That's what he'd heard…

Adriana frowned. "Whoever told you such a thing? Embezzling? My brother-in-law? He would never do such a thing!" There was a note of scorn behind the surprise in her voice. "Never!" she said again. "Don't you know the real reason? Did no one tell you? Didn't you at least suspect…"

"Well, I…"

had thought long and hard about him and remembered now how he had imagined him then, wandering slowly around the deserted office. He was no longer a man, only a shadow. Probably hesitant, fearful, or even, when he was about to kill himself, repentant. Sad, filled with self-pity, he who had once had "such a hopeful future," tearful perhaps, and with an overwhelming desire to be rocked in someone's arms, to be a child again, or, more than that, the mere silhouette of a baby in his mother's protective womb. Perhaps he had half-opened the wooden shutters, slowly pushing back the locks, reining in all his haste and strength, so as not to make a noise. With the light from outside, from a streetlamp or whatever, it would be easier to do what had to be done. But it was possible, too, to do it in the dark and then dissolve into that same darkness.

He hadn't seen that shadow. Indeed, no one had seen it. No one had imagined it. Perhaps only Teresa, but who knows? The major, though, thought about it, unconsciously, on that day, many years ago, when he was still only a second lieutenant, and now here it was back again, standing impassively before him. It was a very calm shadow, imbued with the stillness that all insoluble things bring with them. There was nothing to do. It wasn't even trying to do anything. Or to dream of doing anything—even that was forbidden. No, he wasn't crying. He wasn't thinking about his mother or even his wife. Nor was he thinking—as everyone does at some point—that he had a bright future ahead of him. He was far away, about to enter death, propelled into it, dead and forgotten. He was walking slowly, aimlessly, among the desks, just so he could touch them, feel the rough wood, so that he could accustom himself to the touch. Or perhaps to orient himself, so as not to stumble and make a noise. Or perhaps so as not to hurt himself, to preserve for a few more minutes—or hours—that body on loan to him during his brief sojourn among men. And then he sat down, possibly to ponder purely technical details, only to stand up again and take a few more steps. He was getting closer and closer to the kitchen.

"So, he hadn't…" the major said.

"Embezzled any money? Of course not. The poor fellow didn't even deal with any money in the office. As I said, he was a serious man."

"You mean…"

"Had you never thought about what happened, Major?"

"Not really. A little, yes, but I never thought about it properly. So that's what happened?" he asked without a trace of alarm, but filled with sadness.

"Yes."

He thought about Teresa, who had never been a very influential person in his life, which didn't mean she hadn't been very important once. It was just that her importance had been confined, so to speak, to a matter of months. At the time, he had thought, with all the sincerity of tender youth, that he loved her. Soon afterward, though, indifference had set in, and he had grown tired of her but hadn't known how to break free without inflicting great pain. She was very clingy, and it was the first time she had been in love. If you leave me, I'll kill myself, she would say. And she would beg him to take her far away from there; "there" being the place where everyone knew the mediocre life she was obliged to lead, the husband she had quickly ceased to love, whom she may even have despised—yes, she had despised him, he remembered now—and that very modest, almost rundown house. In the end, he had left her—he had to, taking advantage of being transferred elsewhere—and he then behaved like an errant coward. How else could he have escaped her? He didn't write to her, nor did he receive her letters, because when he left—he couldn't even bear to recall their final parting—he had given her a false address, on a street that probably didn't even exist, number 200. Yes, number 200: that he had never forgotten. Later, he heard that she had been very ill and later still, some time afterward, that her husband had committed suicide. Having been found embezzling money, he had been told. That was enough, and he had never asked any further questions, for fear he might be given another version, one he didn't want to hear. This is why he had never known for certain what had happened. He had been given only hints. Was it possible that… Could it have been… At the time, he simply shrugged off such questions and moved on. He forgot all about the man in the empty office. As the years passed, all memory of him was erased.

"Initially, I would sometimes ask myself, did I do the right thing?" said the woman. "Did I act fairly or stupidly or both those things? That is the problem…or was, I should say. Then things calmed down."

The major said nothing, waiting. She moistened her thin lips with the tip of her tongue, then took a deep breath.

"Five months after our meeting, the one when she talked about Alicinha…"

"There was only that one meeting."

"True. I had turned fifteen and took things very much

to heart, very seriously. I suppose all girls are like that. I mean, of course, that's how girls were then. I don't know what girls are like now. Probably because I don't have any daughters of my own. I lived according to certain preconceived ideas, and I still live according to some of them," she said. "Those that have survived."

"We all do. More or less, even though we may like to think we don't. Or we might even react against them—that can happen too."

"One of those ideas was—and still is—that between a couple, a couple in the abstract sense, there should be no lies. Anything but that—a breakup, separation, divorce, anything—isn't that right, Major?"

"Yes," he said meekly. "Yes..."

"It's true, isn't it? I'm glad to hear you say that. Of course, Teresa and her husband weren't just a couple in the abstract—they were a particular couple, which is as different as chalk and cheese. However, I didn't understand that then, because I was very young. I didn't see the difference. When you left, Major, my sister was utterly distraught. Then, when she received no answer to the letters she wrote to you, she went from being hysterical to deeply depressed. Her heart was broken, as was her pride, but no one knew that. As it happened, the neighbors she had claimed to be so afraid of that afternoon hadn't said a word, presumably because they hadn't seen anything. She wouldn't eat, wouldn't sleep; she was no longer her pretty, lively self, more like her own future corpse. A future that wouldn't be long in coming, if you see what I mean. Her nerves were clearly in a terrible state, that much was clear, but she refused point-blank to see the doctor we were all insisting she should see. My brother-in-law was going crazy. He really loved her, the poor man."

I didn't know that, but what could be more natural, thought the major, taking one last sip of his drink.

"One day, she told me everything," she went on. "Not, perhaps, the wisest choice. Instead of talking to me, she could have spoken to a priest or confessed all to one of her friends, who would probably have been more understanding. But it was a gray, rainy day, and I happened to be there when the mailman once again walked past the house with no letter for her. She then felt a real need to make her confession. Oh, she didn't just tell me what happened. She told me the part she had played in it too. She really dragged herself through the mud. Now that she knew you weren't coming back, Major, she was filled with belated remorse. She looked at me for a long time, as if trying to assess how capable I would be of understanding, then she said, 'I'm going to tell you everything. You're my sister, and now you're a grown woman. You have to understand me.' I said, 'Everything?' and she said again, 'Everything.' That was when you and Alicinha both vanished from the story: Alicinha because she was surplus to requirements and had nothing to do with it; you because it turned out you were completely different from the man I thought you were. A prince? Some prince! All that was left were the brutal soldier and the adulterous woman. How sad. Both of you deceiving a poor man whom I had never particularly liked—he was just that: 'a poor man'—but whom I suddenly saw as the victim of lies and betrayal."

"Those are big words!"

"I know. At the age I was then, you do think in big words. Well, we did then. There were no blurred edges. The colors were all separate and undiluted. Blue and red stood side by side and never made purple."

"Never?"

"Never. Or only in certain twisted minds. But I was a sane and healthy girl."

"And then?" asked the major.

"I spent whole days shaking, afraid of those same neighbors always watching from behind their curtains. They must know and were sure to talk. They were just waiting, but for what? Anyway, we needed to pre-empt them. It was urgent. One day, I went to see her and told her that she should tell her husband everything and ask his forgiveness. He was sure to understand."

"Impossible," said the major.

"That's exactly what she said, that it was impossible. That he would never forgive her. He was a good man, but somewhat limited. And he had too much faith in her. The affair would stay there forever between them, getting bigger and bigger, ever more present, making the air unbreathable. I can see her now, sitting on the bed, looking deathly pale, her hair hanging loose over her shoulders, all the time searching for the exact words to express what she was trying to say. 'Getting bigger and bigger, you understand. Lodged between us forever. No, it's impossible.' She wasn't talking calmly, but excitedly. She was feverish; she barely ate anything and lay awake all night. She was thinking about you, I suppose. And when she thought about what her husband would say, she would weep. 'What's wrong with her, for heaven's sake? What is wrong?' Poor José! The doctor finally did go and see her and prescribed tranquilizers. She didn't take them though. She pretended she did and told everyone that she was taking them, but she didn't. I think she wanted to stay in that febrile state so as not to forget you, so that you would remain there with her. Those pills meant sleep and forgetting. Or perhaps it was a way of punishing herself… Or of taking her revenge, who knows?"

"I never heard anything more about her," said the major, staring into space. "Only about your brother-in-law. That he'd died, I mean, because he'd embezzled some funds."

"A lie."

"Yes, as you said, a lie."

"One day, she did tell him about it. I threatened her. I told her that if she didn't tell him, I would. It was the only way to feel cleansed of all that."

"I see," murmured the major. "I see."

There was an awkward silence, and the major looked around desperately for some diversion. Fontes was coming over, looking even fatter and greasier than he had earlier. "Seborrheia," thought the major with a coolness that alarmed him. He was looking crumpled now and no longer smelled of eau de cologne and Lucky Strike, but of sweat and alcohol. Maud appeared too. "What have you two been plotting all this time?" she asked. Her lips were shiny with freshly applied lipstick, and her blonde hair was neatly combed. Two lines on either side of her mouth, however, indicated how tired she was and even how old. "How old *is* she?" wondered the major. Only a while ago, she had seemed very young, maybe twenty. Now she looked more like twenty-eight or even more.

Fontes was talking to Adriana about Afonso Nobre, who had just left and who had been the guest of honor.

"No one has ever read anything by him," he was saying. "He's very arid, they say. And I always say, well, there's arid and there's arid. And aridity doesn't usually lie in the books themselves, but in the mood we're in when we read them. If we were prepared to think a little, to learn from what we read, rather, of course, than just killing time or—still worse—having decided beforehand that we're not going to like what we read, then Afonso's books would be anything but arid."

He turned to Maud Navarro. "Tell me, my dear, have you read any of Afonso's books?"

"No, I'm completely innocent. I'll swear on the Bible if necessary."

"You see? You see? People are just too lazy to think."

"Don't generalize," she said. "I do read, of course. Whenever I have time. But I don't read Afonso Nobre, and who can blame me? No one has read him, not even you. Well, you might have flicked through one of his books, but the only person who actually reads him, paying full attention, is the proofreader, poor man."

Fontes mentally threw his arms up in the air. "You see? You hear what she's saying?" Maud moved away in search of other interests, having first smiled at the major, and Fontes went to join his wife, who was summoning him over because the fat, bejeweled woman wanted to say her goodbyes.

"What became of her?" the major asked as soon as they were alone again.

"She remarried."

"Ah," said the major.

"She lives in Africa."

"Ah," said the major again.

"In Lourenço Marques."

"A great city!"

"So they say."

"They do."

"Civilized, evolved."

"More than Lisbon, it would seem."

"Much more."

"Isn't life strange?"

"It certainly is."

"And how is she?"

"Teresa?"

"Yes, Teresa."

"Well, she's older of course. She's put on weight. The last time I saw her—she came to visit me in Cape Town—she had dyed her hair blonde, a sort of greenish blonde."

"Goodness."

"There comes an age when women have to dye their hair, and they never choose their natural color, but a different one, sometimes the most unexpected of all."

The major tried to imagine Teresa with her greenish hair, but it was hard work, requiring good will and persistence. He tried to imagine her fat as well, and older. And very happy.

"Is she very happy?" he asked.

She gave an almost imperceptible shrug.

"As for happiness…it's not exactly an immutable state, is it, Major? It changes with time. Teresa might be very happy now. She has money and leads the kind of life she wants to lead. As for love…well, she's over fifty now, dear Major. So..."

"But before?" he asked.

"Oh, before. It was a marriage of convenience really. Her husband wasn't particularly well educated, but I suppose she adapted. I don't know anything definite, only that the marriage had its positive aspects, and that she—not that she's ever said as much—is grateful to me."

The major sighed softly and lit a cigarette.

"When they told me about her husband, the other one, the first one..." he said. "I can't remember now who it was who told me. Someone from Elvas obviously... I thought about him a lot at the time. And yet I still didn't know anything for certain, nor did I want to... I rather balked at certainty. He'd been caught embezzling money, that's what I was told." He exhaled a large cloud of smoke and watched it disperse in the air and the perfumed glow from two lit candles. Then he went on: "The last employee was leaving, turning out the lights one by one until he reached the last one in the corridor. Then he closed the door and turned the key twice in the lock. Then he, or his shadow, emerged from his hiding place. He took off his shoes so as not to be heard and stood next to the locked door. He could still go back, he knew that, but he knew, too, that he wouldn't because there was no point. And he knew that last-minute solutions exist only in cloak-and-dagger stories and B-movies. He was a desperate shadow, but wise too."

Finally, the major went on, in silence now, he opened the door and entered the boss's office. He sat down on the high-backed chair, ran his hands over the desk's glass top, mechanically opened and closed the drawers. Simply to do something or to escape his thoughts for a little longer.

No, he hadn't sat down on that fine, imposing chair, nor had he entered the boss's office—why would he? He had sat down, but in his old swivel chair, very gently so that it wouldn't make any noise. First, though, he went over to open the wooden shutters, just enough to let in a sliver of light. And he began to write. “My darling,” he wrote in a passionate hand. Or “My love”? Or simply “Teresa”? He glanced at the phone, tempted to pick it up. If he called her… Just to hear her voice for one last time, to ask her, to be certain… He even reached out his hand, touched the receiver, only to draw back. Why hear again those simple, terrible words? Besides, shadows can neither speak nor write. Plus they didn’t have a phone at home.

“Did he write a letter?” asked the major.

“Who? Did who write a letter to who?” she said surprised.

“Him. Did he write a letter to your sister before he…”

“I don’t remember. I might have known at the time, that’s possible, but I can’t remember now. There are so many things I don’t remember… Teresa avoided talking about it, which is understandable. She never had what you might call a vocation for suffering. The grief she felt for him was, if you like, sporadic. No, she had no vocation for suffering. And her husband’s death was more of a spur than anything else…”

“Yes…” said the major. “I was imagining him locked inside his old office,” he went on. “A man about to die in a dark house. An old house, wasn’t it?”

“What was?”

“The house, no, I mean the office.”

Adriana explained. “Yes, it was an old office. And the desk he worked at was old too. One of those worm-eaten desks with lots of scratches made with a penknife. To the right there was a lamp. On the wall behind his chair, a swivel chair, was a calendar with a picture of a woman in a swimsuit. But I think the calendar was old too, possibly five or six years out of date. I went there once on some errand; I can't remember what it was. Teresa sent me. He was old too, even though he was only twenty-nine. He had nothing of his own, poor man. No one. I never understood why Teresa… I suppose she wanted to steal Alicinha's boyfriend as a joke, or else just wanted to get married and he happened to turn up."

"It's often not much more than that. I mean, women's 'great loves' often come to little more."

Adriana thought for a moment, then said:

"My conscience is clear."

"Is it?" he asked dully.

"Yes. At first, I wasn't so sure. I felt fearful, uneasy, you see. I wasn't certain, and yet, at the same time… Then I stopped feeling fearful or uneasy, and my clear conscience became definitively clear. Everything turned out for the best."

"For her you mean?"

"Yes, for my sister. If things had worked out differently, there would only have been more affairs. And then she might have suffered, sometimes more, sometimes less. And she would have had a difficult time of it in that stupid, narrowminded town. As it is…well, she may not be *very* happy, but it's better than the alternative. For him too really. He was a poor fellow. What more can a man like him expect from life but humiliations and failures?"

"A little hope perhaps," said the major, but she replied that hope always leads to desolation and bitterness.

The major said "perhaps" and felt a great desire to run away. He couldn't do so suddenly, though, not without a brief transitional period. He looked inside and around himself for some diversionary tactic, but found nothing. The other remaining guests seemed to be engrossed in the conversations they were currently engaged in. On the other side of the room, Maud Navarro was laughing loudly, with her head thrown back and her decolletage getting lower, almost dangerously so, perhaps because *before* she always used to laugh loudly and wear very low-cut dresses.

The major's melancholy gaze lingered on her throat and chest, so white in the light. Then he noticed the sea-green walls and imagined he was in the middle of the ocean. What an idea! With mermaids old and young singing their songs; a mad mermaid with troubled eyes; another made of wax, cold and implacable, without a care in the world; old sharks with big bellies; him… Perhaps he was one of those deep-water fish capable of having whole seas of solitude and silence bearing down on him. Luísa, who wasn't there and who would never come back because the world is large and full of other men: she was one of those bits of seaweed drifting, rootless, at the whim of the tides. And what about José? No, he had died and been devoured. The law of the jungle and the ocean.

He stood up and held out his hand to Adriana. "It's late, and I have to work tomorrow. I must be going. But it was a pleasure to meet you, and to…"

"For me too, Major. Really. I hope we meet again."

He said:

"You never know. Life does occasionally arrange these strange, unexpected encounters…"

"Indeed. And if you ever come to Amsterdam…"

"Which is unlikely. As I said…"

"You never know."

"True, one never knows."

The major bowed, smiled, and walked across the now

much emptier room, threading his way through the other guests, saying, "Excuse me. May I get past?" And, "Thank you so much. See you again soon, Fontes. And thank you, Manuela. No, don't get up."

"Goodbye, Major!" said Maud Navarro. "Major Pencil-Pusher, isn't that what you said? An innocent soldier, with no man's blood on his hands."

He began to say very quietly, "Well, there was someone…" but stopped and merely shrugged. He would like to talk to her about Luísa and about himself and how frustrated he felt not to have had the opportunity to fight for something. To fight, even though he loathed violence. To be necessary. He particularly wanted to tell her about that story, to talk to her about the man who had died one night because of the woman over there with the clear conscience, and because of him, who just happened to be there, and because of Teresa, who was now living a slightly happier life in Africa. In Lourenço Marques, that fine city.

"I'd like to have a longer conversation with you," said the major. "When we have more time."

"Whenever you like, Major."

The major put on his coat and left. He was still well wrapped up even though it was May, because the pleurisy he'd had two years ago had not been without consequences. Out in the street, he thought about the red-haired girl with a touch of regret, because he knew that he would never look her up.

It was a lovely night, and the major decided not to go home, despite the pleurisy and the doctor's advice to take things easy and despite having to go to work the following morning. He spent the night—what remained of it—walking around the city. He sat down on the benches in the parks and studied the ghostly trees giving off their own light, listening to the great silence surrounding him, broken occasionally by the disgruntled barking of some stray dog or other. He didn't look at the sleeping houses or at the river down below, smooth and unruffled in the May moonlight. Nor did he think about Luísa. He was thinking about that man because he needed to think about him. He couldn't just leave him like that, dead and forgotten by everyone, on that night when he had discovered that he had been equally alone in life and death. He once again saw him wandering about the deserted office, and accompanied him to the very end; he even helped him take the pipe and cut it, perhaps with the penknife he doubtless kept in one of the drawers in his desk to sharpen his pencils. Teresa's husband! He shrugged. What was Teresa doing there? She should stay where she was. And it seemed to him that he could hear the gas whistling as it broke free from the red rubber snake imprisoning it.

IN A MAD RUSH

Even then, she'd had that slightly drooping flower-like head and the same troubling brown eyes flecked with yellow and bisected by her upper eyelids, thus leaving the southern hemisphere afloat in the blue-white of the sclera. At the time, though, no one noticed her head or her eyes, or even her small mouth and full lips, the corners of which were squeezed tightly together in order to suppress any sobs, which, once overcome, she drove deep down inside her. She wore a kind of fixed, meaningless smile, more of a grimace really. But again, no one saw that smile. The girl—the child—did not yet exist in detail; it was too early. Her eyes, the smile-that-wasn't-a-smile, her face, were all part of an unknown, mysterious whole. Mysterious? No, not even that, perhaps merely abstract.

Their main feeling at the time was one of perplexity, not knowing quite what attitude to take (should they just behave naturally, or be tenderly and slightly sentimentally protective?), but their main concern, of course, was for themselves; despite being convinced that it was really for that dark bundle, dressed in heavy mourning from head to toe—even down to her brown skin, burned by the African sun, her freckles, her straight, almost black hair—who had stepped cautiously off the plane from Luanda, as if undecided (or wary), and who was coming to stay for good. Nevertheless, there they were, waiting at that airport seething with people either arriving from the outside world or setting off. Yes, the woman was especially concerned. The new arrival was a simple, albeit tragic, creature, who—luckily for her—had not yet grasped the magnitude of that tragedy. Tomorrow, in a week, or, worst-case scenario, in a month, she would feel better or almost. One forgets so quickly when one is fifteen… A fortunate age! But as for her, the woman, what a responsibility and, at the same time, what kudos!

She wouldn't talk to her about her father or her mother, at least not at first—then it would be as if that dreadful accident hadn't happened. And on that subject, what must the child have thought or felt when she got on the plane? Would she have been afraid, poor thing? She was going to help that child to be born again, give her a new life—I mean, how extraordinary was that? If anyone could, she could. She was now embracing the inert bundle and covering it with loud kisses (she had gone for the easiest option: pure, undisguised tenderness): "Leninha! I recognized you right away, but how you've grown, and you look so much older too. And you're so pretty, my love, so pretty." Then she turned to make some soft, quick comment to the man who was with her, before again kissing Lena: "My little girl" (doubtless an unfortunate choice of words). Lena was becoming ever more rigid and withdrawn.

"Hadn't we better be going, Laura? The child must be tired…"

These were the first words Lena actually heard, because the ones spoken by her aunt had become all mixed up inside her and been forgotten almost before she had grasped their meaning. Those last words, however, seemed natural and sensible, even slightly irritated, which is what she needed, accustomed as she was to a utilitarian vocabulary. Hadn't we better be going… She then looked at the tall, well-dressed man with the aquiline nose, a very handsome man, although not that young any more. He looked like, yes, he looked like that French actor, Georges something or other…Marchal or Pascal?

Who was that Georges something or other? The husband of the woman perhaps (and already she was referring to her aunt as "the woman"); no, he definitely wasn't her husband: Her mother had always made it clear that her older sister was single… Unless she had married very recently and told no one… But at her age? Besides, this was a secondary matter. There were more urgent problems troubling her. Would they make her go to high school? Would they let her carry on with her painting? Before, *they*… She thought of her mother and father like that too, as *they*, but for a different reason of course, so that she wouldn't cry. *They* had decided, or, rather, agreed… She refused to see them again as she did in her imagination, or as she now didn't even know how to imagine them. Nor did she want to remember them as they were before they got on that plane to carry them to a nearby town. She didn't want to. *They* had flown off, and she had been left sad and alone, until the day she was, like a trunk, put on another plane, one that *did* reach its destination. And there she was, an as-yet unopened trunk, its contents both banal and unknown. *They*… No, she didn't want to think about her father and mother. She didn't want to. And then she smiled a diligent little smile, brimming with good will, at her aunt and the man accompanying her.

Georges something or other wasn't called Georges, but Pedro, and he was a family friend. Lena had been confused by this expression, because it wasn't one she knew; she had never heard it before. A family friend. Which family? A friend of the family or of her aunt's? No, that couldn't be right. He was so... And she was so... It was impossible. And yet everything seemed to point to that. Good grief, how ridiculous.

Laura decided to devote one afternoon a week to her niece, to talking to her and making her—as she put it—a different woman from the one she would be in other circumstances. A fifteen-year-old girl is so complicated. She could remember it well. So complicated... So natural and, at the same time, so strange.

"Don't you think so, Pedro?"

"Yes, possibly. But she'll turn into a woman with or without your help, and a very pretty woman too. Perhaps she already was when she arrived, and we didn't notice."

This, Laura said, was typical man-think.

"Do you believe that's all there is to it? And what about a person's mind? Goodness, you're such a materialist!"

And nothing would dim Laura's maternal enthusiasm. She dressed Lena from head to toe, she took her to her own hairdresser, she taught her the art of using makeup discreetly, she selected a series of good books for her, she took her to the theater and to concerts.

One day, Lena asked:

"Aunt Laura, can I carry on studying painting?"

"Painting? What an idea! You'll be going to high

school in October. It's all arranged. You're fifteen, and you're already shamefully behind the other girls."

"But I want to study painting, Aunt Laura. I'm not interested in anything else. I just can't concentrate on the other subjects. *They*… My father had already said that I could."

Her little voice did its best to stand up for itself but immediately grew hoarse with the effort. Laura left her chair and went over to give her a kiss.

"My dear, don't ask me for things that, for your own good, I can't give you. You have to study, and we'll talk about painting later. And you need to buck up a bit. I know you've suffered a terrible loss, but that's no reason to spend your days lying on your bed staring at the ceiling. You've got to pull yourself together."

"It's just the way I am, Aunt Laura. I've always been like that."

"Well, change then. It's very simple."

That had been the first shock. Lena's inertia was deep-seated and difficult to shift. You could knead her like clay, and the clay would seem to take on the desired shape, but the moment you let go, it collapsed and she reverted to her usual self. Laura would get irritated; she didn't want to nag, but she couldn't help occasionally looking very annoyed. She recalled what Pedro had said when she told him that Lena was coming to live with her.

"There are boarding schools, you know," he had said. "Why don't you put her in one of those? I would never take on such a responsibility myself. At fifteen, she's not a child anymore; she's a grown woman coming into your home, possibly full of fine qualities, but also, as is only natural, full of defects too. Don't get your hopes up. You don't even know her: She's a stranger."

Now, though, he seemed to have grown fond of Lena. He bought her sweets, gave her tickets to the cinema, and, once, he had even gone to pick her up from school in his Jaguar. The other girls had all rushed over to her the next day:

"Who was that? Your dad?"

Lena had responded angrily—on the verge of tears or loathing, more the latter than the former—that, no, he wasn't her dad; her father had died and her mother too. He was a family friend. And she found herself smiling at the expression, and at something else—quite what she still didn't know, but that made her feel suddenly, bitterly happy.

"I came to pick you up just to show off," he said later, looking at her with new interest. "People will be sure to congratulate me, because you're a real beauty. They might think..."

For, one day, Pedro had discovered her oblique gaze, her large hesitant pupils veiled by eyelids made luminous by the subtle application of eyeshadow, as well as her apparently motiveless smile, no longer pained but amused, very slightly amused, which seemed to linger on her lips long after whatever thought had provoked it had gone.

"What are you smiling at?"

Lena was sitting curled up in the armchair, an open book forgotten on her lap. Her gaze seemed to have overflowed the pages.

"I wasn't smiling, Pedro."

She adjusted the position of her lips, which had formed a kind of sulky pout. She really wasn't aware that she was smiling. It had just happened. More to the point, why were they having that irritating conversation?

"Men!" Aunt Laura said, and that one word had reached her, interrupting her thoughts, which had nothing to do with the book she was reading or, rather, not reading. "Men!" her aunt said again.

Lena looked up then and intercepted the look her aunt was giving Pedro: a long, caressing look, which was accompanied by a smile that made her look older. It was just grotesque.

"Not all men," he said, "not all men. Let's see…how many years has it been, Laura?"

"Fifteen."

"Goodness, fifteen. How time passes. That's how old Lena is!"

He had fallen silent then, thinking, and a deep vertical frown line appeared between his eyebrows. That was when he had looked at Lena and asked, "Why are you smiling?"

"I wasn't smiling, Pedro."

And she had tried to imagine what he would be thinking when, now and then, he glanced at Laura. Perhaps he was thinking that, in those fifteen years, she had lost all the charm of youth as well as the permanent look of mild surprise that *they*, her parents, had mentioned, her wavy blonde hair, her arrogant body. And that look of surprise was beginning to seem ridiculous, her hair was now all too visibly blonde, and her body was growing fatter.

"Cellulite, my dear," he said to her on another occasion. "You'd better watch it, because at your age…" But how old was she? Thirty-eight…and frankly, nowadays, thirty-eight wasn't old at all…

"You mean forty." And he smiled. "Remember, we're

exactly the same age and were born in the same month. Or have you forgotten?"

Laura was looking at him uncomprehending, as if she no longer knew him. Her gaze wandered around the room, from Pedro to her niece, who, at the time, was always, always reading. Deeply absorbed, but not actually looking at her book.

"It's time you went to bed, Lena. You have classes in the morning."

Lena closed her book and got slowly to her feet:

"Goodnight, aunt. Goodnight, Pedro."

They, meanwhile, continued having one of those conversations that, however pointless, are essential for the coming storm. Lena listened to them for a while, before pulling the bedclothes up over her head. Her aunt wept a little, and he consoled her in his slow voice. "Now, now, this is pure childishness," he said. Then they exchanged a rather frosty goodnight. When the front door closed, Lena turned out the light. It was so good, so sweet, to lie in the dark with her eyes open, dreaming. Dreaming about Pedro. Creating a possible life, smoothing away all the rough edges, breaking windows. Dreaming, for example, that her Aunt Laura had died. The darkness was so sweet. The daylight made everything different and difficult; it contaminated the dream. Not the night though. It was a soft, malleable, maternal material that embraced everything you handed it.

One day, he told her, like someone who has just made a discovery:

"You're a woman now. A pretty woman. I'm sure others have told you that..."

"Yes, they have."

"Have many people told you?"

"A few."

"Important people?"

She pouted and shrugged, then looked straight at him:

"No, not very important."

"And…were you pleased?"

"Shouldn't I have been?"

She was a strange girl. She sat curled up in the chair and gazed at him with her large fluctuating eyes and that half-smile he wished he could understand.

Laura arrived then, bursting into the apartment, agitated and perfumed, and the whole atmosphere became saturated with Chanel No. 5. Lena wrinkled her turned-up nose and pursed her lips.

"Oh good, you've been keeping Pedro company. Sorry to be late, but it was so busy downtown…"

And then she would go on the offensive in the conversation. They would sometimes argue; it had become a habit. It could be about some unimportant matter, but, after they had exchanged a few bitter words, that unimportant matter would grow in size and become huge.

One day, after he had left, Laura flung herself down on the sofa and wept uncontrollably. She lay there, abandoned, her face shiny with tears, puffy and old.

"You understand how I feel, don't you, Lena? I can sense him slipping away from me, and it's just horrible."

In a harsh, but very calm voice, Lena asked:

"Why didn't you marry him?"

"I don't know," Laura said, slightly confused. "I just went along with it. Do you think I should have married him?"

"Possibly. But it's too late now, Aunt Laura."

Laura, with her ruined face, stared up at her:

"We never talked about it. Well, he never did. He always said he put his freedom above all else. And I didn't insist, because I was happy with the way things were."

Yes, she was happy. She just needed his presence now and then, to hear his voice on the phone now and then too. People are so different. Lena, for example, was in a hurry about everything; she couldn't make do with a kind of pretend happiness that was thrown to her now and then like a bone to a dog. She had realized this when *that*—the accident—happened, when *they*... She was filled then with a feeling of desperate haste to do quite what she didn't know—not yet, it was too soon—she simply felt in a mad rush to live, even if that meant running down someone who got in her way: her Aunt Laura, for example. But, at that point, she hadn't even met Aunt Laura. She had never even seen her.

"His freedom!" And her voice was clearly mocking her aunt's ingenuousness. "His freedom! Isn't that what all men think? And yet they do marry... Why? Presumably because that's the only way they can get what they want?"

Where had she acquired this knowledge that was making the blood rise in Laura's face, making her feel suddenly ridiculously infantile, even innocent? Lena was sitting very erect in her chair, extremely erect. A faint smile on her lips. Because she had just realized that, in a way, Aunt Laura had died and wouldn't cause her any problems.

HIS LOVE FOR ETEL

To one man, Etel was the most beautiful and desirable of women. She, however, was unaware of this. If she had known—if she'd had even the slightest inkling of what his eyes, when they lingered on her eyes, were silently trying to reveal, or sometimes hide, or, at others, timidly suggest—she would obviously have regarded him differently, slightly astonished at such boldness, or she might have chosen to stop looking at him and speaking to him altogether. Because as far as Lisbon's "upper crust" was concerned—the category to which Etel belonged—Vitorino might be in his last year at business school, but he was still the son of a former hotel cook. However, since she neither knew nor suspected anything, Etel continued to speak to him with a distressing—or consoling—nonchalance and even to ask him, with the friendly but aloof manner of an upper-class girl, if it was true, as she'd been told, that he was still going out with so-and-so. This was one of many buckets of cold water poured over Vitorino's loving heart, but he would nonetheless manage a smile, however forced, and respond in like manner, in the same innocuous, playful tone.

On the days when he'd had one of these rather silly—but to him precious—conversations, he would always return home feeling silent and bitter after that brief burst of excitement and filled with a great desire to die. On days like that, shut up in his modest bedroom with the door locked, he would survey the possibilities, weighing up the pros and cons of the various ways he could put an end to that tepid, tedious existence in which there would never be an Etel: turning on the gas; slitting his wrists with a razor blade; overdosing on aspirin. He also considered in great detail—even reciting to himself some of the more meaningful phrases—the letter he would write to Etel in his final moments, telling her how desperately he loved her. However, he always recoiled while still some distance away from the edge of the precipice. What lured him back was the life yet unlived and the desire to see Etel once more, to talk to her again, even about painfully superficial matters that would lead nowhere.

On calmer days, especially those when he didn't see her, he managed to face up to his situation almost coldly and with the necessary objectivity, and even poke fun at himself a little. How could Etel possibly love him, he would think then. He was ugly, poor, from a different class. He had never been exceptionally good at anything, and even in college, he had only scraped by. He could not think of anyone in the city who really deserved Etel. If she were to love him, he would have to be a different person. Why not simply banish the stupid dream that had taken possession of his body and his heart?

This is what Vitorino thought on those calm days, but then he would meet her, talk to her, or somebody would talk to him about her, and it would all begin again. His mother would sometimes look at him sadly when she thought he wasn't looking. Did she know about his love for Etel? He didn't think so. However, one night, she had planted a longer-than-usual kiss on his cheek when she went to tuck him in, and then sat down on the edge of the bed and spoke to him of a certain very kind, very pretty young woman, a real delight, who would be just perfect for him.

"But I don't want to get married, Mama," said Vitorino with an indifferent shrug.

"Everyone gets married!" she replied, standing up with a sigh of resignation. "Everyone. Sooner or later."

The very next day, he learned that, during the last week, Etel had been seen in the company of an engineer with an English surname, a new arrival in the city, where he now occupied an important post in a large company.

Vitorino had always accepted that Etel would never be his, but it had never occurred to him that another man would win her with such ease. As easy as pie, so to speak, and in such an ostentatious manner that the neighbors were already sharpening their tongues and preparing to wield them with exceptional vigor. This was a terrible shock for Vitorino. "It's just not possible," he would say to himself, as he sat sobbing, head in hands. "It's just not possible."

It was. And he started seeing her everywhere with the engineer—a tall, very smartly dressed man, who seemed to him odiously seductive.

Now that Etel was lost to him and lost too, in a way, to the small world of which they were both a part, his obsession with death vanished. Dying had become pointless really. She was so happy that she might not even notice his disappearance, and any final letter he wrote to her would provoke only an "Oh dear, poor fellow," spoken or thought quickly, in passing. Or she might, almost out of vanity, show it to her fiancé—that, too, was possible. It would be a feather in her cap that few could boast of.

Vitorino continued to live, but he felt no interest in life. He failed his final year at college. His godfather, who was paying for his studies—Vitorino's father had died when he was a child—withdrew his allowance. He should get a job; he was no better than the other boys, and no one had paid for *him* to go to college. Vitorino found a job. Meanwhile, people were born and died, people fell in and out of love. And he still loved Etel.

"Why didn't you tell her while there was still time?" his mother asked him one day, when he finally opened his heart to her.

He did not reply, because this was such a difficult question and he really didn't know how to reply. Speak to Etel? Him? Vitorino? And he knew that there was a good reason why he had remained silent. However, he didn't want to think about that; he feared such thoughts and the conclusions to which they might lead.

One day, the engineer announced that he was leaving Lisbon, and the city's notables put on a farewell lunch complete with lobsters and laudatory speeches. Almost immediately afterward, it became clear that his affair with Etel had ended and that he had asked to be transferred in order to be free of her. Etel felt too humiliated to attend the first ball of the season, and the other girls all smiled discreetly. "Poor thing!" they said without a hint of pity. "There she was imagining herself already married to the engineer, when, for all her pompous ways, she doesn't have a penny to her name." "Whatever was she thinking of?" said the mothers sitting in the wicker chairs placed around the room and all wearing their Sunday-best dresses, which were bursting at the seams because, lately, they had put on weight. They felt almost happy about this romantic setback, because none of their daughters had ever had such an eligible suitor. One of the ladies, the mother of the girl who was "just perfect for Vitorino," took Vitorino aside and made a great show of asking him if he had heard about what had happened to "our Etel."

"No, what?" he said, feigning an indifference he certainly didn't feel.

"She's broken off her relationship with the engineer. Or, rather, he broke it off, which is not quite the same thing."

"Oh, yes, I did hear something about that."

"And is that all you have to say?" cried the lady, revealing very white teeth beneath the thick down on her upper lip. "You men are just like weathercocks... One day, you're facing south, the next north. Poor Etel certainly doesn't have much luck with the men who claim to be in love with her!"

Vitorino gave a little laugh, purely as a way of responding, then off he went and danced with the girl who was perfect for him, and who also spoke to him about Etel in a voice that was, at once, sweet and rather scathing. Poor Etel: She was such a nice girl, and pretty too, no doubt about that, but she just couldn't seem to hang on to a man, had he noticed? Some women were like that, and Etel was one of them. She was genuinely upset for her though, because she was such a good friend of hers.

Full of suppressed rage, he held her very close as they danced. Indeed, he clasped her so tightly to him that, in the end, she pulled away and said she wanted to go and sit down, that she was feeling a little dizzy. Later, she told people that the cook's son had been very forward—the cheek of it!—not realizing that he had been clutching her to him out of pure loathing.

The engineer's departure cheered Vitorino up a lot, but, at the same time, it brought back his old anxiety. At the office, he was often told off because he kept forgetting what he was doing and would sit staring straight through people and walls, wishing himself far away from there.

"So, Senhor Vitorino, where's that letter? Whatever can you be thinking about?"

He was, of course, thinking about Etel, but his boss didn't know that, for he wouldn't stoop to taking an interest in the private lives of his employees, and certainly not in their love lives. Feeling very shaken, Vitorino would always rush back to the old desk he occupied and would write to some limited company or other about something or other that was of absolutely no interest to him whatsoever. Then he would write "yours most sincerely" and get up in order to hand the letter personally to the boss so that he could sign it.

Eventually, Etel started coming to the balls at the casino again, and she laughed and joked as she used to, although hanging over that apparent good humor was a melancholy veil, invisible to most people. "I've heard tell that you're in love with so-and-so. Is that true?" So-and-so was the girl who was perfect for him, and Vitorino said that she shouldn't believe everything she heard, all the while thinking: It's you I love, Etel: only you.

She, however, couldn't hear thoughts, even violent, strident thoughts like Vitorino's. And so she would eye him interrogatively, eyebrows raised, a tiny frown line creasing her very white forehead.

"Bye then!" she said, borne away to the rhythm of a samba in some other man's arms. "See you soon!"

"Yes, see you soon, Etel."

Because he hadn't even dared to ask her to dance with him.

At the end of the year, he was fired for incompetence, and Vitorino found work as a clerk in a draper's shop, but the customers, all of whom were ladies, didn't like him and always wanted to be served by the other clerk—a small, bald man, obsequious and efficient, who was authorized to give them a ten percent discount or run a tab.

Vitorino didn't mind being so ostentatiously sidelined. He was used to that and thought it natural. Being treated any differently would have alarmed, even frightened, him. Besides, the shop was on the street where Etel lived, and he could see her pass by several times a day and even smile at her when she stopped to look in the window.

One day, his godfather died, and, to everyone's amazement and to the indignation of many, he left Vitorino everything. He was suddenly a rich man. What would he do with so much money? He wasn't ambitious, and it had never occurred to him that such a thing could happen, because his godfather had always made a point of saying that he was leaving his fortune to various charities. Vitorino had therefore never nurtured dreams of great wealth—well, he had never been brought up to expect it, which is why he found this new future as a rich man very difficult and awkward. He would have rents to collect, taxes to pay, damn it. And he hesitated over whether to remain working behind the counter in the shop or to set up his own business.

"Why don't you marry Etel?" his mother asked him one day.

Vitorino stared at her in astonishment.

"Marry Etel?" he said.

"Yes, why not? In what way is a girl without a penny to her name any better than you?" said his mother, in her new role as a wealthy woman.

Vitorino felt his heart pounding, and, for a moment, he didn't know what to say or even think. Then, gradually, he began to calm down, and he sat very still so as to put his ideas in order. His mother returned to the kitchen (because she still refused outright to have a maid), while he remained alone with his thoughts. Yes, why not? he thought timorously. Etel was poor, albeit from a good family—"swells," as they used to say—and after that business with the engineer, no one else had sought her out. Why shouldn't he ask her to marry him?

During the days that followed, he continued to hone his thoughts and decided that he would speak to her on Sunday, but as the days passed and Sunday approached, Vitorino's fears grew. What would her answer be? She would, of course, say No; that was only to be expected. Etel was Etel and he was he, a poor fellow who happened to have come into a great deal of money, which he didn't even know how to spend. They had absolutely nothing in common. Etel will say No, but how? What words would she use? Deep inside, though, Vitorino knew that she would, in a way, be happy to find herself loved even by him. She had been so depressed lately… Her good humor was so obviously put on, and there was such an anxious look in her blue eyes…

He called her on Sunday, and his hand was shaking as he dialed her number.

"Hello," he heard her say.

"It's me, Vitorino. Forgive me for bothering you, but I have something important to ask you."

She was taken aback.

"Important, you say?"

"I love you. Will you marry me."

He blurted this out, like someone issuing an apology, afraid that he might change his mind and allow his timidity to get the better of him and stop him saying everything he needed to say. There was a pause at the other end of the phone, and then in a rather faint voice, Etel asked:

"Is this true?"

"It's always been true. Ever since I first met you. But I was afraid. And I would find it perfectly natural if you were to…"

Etel interrupted him and said:

"Yes, I think I will marry you, Vitorino."

He heard these words and froze, his mind empty of thoughts and words. When he was able to speak, when speech was once again possible, he muttered something intended to show how happy he was and then quickly hung up. Something along the lines of, "I'm very happy, Etel. I'll see you tomorrow."

That was it. Then he put the phone down and collapsed into a chair. He stayed like that for a long time, as if stunned, and he felt sad, disconsolate, arid. His mother appeared, wiping her hands on her apron, and asked if he had spoken to her. Seeing him so downcast, she assumed that Etel had rejected him. "What did she say?" she asked anyway, feeling angry on his behalf.

He said nothing, perhaps because he hadn't even heard her question. The last words that had stayed with him were not his own "I'm very happy, Etel"—him, happy!—but the words she had said to him, words he never thought he would hear: "Yes, I think I will marry you, Vitorino." How was that possible?

His mother was standing in front of him, talking. Suddenly, he heard her tell him not to take it to heart, that the silly fool (by which she meant Etel) was hardly much of a catch: She was, after all, nearly thirty, and there had been a lot of gossip about her and that engineer. He, Vitorino, could do better than that. And all of a sudden, Vitorino realized that Etel was indeed as old as his mother said, that she wasn't as beautiful as she had always seemed to him, and she had indeed been the subject of a lot of talk. He felt, too, that he had stopped desiring her and that her face, which he knew by heart, and her voice—which, only minutes earlier, had spoken into his ear the words he had so often dreamed of hearing—had suddenly ceased to have any profound meaning for him, and were just like any other face and voice.

IN THE FIRST FLOWER OF YOUTH

The man is walking unhurriedly along, heading nowhere in particular. Sometimes he slows right down, almost stops, looks indecisively left and right, hesitating like someone unable to decide which road to take. It's as if he were walking for walking's sake, perhaps to kill time or because he has no alternative, but any of those reasons seem strange at that hour in the morning and on a very cold winter's day, when the unemployed and the elderly are unlikely to be out wandering the streets. Apart from him, everyone else is walking quickly, urgently, heading for a particular place—each with their own destination.

He's an ordinary-looking man, carrying a suitcase in one hand. Very pale—haggard—and ageless. Yes, it's impossible to tell what age he is. In his thirties but old before his time? A well-preserved fifty-year-old? He's wearing a strange outfit. A dark-blue overcoat, very long and slightly waisted; a pair of baggy trousers that come down almost over his heels; and a hat with a more than usually wide brim. The suitcase is a good-quality one, but time has taken the shine off the clasps and hardened the leather, covering it with dark stains.

The man's hands must be frozen, because he suddenly stops, puts down the suitcase, and rubs his hands together for some time to get the blood moving. Then he looks around him and, on the other side of the street, beyond a passing vehicle, he spots a small café that is, just at that very moment, opening its heavy iron eyelids. After a brief expectant, or rather, meditative, pause, he crosses the road, slightly bent beneath the weight of the suitcase.

He has set it down beside him now, carefully, as if it were very fragile, then he sits and waits. He doesn't snap his fingers or try to attract the eye of the waiter. He waits there placidly, like someone accustomed to long, infinitely long waits.

The waiter approaches slowly, opening his mouth to speak, but first wipes the table with a cloth. This is doubtless an automatic gesture, because, at that hour, no one will have had time to dirty anything. This is what is going through the man's head as he hears the waiter commenting, "What weather, eh?" and as he answers, "Yes, terrible," without even thinking about what he's saying, although he says it with relative enthusiasm. The waiter goes on:

"It's been like this for two weeks now. When will it change?"

The man says:

"Yes, when?"

"Anyway, what can I get you?" the waiter asks.

At first, he doesn't know what he wants or if he wants anything. What he most wanted, when he went in, was to be able to sit in a quiet, warm place and talk about simple, real things like the weather. He ends up asking for a brandy and drinks it in slow, pensive sips. The taste brings back memories, and he allows himself to be drawn along by them, to be lulled by them. Then he gets up and goes over to the phone.

He dials a number but immediately hangs up. Then he dials another, and his heart beats faster. When he says the name of his old friend, he feels his voice tremble, and he has to repeat the question because the person at the other end doesn't understand. A cheerful, slightly sleepy voice, which he knows well, even after all these years, says:

"The last thing I would have expected—the very last thing—is for someone to call up asking for him, just like that. Asking if he's here… It's just incredible. Who are you, anyway; what's your name? I seem to recognize your voice… Are you a friend? If you are, what are you doing asking me if he's here?"

The man avoids giving a direct answer and says that, no, she doesn't know him, and his name will mean nothing to her.

The voice isn't so sure: "Nothing?"

"No, nothing." To be honest, he isn't really a friend, more of an acquaintance who needs to speak to him urgently. Would that be possible?

The voice gives a short laugh. "Speak to him? That won't be easy. Perhaps you should go to the lost and found."

"You mean you've lost him?" says the man, slightly perplexed.

"You could say that. It's a long story."

"I don't wish to be indiscreet; I merely wanted…"

There was a long sigh:

"Well, seeing that you're a friend of his or an acquaintance… We got divorced, there you have it. Ten years ago. All I can tell you is that he's in Africa. Leopoldville, Stanleyville, Brazzaville, or somewhere like that. I've always been useless at geography! As you see, I'm not much help."

The man apologizes, and she laughs again, rather affectedly this time and not sleepily at all. "Don't worry, I made a similar blunder once, when I asked a widower how his wife was. So you're not alone."

"No, you're right."

The man pays and leaves the café. The cold again descends on his body, and he allows it to enfold him. He's thinking about that friend who just up and left, without even trying to see him or at least send word, asking his sister (or his mother, who was alive at the time) to pass on a message. He simply got divorced and left and now lives in an African town ending in -ville. "I've always been useless at geography!"

There isn't a scrap of blue in the sky; it's all gray clouds and a cold, harsh, cutting wind against which he has to fight, but he's suddenly terribly tired and incapable of fighting, even against the wind. He feels he can't take another step. He is also, and this is a strange sensation, very slightly tipsy, but he doesn't know if it's the brandy he drank—very little—or the gusts of air entering lungs unaccustomed to being out in the open, or in the midst of such agitated, unquiet air. Then he hails a cab and asks to be taken to his sister Maria's house.

With one cold, white, bloodless finger he presses the metal button of the doorbell, and the door opens. Through the growing crack, which stops growing at a certain point, he sees her face, the middle section only—eyes, nose, mouth half-open in amazement—and hears a muffled cry, which becomes her voice, hoarse with emotion and amazement.

"Good heavens, it's you!"

"Yes, it's me," says the man. "I wanted to surprise you. I called earlier from a café, but then changed my mind. I wanted to surprise you, Maria."

The door opens wider, and she says, "Come in. Quickly."

The man enters a broad hallway where the atmosphere is warm and the décor welcoming and cozy. Her plump arms encircle his neck and her hands draw down his head, and he feels on his cheek the gentle pressure of her cool lips. Then she leads him into the living room and invites him to sit down in an armchair. His suitcase is still in the corridor.

"What are you going to do now?" he hears her ask.

"I don't know yet. It's early days."

"Ah."

"You probably think…"

She interrupts him:

"What?"

"That I must have had plenty of time to make plans and to ponder the pros and cons of all of them," the man says. "Well, yes, I did. But I still don't know."

There is a silence, and the man takes the opportunity to look around; he recognizes the circular table with the marble top, the rocking chair, and the photo of a woman, where his gaze stops.

"She suffered a lot, didn't she?" he says.

Maria nods. "How happy she would have been today though," she says. "She was never the same afterward, you know."

He bows his head. “Of course,” he says. That’s what he always says when he doesn’t know what else to say. Of course. Finally, he finds a few words. “She never understood…”

Maria interrupts again:

“You couldn’t really expect her to, could you?”

“No, probably not. There will always be a gap between parents and their children. Sometimes there’s only a twenty-year age-gap, but it makes no difference. The gap is still there, just from the fact of being parents and children.”

“I never noticed it,” says Maria.

“Of course,” says the man again.

She is staring at him hard, then looks away as if embarrassed. What about? thinks the man, smiling rather sadly. However, he sees her clasping and unclasping her hands, her small childlike hands, and his smile disappears, because he knows that, in her, this is a sign of genuine distress.

“I would love you to stay,” she says in a tremulous voice. “I would love that. I never understood either, but I would love…”

“It’s your husband, isn’t it?”

The man sees her glance at the clock and hears her say, “We still have time. He never gets back before noon. Tell me about you.”

He gives her a long, weary look. He is neither irritated nor hurt. The smile lifting the corners of his mouth is simply a smile, nothing more. He is sitting in a familiar armchair in the home of his sister, who is all the family he has left, and he looks at her long and hard as if he were only now really seeing her. When it happened, she was a child, and he was, as their mother would say, in the first flower of youth. Afterward, he saw her several times, not often and never alone. He knew that she had finished high school, then that she had met a very nice young man, then that she was going to get married, and later, that she had married. He had never noticed, though, during those visits—infrequent and growing ever rarer—he had never noticed, even though he knew she was married, that she had become a grown woman, and he is now amazed to find her so female, so blossoming, so sensible that she is asking (indirectly of course) her newly arrived brother to leave before midday, so as not to trouble her husband's peace of mind with his unwanted presence.

"But you're happy, aren't you?" he asks.

"Yes, I'm very happy."

"That's good, Maria. That's what matters."

He asks after various mutual acquaintances, but they have all pretty much disappeared from her world. And she has little to do with those who remain.

"What about Dina?"

"She has three children, and she's put on a lot of weight."

"Ah."

"Tell me about you," she asks again.

"Me? There's nothing to tell. Really nothing. I got out today and dropped by to say hello, that's all. And now I must be going."

She is almost crying and still desperately wringing her hands.

"I'd love you to stay. If it were up to me…"

"I know, Maria. Don't worry, it doesn't matter."

He stands up and stoops a little to kiss her.

"It's still so early," she says.

"It's time. I have things to do."

"Really? I hope that now at least…"

"Yes, of course."

"Do you need anything. I can lend you some money. Not much, because we're not exactly rich…but…"

"Thank you, that's not necessary. See you again some time."

He kisses her again, picks up his suitcase and goes down the stairs.

Once more that sharp, penetrating cold piercing the flesh, along with the rain that has just begun to fall. The man starts walking, again with no specific goal, and he thinks of other people from his youth who it also won't be worth seeking out. Dina, his former girlfriend, who married two years later; his colleagues, who perhaps have good jobs and are doing well, who knows? And who may well be living quiet, problem-free lives, enjoying the almost sacred peace of good digestion. Big bellies and gentle laughter. Buddhas, in short. He will seek them out anyway. He needs to eat and therefore to work.

He glances at a ragged woman selling plastic rainhats and who is grinning from ear to ear. She's laughing at him. What a sight, eh? And that hat! The kind of hat a clown would wear…

The man is smiling at nothing at all and he walks on, battered by the rain, weighed down by the suitcase, uncertain as to where he's going.

I CARRY YOU ALL IN MY HEART

They were light, soft massages given by skilled, invisible hands, that came, lingered, then left only to return again five or ten minutes later, or half an hour on his better days. Waves of pain that grew, rose up, then broke and fell back. He would moan faintly, softly, sometimes impatiently—like a strange form of background music. This was followed by a sigh and silence. He would wait for them to come back, those cruel, amorphous hands. He would half-close his eyes while he waited almost anxiously, and there was already an anticipatory grimace on his face. They never let him down; they always came back.

This process evolved slowly, until one day, he couldn't even stand up. He sat in his big leather armchair with one leg bent and the other straight, staring glumly at the wall or into the street beyond the windows. Becoming used to this wasn't easy for him or for those he lived with. He had been a cheerful, active man. However, his good humor, along with all activity, escaped from the room they chose for him, because it was lighter and had large windows, but that, nonetheless, had strictly limited, static horizons.

In the early days, friends would often visit, which helped make the long hours shorter. Little by little, though, those visits became less frequent and briefer too. His friends always, inevitably, had some urgent matter to deal with, and they genuinely did. To distract him, however, they would bring him the latest bestsellers—"really good and very interesting"—which he would leaf through briefly before adding them to the pile on the small table beside him, next to the radio.

His sons came every day, sometimes bringing with them their wives and crying babies in flowery bassinets. But his daughters-in-law only ever talked about children, and his sons' sole topic of conversation was the office, which he, so to speak, had abandoned. Well, if they didn't take charge of it… And Bernardo would say, "Yes, of course, you're quite right. The office, yes…"

The truth is that the office had completely ceased to interest him. Just like that. From one day to the next. Then again, many things had ceased to interest him since he had become ill, and the office was one of them. When his sons came to ask his advice about matters they considered important, he would merely shrug and tell them, with the faint smile of someone who can't quite believe what he's saying, that he had absolute confidence in them and that they should do whatever they thought best.

"You should help them," his wife, Augusta, said one day, looking up from her never-ending knitting, which she did now in order to sit with him and keep him company. "They're just starting out, and they know nothing about certain traps that you must know well. They might fall into them."

"Yes, they might," he said, opening the newspaper.

"Is that all you have to say?" Her voice took on the slightly acidic tone she adopted on one of her bad days—a tone that, because she was basically a kind woman, she had set aside since he fell ill, although it still resurfaced whenever she felt the need to defend her sons from his indifference.

"It is," he said.

His wife put down her knitting and asked:

"Why do you take that attitude? It's as if you had something against us. Has anyone offended you? Is anyone to blame for your current situation?"

Bernardo said no, no one was to blame, and this seemed to reassure or at least soothe her. And she resumed her knitting.

The waves of pain were less frequent now and less intense, thanks to the honey-colored capsules and the various other pills he took, as well as an injection each morning. The days, though, were immense, and the room in which he sat from morning to night was becoming ever smaller and more devoid of mystery. He knew its every detail, details that had always gone unnoticed before. It was as if the inanimate objects were taking their revenge for the thirty years during which he had paid them no attention and were now obliging him to look at them, study them, then close his weary eyes, exhausted. However, he always returned to them; he had no alternative when he grew bored with the street and the things of the street and even with the binoculars he had asked them to buy so that he could see those things more clearly. He had his books, of course, and the newspapers, which he either read from first page to last or flung down angrily when he was only halfway through on those days that refused to progress, that paused absentmindedly, that never seemed to advance. On days like that, what did he care if the millionaire Kennedy and the proletarian Kruschev had reached an agreement? What use was such an agreement to him? Let them set off a bomb if they wanted; let them blow up everything, including him and his eternally immobile legs.

On such days, his wife carried on with her knitting—why would she not? And, as always, she did so serenely, her lips moving slightly as she counted the stitches, as if she were praying. And there was no reason why she shouldn't count the stitches. She had never been a great talker—this had even been one of her virtues—but the misfortune, which is how Augusta usually referred to Bernardo's illness, seemed to have deprived her of the power of speech. Her voice was only ever heard when there were important things to discuss, things that *she* considered important: for example, the fact that he didn't draw on his experience to advise his sons (the poor things were so honest they could easily be deceived!) or when he occasionally forgot to take his medicines at the right time. The rest of the world seemed to have disappeared, and her hands moved nimbly in the vacuum, perhaps simply to prove to themselves that they existed. And she inundated the whole family with sweaters and pullovers.

Bernardo would close his book; throw the newspaper down on the floor or read every last word of it, including the ads; and escape from that small room cluttered with objects (he and his armchair, the sofa, three other chairs, the writing desk, the paintings). He would escape by closing his eyes. He had never been a man of great imagination, which is why, however hard he tried, he could never invent stories. He had to make do with what he had on hand and return to past events, long since forgotten. The chorus girl he had once set up in an apartment—a foolish fancy; the time he flew to the United States and one of the engines failed, and the Englishwoman sitting next to him started screaming; the sound of gunshots and a woman collapsing almost at his feet, covered in blood, at the door to the hotel on Rue Vavin. Things like that. Sometimes he would go even further back in time or perform a complete backflip that found him taking his first steps to happiness (and relative prosperity) to the tune of the wedding march, arm in arm with Augusta, looking fresh as a rose and with her veil trailing behind her. His father-in-law introducing him to the guests. And with great excitement, he found himself shaking various hands with blue (or blueish) blood in their veins, and even, from time to time, the condescending hand of a government minister. And everyone was smiling at him fondly, as if they loved him, and wishing them every happiness. His father-in-law had certainly helped him with his contacts (which was all he had), but he had gone on to make his own fortune and was now a rich man—a disabled rich man, to be more precise. Anyway, his sons would not be left wanting when he died. They could even, for now, allow themselves to make a few honest mistakes; it would do them good.

One day, a friend visited him and, when they were alone, spoke to him about a woman named Sofia. Bernardo blinked, perplexed, because he had always avoided, as being too unpleasant, any mention of that woman, and all his friends knew this and respected his wishes. They had been married many years before, but it hadn't lasted, and they had each gone their separate ways. So widely had their paths diverged that they had never met again. Bernardo had always regarded that first marriage, fortunately a registry office wedding hastily arranged, as a youthful error. The real marriage had been the second one, years later, with the bride all in white, high-class guests, and solid plans for the future. Now that his friend was talking to him about Sofia—"Do you know who I met yesterday? Sofia, your first wife"—now that his friend was talking about her, he remembered the terrible arguments they used to have, the passionate reconciliations, and even the evening when he arrived home for supper and found the apartment empty and, in a prominent position on the bed, the letter in which his wife, in her hasty scribble, full of spelling mistakes, told him that she had finally—finally!—found the love of her life.

"She must have found many more," said Bernardo's friend. "That's what she made me to understand. One hell of a life. Now, though, she's old and lives alone, with two cats."

"I find it hard to imagine her old," said Bernardo thoughtfully. "Well, that's only natural. I haven't seen her for over thirty years, because I've been married to Augusta for thirty years. I can't imagine Sofia living alone either."

"The reason I'm talking to you about Sofia is because I have a message to give you. She asked me to tell you..."

"What?"

"That she would like to see you. That she would *love* to see you."

"And why not?" murmured Bernardo unthinkingly. "Why not? That's just like her," he went on. "She always loved parties as well as visiting the sick and attending funerals. She's coming to see the invalid, to distract him.

Let her come then."

"What about Augusta?"

"Tell Sofia to come on Monday afternoon. That's the day Augusta goes downtown. It's an old habit of hers apparently, but I've only just realized it. Can you imagine anyone going downtown every single Monday afternoon?"

The friend left, and Bernardo climbed up the hills blocking his view and ended up a long way away, at Sofia's side, at the point where that wall had started to rise up between them, an invisible wall that grew higher and thicker with each day that passed. She talked (a lot) and he talked (a little), but they never listened to each other; they only heard their own voices, but, at the time, they didn't see this. Then the fights began, perhaps because she would arrive home late (or was it for some other reason?), and she would have an absent, slightly mysterious look on her face, the look of someone happily installed in some faraway place. One day, she didn't come home at all because she had found the love of her life, or thought she had. They were both twenty-three at the time.

On Monday afternoon, a lady with white hair, immaculately dressed and wearing a black felt hat—an old lady making no attempt to conceal her age, doubtless because she had realized one day that this simply wouldn't work—anyway, this lady confidently rang the doorbell and told the maid that she was expected.

The maid showed her into the living room and shut the door. For the next two hours, the visitor's strident voice and loud, liquid laugh could be heard coming from the room. Then there was a whispered conversation, and the visitor left.

"Who came to see you today?" Augusta asked that evening, as she began work on a pullover for one of her two sons with wool she had bought that afternoon.

"A former secretary of mine."

"It seems she was very old," said Augusta, whose face was still fresh as a rose.

"Very," he said. Yes, very. Who would have thought it?

Then a week passed, and the following Monday, Sofia again rang the doorbell. This time, however, she didn't come alone. She was accompanied by two men carrying a stretcher. Bernardo was ready and even impatient to leave. The two male nurses picked him up, and the maid was just about to open her mouth and scream hysterically when Sofia shoved her inside the pantry and locked the door. Then they left. Bernardo had placed his letter on top of the radio. He had written it the night before and it read as follows:

My dear Augusta,

It is the custom—as I know from personal experience—to leave a farewell note. Putting my feelings into words has never been my strong point, but I hope you will believe me when I say quite simply that I love you and our sons, and always have. This indisputable truth has nothing to do (and I want you to be quite sure of this) with the decision I have made. The fact is that I have been terribly bored. I had never realized before—I didn't have the time—how very bored I've always felt in your company. Now, though, I have had more than enough time to think, and I realize that what awaits me are more hours of silent knitting and tedious conversations about baby bottles, baby food, and the office. I also realize, Augusta, that the (painful) days I have left are few in number, and that I ought to spend them in the most pleasant way possible, as long, of course, as it doesn't harm you in any way. I repeat that what I am doing in no way diminishes the love I feel for you all, and that love remains unchanged. I carry you all in my heart. Tomorrow, I will write a business-like letter to our sons, as I know they would like that. I intend to arrange things so that everyone is happy. I don't need much. I need only enough to pay for my care and my accommodation with the lady friend who has so kindly agreed to take me in.

With much love from your husband,
Bernardo

ADELAIDE

"You'll laugh when I tell you," he'd said at the time. Her voice was barely audible, and she was looking at him with that hesitant, slightly cross-eyed gaze, already lost, already adrift, a gaze he would not easily forget. "No, you'll laugh," he said again. "It doesn't get much worse, believe me."

Doesn't it? Possibly. The fact is, the other men *had* laughed when he told them. Even he had laughed. Not just to join in with the crowd, but as a way of washing himself clean of any hint of the ridiculous, with which he might, inevitably, have been spattered. "You'll laugh when I tell you." He could still see her and hear her. He would continue to see and hear her for some time, standing motionless at his front door, skinny and uncertain, as if bent beneath the weight of her long hair or her suitcase or her pain. At that point, she still wasn't trembling or crying or feeling afraid. All that would come later, intermingled with a clear desire to die and an obscure fear of actually seeking her own death. That's precisely why he wanted her to leave quickly, before she started crying and trembling and feeling afraid. Before all of that.

"You must go back home at once," he had said. "Don't wait. Your husband won't know anything about it. If you like, you can leave your suitcase here and come for it later, when there's no one expecting you at home."

"But I told him everything. I obviously made a mistake. But I assumed... You said..."

She wasn't accusing him; she didn't yet know what the truth was. She was speaking like someone apologizing or asking forgiveness for having done the opposite of what she should have. Perhaps she could see in his eyes the eyes of others—her mother, her father, her teachers, her husband. Perhaps. I assumed... That's what she had always done, poor thing, all her life.

He had felt like killing her, yes, killing, or at least hitting, her, shaking her, calling her every name under the sun, telling her the harsh truth. I never loved you, never, do you hear? I said all those things simply because I happened to sit next to you, do you understand? *Do you understand?* I find you unattractive and stupid—above all, stupid. You know what that means, don't you? Stupid?

But she had already understood, and why hurt her even more? "Anyway, you must leave now," he had said at last, in a tone of voice that he was trying to make persuasive, the tone of voice in which you would speak to a child. "Your husband's a good man; he'll forgive you, you'll see. You'll come up with some explanation: Tell him you thought it all over on your way here and realized that he's the only one you love...any excuse will do. But you mustn't delay, and he mustn't for one moment know that you've spoken to me. That's the important thing. There's a taxi stand just over there. Come on, there's no time to waste."

She was looking at him uncomprehendingly, but she had looked at him in just that way two weeks ago, at the gathering where he had started talking to her simply because there happened to be an empty chair next to hers, and he was tired of standing. That night, she had an air about her of a slightly backward child. Not particularly pretty, not particularly elegant, and certainly not particularly bright. Her husband had seemed more interested in the blonde in the green dress and completely oblivious to the fact that his wife was just a few feet away. Seeing this, he had struck up a conversation with the wife, and they had exchanged a few banal, insignificant words. Then someone had mentioned the name of Einstein: "Isn't he a German doctor, who discovered something or other?" she asked innocently. He set out to explain to her in simple language what that something or other was, but then he heard her say, "It's all a bit too abstract for me." And he had given up. The red-headed poetess was talking loudly about a cruise she was going on in the summer, and then he had turned to her (he still didn't know her name—"I'm sorry, what's your name?" "Adelaide"), he had turned to Adelaide and asked if she liked to travel.

"Do you like to travel, Adelaide?"

She had blushed slightly, perhaps ashamed of her own limitations and her mediocre life.

"To be honest, I don't know. I've never left Lisbon. I imagine it must be very nice to travel. And I would love to travel. Do you know what my dream is, the place I would really love to visit?"

"The South Sea islands?"

She stared at him, open-mouthed.

"Good heavens, how did you know?"

"I love you, Adelaide, and I'd love to go with you to Kauai."

Why had he said that? Because her husband was sitting there, flirting with another woman? Because she seemed such easy prey? Because he felt sorry for her lonely state? Yes, for all those reasons, but mainly because there had happened to be an empty chair beside hers.

She had turned and again stared at him open-mouthed. She didn't know whether to laugh, to pretend she didn't believe him, or to join in the game. If she should say to him: Really? That's wonderful. I had no idea; how could I not have noticed? You will forgive me, won't you? Or else have the wit to say out loud to her husband: Darling, prepare yourself for a shock. Someone has just made a declaration of love to me. I'm not sure what to do; what do you think? And this would have been followed by much laughter, and it would all have been very funny.

However, she didn't know how to do any of those things. She led a very quiet life; her husband had found her in the provinces; she didn't know anything about such elegant games. Her mother was so bourgeois that she didn't even know that she was, and didn't even know what being bourgeois meant. This is why every part of her was staring at him open-mouthed.

"What? What did you say? You're joking, aren't you?"

And when he saw her sitting next to him, so very vulnerable, he thought that it was true, that he really did love her, that she was the love of his life, despite Einstein and the South Sea islands. Then he said many things, such crazy things that no woman would be totally taken in by them. No woman, apart from Adelaide.

He repeated them the following day and the next and

the next, this time over the phone. She listened in silence on the other end of the line. Sometimes she would ask, "Do you mean it? Do you swear that you mean it?"

Then one day, that day, she had appeared at his door, suitcase in hand. That had been a very awkward moment.

"I'm here. Isn't that what you wanted? Didn't you say that you'd like to go with me to…where was it now?"

He didn't know or care. It might have been the South Seas. But he needed to nip this situation in the bud right there and then. Yes, that must have been what he'd said: the South Seas.

"I assume you haven't said anything to your husband," he said brusquely.

"Of course I have."

Of course. He could no longer remember what words he used then. He had perhaps been cruel, but at the time he wasn't aware that he was being cruel. He had told her everything that he hadn't yet told her. She didn't quite understand; she just stared at him. She stood there before him, and only then did he realize that she hadn't moved from that one spot, his front door.

"You're joking, aren't you?" she said fearfully. "You're trying to frighten me, but why?"

He hadn't responded, and then she understood. "Ah, so it's true," she had said.

There had been no recrimination, no hint of regret or tears in her voice. She seemed like a different woman, and this was what he found especially hard to forgive.

He watched her bend down a little, pick up her suitcase, and once again stoop slightly beneath its weight—was it really that heavy?—then he saw her turn and leave, looking very dignified and without saying a word. The street door slammed, and he went over to the window and peered out to watch her leaving. He saw her slowly cross the street, without looking out for cars; he saw her put down the case as if to catch her breath; then head off along the street until she was lost among the crowds. An ant in an anthill, that's what she was. A poor ant laden down with her belongings and with nowhere to go. That's why she was walking so slowly; that's why she didn't hail any of the passing cabs. She had no address to give them.

He had a strange feeling in his throat and a need for someone to tell him he'd done the right thing, for someone to tell him he was right. His friends all agreed that he was. And that's when he started laughing and finding the whole thing ridiculous. But once everyone laughed their fill, the ridiculousness wore thin, and then he saw two very clear images—of her and of him—and he began to feel remorse. Nothing too serious, of course. Nothing that would last.